I0657997

CRYSTALBORNE SIGILS

BOOK 1 OF THE DELIBERIA CHRONICLES

S. LYNN HELTON

Crystalborne Sigils is a work of fiction.
Names, characters, places, organizations, and events are either products of the author's imagination or are used fictitiously. Any resemblance to actual persons, living or dead, organizations, events, or locales is entirely coincidental.

Copyright © 2022 S. Lynn Helton
Cover illustration © 2022 R. M. Helton
Cover design by S. Lynn Helton

All rights reserved.
No part of this book may be reproduced, or stored in a retrieval system, or transmitted in any form or by any means, electronic, mechanical, photocopying, recording, or otherwise, or used in training AI software, without the express written permission of the publisher, excepting brief quotes used in reviews.

The scanning, uploading, and distribution of this book via the Internet or via any other means without the permission of the publisher is illegal and punishable by law. Please purchase only authorized electronic editions, and do not participate in or encourage electronic piracy of copyrighted materials.

Thank you for respecting the hard work of the author.

ISBN (Paperback): 978-1-7348581-2-9
ISBN (eBook): 978-1-7348581-3-6

Scripturio Books
www.ScripturioBooks.com
24.04.03

Dedication & Acknowledgments

For Elaine, Mark, and Vickie, marvelous beta-readers!
Without your insightful input, my stories would be much
rougher and less coherent. So thank you, as always!

CHAPTER 1

The dark ship that sailed into the harbor at sunset should have fallen apart long before it reached shore… from all appearances, anyway. For some inexplicable reason, the ship demanded Gyasi's attention more than all the other ships already docked – beyond the fact that ships seldom arrived so late in the day.

Gyasi habitually watched the incoming ships from the second floor of his family's modest storehouse located on a hill near the dock. He hoped for some newcomer who might be interested in a trade arrangement for the goods stored in the single large room of the building's ground floor. The storehouse occupied the end of a row of similar storehouses, the others all larger than his, with only the shoreline beyond to the west.

This ship looked unlike any he had ever seen – certainly not like any of the merchant ships with which he had dealt since he had inherited the running of the business after his mother's death a little more than a year before. Even since he had first begun to watch the incoming ships as a child, this ship was easily the most distinctive, with four masts and the deck built up both fore and aft.

Gyasi watched the ship ease up to the dock—the ship's sweeps maneuvered it expertly—and imagined he heard an echo of Toabi's words of a few days earlier. "There's going to be a change," Gyasi's younger brother had murmured as they both watched the sunrise from the other side of the storehouse.

Gyasi folded his arms and leaned on the windowsill with a soft sigh. He had not felt what his brother had, in the secret magic they shared. *What had Toa felt, truly? Could it be just wishful thinking on his brother's part? Could he know something?*

The new ship dwarfed the others at the dock. In the dim orange-tinted light, Gyasi struggled to determine the colors of its sails, but he saw that a subtle and unique pattern decorated them: a series of intertwined curves and flourishes. Obviously built for the sea, the ship looked to be swift, except for a damaged mast, a gaping hole in the deck near the stern, port side, and numerous other smaller holes, smashed timbers, and tears in the sails. From his vantage, Gyasi saw only a few people on the deck. By the way they moved, he guessed they were injured.

After Gyasi watched the damaged, listing ship limp to a berth in the harbor, he ran downstairs. His presence would be expected, even required, and it would not do to be late. *He did not want the attention that would bring. Besides, he wanted to get a better look at this newcomer and her crew.*

He grabbed his reed pens in their protective wooden case, a small jar of ink, and a blank tally scroll from the small supply on the shelf. *Need to see about getting more scrolls soon.*

Tucking his supplies in a small satchel, he slung the bag over one shoulder and stuck his other arm through the strap, so the bag hung cross-body, freeing his hands. Then he dashed out the door.

By the time Gyasi arrived at the end of the newcomer's pier, a crowd had already gathered there. Most of the dock workers, it looked like. The Harbormaster himself faced the damaged ship from a few steps in front of the crowd. As the designated Harbor Tallymaster for the town of Hawei, Gyasi was given room to move through the crowd to the front – plenty of room so no one would come into contact with him, perhaps fearing they might catch his Blight by touch alone. Although he worked alongside many of these people, he still kept his gaze turned away from theirs, not offering any potential threat. *Better that way.* Someone had lit the lanterns along the dock which let Gyasi see the ship more clearly and he shivered as he examined it.

The ship's hull and decks looked a glossy black in the lanternlight, and the sails were a red nearly the color of blood, with the strange pattern on them in some darker color. Gyasi heard murmurs from the crowd around him about 'death ships' and 'evil omens'. *Nonsense, of course.* But he had to admit to himself that if anything portended a change, and not for the better, this ship certainly fit the sort of harbinger one might expect.

Kalbei, the Harbormaster, shifted his feet and darted glances all around while he waited for someone from the ship to come meet him.

Before too long, someone came to the ship's rail. "Permission to come ashore?" the person called out.

The words were heavily accented, with a lilt that Gyasi found unfamiliar. *Unusual.* While not the largest port town in the Atturei Empire, Hawei still saw many ships from the other lands the Empire traded with. Gyasi had grown up hearing many different accents throughout his score and two years.

Kalbei beckoned to the figure with a wave of a hand. "Come ahead," he called, then turned slightly toward the crowd that stood a few steps behind him. When he spotted Gyasi, he motioned him closer.

"Join me, Gya. Maybe you can tell me something about these strangers."

Gyasi hurried to take his place next to the Harbormaster as people on the ship wrestled their gangplank into position.

"I haven't seen the like of their ship before," Gyasi told Kalbei in a quiet voice.

Kalbei grunted an acknowledgment as two figures eased down the gangplank to the dock and the waiting crowd. They walked with that gait peculiar to those who spent long days on the ocean. In the uncertain light, Gyasi struggled to see any details about them. He narrowed his eyes against the spray that blew off the water in the wind that had gusted several days – often the sign of storms to the north.

The newcomers stopped a few paces away in the light from the dock lanterns and Gyasi let out a soft sigh. *They were just men.* A number of years older than himself, he guessed. They stood a little taller than the average. Their hair was of diverse shades of brown—far less curly than Gyasi's own pale-yellow hair—and their skin rubicund. Quite unlike most of the Empire's people, but still just men.

Both men were cleanshaven, unlike the men of Gyasi's acquaintance who all, himself included, wore beards and mustaches, usually close-cut. The newcomers' clothes had an exotic look to them – hip-length tunics with sleeves that reached down their arms to their elbows and loose trousers gathered at the ankle. The clothes showed signs of much mending, places where the cloth looked like it had been cut. *Could that damage be from swords? Might they have been set upon by pirates?*

Their low shoes looked much like Gyasi's own, but the strangers' clothing was exceedingly plain next to the bright patterns that decorated the cloth that made up the sleeveless knee-length and longer tunics and wide-legged trousers worn by the Hawei workers and residents who had gathered on the dock.

After they scrutinized the people who had gathered, the

strange men bowed to Gyasi and Kalbei, their hands clasped before them.

"Our thanks for allowing us to put in at your harbor," one man said, the older of the two. "What fees do we owe?"

Kalbei stood dumb, apparently nonplused by this ordinary question. Gyasi cleared his throat and nodded discretely to the newcomers when Kalbei glanced at him. Kalbei shook himself and told the strangers the rules of the dock and explained the various fees to them.

Kalbei and the man who had spoken then dickered about fees while Gyasi and the other man waited. Gyasi studied the other man while he looked around, openly curious. When they caught each other's eyes, the man smiled slightly at Gyasi before Gya dropped his gaze away.

"It has been a long time since we last put ashore," the stranger said, his voice soft enough that he did not interrupt the dickering.

"Then I'd expect you'll want to visit a good tavern, maybe even an inn, and spend a few days here." Gyasi kept his voice as quiet.

The man smiled. "That would be very welcome. Also, if there is a healer—" He broke off at a sharp word from his companion.

The two argued in a language foreign to Gyasi, and Kalbei's expression grew worried as the argument turned intense. A sudden loud word from the direction of the ship silenced the two men.

Another figure descended from the ship. This figure wore a wine-red cloak with the hood pulled far forward. The cloak enveloped the figure and brushed the ground. Gyasi noticed a pronounced limp as it came toward them. A few more harsh-sounding words from the newcomer and the two strangers each dropped to one knee where they stood and bowed their heads. Both Gyasi and Kalbei peered curiously at the newcomer while the crowd behind them murmured and shuffled their feet.

Apparently ignoring the two kneeling men, the figure moved closer to Kalbei.

"My apologies, good sirs," the figure said in a tone unlike the previous harsh-sounding words, the voice feminine. The woman pushed back the hood with slender hands, revealing striking features unlike anyone Gyasi had seen before.

Her smooth, straight hair, a black so dark it had blue hints in it, fell only to her shoulders. Her skin was a golden brown, if he could trust how it looked in the lantern-light, shades lighter than Gyasi's own dark-brown skin. She was thin, not at all like the women of his acquaintance with their strong, stocky builds and generous curves. Although this woman did have her own curves, Gya saw as the wind momentarily plastered her cloak against her before it whipped it away again to reveal the simple ankle-length gown she wore beneath it.

She was nearly of a height to look Gyasi straight in the eyes. Something made him think she was some years older than he, but he could not pinpoint what gave him that impression. And her eyes…. They had a slight tilt upward at their outer corners and were the darkest he had ever seen, quite different from the light browns, ambers, or pale blues most common among the people of the Empire.

From the differences in their appearances, Gyasi decided she and the two men who knelt behind her did not come from the same people. The woman's accent sounded different from theirs. When Gyasi realized he had been staring, he shifted his gaze away.

The woman handed some coins to Kalbei. "I hope that those will allow us to stay here for a while."

Kalbei's eyes widened as he examined the coins that glinted in his hands, each one gold and perhaps two-thirds the size of a gold-spisha, the Empire's most valuable coin. The woman had given Kalbei three of them.

"Four months!" Kalbei stammered. "This would pay your fees for a whole four months."

The woman raised her eyebrows. "I doubt we will need so long a time. Perhaps two months for now, and then see if we need longer?"

Kalbei nodded agreement and returned one of the gold coins. He pulled a small pouch, stamped with the Empire's symbol, from a larger one on his belt and poured a stream of silver-spishas into one hand. He counted out thirty-four of them into the woman's hand. "And that's a confirmed arrangement," he told her as he put the pouch away again. "Paid for two months and we can talk again if you wish to stay longer."

The woman tucked the coins away somewhere beneath her cloak and turned to Gyasi. "I believe I heard mention of a good tavern or inn, and a healer? We would like to replenish our supplies, also."

"There are several wonderful places that cater to the ships," Gyasi told her. "Although you'll need to wait until tomorrow for supplies as most places have ended their day already. I've an arrangement with a healer for my own people. I'm certain he'd be willing to look at yours."

She nodded and motioned to the still-kneeling men. They got to their feet and moved to stand behind her, one at each shoulder.

"Please tell Narain here how to get to the nearest inn." She indicated the man who had spoken with Gyasi. "Then if you would take me to see your healer friend…."

"Of—"

"Hold a moment," Kalbei broke in as he directed a pointed look at Gyasi.

No doubt to make sure I remember the laws, Gyasi grumbled to himself, annoyed at the older man. He kept his thoughts from his expression and simply gave Kalbei a meek nod, acting the compliant citizen, the role he had made for himself to stay safe, when he longed to be just the opposite. *If only it would do any good.*

The newcomers exchanged glances and all three of them made aborted motions that looked like they reached for weapons, which they did not carry. Kalbei drew himself up at their suddenly wary expressions and clenched and unclenched both fists.

Gyasi stepped between them, with a second nod to Kalbei. "As I was saying… of course we wouldn't send you off with only directions, unfamiliar with our town as you are."

"I'll show the way to Shala's Inn," Kalbei said. "She's got an exceptional place, not too far. She should have rooms available, too."

"I'm happy to take you to the healer," Gyasi said.

"But we still have business first." Kalbei held out an arm to block anyone from walking away.

Again the newcomers exchanged concerned looks. One of the men glanced back at their ship and edged that direction.

"You just need Hawei tokens," Gyasi hurried to explain. "The tokens for our town."

Their concerned expressions changed to ones of confusion. Gya pulled his token from beneath his shirt by the cord it hung from around his neck and eased closer to one of the lanterns. He held out the token for the strangers to see in the light.

The woman followed him and, with a glance to ask permission, leaned closer to examine what he held. Gyasi's token was a square ceramic piece, roughly half the length of his thumb across, with a hole in one corner for the cord. The Empire's symbol of the crossed sword and scepter in front of a single flame was stamped and tinted on one side and a few words were pressed into the other, also tinted to make them stand out from the gray background.

"What does this say?" The woman pointed to the token.

"That side identifies the bearer and which sanctions are allowed to him or her," Kalbei said.

Gyasi tucked his token away again as the Harbormaster

handed each of the newcomers two tokens, a gray one on a cord, much like Gyasi's, and a second one, slightly larger and black, with a hook on one corner.

"This token on the cord identifies you as travelers, visitors to Hawei," Kalbei explained as he indicated the smaller of the two tokens he had given out. "See here, this word is Hawei, the name of this town. Wear those as long as you are in our town. The second token allows you to be out later at night, if needed to finish your business tonight. Hook it onto your town token's cord. You have until the second hour after midnight, after which you must be either in an inn for the rest of the night or back on your ship. Give those tokens to Gyasi here when you're settled, or you can return them to me tomorrow morning."

Kalbei handed Gyasi one of the black tokens. "So you can see them settled."

He then motioned to Narain and the other man to join him and turned toward town while he muttered under his breath about four months.

The woman watched her companions and Kalbei until they left the dock area, then turned those amazing eyes to Gyasi.

"Is there some threat in the night, that people need special permission to go about after dark?"

Gyasi shrugged. "It's just the law. And it's only between midnight and the sixth hour after."

She frowned and took a quick look around. Gyasi followed her gaze but saw nothing unusual. Already the onlookers had returned to their tasks or headed home for the night, although a few dock workers still lingered – the Keepers too, of course, who were always around town. One Keeper watched Gyasi and the woman, but when the Keeper met Gyasi's gaze, she only gave them a slight nod before she turned her attention toward the ship.

After she perused the woman as she watched her ship, the stranger turned back to Gyasi.

"The healer?"

With an effort, Gyasi drew his gaze from her dark, dark eyes and turned his attention back to the matter at hand. "Yes, of course. It's not too far to Candwi's dwelling. Up the hill into the town proper. I can get a wagon for you."

"My thanks, but that will not be necessary. Our healer told me walking would help. Please, let us go."

Gyasi glanced sidelong at her. *What a formal way of talking. Could that be how her people spoke in their own language? Or, more likely, she and her people had little practice before this in conversing in the Empire's tongue.*

"Of course. This way." With a quick look around to see if any of the Keepers paid them more than the usual attention, Gyasi led the woman toward town.

"Oh!" The woman's exclamation broke their silence as they came in sight of the edge of town, the somewhat rundown shops and dwellings closest to the harbor.

"What is it? Should I get that wagon?" Gyasi studied her, but she did not seem to be in pain. She stared at the buildings however, her expression something that looked like shock. He followed her gaze but saw nothing of concern. While the shoreline smells were perhaps a little stronger there than they had been at the dock, she did not look like that was what had stopped her.

She met his gaze. "What? Oh, no, I have no need for the wagon. It is just…." She waved a hand toward the buildings. "They remind me of my own village. The sturdy brick walls, always in need of a bit of repair work. Sloping roofs for the rain to run off." Her voice held a wistful note in it.

Gya scanned the buildings and tried to see them as she might be. A number of candle-lanterns on poles lined the streets and provided a good amount of light. Constructed of fired mudbrick, often stuccoed then painted in pale colors, the buildings were roofed with darker, reddish tiles from some of the many potters in this town known for its pottery and ceramics – and its good harbor. The streets boasted a layer of gritty dust, as usual. Any cleansing brought by the infrequent rains seldom lasted long.

Many of the buildings near the harbor needed repairs and their paint flaked to show the light sand-color of the bricks beneath. The poorest of the town comprised most of the people who lived in those buildings, located so near busy storehouses and the frequently odorous harbor.

The woman stared at the buildings several seconds longer before she shook herself free of her fascination and resumed walking.

"You perhaps wonder why I wish to see a healer when I just mentioned ours?" she said.

"It had occurred to me."

"She died. Just a couple of weeks ago. Not long after I was injured, but before most of my crew were. They need to be tended properly, before I lose more of them."

"Candwi is good. Also, he's treated battle injures before."

The woman looked at him sidelong. "You think we have seen battle?"

Gyasi glanced at her. "That would be my guess. Your two men's clothing looked like it had been sliced by blades and poorly mended. I could see what looked like bloodstains in the material. The deck of your ship bears the marks of flames, and it's devilishly difficult to do such damage to a mast of that size, unless it's been hit by something like a large rock, say, from a catapult. Same as what made the hole near the stern, possibly. Also, your man Narain has a mostly healed, but recent, blade wound across his forearm. Shall I continue?"

She laughed. "No, you have pretty well covered it. Are you a town guard or something like that here?"

"No. Just the Harbor Tallymaster. And a merchant for now, too. But I keep my eyes open. Our harbor sees ships from many lands, and some have come in looking almost as bad as yours."

"I see. Well, my observant Tallymaster/merchant, you have the right of it. We were attacked and came off much worse than is our usual wont. I believe we entered some forbidden waters."

"Hmm. Not pirates then. You were attacked from shore?"

"Yes. An area with tall cliffs and white beaches."

"The Yuyur lands. Those barbarians dislike all outsiders. Why would you have sailed to them?"

She looked away into the night. "It was unintentional. We came out of the gale almost ashore there."

What an odd way to say a sea storm ended. Gya peered at her. *With her odd accent… must be the way they phrase such things in her own language.*

"Forgive me for prying," he said when she added nothing further.

"There is nothing to forgive. You are naturally curious. Perhaps I can explain it to you better sometime. May I know your name?"

"Oh, my apologies for the oversight." Gyasi's chuckle sounded more nervous than he wanted. "I'm Gyasi K'rond. As I already mentioned, I'm Harbor Tallymaster of the Docks and currently also a storehouse merchant of Hawei."

"Ah, Gyasi K'rond. I am grateful for your help. I am Alorsha Tavano, acting Ship's Master until her true master recovers. I also happen to be one of the owners of the ship."

"Please, call me Gya, Master Tavano."

She chuckled. "Acting master only, as I said. Please just call me Alorsha."

"Certainly. So, you own the ship. Is it customary among your people for the owners to sail with their ships?"

Alorsha shook her head, with a slight smile that seemed to hold a hint of sadness. "Mine is a unique situation."

When she explained no further, Gya changed the subject. "I'll need to tally the cargo you've brought for sale. Tonight would be best, if it can be managed."

Alorsha gave him a strange look. "You tally the cargo of every ship that docks here?"

"Of course. Part of the Empire's strength is its attention to details and information. To keep us all safe."

Alorsha nodded, but her expression held more than a hint of doubt. "I had hoped to gain the healer's services this night then manage some sleep. Our recent journey has been... difficult."

Gyasi glanced at her and shrugged to himself. "As Tallymaster, I'm required to look over your goods, but if you can give me a description tonight, we can delay the visual look-see until morning."

Alorsha frowned. "We are not a merchant ship, although many of the crew create items to trade or sell. The cargo we carry is food and goods for ourselves and for maintaining the *Deliberia*."

"*Deliberia*." Gyasi stumbled over the unfamiliar word. "That's what your ship is called?"

She nodded, with a slight smile.

"Ah. Then why have you come to the docks of Hawei?"

"We are looking for someone—" As Alorsha spoke, they both turned the corner around one of the town's larger buildings and ran into another person.

After a startled moment, and another to untangle themselves, Gyasi and Alorsha faced the man they had nearly run over.

Gyasi recognized him of course, one of the town's Keepers. While Usrai stood barely a couple of finger-widths taller than Gya, he projected an imposing toughness as he loomed in his fitted brown uniform of hip-length coat over snug trousers, with shiny black calf high boots and gray backless gloves. Gya shrank in on himself, always small around him, although they were both stocky and his years helping in the storehouse as he grew had given him muscles and strength.

It had been the same even back when they took

schooling together, Usrai a year ahead of him. Usrai always stood too close as he liked to do to dominate another. He wore his near-white curly hair almost as short as Gya's and was not someone Gya wanted to cross.

Usrai's expression changed from irritation to something darker when he recognized Gya and saw the woman with him. Not needing to pretend at the apprehension that everyone struggled with when singled out by the Keepers, Gya yanked out the cord with his two tokens before Usrai demanded to see them.

The Keeper looked Alorsha over while he mostly ignored Gya.

"Well, here is a pretty out and about in the dark of night," he said. "Whatever is to be done?"

"It's all sanctioned, Usrai." Gyasi held his tokens closer to the man. "Her ship just made port and Kalbei cleared us to go see Candwi."

Usrai stepped closer to Gya and frowned at him before he gave his tokens a cursory look while Alorsha belatedly dug hers out from under her shirt. The Keeper scrutinized both of Alorsha's tokens, front and back, before he let them drop to hang from her cord.

"All in perfect order, as I would expect from you, Gya." Usrai's tone held a hint of a sneer. "You've always been good about knowing your place." In a swift motion, he grabbed Alorsha's hand as she started to tuck away her tokens and grinned at her.

"When you've finished your mission of mercy for your ship, if you still have time before your token's pass runs out, come find me at The Ample Flagon. It's a couple streets over. Ask for Usrai." He rubbed his thumb across Alorsha's hand in a rough caress. "I'm much more fun than this shrinking list-maker here."

After a quick glance at Gya, Alorsha gave Usrai a slight smile that held no warmth. "I will keep that in mind." She pulled her hand back, tucked away her tokens, and turned to Gya. "Is the healer much further?"

Usrai clapped Gya on the shoulder, hard. The blow masqueraded as an affable gesture but caused Gya to stumble a step. Then Usrai grabbed his arm in a clench too tight to be friendly. Gyasi fought the sudden panic that gripped him and hoped it did not show.

Had the Keeper somehow learned his secret?

In the next instant, he forced himself to give Usrai merely a questioning look.

"Keep us apprised about this ship." Usrai leaned close with a glower on his face. "And keep an eye on that brother of yours. He pushes the sanctions too much more and it'll go hard for him." He shook Gya's arm, once and hard, before he released it.

"Best be getting on," the Keeper said with a satisfied grin and turned back the way he had come.

Gya rubbed his arm while he led Alorsha the same direction, at a slower pace to avoid catching Usrai. "Just another block to Candwi's. You should know that Usrai has several lovers already. They're rather possessive of his attentions—"

Alorsha's laugh interrupted him. "I thank you for the warning. I have no intention of joining them or challenging their places."

With a nod, secretly pleased at her answer, Gya led the way to one of the shuttered shops and up the stairs to the door to the dwelling on the second floor. "Here's Candwi's place." He knocked on the plain door.

When the healer's wizened face appeared at the crack of the barely opened door, Gyasi introduced Alorsha and explained their purpose there.

Candwi nodded, his motion abrupt. "I'll come to the ship. Let me just finish here and get my things." He closed the door again.

"Is he not going to need one of the tokens?" Alorsha said.

"Healers, and Keepers too, have special tokens that allow them the sanction of free travel within Hawei, no matter the time of day," Gyasi said. "Candwi always keeps his close at hand in case he's called out late at night."

They waited many long minutes before Candwi opened the door again. He carried a bag in one hand and ushered two women out ahead of him, one of them leaning on the other.

Candwi gave the leaning woman a stern look as he closed his door. "Now you do as I said, Razaya. When you get back home, stay off that foot and rest. Keep it wrapped. No evening tavern visits for a while."

The woman's expression soured, but her companion nodded. "I'll make sure of it," she assured the healer.

"That means you'll just have to get me my drinks for the nights," Razaya told her companion, her speech slurred. "Promise me, Omondu, my love?"

"Uh, surely. Let's just get you back home for now."

Gya, Alorsha, and Candwi watched the two women stagger down the stairs and along the street, until they rounded a corner.

"Will Razaya be alright?" Gya ventured when Candwi turned his attention back to them.

"More drunk than hurt," the healer muttered. "Nothing new there. She'll be fine if she does as I told her. The drunken fool started early tonight and managed to trip off the tavern steps. Twisted her ankle."

With a shake of his head for Razaya's injury, Candwi nodded to Alorsha and Gya to lead the way. They headed back to the dock and Candwi quizzed Alorsha the whole way about the injuries of the crew.

Before Gya left them at the ship, he learned a few details from Alorsha about any goods the ship-folk might want to sell. Then he watched until both Candwi and Alorsha were aboard. He exchanged nods with the two Keepers who stood at the bottom of the plank that led to the strange ship and headed to the dwelling he shared with his brother on the second floor of their storehouse.

CHAPTER 2

ELSEWHERE, IN A PROVINCIAL CAPITAL OF THE ATTUREI EMPIRE

The stranger walked into the small building as if he owned the place. In fact, from the quality of his clothes and the way he carried himself, Triloa felt certain that he could have owned it if he chose. He paused in the doorway and scrutinized the small room. Triloa in turn, looked him over as well in the light of the lanterns spaced around the room, lighting it against the late hour. *Unusual to have someone come in so late in the day.* They themselves seldom stayed this late.

At first, with his too-light brown skin, she assumed the stranger came from one of the portions of the Empire that lay further north, perhaps the Layakei region, which bordered Yuyur, land of the barbarians. But no, he stood too tall and his clothes did not match anything customarily worn in that wild region.

She looked more closely – his clothes did not match any style that she had ever heard of. He wore long robes of some sort, of a deep blue-green, a couple of layers it looked like, and slit on the sides from the bottom nearly to his waist, to show matching trousers beneath. The stranger bore no weapon, but she saw two rings on his belt from which a scabbard might normally hang.

Triloa guessed that he had seen close to a score and ten of years. She had never before seen hair of the deep red-brown color that his was. She caught sight of his eyes—a blue-green almost the color of his robes—and they held her motionless as she came under his scrutiny.

When his gaze released her some seconds or hours later, after a light touch of his fingers to the back of her hand, her curiosity had fled, leaving her only with the certain knowledge that here was someone important. It never occurred to her to wonder where this knowledge came from. With a bright smile for him, she stood up from behind her small desk and smoothed her uniform coat, not unintentionally showing off her generous curves. He looked her over from head to toe and smiled in appreciation.

She inclined her head to him. "May I escort you to see the minister, sir?"

With a negligent wave of his hand, he glided toward the hall that led to the minister's office. "That won't be necessary. I can find my own way."

She shivered at the sound of his voice, a deep, soft thing with a strange accent. It hinted at secrets, power, and forbidden knowledge.

"See to my companion's needs while he waits here for my return," the stranger added as he swept past her with a faint whisper of the bottom of his robe across the floor and an odd scent of burnt wood. Then he was gone down the short hall.

Only then did Triloa notice the second man who had entered in the first one's shadow. He stood in the doorway, his posture hesitant. His clothing resembled the other man's, but was made of coarser material and duller colors, variations of brown. *Perhaps a poor relation that the first man graciously allowed to travel with him?*

At a second look, Triloa decided he was no relation

after all. True, his hair was also a strange color—gold-brown in his case—and his eyes were green, not at all as penetrating as the other man's. His features were not at all like the first man's and he looked to be a little shorter than the other. He had a beaten look to him, as if life was almost too much for him. He barely glanced at her before his gaze slid away from hers.

"Is it all right if I sit?" he mumbled, his voice harsh and jarring after the smooth, rich sound of the first man's.

"Of course." Triloa indicated a chair for him. "I'll get you a bit of water to drink."

~ ~ ~

Imperial Minister Arizu B'Jen looked up as the stranger entered her office. *What interruption was this?* She had hoped to finish up and go home soon. *Hopefully, she could address whatever his concern was and get him on his way quickly.*

The man closed the door behind him and drew himself up straight, his eyes boldly gazing at her. Then he extended his right arm toward her, the back of that hand properly facing her.

At least he knew the proper, civilized greeting, even if he was obviously from out-Empire.

She rose and stepped around her table to approach him. Extending her arm even as his was, she touched the back of her hand to the back of his to complete the greeting. "What brings you to me?"

He calmly seated himself in the chair closest to the door. She took one that sat at an angle to his.

"I have some information that you should find useful." The man's deep voice, while not much louder than a whisper, seemed to fill the room.

Arizu merely nodded, for some reason not inclined to question the stranger, not even about what information he offered. She assessed his exotic looks with a slight smile. Under his intent gaze, she preened while he continued.

"A dangerous traveler is headed to your lands. She might even have already arrived, almost certainly at one of your port towns. To the west, roughly, I believe. I don't know which town that might be, but it's likely whichever holds your largest port in that area."

"That would be Hawei."

"Hawei," the stranger repeated, seeming to taste the word and find it strange. "This traveler brings with her the forbidden knowledge. I believe she means to spread her contamination throughout your lands. I thought perhaps you'd be interested."

At his words, Arizu shuddered. *To think that after all their work, hers and the Keepers' and the Imperial Council's, an outsider would come here to spread the Blight, the abomination of magic, to again contaminate the common people of the Atturei Empire. Those who had no business with magic.*

"Y-yes." She flushed under his gaze, her brown cheeks slightly darkened. "You have my gratitude for bringing me this information. If there's anything I can offer you in return…."

The stranger smiled and let his gaze rove over her. "There's no need for you to offer me anything, although we might find something we can offer each other."

He shook his head, the motion slight, and Arizu took a deep breath as if released from some constraint.

He still smiled at her. "Later. But for now, perhaps there *is* something yet that I can offer you. I assume you'd find this person's name useful."

"Oh yes, of course."

"She is known as Alorsha Tavano."

"Alorsha Tavano? I've not heard a name like that before."

"Of course not. She's not from your lands or from anywhere even near your lands. But she brings the forbidden with her to pollute the great Empire of Atturei."

"Thank you again for this valuable information. And I *am* sincere… if I can offer you anything in return…."

The stranger smiled at her again—a smile that seemed full of promises—and stood to leave. "If you'll simply stop her, that will suffice in return for the information I've brought you. Anything else we might decide on will be just something special between us two."

"Of course. We have tamed Magickas, tied to the Empire, who can deal with the threat. I'll see to that right away." Arizu found herself speaking that last to the closing door.

Outside in the hallway, the stranger eased the door shut behind him and chuckled to himself. This Empire that claimed to want to eliminate all magic had taken those who worked magic and made them its vassals.

He shook his head in amusement as he read the hand-painted sign that hung on the wall next to the door: 'Ministry for the Containment of the Abomination of Magic'.

That should keep Alorsha occupied.

CHAPTER 3

Gyasi again stood at the window that overlooked the harbor. In the pale morning light, the *Deliberia* looked far more benign than the previous night, although still just as imposing. Gyasi saw that the wood of the ship was not truly black, but rather very dark, with an exotic reddish tint to it.

If they carried more of that wood and would be willing to sell it, he knew some people who would pay a premium price for it. They would probably take it to the Imperial Capital and get their money back and more there.

Well, he would know soon enough if the ship had any to spare. As soon as he saw movement on the deck, he planned to go there for his tally-work.

The door opened behind him and he heard the familiar sounds of his brother stumbling in after all night out. Toabi joined him at the window, rubbing a hand over his short hair that was a shade darker than Gya's.

"That's quite the ship," he muttered as he leaned against the window casing. "Certainly, a harbinger of change, if I've ever seen one. They call you out last night to log her in?"

"Sort of," Gyasi muttered. "Where were you, Toa?"

The younger man grinned. "Celebrating Zawdi's name-day, of course. You should've come."

When Gya did not respond, Toa sighed. "So, did you make it to the meeting?"

Gya frowned and, although he knew they were alone in the building this early, he looked around to ensure no one was close enough to eavesdrop – a precaution that had become habit.

"Not so loud, Toa."

Toa waved a dismissive hand at him. "Don't worry so. No one's here. Certainly not in our dwelling. No one will find out."

Gya's frown deepened but he nodded.

"I couldn't get away to meet," Gya said. "So we'll have to wait for the sign for the next one." He peered at his brother. "You should come more often. Learn to better use, and hide, the magic."

Toa plopped into a chair. "What's the point? Why hide it. Why even bother learning any, if we're only going to stick to the smaller, simpler ones?"

"Someday we'll not have to fear the Keepers. Someday we'll be able to use our magic openly, like when our parents were children."

"And *someday* we'll not have to fear being dragged off to who-knows-where." Toa imitated Gya's voice. "Subject to who-knows-what the Empire does with all the Magickas that it finds and hauls off." Toa shook his head. "I've heard this all before. What good did hiding the magic do for father? It didn't help when they came for him! It only made it easier for them to take him, leaving mother stuck with us, two children, when he never came back. If we're going to actually learn the magic, we've got to go all in. None of this extreme caution and hiding. We should learn to really use it, so it'll matter!"

Gya sighed and rubbed his forehead. "How I wish, but

we've been over this before. We can't do that. I can't. It'll just make things worse."

"It's always the same thing. Hiding your magic won't help you get the Council to allow you to wed, get them to choose a wife, the one you hope for."

Gya winced at the reminder. With their history of the Blight of magic in the family, he and his brother were at the bottom of all the lists. Lists for access to the better sanctions, lists for those allowed to wed so their family line would continue. Although as far as most of the people of Hawei knew, he and Toa had no magic.

Toa waved a finger in Gya's face. "You should come with me, instead. I know a couple of women who would like to get together with you."

"Oh, stop."

Toa chuckled. "Still pining after her, are you?"

"I don't pine."

"Have you even spoken with her? Anything beyond comments about on what a fine day it is?" Toa grinned at his older brother's expression. "That's what I thought."

Gya shook his head with a sigh. "It wouldn't be fair to her to even hint at something we might not be allowed. A home together. Perhaps a family."

Toa imitated his brother's head shake. "You've got it bad, don't you? Definitely pining. Just do it, if she'll have you. Marry. We shouldn't need to have the town council's say-so for such a thing."

"We'd have to leave. Run."

"So find someplace new to live. Better. Where we don't have to hide who we are, what we can do." Toa's voice was little more than a whisper.

Gya matched his tone. "We shouldn't *have* to run. There's got to be some way—"

"But that requires actually *doing* something," Toa countered. "Not just secret, hidden meetings with the others. Not just going over the same simple magics again and again. Not just talking."

"We can't risk more right now. Can't risk being discovered if we can't oppose them." Gya waved a dismissive hand in the air. "But enough. We have things we need to do. Come with me to the ship. At least do some work around here today. Soon enough, you'll have to take charge of the storehouse and the rest of the business like you're supposed to. You've nearly a score years. Time to get serious. I can't keep doing this and being Tallymaster for much longer. The other merchants won't stand for it."

Toa held up his hands in a placating gesture and bowed to Gya. "As you say, oh eldest of the family. I'll just wash up and change."

"Please do. You reek. Did you drink the pom wine, or pour it over your head?"

Toa laughed before he gave Gya a stern look. "Take care you're not turning into the meek town worker you pretend at."

With a casual wave at Gya, he headed to their small bathing house that sat tucked behind the storehouse.

Gya stared at the empty doorway long after he had gone. *Had he become the meek town worker that had only been supposed to be a façade to hide behind?*

~ ~ ~

Toa caught Gya as he neared the ship's gangplank. Together, they walked closer and had nearly reached it when Alorsha appeared at the railing.

Toa whistled under his breath. "On second thought, brother, maybe I *should* be doing my work in the family business."

Gya sighed to himself. *Toa would never change.* "Be careful here," he warned his brother in a whisper. "She's one of the ship's owners, she told me. I'd say she's probably a couple years shy of being a score and ten years old."

Toa shrugged and grinned. "Not *that* much older than

me. It's said that among the elite of the Empire, the women often prefer a younger man," he whispered back.

"You're not one of the elite," Gya hissed. "And she's not of the Empire. We don't know her people's customs."

"You worry too much. I'll just be my usual charming self."

Gya snorted.

On the deck, several crewmembers awaited their arrival. Some carried bags and some had spread out some of their goods on the deck around them. Others continued with their duties. Gya noted that the crew seemed to consist of roughly the same number of men as women.

After introductions, Alorsha led Gya and Toa to the waiting crewmembers, a diverse group of people. As with the crewmembers Gya saw in passing, all hard at work at their various tasks, the small group that waited for him exhibited all shades of hair, eyes and skin. Much more variety than Gya saw in Hawei most of the time and several with skin much lighter than he usually saw, except for the rare ships that came from the far north. He had the feeling that *Deliberia's* crew originally hailed from a great variety of lands before they had sailed with the ship.

"As I told you, we are not a merchant ship. But these people do have a few things they would like to barter or sell." Alorsha smiled at her crew and they returned the expression.

Gya looked at the list he had created the previous night based on what Alorsha had told him her crew had to sell. Yes, he had remembered everything. So he went from one crewmember to another and marked on his tally scroll how many of their items they had available and their names and any other details about the goods that they offered. Toa and Alorsha followed along, with Toa trying to engage the *Deliberia's* Acting Master in conversation.

After he had spoken with the last crewmember, Gya turned to Alorsha.

"Now, if you would show me your ship. I need to

make note of what else you carry, even if you will not be selling it."

"Is that necessary? We just want to heal and make repairs." Alorsha frowned and looked around the deck, perhaps looking for someone.

Gya nodded. "It's one of the requirements to be able to dock here."

Alorsha pulled one of the crew aside and spoke to him briefly, then smiled at Gya and Toa, her smile a little strained.

"Please come with me."

The brothers followed her as she took them throughout the ship, where they found all the usual rooms on a ship: quarters for the crew, the galley and an eating area, rooms for the sweeps and the various rooms that stored the depleted provisions for the crew and materials for repairs to the ship. Nothing more than what she had said.

But beyond those, Gya also saw rooms set aside for activities he had never expected to see aboard a ship. Weavers occupied one room, with some people sewing clothes in the adjoining room. One space belowdecks held a mill, smaller than any Gya had seen before, with two crewmembers turning it to grind grains. In another room, two people seemed to be mending shoes while another worked on a belt. Gya even discovered a small room that seemed home to some small birds similar to chickens.

He shook his head at that last discovery. *The ship's more like a floating town than anything else.*

Gya would have liked to linger at storerooms that held pieces of that red wood, but Alorsha hurried them along. Everywhere they went belowdecks, Gya detected a faint spicy scent that reminded him of cinnamon. But the ship did not seem to carry spices other than what they used in the galley. *Curious.*

Last Alorsha took them to the raised decks at the bow and the stern of the ship. The single raised deck at the bow served as roof for more crew quarters. Gya guessed they belonged to those of higher rank among the common crewmembers. The stern featured two raised decks.

Two large items bundled in canvas sat on the raised deck at the bow, and Gya spotted another two on the highest deck at the stern. Gya peeked beneath the edge of one and found a large contraption that looked somewhat like a crossbow, but much larger. He had seen something like this before.

"Ballistae?" Gya gestured toward the others. "Four of them?"

"Not all waters we have sailed have been friendly." Alorsha directed a pointed glance at the damage visible from where they stood.

Gya shuffled his feet. "Oh, of course. Shall we continue?" He gestured toward the raised decks at the stern and followed as Alorsha led the way. As they passed the ship's masts, a short pole attached to the rigging of one caught Gya's attention. *Wonder what that's for? Looks out of place – maybe just another broken part.* He shrugged to himself and chose to keep his peace to avoid asking a potentially laughable question.

The lower floor at the stern, on a level with the main deck, held several cabins, one of which belonged to the Ship's Captain. The others belonged to others of the crew who seemed the equivalent of officers from what Gya knew from other ships. The upper floor held just two cabins, Alorsha told him.

"The cabin belonging to our Ship's Master, Saevalde Eztevo, is in here, and my cabin, also." Alorsha paused outside the door. A double door, Gya noticed. "Your healer said our Ship's Master needs her rest." She gave Gya a pointed look.

"I'm sorry. I must inspect everywhere."

Alorsha nodded and eased open the left door. She leaned in and spoke in a quiet voice to someone inside before she opened the door wider.

Within, Gya found a cabin more simply furnished than he expected: bed, table and chairs, and low cabinets along the walls for storage, situated beneath a lot of windows.

A stocky woman with browned and weathered skin, brown wavy hair and light-blue eyes lay on the bed, which sat left of center in the room. She wore a simple shirt and trousers and an annoyed expression. Bandages tightly wrapped one of her legs, that leg of the trousers sliced open.

For ease of tending the wound, Gya assumed.

The woman squinted at them as they entered.

"So you are the ones tramping all over the *Deliberia*," she said with a scowl. "Well, look around lads, but be quick about it. We do not have all day to show people around."

Gya nodded his thanks to the woman. He took a quick look around the cabin and peeked into the cabinets under Alorsha's watchful gaze. Toa stood in the middle of the room and just watched Alorsha.

Gya spotted a door at the back of the room, a single one positioned in the center of the wall. He headed toward it while he gave Alorsha a questioning look.

"My cabin." She joined him at the door and opened it herself.

This room was furnished much like the outer room, but what looked like dried plants covered nearly every available surface. Amidst the clutter, several live plants grew in pots of various sizes. One plant in particular caught Gya's eye, a flower unlike any he had seen before.

A single stalk grew from the midst of a small bush that reached only as high as the length of his hand. A flower much the same size as the bush topped the stalk: one deep-red bloom, with gold edging the scalloped petals.

"It's called a chervynai," Alorsha said as he peered at it. "Not the easiest to grow, but I love it. A small remnant of my home."

Gya examined it a minute longer. *The gold on the petals*

looks almost real. Would that even be possible?

He drew his attention back to his purpose there and moved cautiously around the clutter while Toa followed close behind.

"What are all these?" Gya waved a hand at the various bits of plants scattered about, mostly leaves. None of them looked familiar.

"I study them."

"Ah," Toa said. "To find which are sweet or bitter or spicy? To enhance shipboard food?"

Alorsha stared at him, her expression one of confusion. Then she shook her head.

"Not for food, although many are edible," she said. "To discover their properties, to try to draw out their ma—"

A loud cough from the door interrupted her. A crewmember stood there – a man with weathered skin, a slightly lighter brown than Alorsha's, who wore his long brown hair in two plaits. He stood close to a head taller than Gya. A sling held one of his arms, but Gya had the impression it would not hamper him in the least if he needed to oppose some threat. He wore a sword at his side and carried tucked in his belt a strange item that looked like a hand crossbow without the bow and string parts. Gya suspected it was still a weapon of some sort.

Alorsha introduced the imposing newcomer as the Ship's Captain, Mikolus Ludek.

"Pardon the interruption," Captain Ludek said with a slight bow of his head to Alorsha. "A matter below-decks would benefit from your attention."

Gya grabbed Toa by the arm and headed toward the door. "We were just finishing," he said as he sidled past the tall man at the doorway. "We certainly don't wish to keep you. I'd appreciate it if your crewmembers who wish to sell their wares would stop by our storehouse. We might have some barter arrangements they would be interested in. Either with us, or for some of the other merchants."

Gya glanced back as they stepped back onto the deck and saw the Ship's Captain in earnest conversion with Alorsha, whose expression seemed worried.

As Gya hustled Toa from the ship, he cringed under the harsh gazes of everyone on the docks who scrutinized the brothers as they passed. He resisted the urge to glance back at the Keepers stationed there, to see if they knew.

When Toa started to speak, Gya hushed him. "Back home."

~ ~ ~

Gya and Toa slipped inside their storehouse. With a quick look behind them, Gya closed the door and pulled Toa to one side, behind a double stack of barrels. Fortunately, some of their workers were occupied loading a wagon near the big double doors at the front of the storehouse. The noise would keep anyone from overhearing the brothers.

"Was she going to say magic?" Toa said, eagerness clear in his expression. "Did they bring magic with them? This could be the chance we've hoped for."

"Quietly," Gya reminded him. "It seemed like it. But we can't just assume."

"This changes everything!"

"Toa! We don't know these people. What if it's some trap for hidden Magickas like us?"

"You're thinking Imperial Seekers?"

"Could be. I've heard they do such things. And worse." Gya shuddered. He had never encountered one of those elite Keepers himself. But he had heard plenty of tales about the brutal treatment Magickas received from that group attached to the Empire's Ministry for the Containment of the Abomination of Magic.

Toa turned toward the harbor, his gaze distant as if he looked through the storehouse's walls. "I don't see it. They aren't known for being subtle and don't use people from out-Empire. And we'd have noticed strange Keepers in town. I've heard their uniforms don't look like regular Keepers' anyway."

After Gya considered Toa's words, he nodded. "True. I can't argue with that. Still, we have to consider that she could've been going to say something else."

"So we find out. I'll talk with her." Toa grinned. "She might like to join me at Shala's Inn for a meal or two."

Gya frowned at his younger brother. "You don't even know if she'd be interested. Or is unattached."

Toa's grin grew and he shrugged. "You should at least tell the others what we suspect. Find out when we're meeting next, too."

"We? So you'll come this time?"

Toa clapped his older brother on the shoulder. "Things have gotten a lot more interesting. Of course I'll try to be there. Just let me know where and when."

Gya watched him saunter back out the door, leaving it open. With a shake of his head, Gya headed out too. Time to get on with the day's tasks, starting with his tally report for Kalbei so any interested merchants could see what the ship had to offer. He also needed to return the tokens from the previous night.

CHAPTER 4

Late in the afternoon the next day, Gya headed for Ifeoma K'lar's bakery in town. She baked the best breads and pastries, and also belonged to their secret group.

When he entered the shop, he found her wrapping some sweets for Wambua and her girls. The air in the shop carried the mouthwatering scent of freshly baked bread goods, as it always did. Gya's stomach rumbled at the scent.

Ifeoma wore her favorite ankle-length dress of pale blue with bright blue swirls and flower designs, a nice contrast with her brown skin—lighter than Gya's—and light brown eyes. She wore her curly black hair, with its few strands of white, as short as Gya did his. Bright, beaded bracelets decorated both bare arms just above her elbows.

Ifeoma acknowledged Gya with a nod of her head while she finished helping Wambua put all her purchases in the cloth bags she carried. As she passed him on her way out of the shop, Wambua pulled her daughters close with a fierce look for Gya, as if she needed to protect them from him, guard them from the Blight of his family.

He lowered his gaze and backed away to give her plenty of room to pass by without any risk that she might touch him.

After the door closed behind Wambua, Ifeoma enveloped Gya in a quick hug. Her strength belied her stature as she stood almost a head shorter than he did.

She looked at him with anticipation. "The ship? Is that why you missed the meet a night ago?"

Gya nodded. "Had to be all official with its arrival and couldn't get away in time."

She gave him a shrewd look. "There's something more, I think. The lady captain, perhaps?"

Gya glanced at her. "She's the acting Ship's Master, and I walked her to Candwi's. That's all. There are injuries among the crew."

"And?"

Gya rubbed his forehead. "The next morning, yesterday morning, Alorsha—that's her name—seemed to be about to speak of magic. But we were interrupted."

Ifeoma nodded and gathered some small rolls of bread for Gya, so his visit would not look unusual. "Have you yet looked at the ship itself? Through a seeing-stone?"

Gya shook his head and added one of Ifeoma's special spicy breads to the collection. Toa liked those best.

"You should," Ifeoma urged. "You'll find it very interesting."

"Find what interesting?" Gya frowned when she just shook her head. "You're not going to tell me?"

Ifeoma smiled. "Ah, the impatience of youth. See for yourself. Decide what you think of what you see. Then we'll talk."

Gya gave her a mock glare and shook his head. "Your way, as always."

She smiled, counted the coins he handed her, and returned ten of the small copper ones. "Next time maybe try one of my twisted sweet breads. I plan to make a fresh batch in two days in the cool of the evening. It's my grandmother's recipe and can be a lengthy process and mustn't be rushed."

Gya nodded as he deciphered the code in her words and actions that told him when the next meeting would be: at the second hour after sundown in ten days, in the location they used the most often, a cave near his storehouse.

"And I might try a little something special, soon, too," Ifeoma added. "Although I'm not sure it'll work out. I'll let you know."

Gya knew that meant one, or perhaps more, of the others hoped they could meet sooner, even if only briefly, but suspected they might not be able to manage it.

"I'll look forward to it," he told her.

As he opened the door to leave, he nearly hit Usrai with it. The stocky Keeper grinned at him and pushed into the shop.

"We seem to keep meeting," he said to Gya. "I might start thinking that you're following me."

Gya shifted his feet and kept his gaze away from Usrai's. "I'm not. I just needed some breads."

Usrai laughed. "You're too amusing, Gya. For a lowly, shrinking merchant. Too bad really that you're from a Magicka family. Otherwise, we could've made quite the pair and had an enjoyable time together."

Gya shook his head. "I'm afraid I'd not suit you at all." He hurried away from the shop and imagined he heard the Keeper's laughter following him.

Gya rounded a corner, his attention more behind him than on where he headed. He slammed into someone hard. The squeak of surprise, and possibly pain, told him exactly who he had run into before his vision cleared enough to see. The first person he would want to see and the last he would have wanted to crash into.

He reached out to the woman, who stood only a little shorter than he did, but hesitated to actually touch her hand. "Chizoa! I'm sorry. I'm so sorry. Are you hurt?"

Chizoa N'lela's beautiful, dark-brown skin seemed a little darker on her cheeks as she shot him a sidelong look. Even that quick glance allowed him to take in those glorious amber eyes of hers, and from much closer than he had dared before to meet them.

Then her brilliant smile caught his attention: it lit her whole face, as always. So she must not be too upset to have him run into her. Literally. She had been carrying several new shirts—she was a garment maker—which lay scattered around the two of them after their collision.

Chizoa brushed her long, thick hair away from her face and smiled again at Gya. He smiled back. "I'm fine. Startled more than anything else." She reached a hand toward him but stopped short of touching him. "Are *you* all right?"

"What? Oh, I'm fine. Are you sure I didn't hurt you?"

She shook her head, still smiling. "No. Just surprised me, as I said." She bent to gather the clothing and Gya helped. "Thank you, but I can get them. You seemed in a hurry."

"It's nothing. I should've been watching where I was going."

After he handed her the last item, he turned to go, but stole another glance at her.

"Have you heard that Ifeoma's going to make some twisted sweet breads? And possibly a little something special." Without saying the words outright, his question asked if she knew about the upcoming meeting and the chance of meeting sooner.

She smiled. "I'd heard the first but not the second. After I deliver these shirts, I plan to go see her." With that statement, she told him that she did not yet have the details about the meetings but would soon. And she had not heard before about meeting sooner.

Much as he would have liked to linger in her company, he could think of no plausible reason to let him do that, so he wished her a pleasant day. They said their good-byes and he headed back to the storehouse.

~ ~ ~

Something woke Gya. He slowly turned over and looked around his room, dim in the light of the two moons that barely shone through his window. Nothing moved. He held his breath to listen better and heard a slight sound. From Toa's room, it sounded like.

Now what was his brother up to?

With a small sigh, he climbed out of bed and wrapped his blanket around his shoulders. He padded into Toa's room and found him crouched by his window.

With its west-facing window, Toa's room was much dimmer than Gya's.

Toa glanced over his shoulder and beckoned Gya closer. "You've got to see this," he whispered.

He held one of the brothers' best seeing-stones in one hand, a clear, flattened, blue-tinted kri-stone crystal—the naturally occurring magic stone used by all Magickas—and knelt within a large sigil traced on the floor with powdered blue kri-stone. Gya smiled to himself. At least Toa worked the magic correctly.

"What is it?" he said as he joined his brother, careful to avoid disarranging the powdered lines as he stepped around them.

Toa nodded toward Alorsha's ship, visible below.

As Gya perused the ship, he saw an odd-colored flash of light from the stern, a kind of bluish-white. *From Alorsha's cabin?* He saw another flash. He turned to give Toa a questioning look.

"I see the flashes, too," Toa said. "I think we're the only ones who would see them. No one else lives down here toward this end of the docks, so no one should be seeing those. Now look at the ship through the seeing-stone."

Gya held the stone in front of one eye and closed the other. Then he gasped and nearly dropped the stone. The whole ship glowed a faint red-gold. The whole thing!

He met Toa's gaze.

"But how?" Toa said. "How could a wooden ship glow with magic? Did you see any kri-stone crystals there? Any sigils traced from their powder?"

Gya shook his head. "Nothing of the sort. That one crewmember had those pieces of jewelry. But he had nothing that looked like any kind of crystals I've ever seen, or any other stones I've seen either. But the ship comes from somewhere unknown. Perhaps they use the crystals differently somehow. To result in that." He waved a hand toward the ship.

"Shouldn't we warn her?" Toa pulled a blue kri-stone crystal from a small leather bag that sat on the end of his bed. He bent to tap one end of the crystal to one of the lines of the sigil. He then traced a loop in the air with the crystal and pointed the narrower end of the crystal to the small bag. The powdered crystal streamed up from the floor and into the bag, a thin line that followed the path he had inscribed in the air.

Gya watched to be certain all the powder returned to the bag. Sometimes Toa's magic was a little sloppy and performed incompletely. "I've a feeling that her Ship's Captain might have done that already… when he interrupted whatever she was going to say."

"But the flashes. If she'd been warned, would she still work magic?"

Gya directed a pointed look at the seeing-stone Toa still held and the small bag that now held all the blue kri-stone powder and the crystal.

Toa grinned. "I see your point."

They stashed the magic materials in the cubby hole they had created for that purpose alone.

"I still think I'll warn her tomorrow," Toa said with a grin. "I'll also ask her if she'd like to join me for a delicious meal at Shala's Inn.'"

Gya just shook his head and wished Toa a good night.

~ ~ ~

Toa was already gone when Gya woke and then started the morning's work in the storehouse. Unusual for Toa, but he would even forego sleeping late, something he loved to do, when involved in the pursuit of a woman.

About mid-morning, while Gya leaned against the storehouse wall to rest in the sunshine, after he had sent off two heavily laden wagons, he saw Toa leave the *Deliberia*. His brother waved and headed into town.

As he watched him, Gya spotted one of Hawei's councilmembers coming from the town to the docks. He straightened and brushed down his work clothes to try to look more presentable when he recognized Bayo, head of the council.

The elderly woman walked briskly toward him. Her bright orange, ankle-length tunic stirred dust eddies in her wake. Although her hair had turned white—with no sign left of its former dark color—and deep wrinkles crisscrossed her dark skin, she moved like a woman much younger than her true years.

Gya touched the back of his right hand to the back of hers in formal greeting as she joined him.

"Councilor Bayo, your visit honors me."

She gave him a slight smile.

"I'm afraid you won't feel that way when you hear my news. Come, let's sit." She led the way to one of the low benches that Gya kept placed near the large double doors of the storehouse. Gya waited until she had seated herself before he joined her.

She reached out and patted his hand, sympathy clear in her expression. "I can't tell you how sorry I am. The Council cannot grant your petition to wed. Nor Toa's either."

Gya hung his head. "Why not? Neither of us have shown signs of the Blight."

She patted his hand again. "It's not that. Haven't you heard about the newest mandate? No one with any signs of the Blight of magic anywhere in the family line is allowed to wed, not even to someone from another family with the Blight. The mandate arrived from the Imperial Capital just a day ago. I *am* sorry."

Gya shook his head. "But… but even father's Blight was so slight that it was hardly evident. Even the Keepers who were there to take him said they did not know why they bothered."

"I know. I remember. But still, it's there. You and Toa might not be actively Blighted, but your children—"

"Doesn't sound like there'll be any," Gya cut in, his tone bitter. He rose and bowed to her, his action stiff and formal. "I thank you for coming out here to tell me."

Bayo got to her feet and laid her hand on his shoulder to offer commiseration.

"It's just the young Emperor showing his control now that he's grown and able to rule in his own right. He's issuing all sorts of mandates right now to show his power. Word has it we can expect more soon. But it'll ease, I've no doubt. Just give it time."

Gya frowned, but nodded, and she headed back toward town without another word.

Gya stood a long time and stared first at nothing in particular, then looked at the *Deliberia*. He was certain the news would be all over town soon, if not already. This made their upcoming meet that much more important. And maybe even more important to meet sooner, if they could.

It seemed clear that the Empire planned to kill off by attrition any who might be able to work magic. An inability to continue their family lines meant the death of them all. *And what more would the new mandates inflict on them?*

Could Toa have been right? Should they now be doing more than merely practicing working the magic in secret, they and the few others in Hawei? Should they be planning some action against those who would see their families wither and die?

Should he and Toa seek to learn about the magics of the Deliberia?

How could he be sure that wouldn't just make everything worse?

CHAPTER 5

IN A PROVINCIAL CAPITAL OF THE ATTUREI EMPIRE

Arizu watched the stranger pace around one of the Ministry's small meeting rooms. He had only lightly sampled the fine array of foods she had directed the attendants to prepare for them. His restlessness seemed to infect her, too and she found she had little appetite. Strange how his mood so resonated in her. Now if he would just share his name with her.

"You *have* sent the messages?" He paused in his pacing to pour some wine into an earthenware mug and drink it.

"Yes. As I've said. I sent them that very night we first spoke." She let some of her exasperation color her words. "I'm Minister in this province, but some things must come from the Imperial Capital, not this provincial one. And even with our special couriers, swift as their horses are, it takes days to get a message there from here."

He sat in the chair next to her and leaned forward, brushing his fingers lightly across the back of her hand. The remnants of the thoughts of what his name might be slipped away with his touch. *She didn't really need to know his name, did she?* For the briefest moment, that thought felt odd. But it too drifted away.

"Don't let my sour mood burden you."

And with those words of his, it no longer did.

The stranger waved his man over to serve them and continued to stroke the back of her hand. Arizu did not know the man's name; the stranger had not said. *It didn't really matter. He was just an attendant of some sort, such as she had. Of course the stranger was someone who would have an attendant.*

"I find I've little patience sometimes," the stranger said as he sampled the delicacies. "Especially in this sort of situation. When it feels as if nothing can be done and yet the danger from that traveler looms."

"The messages will get through in a few days. They'll understand the danger, and the importance of taking steps. Something will be done."

"But not for some time, from the sound of it. Isn't there something that can be done sooner? Perhaps you know of some of the Empire's tamed Magickas who are nearby? Perhaps they could do something from here? Something these Magickas can do at a distance?"

Arizu considered that. She had little knowledge of the details of what Magickas could do and preferred it that way. Still....

"I *have* heard that some can do an 'influence' I think they call it. Some of the more powerful or knowledgeable ones, I think."

"An 'influence'?" the stranger prompted when she did not elaborate.

Arizu nodded. "It's something that can affect an area with an overlying... mood, I guess you might say. No... more of an ambiance."

"An ambiance? I wasn't thinking of something to make the townsfolk feel contented or happy or something like that."

Arizu chuckled, then stifled her sudden humor at the stranger's severe expression. "It's not like that. I've heard they can place an influence like misfortune." She gave him a meaningful look.

His smile grew slowly and made her feel warm. "Ah. Everyone starts having bad luck—"

"And with the only new thing in the area being your Alorsha, they'll soon blame her for everything that goes wrong." She smiled broadly at him. "That should make it near impossible for her to spread her vile contamination, I'd think."

The stranger nodded. His smile matched hers as he held her gaze with his own and clasped her hand with both of his. "Splendid. And in the meantime, we can begin our journey to the Imperial Capital. There I know I'll be able to convince those who need to be convinced of the danger and need to do something."

What a wonderful idea. She should have thought of that, but of course he would. Arizu nodded, her enthusiasm clear in the gesture. "Yes. Of course. That will do it."

CHAPTER 6

Gya found no opportunity during the next week to return to the ship as he would have liked. Several trader ships arrived and kept the storehouse busy with people leaving and picking up goods. A few even traded some goods for others he held in the building.

Each day he sent several carts to smaller towns near Hawei to deliver items there. Toa ran errands into Hawei, mostly to bring back food—which included some of the twisted sweet breads from Ifeoma's bakery—and he also delved more into the business at the storehouse.

While Gya did see people leave the *Deliberia* and return later with bundles of goods, he did not see Alorsha during that time. Those crewmembers he noticed seemed to complete their errands quickly and return to the ship. Toa shared with him the gossip that the crew of the *Deliberia* stayed mostly to themselves when in the town and seemed to particularly need nails, from what he overheard. They came into town for many meals, but none of them had chosen to take rooms at the inn. They also made arrangements to get a variety of foodstuffs for the ship, some that would be coming from other towns.

The last day of that busy week, Toa returned from a short visit to town with word that the Magickas still planned to have the next night's meeting. "Still in the cave, too," he told Gya. "Seems the others don't feel it's wise trying to meet anywhere in town, not even the cellar under the bakery."

Gya frowned. "So we've just the cave left for meeting?"

"Seems so. Anyway, the usual time: second hour after sundown. Didn't sound like they're planning to practice any for this one. Said there's information to share. And planning another meeting to actually work magic in probably another ten days or so."

"Will you be able to come to this one?"

Toa shrugged and looked away. "Sounds like just more talk without actually doing anything. You can let me know all about it later."

"Toa…." Gya grasped his shoulder.

His brother shrugged him off. "I'll get back to work. Those carts need loading and we're missing a couple of workers today."

~ ~ ~

The next day, Toa left without a word after they had sent off the last cart for the day. He did not join Gya for the evening meal, nor did he return before the time came to go meet the others at the cave.

Gya checked that the storehouse was secure for the night. Upstairs in their dwelling, he set a spill to the embers of the fire in the kitchen and lit a lantern for his bedroom, as he habitually did. He set the lantern in its accustomed place on a low table near the bed. With one last look around, he slipped back downstairs and out the storeroom's side door, locking it behind him.

He paused in a shadow to look and listen. When he heard nothing unusual and saw no movement, he sidled around the storehouse wall to the outside entrance to their personal stores beneath the building.

Again locking the door behind him, Gya found his way by touch to the back wall of the cellar. There he slipped the locking kri-stone crystal into the secret keyhole at the base of the wall—designed to look like nothing more than a broken section—and traced the proper sigil on the wall above it with a finger dusted with powdered kri-stone.

He pushed on the panel to open the hidden door. After he gathered the powdered stone that clung to the wall, he closed the door behind him and leaned against it to take some deep breaths to calm himself.

With the small tinder box set there for just that purpose, he lit the candle he and Toa kept close inside the door and followed the tunnel to one of the small caves at its other end.

This tunnel had existed for a long time, known only to the K'rond family. Family stories claimed they had been involved with smuggling in the past, perhaps a couple hundred years earlier. Certainly, the caves might have been used for such a thing since they perched in the low cliffs that bordered the sea, close to Hawei but a distance west of the town.

As he approached the cave where he and the other Magickas held their meetings, Gya paused to listen. No sound of voices. He must have arrived first, as usual. That suited him.

He snuffed his candle and pulled out a white-edged seeing-stone, a crystal a little different from the one he and Toa had used to look at the *Deliberia*. This one, when used with the proper sigil, would let him see in the dark. For a short time.

He dipped his smallest finger into the small pouch of powdered kri-stone that had held the crystal and traced the proper sigil on one side of the seeing-stone. Holding the seeing-stone to one eye, he made his way the rest of the way to the meeting cave.

Another door closed this end, this one made of rock. Gya opened it the same way as the one back at the cellar and closed it behind him. He and Toa were the only ones who knew of that particular entrance.

If he had heard any voices earlier, he would have taken a side passage to a different cave and followed the shoreline to enter this cave by its mouth.

After he made certain the door had latched behind him, Gya stepped to the cave mouth and crouched there to wait. He judged the others should arrive in less than half an hour, so he spent the time reviewing what had happened and trying to decide what their next steps should be. Part of the time, he also worried about Toa. *If only he had made himself more a part of their group; he might have been happier if he had known that they* did *plan to make changes. Working with other Magickas. They just couldn't risk moving too quickly.*

The others arrived and Gya moved inside the cave. He lit a candle off to one side to give them minimal light that should not be visible from too far outside the entrance.

Their small group numbered seven, including himself and Toa. Everyone except for Toa came to the cave this night. It had been that way for many recent meetings.

What might Toa be doing that he hadn't come to this meeting? Or planning to do? Gya tried to push that concern from his thoughts, at least until he returned home later.

After all the others had settled on spots on the dirt floor, Gya joined them. He gazed a moment at the diverse group who ranged in age from Chizoa, a bit more than a year younger than his own score and two years, to Dakrei M'bweyo, who had more than three score years. If Toa had been there, he would have been the youngest by nearly a year.

Chizoa and Dakrei contrasted sharply with each other. Chizoa was brightness. She had dressed up, with her rich hair slicked into a bun on the back of her head. She wore a simply styled but well-made dress of light cloth in a yellow and orange design. In her bun, she wore a fancy, carved wooden hair stick. A favorite of hers, Gya remembered. It had once belonged to her mother.

Dakrei, in contrast, was all faded… faded loose shirt and trousers of a light green with a blue swirl pattern— thin and worn—faded brown skin and fading, graying brown hair. His age showed clearly, although his pale-blue eyes were still sharp.

The other three were Ifeoma, the baker; Ekosua T'narm, a woman some years older than Gya, shorter and stockier than any of the others there, with skin and hair a shade shy of black and light-brown eyes; and Ayaru V'sar, a tall woman somewhat younger than Dakrei, with skin and hair that nearly matched Gya's in color, but eyes much lighter brown than his.

Both Ekosua and Ayaru wore their hair in many thin braids, Ekosua's much shorter than Ayaru's. All three women wore loose shirts and trousers much like Gya's and Dakrei's, but less faded.

Ifeoma frowned. "Again no Toa?"

Gya shook his head. "He thinks we do too much talking and not enough working magic to make things better."

"Now, if only it were that easy," Ayaru said.

"And we've things to talk about this night," Dakrei said.

"The new mandates?" Chizoa said.

"Not much to say there," Ekosua said. "Things are getting worse. More rules against us *Blighted*." She sneered the last word. "Another new one just today: non-Blighted merchants are supposed to sell their best goods only to the non-Blighted. They're to set aside the poorest goods for the Blighted, and those are the only goods any Blighted can now purchase from them. Those merchants can sell them for the same cost as their best goods, too, or even more."

"And they're saying more mandates are coming,"

Chizoa said. "What are we going to do?"

The fear and worry in her voice pierced right through Gya. *If only he could comfort her. If only he dared try.*

"Continue to be careful," Ayaru said. "Do nothing to draw their attention. After this new, young Emperor has flexed his muscles some, I'd not be surprised to see things go back to what we've been living with already."

"Should we meet more often? Practice more and start working the harder sigils?" Gya said.

"That's a thought," Ayaru said. "Have to reflect on that. On if we can manage it."

"I've some news," Dakrei said then. "Limbani got me a message that his group in Ikkavai has connected with two other groups, one in Yakwes, the other in Pumza."

"How many of us is that now?" Chizoa said.

"Fifteen groups, I think," Ayaru said. "With these two new ones."

"How many do these new groups have?" Gya said.

"About the same as us," Dakrei said. "Sounded like the one in Pumza might reach ten, if they convince other Magickas in their town to join them. Would make them the largest yet."

"Is that enough?" Ifeoma said.

Everyone exchanged looks.

"Well now, if we have to make a move, it'll have to be enough," Ayaru said.

After nods of agreement from everyone, Ekosua said, "What of the ship, Gya? They're from out-Empire, right? Do they bring new magic knowledge we can learn and use?"

Gya frowned. "Maybe. I'm not sure, yet."

"Could be a trap," Dakrei said. "The Empire's itching to grab the last Magickas, wipe us out. Maybe they sent this ship to trick us into revealing ourselves."

"Maybe," Gya agreed. "I'll be careful, but I don't think they're a trap for us. There are too many strange and different things about them. I somehow doubt the Empire would go to that much trouble. I think they've come from very far away."

"Maybe they'll join us. They could make a difference," Chizoa said.

"See what you can learn of them," Ayaru instructed Gya, who nodded his agreement.

"Did everyone hear about Omondu's broken foot?" Chizoa asked after a moment.

"What?" Gya shook his head. "No, it was her spouse's ankle. And I don't think it was broken."

Chizoa frowned at him. "No, I know about Razaya's ankle. I'm not talking about that. Now Omondu's got a broken foot. She dropped something on it, from what I overheard."

"Some bad luck for those two, certainly," Ekosua said. "Razaya's still not getting about yet."

"A few other residents have also had some odd accidents recently," Dakrei said. "Tripping over something, things falling off shelves."

"Funny how sometimes that sort of thing seems to happen in a clump," Ayaru said. She levered herself to her feet. "Time for me to be getting back. Couldn't set aside much time for this tonight. Everyone be safe."

Dakrei rose and with quick good-byes to the others, accompanied her out of the cave. Ifeoma and Ekosua then said they needed to go, too. Chizoa rose with them, but then glanced at Gya, who immediately jumped to his feet. *Should he offer to walk with her back to town? That might be too bold. And besides, Ifeoma and Ekosua were there to walk with her.*

Hating that he feared to even ask, he wished all three women a good night and watched as they walked out of the cave.

With a sigh at himself, he blew out the candle and headed back to the storehouse the way he had come earlier.

~ ~ ~

The next four days, business activity at the storehouse grew progressively less and less, which let Gya head into town while Toa minded the little activity at the storehouse the morning of the fifth day. Along the way, the normal squawking background of seagulls seemed more raucous than usual. Gya gave the noise little thought, other than wondering, in passing, what had the birds so upset.

Gya's steps slowed as he approached the center of town. More people lingered in the streets than usual for late morning, gathered in small groups and engaged in heated conversations. Gya caught some of what was said. Something about a run of bad luck. Then he heard something he had never thought to hear.

"Maybe we shouldn't be getting rid of the Magickas," Gya overheard as he turned a corner and almost ran into one of the clusters of people. At their startled looks, he backed away, and received his second surprise.

"Wait." An older woman held a hand out to him. She dropped her hand when Gya stopped, but none of the group sidled away as the townsfolk usually did.

"I'm just getting some provisions for me and my brother," Gya told them. "I won't be in town long."

The older of the two men in the group waved a dismissive hand. "Nothing about that. You're from a family of Magickas. Can you do something to ward off bad luck? Or break a curse? Maybe your brother can? Or you know a Magicka still in hiding?"

Gya looked around. *What was this? Some sort of trap?* He spotted one of the Keepers further along the street. The woman met his gaze then turned to scan the rest of the street and the other gatherings.

Gya stepped back. "I-I don't understand," he stammered. "The magic is forbidden, even if we *could* do it."

A younger woman in the group gave him a friendly smile. "Don't you know what's happened?"

Gya shook his head. A quick glance around showed him a second group had come close enough to hear. He took another step back, his legs and hands quivery. *Could he outrun all of them?*

"Don't go," the woman said. "Maybe you can help."

Gya shook his head. "I don't do magic."

"We need something," the woman persisted. "It's been horrible."

"The milk on Jwanu's farm spoiled four mornings ago," the younger man in the group broke in. "And again a day ago."

"All the pots at Hakizi's Pottery were ruined in the kiln two days ago," the older man said.

"My nephew's horse came up lame last night," the older woman said. "But it was fine and frisky before the evening meal."

"No more than an hour ago, the entire morning's baking caught fire at Ifeoma's bakery. Like to burned the whole place," a woman from the second group added.

"What?" Gya spun to face her. "Is she all right? What happened?"

The woman shrugged and pointed to a faint plume of smoke visible in the clear air. It drifted into the sky from somewhere a few blocks away. Frantic, Gya pushed his way through the group that blocked his path that direction and ran, pleading silently with whatever spirits might hover nearby, if any, that Ifeoma was safe.

Gya dashed through the streets, heedless of the people he shoved past and the attention his frantic passage drew. The Keepers he passed only looked at him. None followed or called out to him to stop.

Had they set this up somehow? To force him to reveal himself as a Magicka? His breath caught at the thought and his stomach clenched.

He rounded the corner onto the street with Ifeoma's bakery, fearing what he would find.

A wisp of smoke drifted out the open door to the

place, but otherwise everything looked normal. The smell of burnt bread assailed him as he skidded to a stop at the open door.

"Ifeoma?" he called into the hazy interior. He called again, louder, when she did not answer right away.

He heard the bang of a door hidden in the gloom at the back of the shop and Ifeoma shambled toward him through swirls of smoke. He caught her in a quick embrace and helped her outside into the clearer air, heedless of the black smudges on her bright orange tunic that transferred to his own clothing.

After several deep coughs, she sank down next to the front of her store and waved away his hovering concern.

"Lost the morning's pastry breads in the big oven." Her voice had a raspy tone to it. "But nothing worse. Just a mess to clean up." She coughed again.

"But you're all right? Shall I get Candwi?"

Ifeoma waved that suggestion away. "It's just a little smoke. I'll be fine once it clears from me and the shop. Got both doors open now so the shop'll be good in a few."

Gya peered back inside. The smoke had already cleared considerably. He took the time to visit one of the neighboring shops to get some water—given grudgingly— before he sat next to her. A few passersby peered at them, but no one stopped.

"What happened?" Gya asked after Ifeoma drank some the water.

She shrugged. "Can't really say. The morning was going along the same as most mornings, better even. The next I knew the breads in the ovens were all burning. On fire, not just getting overcooked. I doused the fires beneath the ovens and the breads burned out after a few minutes. Now I've all this smoke."

She coughed again and finished her water while she watched the passersby. Then with a motherly pat on Gya's knee, she hauled herself to her feet.

"Best get started on the clean-up."

Gya jumped up. "I can help."

But she stopped him with a hand on his chest. "Kind of you, but you'd best get back." She leaned close and whispered, "I've just got a feeling it's best to stick close to home this day. For all of us."

With a quick look around to see if anyone was close, Gya leaned toward her. "You've worked a seeing sigil?" he whispered.

She shook her head. "No. And it's nothing as clear as I might get from that," she whispered back and patted his shoulder. She gave him a slight push away from the shop and went inside.

Gya stood outside and watched her through the grimy front window. She stopped in the center of her shop and scanned the smoke damage before she waved at him and followed that with a shooing motion. He waved back and headed down the street. Ifeoma's concern dogged him. *Perhaps he did not need those extra provisions just yet. Perhaps he should just return home.*

Lost in thought, he paid little attention to his surroundings, just enough to avoid bumping into anyone and enough to feel the regard he gathered, more than the usual whenever he was in town.

How could the townsfolk want the Magickas to help them with this 'bad luck'? It *had* to be some sort of trap set up by the Keepers. Or maybe even higher officials in the Empire.

But if it wasn't?

A clatter of rocks drew him from his thoughts. *Were children throwing pebbles at him again?* They had done so before.

A shout next to his ear startled him and someone shoved him hard. He stumbled and tried to remain upright but still fell on the hard roadway. He scrambled back to his feet and froze, stunned by the sight before him. With an earsplitting roar, the large storehouse he had been passing crumbled and collapsed into itself, spewing chunks of mud brick and pottery roofing onto the street.

"The building wasn't that old," Gya murmured, unable to think of what might have happened.

Someone gripped his arm. "Are you all right?" It was one of the newest Keepers. "Sorry about pushing you, but you didn't seem to notice the building crumbling."

Gya disengaged his arm and brushed himself off. "You have my thanks for the push, then. I'm fine."

Together they turned to survey the ruin. "At least everyone got out," the Keeper murmured before he approached two other Keepers who arrived at a run. The three conferred, with several glances Gya's direction, before they moved off to deal with the aftermath of the disaster.

Without warning, a seagull swooped from a nearby building at one of the newly arrived Keepers. The man ran for the shelter of an overhang on an adjacent building, using his arms to protect his head. The bird followed, squawking stridently, before it veered away, clipping a wing on the corner of a roof as it flew off.

Gya watched the bird until he could not see it any longer, then lingered a few minutes more to see if he could help with the mess from the fallen building. He noted a group of workers who huddled nearby, shaken at their near miss. When the Keepers made it clear his help was unwelcome, Gya headed home, anxious about the apparent run of misfortune that seemed to be continuing.

Maybe he could find something in his few codices that he could do to help end it, or at least keep it from getting worse. But only if it was a magic he could work at a distance, hidden from view.

He still was uncertain this was not all some ploy to trap any remaining working Magickas.

CHAPTER 7

The next few days, Gya stayed close to the storehouse, although not very busy with only a few goods arriving and departing. Toa stayed close too and ventured out only a couple of times. When he returned from those quick trips, he brought with him tales of more mishaps and ill fortune in Hawei: dogs suddenly running off terrified of nothing anyone saw, donkeys turned crazed and unmanageable, additional broken and burnt goods, and more.

"Hundreds of mice have swarmed the T'rojim storehouse," Toa told Gya the afternoon of the third day after the fire, as they sorted through some of the pottery to send on a ship due to leave that evening.

That day had also seen the new mandate that the Blighted could not have any of the non-Blighted as workers, as of the end of the day, so Gya and Toa had only a few workers left to help them with the storehouse's remaining business.

"The T'rojims don't keep any food in there," Gya said. "Why would a horde of mice gather there?"

Toa shrugged. "It's like there's a curse of some sort on

Hawei. A lot of townsfolk are saying that, too." After he looked around, he leaned close. "Some are trying to blame Magickas, but others are saying it's that ship."

Gya frowned. "We should warn them."

"It's just muttering. We should *do* something about all these strange happenings. Have you found anything in those codices you've got stashed away?"

This time Gya looked around. When he located all their workers, all too far from them to overhear them, he shook his head.

"Haven't had the focus to look thoroughly. You know how hard some of it is to read. What if we try something and make it worse?"

"Thought that's why we've been meeting. To learn how to use the ma—"

"Hush," Gya gripped Toa's arm and again looked around. "We can't get careless."

Toa pulled his arm away. "We can't keep being so careful we scare ourselves into immobility." He grabbed the last box for that load and carried it to the wagon that waited outside the large double doors. He and Gya tied down everything and Gya checked off the list.

"That's all of it," he told the driver and watched the woman double check all the tie-downs before she climbed into the wagon's seat and urged her pair of horses down the hill from the storehouse to the harbor.

He returned to the storehouse and had started on the next load when a shout followed by crashing sounds sent him racing back to the road.

Just shy of the harbor, at the steepest part of the road that led down from the storehouse, the wagon had somehow overturned and rolled the rest of the way down the hill. The boxes it had carried were as smashed as it was. Gya could not spot the driver but saw some dock workers trying to catch the horses who were running from the wreckage.

Gya called for Toa and his few remaining workers as he

rushed down the slope, heedless of any danger of falling. As he arrived at the section of road where the wagon had foundered, he spotted the driver pulling herself from a clump of thorny bushes at the side of the road. She shook off his helping hand with a growl.

"I'm done. This arrangement's not worth it. Find one of your own kind to haul your stuff." She stomped off to help catch the horses. "Also, you now owe me the cost of my wagon and care for any injury my horses might have taken," she called back over her shoulder.

Toa skidded to a halt at Gya's side in time to hear her words. He surveyed the wreck of the wagon and the pottery shipment and sighed. "This is going to hurt. She was the most reliable driver who'd work with us. Now we won't get any profits from selling those pots either."

Gya shared a look with Toa.

"What's causing all this? That wagon was fine, and the road's fine. Might something have spooked the horses?"

Toa looked around. "Don't see anything." He turned to study the *Deliberia*. "Is it possible they're responsible?"

Gya scrutinized the ship, too, and noted the activity on deck. Looked like they were hard at work on repairs. "I don't think so. Why would they do that sort of thing? What would they have to gain? Has anyone even seen any of them near any of these mishaps?"

Toa shook his head. "From what I've heard, they've spent most of their time right over there. Working to fix their ship. When they're not getting more supplies."

The mess below them drew Gya's gaze again. He shook his head. "See if you can grab some workers to help with this. Maybe we can salvage something."

He headed down the slope to clear the wreckage of the wagon.

~ ~ ~

Early the next morning, before the time he usually

opened the storehouse for business and well before he wanted to deal with anyone after the disaster of the previous day, Gya heard a tapping on the large double doors. Visitors that time of day all too often meant Keepers at one's door, there to find some fault and require some bribe to let it pass. Still, not answering would make things worse.

Toa had not yet returned home from the night before. How he had the energy to go out after the hard work clearing the broken wagon and shipment, Gya did not know. But he had gone off as usual, so Gya was left to answer the knocking.

He shoved the last of his breakfast in his mouth and chewed as he hurried downstairs to see who knocked on his door. He wiped his hands on the sides of his trousers, then swung open one of the double doors.

But instead of Usrai or some other Keeper, Gya found himself facing Alorsha. Captain Ludek stood there too, close behind her left shoulder, and six other members of the *Deliberia*'s crew ranged behind them. Gya's tension dissolved into something like happiness and he smiled warmly.

"Good morning. This is before the time we usually open the business for the day, but you're welcome to come in."

Alorsha inclined her head and led the others inside, walking much better than before, her limp nearly gone. The Captain no longer wore his sling. Gya closed the door behind them but did not latch it again.

"I apologize for arriving so early. You did say my crew could speak with you about some possible barters?" Alorsha stepped to one side to allow the crewmembers to approach.

"Of course," Gya said.

He led the others to a table that sat to one side and he and the crewmembers—a mix of men and women—settled in to haggle and see what deals they might make.

Alorsha and the Ship's Captain stood nearby, but off to the side and out of the way to allow Gya to grab as yet unsold goods from some of the boxes nearby to offer.

When they finished, more than an hour later—and after the rest of the day's meager business had gotten going—Gya had a nice collection of exotic goods and the crewmembers had some of the Empire's coins and various cloths and pottery goods that seemed to please them.

With nods to Alorsha and the Ship's Captain, the six crewmembers left.

Gya gave Alorsha a questioning look. "Is there something else?"

"Might you have any sail canvas?"

Gya reluctantly shook his head. "We don't. Not at the moment, anyway. But I'm happy to ask around."

"My thanks."

He nodded acknowledgment. "I noticed your ship is constructed of an unusual wood," he ventured. "It's like nothing I've seen before. If you've got a few pieces, even scraps, that you don't need, I think I can get you a very good price for them."

Alorsha and Captain Ludek exchanged glances, their expressions odd.

"Perhaps." Alorsha's slight smile barely curved her lips. "I'll consider that and see what I might have when I get back to the ship."

As she turned to go, the side door banged open. "Gya! Have you—" Toa pulled up short at the sight of the people from the *Deliberia* and gave Alorsha a big smile. He stepped close to her. The Ship's Captain took a step toward Toa, a stern expression on his face, but subsided at a look from Alorsha.

"Are you looking for me? You've reconsidered?" Toa said.

Alorsha shook her head with a slight smile. "Your attentions flatter me, and I thank you for them. I'm not at liberty to join you for entertaining evenings."

Toa frowned in irritation. The next moment his bright smile replaced that expression while he closed the space between them even further. "If that changes, I'll be available."

Alorsha's expression did not change, but she shook her head again and pulled her hands away when Toa reached to clasp them. Gya noticed then that Alorsha wore two identical rings in a pink-gold metal, both with detailed sculptural relief embellishments, one each on the third finger of each hand. She wore another ring on her left thumb, this one plainer and of a coppery metal, with a small gray disk in the middle of it. It looked somehow unfinished or incomplete, but Gya could not think why it seemed that way to him.

The only other jewelry Alorsha wore was a chain around her neck with two pendants hanging from it: a goldish disk with a similarly colored stone shaped like a bird of some kind, and half-hidden behind that, a pendant that looked like some kind of double frame, the outer of elaborately carved wood that resembled the wood of the *Deliberia*, and the inner of the same coppery metal as her thumb ring. A round stone sat in the center of the double frame and matched the outer, wooden part of the frame in color.

With a shrug and a jaunty wave, Toa headed toward the stairs to their upstairs dwelling. Alorsha followed Gya's gaze to her two matching rings.

"Ah. Among my people, these signify that one has a life partner. He wears identical rings."

Gya glanced at the Ship's Captain but saw no rings on his hands. The man chuckled.

"Not me," he said. "My people have a different custom anyway."

"I didn't mean to pry," Gya said.

Alorsha laughed, and Gya tried not to notice how pleasant he found the sound. "You're naturally curious. You haven't pried."

She glanced around the storehouse and lowered her voice.

"We, too, are curious, and have some questions…."

Did they want to talk about magic? Feeling that might be the case, Gya also looked around. No one was close enough to hear them, but he still preferred to be cautious.

"This is not a good place for a discussion," he said.

"After refusing your brother thrice now, I think meeting for a meal would be unwise." Alorsha's expression held a hint of humor.

Gya nodded, not sure how to respond to the humor.

"Your plants, perhaps?" Captain Ludek murmured as he leaned close.

Alorsha nodded and spoke in a normal voice again. "Of course. Merchant Gya, might it be possible for you to point out some of the more interesting plants that grow near your town? I'd be particularly interested in anything that adds flavor to a bland meal, or perhaps can be used as a dye."

Gya gazed at her blankly, then nodded when he realized she had offered a way for them to talk. "While not my specialty—I'm no grower—I do have a bit of knowledge of such things, as they are often traded to other towns."

"I'm sure your knowledge will be helpful," Alorsha said. "Must we get another one of those tokens to step outside the town's confines?"

Gya shook his head. "Not if we go during daylight. We just must register with the gate Keepers both when we leave and when we return."

Alorsha nodded, with a thoughtful look. "We'll meet you then at the gate. Which one and when?"

Gya looked around the storehouse to judge the workers' current activity and the day's tasks.

"I need to see some things finished here this morning. This afternoon? Starting at the second hour past midday, perhaps? The inland gate is closest to the greatest variety of wild plants. Perhaps you might find something there."

Alorsha and Captain Ludek exchanged glances and the Captain nodded slightly.

"That should be fine," she said. "Until then."

~ ~ ~

Gya hurried to the inland gate, striving to look like he was *not* in a hurry, but worried that he was too late and had missed Alorsha. But no, there she stood, waiting by the Keeper assigned to the gate this day. She had brought Captain Ludek with her. He still carried the sword at his side and the strange not-a-hand-crossbow item in his belt.

As he strode to them, Gya worked to slow his breathing. No need to give the Keeper any reason to think this little expedition was of any importance.

Gya nodded a greeting to the Keeper. "I'm taking them to see about some herbs for spicing up their meals. We'll probably need a couple of hours."

The Keeper scowled at him, his expression uncertain, but he let them pass through the gate. He watched them until they moved out of sight into the sparse trees that grew a short distance from Hawei.

"There's a creek this way," Gya said. "Of course, that area is much more verdant than here further from any streams. I've heard it's a particularly good place to find some of those plants."

Unlike most towns of the Empire which clustered along the waterways and avoided the relatively barren lands between them, Hawei had been built further from the closest natural stream so it could command its excellent natural harbor. So the three walked for almost half an hour to reach the creek. Along the way, all of them periodically looked around to see if they were followed.

The plants around them grew lusher as they approached the stream, changing from the somewhat-arid landscape to the streamside greenery, as was the pattern throughout much of the Empire. Birdsong periodically drifted through the air around them. The warm smell of rich earth and growing things replaced the dustiness of the drier lands. When they reached the creek bank, Alorsha gave Captain Ludek a questioning look. He shook his head.

"We can talk here," Gya said, then blurted out, "What's the magic of your ship?" He had not planned to mention that first, but the image of what he had seen through the seeing-stone had stayed with him.

Alorsha and the Captain exchanged looks before Captain Ludek took a step back and turned slightly to look around. Gya saw him place one hand on the hilt of his sheathed sword.

"From what we've heard, magic here is a forbidden thing. Something not to be discussed." Alorsha turned her gaze to a cluster of plants near her feet. She bent to run her fingers along the stems and leaves. Her slight smile appeared and vanished so quickly that Gya was uncertain he had even seen it. "What is this plant?"

Gya looked it over, then wet a fingertip and touched a leaf. The slight sting told him what he needed.

"It's igyelan. Named, in a dead language originally, for the sting you feel when you touch it. So I've heard. The leaves can be dried and used to add a lot of spice to a meal. But not the stems. They're poisonous and can make a person very sick."

Alorsha nodded and turned to him.

He was almost lost in those amazing eyes of hers, but after a moment he came to himself, again. He cleared his throat self-consciously.

"Uh, if you'll permit...." He pulled out a small bag that held white powdered kri-stone and one small white crystal. Risky to carry such things with him, but he had wanted to be able to show Alorsha some of his magic.

Alorsha looked on, her curiosity evident in her expression. Gya also felt Captain Ludek's attention on his actions, but the man also scanned the area around them at regular intervals. Gya worked with great care—he hoped he remembered the sigil correctly—and drew a small sigil on the dirt with the powdered stone. He placed the crystal in the exact center of the spiral-shaped sigil and grinned as the magic made the crystal glow softly.

Then he dared to glance at Alorsha.

She looked from him to the glowing crystal and back, and exchanged looks with the Captain.

"I agree." The Captain turned so his back was to them and continued to watch their surroundings.

Alorsha found a rock to sit on and gestured to another nearby. Before he joined her on the rocks, Gya reclaimed his crystal—its light faded when he removed it from the sigil—and made the circular gesture that directed the powder back into its bag. He dropped the crystal in on top and tucked the bag away in a hidden pocket. With his shoe, he scuffed the patch of dirt where he had drawn the sigil until that patch was indistinguishable from its surroundings.

"Why is magic forbidden here?" Alorsha kept her voice quiet.

Gya perched on his rock as he considered how he might answer. "I don't know. It's been so in the Empire since before I was born. But not always. Sometime more than about a score and ten years ago, the Empire forbade magic. At first, so I've heard, they only required all known Magickas to wear a badge that declared what they were. Of course, they weren't supposed to practice any magic or teach it. Soon the Magickas had to pay extra fees for their businesses, then fewer and fewer people came to their businesses. Then the Magickas began to disappear, taken by the Empire, by the Keepers, for the safety of everyone."

"What did they do with the Magickas?" Alorsha asked.

Gya shrugged. "No one knows. They've never returned."

"But your business has seemed to be thriving and you're—"

"Yes, I'm a Magicka. And the business is managing. It was many years after they rounded up the Magickas and took them away that I learned that I could work magic. I'm certainly not going to let people know. Even now, the families that had a Magicka are watched closely, are considered Blighted because they have a Magicka somewhere in the family line, have fewer sanctions allowed to them. Some people will deal with us, but still many won't."

"So why show me you know magic?"

"You're not of the Empire. Of that I'm certain. Also, your ship glows with magic. I've seen it through a seeing-stone. I think you work magic yourself. Maybe you could help us."

Alorsha looked thoughtful and would not meet his gaze.

"We're just visitors, not staying long. We have a weighty need of our own. If we get sidetracked, it might mean something even worse than your Empire is now."

Gya gave her a look of disbelief. "What's this weighty need? You've not seemed to be in a hurry to pursue it."

"We must have a whole ship and crew," Captain Ludek said.

Alorsha nodded. "Anything less could see us fail. Maybe even get us killed."

Gya stared at her. "So what *is* this weighty need?" he repeated.

Alorsha did not answer right away. When she finally spoke, her voice was not much more than a whisper. "We seek two men from my homeland. One stands about a half-head taller than me, the other just a little shorter than that. The first is thinner than the second and has auburn hair, blue-green eyes and skin of a light brown, lighter than mine. The second has gold-brown hair, lighter skin and green eyes. He might look like he's in a daze or ill."

Gya shook his head. "I've not seen either of these men. Why do you seek them?"

"The first I described is a fugitive from my homeland. His name's Devrand Charnov. He's dangerous. The man with him doesn't accompany him by his own will. His name's Jarthan Tavano."

"Tavano? He's…. Is he your life partner?"

With a sad smile, Alorsha nodded.

"Do you know that they came through this area?" Gya said. "Perhaps they went to the Imperial Capital instead."

Alorsha rose and paced. She brushed each plant she passed with her fingertips, her expression distracted.

"A magic that I can work helps me follow them." Her voice was little more than a whisper. "But it lacks in details. I learned that they're somewhere this direction relative to our ship as we sailed." She extended an arm toward the southeast. "Your town's along that line, so it was possible that they'd passed through it."

"I can check with some friends," Gya said. "But by your description, they're exotic enough that if anyone had seen them, I'm sure the whole town would've been talking about it."

Both Alorsha and Captain Ludek chuckled. "So very true of villages and small towns," Alorsha said. Then she knelt by one small, low-growing plant with tiny yellow flowers to examine it more closely. She closed her eyes and laid her whole hand on the plant to cover it completely but did not press on it.

"Are you working some of your magic?" Gya said.

"Sort of." She kept her eyes closed. "I'm what is known in my homeland as a coppice-mage. I can reach into a plant's magic, work with it."

Gya stared at her. "Plants have magic?" *How had he never thought of such a thing?*

She glanced at him sidelong. "You only work with the stone?"

"It's called kri-stone. All Magickas need kri-stone in

some form to work any magic. Crystals, powdered." His voice trailed off as he realized he had not seen her with any kri-stone. He gave her and the Captain a quizzical look.

At that moment, Captain Ludek hissed, a soft warning sound. "Someone's coming," he murmured.

Alorsha hurried to pluck a few leaves and flowers from plants nearby, and moved back to the one Gya had led her to first.

"What dishes does this work best in?" She acted as if they had been discussing it all along.

"Ah, mostly meat dishes, I understand. I'm no great cook though, so you might want to talk to—"

"There you are, Gya," Usrai called from several paces away as he emerged from a denser cluster of trees. "You must return to Hawei. Didn't you read the latest mandates?"

Gya shuffled his feet and looked at the ground as he pulled his meek persona over his irritation. "I'm sorry. No, I didn't see them."

"They're posted at the council hall. Like always. You need to check there every day. I'll let this slip this once. I imagine you were distracted." He glanced meaningfully at Alorsha. "But you should know that no one from a Blighted family line has sanction to leave their town or village without a Keeper with them at all times."

Gya saw Alorsha pocket some of the leaves and stems from the plant they had been discussing, then she stepped closer to Usrai. "Blighted family line? What's this?"

Gya silently applauded her act of ignorance of the subject.

Usrai's expression morphed into surprise. "I'd thought the Blight was being fought everywhere, even outside the Empire's current reach."

Alorsha gazed back at the Keeper, her expression bland and unreadable. "Perhaps we know it by another term."

Usrai scrutinized her for a tense moment before he

shrugged. "Odd. I speak of the Blight of magic, of course. It runs in certain families, although not everyone in the family seems to inherit the ability to actually use magic." He gave Gya a hard look and the shorter man dropped his gaze.

"Ah, I know of what you speak," Alorsha said. She shook her head, her expression serious. "Quite the thing, that is. But shouldn't we be getting back to town?"

With that, she headed off toward Hawei, Captain Ludek walking at her side.

Usrai whirled on Gya and stepped right into his face. "Watch yourself if you wish to continue to enjoy the sanctions you *are* allowed in my town. Step out of your place again…."

Gya held up his hands in a placating gesture. "I'm properly warned." He managed to put a squeak of fear into his voice although he secretly seethed. "Again, I'm sorry. A misstep on my part. I assure you; it won't happen again."

With an abrupt nod, the Keeper turned to go, but whirled back just as fast. He yanked on the cord that held Gya's token and pulled it from beneath his shirt where he normally wore it.

"This stays out and visible at all times now," Usrai growled. "Another of the new mandates. And you'd better keep a firm hand on that brother of yours. I know he's one of the ones who've been tearing down the mandates at night. We manage to catch him, or catch him out and about in the late night… well, who knows what might happen."

CHAPTER 8

AT A RELAY STATION NORTH OF THE IMPERIAL CAPITAL

Arizu cringed at the sight of the stranger's ire. His foul mood filled the barely adequate guesthouse room in which they planned to spend the night before continuing their bumpy journey in a Ministry carriage to the Imperial Capital. The next instant, she basked in his placating smile. She needed to stop thinking of him as 'the stranger'. *He had told her his name. Dev, he was Dev.* Still, she knew nothing further of him, so he was still a stranger in many ways.

"My anger is not for you," he assured her, with a light touch of his fingers to her cheek. "Your colleagues, however...."

Her uneasiness at his ire slipped away with his touch and she focused on his concerns.

"Unfortunately, so many things take so much time in the Empire," Arizu said.

Dev nodded absently. "I'm concerned that this threat to your Empire isn't receiving the consideration it deserves. We should have at least come across a return courier by now. The longer Alorsha is left largely unopposed in one of your Empire's towns, the more chance she has to draw your people to her. She has proven adept at such things."

"I'm sure they've got the Empire's best Magickas working on something. But they need time. None are anywhere close to Hawei."

"What is it they need time for? It's magic. Just do the magic, right?"

Arizu sighed. "You're fortunate to not have encountered any Magickas. I just wish I could say the same. I still feel contaminated and I've only encountered any of them for a very short time. Much of what the Empire's best Magickas do is new and so requires time and preparation. There are also some things only a few of them can do. I cannot tell you more."

"Cannot? Or will not?"

Arizu grimaced but stayed silent.

Dev studied her expression and nodded. "I see." His own expression turned bland and he turned away.

She jumped up and hurried to him. "Still, we could increase the town's misfortune ambiance. I'll send word to the nearest Provincial Capital, to the Ministry representatives there to see that it's done. A messenger can reach them before dawn."

Would that be enough for him for now? Surely it would. And soon they'd be at the Imperial Capital. The relief that washed through her when he turned back to her with a smile weakened her knees. He sat on a corner of the bed.

"Yes, do that. And I'll await you right here."

CHAPTER 9

Midday the day after he had taken Alorsha outside the town, Gya decided he needed to see what the latest mandates said, with new ones coming from the Imperial Capital more and more frequently, brought by the special couriers on their special horses that had been bred for speed. Gya had heard that messages and mandates could make it all the way out to Hawei, one of the western-most large towns, in little more than a week, if the couriers pushed the horses.

The morning had been slow at the storehouse, with few people coming in to trade or pick up goods that had arrived on ships the previous day. With Toa grumbling about mandates and sanctions whenever they were alone, Gya was glad to escape the building, even to go read what was likely more bad news.

On the walk into the town, he saw fewer people than usual. The closer he got, the more he had a sense of something wrong. The few people he did encounter gave him strange looks, some of them hostile, as they edged away to keep a distance between him and themselves.

In the town proper, it only got worse. People he encountered deliberately moved across the street to keep a distance between him and themselves, many of them stumbling in their haste to get away. Angry mutters seemed to follow him.

At the center of town stood the council hall, with a pole outside that held posted mandates. It was so full of papers nailed to it that Gya could not see the wood of the pole from the height of his knees to above the highest point he could reach. New mandates had just been placed atop older ones, filling the pole.

Gya tried to shake the shivery feeling that gripped him. He felt that everyone glared at him. When he glanced around, he found that was not too far from true. When his gaze met theirs, the townsfolk, people he knew and had grown up with, all of them turned away.

He stepped close enough to the post to read the notices that hung there. With each new one he read, his anger, sorrow, and fear all grew.

Magickas could no longer sell goods to non-Magickas, Keepers and other officials of the Empire could take any goods from Magickas without payment, non-Magickas need not sell anything or provide any service to Magickas if they chose, and on and on.

Almost sick with anxiety and dread after he finished reading the last of the mandates, Gya struggled to hide the feelings. A nail fell from somewhere on the post as he turned away, drawing a long scratch down one arm. A step from the post he tripped and only just managed to keep to his feet. When he looked to see what had tripped him, nothing was there. And no one nearby.

Gya struggled to walk normally away from the post. The fear and meekness that he had worn as a cloak now felt like his reality. He did not want to draw anyone's attention. He just wanted to scurry back to his dwelling and huddle inside.

In his need to get away from the town, he plunged into

a group of people before he realized they were there.

He kept his gaze on his feet as he struggled to get away, but then the voices penetrated his self-imposed haze, and he realized this group was from the *Deliberia*.

"Gya, ease up there." That was Narain, he recognized his voice. "What's wrong?"

Gya glanced at the people around him, only four of them and all clearly from the ship. Narain's was the only name he remembered.

"I-I just need to get back to the storehouse." Gya looked around wildly, feeling trapped, even with these friendly people around him. "A-and you should go. You shouldn't be talking to me."

He took in their puzzled looks and added, "The mandates." He waved a hand back toward the pole with its damning notices. "Haven't you read them?"

The *Deliberia* crewmembers exchanged looks and looked at the post.

"Ah, we can speak your language," Narain said after a moment, "but we can't read it."

Then Gya heard the voice he dreaded.

"You there. Magicka," Usrai shouted from down the street. "Get away from these honored visitors to the Empire."

With an apologetic look at the *Deliberia* crewmembers, Gya hurried away from them.

"Of course," he told Usrai as he hurried past. "No harm. They haven't been able to read the mandates."

Usrai scowled at him and shoved him further away.

"Just you mind your own business. Scurry back to your storehouse and prepare for a visit from Keepers. As per the mandates, we'll be removing the goods that you shouldn't have there and looking through the rest."

With that threat, he sauntered to the group from the ship and spoke with them, pointing an angry finger toward Gya, who took himself off, away from there.

The trip back out of town was worse than his walk into

Hawei. This time, people openly sneered at him, and some young children threw rocks at him while they dogged his steps for a long while. Few of the rocks hit him, but those that did hit him hurt, and might even have hit hard enough to bruise.

At the edge of town, he finally had enough of it and turned toward the children with a snarl of frustration. They froze, their mouths open, rocks in their hands.

He took a single step toward them, going no closer, and shouted at them to stop.

With shrieks, they dropped their rocks and ran back into town. Gya shrank into himself as he realized what tales they would likely carry. He dodged a puffed-up cat that chased a small, terrified dog, nearly losing his footing, as he began the climb up the hill to the storehouse, his thoughts on the children. *Had he just made things worse?*

~ ~ ~

Gya found a frenzy of activity at the storehouse. Several Keepers were already there, and they ordered his workers about. One strong Keeper held Toa by the arms off to the side while his brother screamed at them. Toa's face and arms were bruised and one of his eyes had swollen nearly shut.

Gya stepped into the midst of the chaos.

"What's all this?" he shouted, getting everyone's attention momentarily, before most of them resumed their activities.

One Keeper trudged to him and handed him a paper.

"You are not to handle any goods for non-Magickas," he told Gya. "Nor are you to have any dealings with non-Magickas except the Empire's appointed representatives, such as us. We're removing all the goods that belong to non-Magickas to an un-Blighted storehouse. And you will hand over all your tallies to this point."

Gya exchanged a look with his brother, who had

stopped shouting and stood glaring in the Keeper's grasp.

"But we haven't been paid for those goods yet," Gya protested. He crumpled the paper without reading it. "We have arrangements—"

"Not any longer," the Keeper cut him off. "You deal only with your own kind, now. Others with the Blight. Or, like I said, with us. And only your own immediate relatives can work for you now. No others. As for your 'arrangements', here is your new arrangement."

The man handed Gya a handful of spishas, worth less than a third of the goods the Keepers were removing.

"You're also no longer needed as Harbor Tallymaster," another Keeper told Gya with a toothy grin. "The town will be finding someone much more suitable for that task."

Hot anger rushed through him. Gya flung the coins to the ground and lunged at the grinning Keeper. A hard fist in his face stopped him cold, and the next instant he was held much as Toa.

Although he struggled, and almost broke free at first, Gya ended up helplessly watching as the Keepers emptied the storehouse, except for a few lonely goods that had come from other merchants who numbered among the Blighted. The Keepers also gathered all the years of tally scrolls from the shelves and bundled them carelessly into a large bag.

The Keepers who held the brothers shoved them hard into the echoing storehouse then left with the others, pushing their last few workers ahead of them, headed back to town.

On hands and knees, Gya watched the carts roll away until he could not see them anymore. Next to him, Toa cursed nonstop until the carts rumbled out of sight. Gya shifted around to sit on the floor and gingerly touched his nose. *Bloody and painful but probably not broken.*

Gya hauled himself to his feet and held a hand out to help Toa up. "We'd better see a healer," he muttered.

Toa waved him off and scrambled to his feet on his

own. "Good luck with that," he scoffed. "Candwi's not from a Blighted family. He won't help us now."

Gya frowned. "He's always been a friend to our family."

"He can't be a friend anymore. The mandates won't allow it," Toa shouted. He spun around and stared at the nearly empty storehouse then headed for the door almost at a run. "I can't stay here right now."

Gya tried to catch his arm but missed. "Where are you going?"

"I don't know," Toa called back. "I don't really care! Along the shore, I guess. I'll be back. Sometime."

Gya followed him to the door. He squeezed his nose to try to stop the bleeding and watched through watering eyes as his brother ran west toward the shore, away from the town and harbor. It was something he had done when things were bad ever since he was small. Gya worried but knew his younger brother would not welcome company for a while. So he looked back into the storehouse.

The Keepers had left a mess. They had not been careful and so Gya faced broken shelves, boxes and barrels. Of the few goods that remained, Gya guessed that half might be too damaged to salvage.

With a sigh he turned back outside and gathered the coins that lay in the dirt. He had a feeling they would need every last one of them. Then he headed to their bathing house to clean the blood off himself before he turned to the work to salvage what he could in the storehouse.

CHAPTER 10

"It isn't right. It's not fair!" Toa slammed a hand atop the table they used for meals in their dwelling. "We should be able to make our own choices, do business with who we want, have the chance to wed who we like. The Empire shouldn't be telling families how to run their lives!"

Gya nodded tiredly. Toa had raged off and on ever since the Keepers had emptied their storehouse two days previously. In that time, they had compared what they knew of all the new mandates that ate away at the sanctions allowed them – something that had not improved either of their moods.

"We can't wait any longer." Toa stomped around the table. "Something's got to be done!"

"But what? And how?" Gya folded his arms on the table, tempted to lay his head on them but he resisted. "There are only the few of us in town with magic. Since most of the codices that tell us how to use that magic are gone, have been taken by the Empire, we're poor Magickas. We're not strong enough to stand against the Keepers of Hawei, let alone the rest of the Empire. We can't even manage the more complex magics in the few codices we *do* have until we've mastered the simpler ones."

"Others in town must see how things are going wrong. Even those without the magic Blight face new mandates all the time, too. The best of everything must go to the Imperial Capital. No going out after dark. They treat us all like children. Others must be willing to join with us, if only we talk with them."

Gya shook his head and dropped it into his cupped hands. "You've been saying that. But how can we do such a thing? All it takes is one person talking to the Keepers."

Toa growled and whirled to the door. "You with your worries. You'll just sit there and dither and let them wipe us all out." He slammed a hand onto the table again. "This is useless. I'm going out."

"Wait! What of the meet tonight?"

"You go and talk-talk with the others. Practice your little magics together while you dream of how it used to be. Or how it should be. Whatever! I'll let you know when something real's going to happen."

He stormed out the door.

Gya sighed. He cleaned up the remnants of their evening meal and lit his customary lantern in his bedroom before he secured the storehouse for the night. With everything going on, the meeting had been postponed and it had now been almost two weeks since he had seen the other Magickas for anything more than just a casual greeting in passing.

Watching for any movement, he scurried out the storeroom's side door and to the door to their personal stores.

Inside, he sighed again at the sight of the meager amount of food stored on the shelves. *How were they going to get through this?*

Through the hidden door and tunnel, Gya soon came to the meeting cave, first again, from the lack of any voices. Inside the meeting cave, he tucked himself off to the side to wait, in a spot from which he could see the cave opening but not be seen himself immediately. *Would the others even come, with everything that was happening?*

The others did come, together and not long after Gya had settled himself. When they joined him inside, he lit the candle, as usual. *If only things really were going as usual.*

Gya set the candle to one side, mostly shielded by some rocks so it barely lit the cave and no light extended out into the dusk. The other Magickas' expressions looked tense, worried. *Did he look the same to them?*

"Toa?" Ayaru said after they had all found spots to sit on the ground.

"He's off angry again." Gya wrapped his arms around his knees and rested his chin on them.

"That's not surprising." Ekosua shook her head, her expression sad. "With the new mandates…."

They took several minutes to talk through the latest mandates from the Imperial Capital as well as the continuing bad luck that plagued the town.

"Enough." Dakrei slapped a hand on the dirt floor. "We *all* know it's bad, getting worse. How soon can we move? Everyone feel strong enough in their magical knowledge?"

Mutters and shakes of heads flowed around the small circle.

"Thought not," Dakrei said. "So let's not waste the little time we have with talk of things we already know."

With a shrug, Gya pulled out one of his small bags of powdered kri-stone. "We *should* get some magic work in while we have a chance."

They paired off to work on coordinated magic. Ayaru and Dakrei paired, and Ifeoma with Ekosua, which left Gya and Chizoa to pair with each other. Chizoa gave Gya a pleased smile as she joined him off to one side. And while they worked on the magic, Gya spent almost as much time stealing sidelong glances at her and fidgeting when her gaze met his or their hands brushed as he did with the magic.

Still, they worked together for close to an hour as they tried to get the sigil drawn just right and the crystals placed just so for a trap that would immobilize someone for as long as an hour. Gya had found that sigil in one of the few codices he had left from his father. He and Chizoa had nearly finished redrawing it for the fourth time when she stopped and looked toward the cave opening.

"I hear something."

Everyone in the cave froze and listened to the sounds of footsteps approaching the cave. Then they heard a low whistle, the last several notes of a popular song.

"It's Toa." Gya went to the entrance to greet his brother, relieved that he had remembered to take the side passage and not come out directly in the cave.

Toa's expression was strained, and he held up a hand to forestall Gya's questions. "I'll tell everyone at the same time," he said shortly and hurried into the cave.

Within, he paused and looked around uncertainly.

"Just speak the words, son," Dakrei urged.

Toa's gaze settled on Chizoa. "I'm so sorry, Chizoa. The Keepers've taken your grandmother. Vabena didn't look hurt, at least."

Chizoa gasped and reached blindly behind herself for some support, only finding it when she ran into the wall. The others stared at Toa with varying expressions of disbelief.

"But why?" Chizoa said. "She's never been able to work magic."

"I don't know. But I did see them carrying out some things from her house."

Chizoa shrank in on herself.

"Oh, no!" she wailed. "It's my fault. I must've left something in her house."

Gya placed a gentle hand on her shoulder while he wished he could offer her more comfort. He peered at Toa. "You were there?"

Toa shuffled his feet. "Not there. I was just leaving Zawdi's."

"Didn't see you, did they?" Dakrei said.

Toa shook his head. "I was very careful. Besides, they were focused on Vabena and the house."

"Better get back to our own homes," Dakrei said as he packed away their supplies. After a moment of hesitation, he slipped everything behind and somewhat under one of the large rocks that lined the back wall of the cave.

"Just in case," he told everyone at their questioning looks. "And better be extra careful to brush away any marks from our shoes outside. Be sure to watch out for the Keepers in the night. Can't let them know any of us have been out after dark, against the mandate."

The others followed his example, tucking their magical materials away around the cave. One by one, they slipped out into the night.

Gya took a last look at each one. He hoped it would not truly be the last time he saw them. Chizoa gave him an anguished look, then turned away as Ifeoma told her that she could stay with her that night.

When the others had gone, Toa and Gya slipped behind the rock door in the cave and followed the passage back to their cellar. After they double-checked that everything was secure, they hurried to their second-floor dwelling.

"How bad?" Gya poured a drink for each of them.

"Not sure. I did see some Keepers that I didn't recognize. Maybe they came from the Imperial Capital, although I'd not heard that any had come to Hawei. While they cleared things from Vabena's house, they didn't say anything about going after anyone else – at least not that I heard."

"We'd better make extra certain we've got all our magic supplies well hidden. And away from here in case they *are* found."

Gya shuttered the lantern he had left lit earlier,

dimming the light in the room as he would normally be doing about this time of night. He took a quick look out the window and saw a few dim lights on the *Deliberia*. With only a passing thought to wonder what they did there, he joined his brother. Together, they hurried to gather anything that could possibly be considered related to magic.

They pulled their variously colored crystals, the few codices of sigils they had left from their father, and their carefully stored bags of powdered kri-stone from all their hiding spots and carried everything back to the tunnels, to hiding places there, using some of the other side tunnels they knew about.

By unspoken agreement, they also put together packs for themselves with some clothes and food, and in Gya's case, also a map of the Empire that he had gotten from a trader along with some jars of ink and a set of reed pens. They hid these packs too, in case the time to run was soon.

~ ~ ~

Without the usual bustle of business at the storehouse, the following morning was quiet. Gya struggled to continue the clean-up, under a cloud of dread that something bad approached, a feeling of waiting for something. Toa acted unusually sluggish and stayed close to the storehouse with Gya.

As the morning wore on, with no ships coming into the harbor and only a few merchants stopping by to get their goods and trade for some others, Gya began to feel restless.

He paced to the storehouse's big double doors, open in the warm weather, and peered at the *Deliberia*. There seemed to be a lot of activity on the deck and from his vantage much of the damage seemed well on the way to being repaired.

He watched the distant figures for a while.

How had they repaired so much so quickly?

He had not heard of any crewmembers seeking out wood for repairs. Only the nails and sail canvas. From what he saw, the repaired areas perfectly matched the rest of the ship.

Had they carried so much of their own wood with them? He did not remember seeing much extra wood onboard.

He frowned as he continued to watch the activity. Another mystery about the ship.

"Think I'll head into town for a little while," Gya said over his shoulder to Toa, having grown tired of the observations and speculation running through his thoughts.

When Toa did not immediately respond, Gya turned to find his younger brother giving him a knowing grin. "Going to make sure Chizoa's all right?"

With a mock glare for his brother, Gya nodded. "See how she's doing. See if they've heard anything."

"Just be sure you don't talk only about the weather." Toa waved a finger at Gya.

"What? We've talked about more than the weather," Gya sputtered.

"Hah!" Toa deepened his voice slightly to imitate Gya. "Hello, Chizoa. What fine spring weather we're having this fine spring day, wouldn't you say?"

He next made his voice high pitched and breathy. "Why yes, Gyasi. You've described this fine spring day just fine. I've not seen a finer day." Toa's teasing dissolved into laughter, and after he hung onto his irritation with the teasing a little longer, Gya joined him. It felt good to be able to laugh.

"We're not really that bad, are we?" Gya choked out around his mirth.

"Maybe not quite. Still, don't talk about the weather." Toa sobered and gave him a significant look.

Gya sighed. "I'll try."

"And since you're leaving me stuck here, be sure you

bring back a few of those pastries I like." Toa returned to separating a few goods that needed to go to two different merchants.

"I will," Gya said to his back and headed across the slope of the hill.

In town, Gya hurried to Ifeoma's bakery, hoping he might find Chizoa still there. But Ifeoma stood alone in the shop. She greeted Gya with a slight smile.

"She should be back soon," she told him. "She just needed to be at her grandmother's shop for a couple of customers this morning."

Gya nodded his understanding. Chizoa often worked with her grandmother, both of them accomplished garment makers. Many townsfolk hired them to make clothing, especially fancier items. Or at least many used to hire them. *The mandates would likely hurt their business too.*

"Any word about Vabena?"

Ifeoma shook her head, her expression sad. "Nothing at all. I suggest you don't talk about it with Chizoa, either, unless she mentions it first. She's understandably upset."

Ifeoma handed Gya a hot cup of tea and waved him to one of the small tables she had for people who wanted to eat in the shop.

When he had finished about half his drink, Ifeoma brought Gya a small warm roll, fresh-baked, and a flower-shaped pat of butter in a small bowl. She patted his shoulder as she passed him to return to her baking.

As Gya sipped a second cup of tea, the door opened and Chizoa slipped inside. She ran to Ifeoma, oblivious to Gya seated off to the side.

"Have you heard anything?" Chizoa asked the older woman, her expression anguished.

When the other woman shook her head, she slumped into the nearest chair. "No one knows anything," she said. "The Keepers won't even admit they took grandmother."

Ifeoma gave her hand a comforting squeeze and slowly turned the younger woman toward where Gya sat.

"You have a visitor," she told her.

Gya rose to his feet as the two women turned toward him. He froze in surprise when Chizoa dashed into his arms.

He stared at Ifeoma in astonishment but wrapped his arms around the shaking woman who clung to him. It felt natural and right to stand that way.

While his sadness nearly matched Chizoa's about what had happened, a part of him was thrilled that she turned to him for comfort. He wished he could offer more.

They stood that way many minutes before Chizoa eased back and wiped her tears away. Gya pictured brushing them away for her but hesitated and the moment was gone.

Chizoa sank into the chair next to his. "Thank you for coming to see me," she murmured, her gaze on the tabletop.

"I wish I could be of more help." Gya seated himself again.

Chizoa shrugged and seemed to struggle again with tears. This time she won the battle though.

"I don't know what to do. What any of us can do."

Ifeoma brought her a cup of tea. "Drink up. Try not to dwell on it. We might yet find something we can do."

The younger woman nodded and drank her tea in a few quick gulps. Gya doubted she even tasted it.

She reached across the table and clasped his hand briefly. "I just can't sit still and do nothing. But there's nothing I *can* do. I need to move…. Will you walk with me? Do you have to get back soon?"

Gya gave her a startled look and looked away again as his face grew warm. "I-I'd like that. I don't have to get back too soon. Not much business and Toa's there, anyway. Oh, that reminds me." He turned to Ifeoma. "Toa asked me to bring back some of his favorite pastries."

Ifeoma chuckled. "Of course. It happens I have some baking right now. They'll be ready for you when you return from your walk."

Chizoa and Gya started to clear their table, but Ifeoma shooed them away. "Go. I've got this."

So, hands clasped, Gya and Chizoa sauntered through the town. In her company, Gya found he could mostly ignore the harsh looks from the townsfolk.

He and Chizoa kept their conversation light and away from their worries. She told him of the decorated dresses and shirts she was making for a girl's coming of age celebration. He told her about some of the strange goods he had seen people bring to his storehouse in trade.

Gya was pleased with himself that not once did he mention the lovely weather. Although, with Chizoa next to him, their hands clasped and their arms brushing now and then as they walked, the day seemed even brighter and prettier than it had before.

As they walked and chatted, he stole glances at her from time to time. When his glances met hers, they both quickly looked away, then both stole glances again.

In this pleasant manner, close to two hours passed before they returned to the bakery.

There Chizoa reluctantly told him she needed to get back to her sewing. "But I hope we can do this again."

Gya felt like he was grinning like a fool. "Y-yes, me too. I'd like to."

Distracted by thoughts of seeing Chizoa again, he nearly dropped the package of pastries when Ifeoma handed it to him. Then he was out the door, with a wild desire to skip, or perhaps run – he could not decide which.

CHAPTER 11

IN THE IMPERIAL CAPITAL

Imperial Minister Arizu led the way to the chamber used by the Imperial Council, those members of the Imperial family who bothered themselves with practical matters in the Empire. While larger in the past, the Council currently numbered only three, two men and one woman, siblings who all clearly carried three score or more years, great-aunt and great-uncles to the current Emperor, as Arizu remembered. Most of the family preferred to stay apart from the mundane business of running the Empire, but these few preferred the control.

Arizu had explained all this to Dev, who walked a step behind her.

She glanced back at him and he smiled at her, but the expression did not reach his eyes. They both wore rich clothes for this meeting, shirts and matching trousers in bright colors and made of the finest linen. Arizu had chosen to wear reds and oranges; those colors set off her dark brown skin and black hair. Her companion wore blues and greens and the colors set off his eyes to great effect.

Arizu momentarily lost track of her surroundings in a reverie of gazing into those eyes. At a questioning sound from the attendant stationed at the door to the council chambers, she pulled her thoughts back to the present.

"Please announce us to the Council," she told the man. "Minister Arizu B'Jen and esteemed guest."

With a slight nod, the attendant cracked open the door and announced them. He then stepped to the side to allow them to enter and closed the door behind them.

The Council had invited them to one of their smaller meeting rooms, so the table sat just a few steps inside the door. Dev glided to the table and greeted each member of the council with the proper formal touch of hands back-to-back before he took a seat. His man who followed so silently stood at his left shoulder. Arizu took the seat to Dev's right when he gestured for her to do so.

Dev spoke first. Arizu smiled at the rich sound of his voice. She would be content to simply sit and listen to him talk.

"Councilors, I know you've all heard of the information I brought, of the threat I warned you about."

Arizu's smile widened when she saw all the councilors nod, almost at the same time. *Smart of them to recognize Dev's importance.*

"I am, of course, gratified by your burst of activity preparing to face this threat. It would have been preferable to have learned of it before we finally arrived here," Dev continued. "However, it's unclear what all your activity's accomplishing."

He gave the Councilors a look full of challenge. Arizu shivered, glad that harsh look was not directed at her.

The Imperial aunt scowled right back at Dev. "We've been readying some of our controlled Magickas to send to Hawei. It takes time to prepare for this sort of magic. Not to mention that it's a new magic for most of them. We've also had some setbacks. As soon as they're ready—and they nearly are—they can open some sort of magic gateway and be there almost immediately after. Although they'll need some rest before they can do their magic again."

Dev waved a hand in dismissal of those concerns.

"The one I warned Minister Arizu about, the Magicka—as you call them—that you are after won't stay in Hawei waiting for you to overcome your setbacks. The Minister gave me the impression that you could send your Magickas right away and yet you have delayed and delayed."

Now the older man to the Imperial aunt's left also scowled at Dev. "It wasn't the Minister's place to promise that action. It most certainly wasn't her place to do so without sanction from the Council."

Dev shook his head, his expression saddened. Arizu felt a sudden urge to brush her fingers across his face, to smooth the sadness away. He gave her a quick, sidelong smile, almost as if he knew her thoughts. Then he turned his stern gaze on the Council again.

"At least now you've rectified your error in initially thwarting the Minister's actions," he said.

"Assuredly," the Imperial aunt hastened to say. "The Magickas will be able to open the gateway in a couple of days, at most."

"Perhaps you can increase your efforts and ensure it happens even sooner." Dev's voice held a deep displeasure that made Arizu shiver.

All three Councilors nodded their heads in unison, their expressions concerned but eager to do as he needed.

"After the Magickas have gone through, with a number of Keepers to watch them and also secure the town, they'll need some hours to recover before they go after *your* Magicka," the third Councilor, the youngest of the three, said. He shrank under Dev's gaze, but still continued, "I thought you should know."

"This will all be taken care of to your satisfaction," the Imperial aunt assured Dev.

In a heavy silence, he studied the Councilors while they exchanged uneasy glances. Then with an abrupt nod, he rose to his feet, Arizu an instant behind him.

"I look forward to the resolution of this problem. I'm pleased that you're taking this as seriously as it must be taken." The Councilors preened at this sign of his approval.

Dev then leaned on the table to gaze intently at each Councilor in turn. "We'll meet again in a few days to review your progress."

With Arizu and his silent companion following on his heels, Dev left the Councilors staring after him, their expressions mixtures of awe and consternation.

CHAPTER 12

As Gya tried to go about business as usual the next day, the little business they still had, he regularly startled at sudden noises. Overnight, his joy at being with Chizoa had given way to an almost paralyzing anxiety. When it got bad enough late in the morning that Toa gave him odd looks, he left his brother in charge of the storehouse and headed into town.

He tried to keep his pace and glances casual, but what he saw did nothing to ease his worries.

At least twice the number of Keepers as the previous day hovered around town, and Gya did not recognize most of them. The other people he saw acted nervous and clustered at street corners to exchange news. They split apart to hurry about their business if it looked like a Keeper took any interest in them.

Every street he walked, Gya felt people watching him. If he passed close to a group, they stopped talking to stare at him until he moved off. He started to feel twitchy at all the attention and so took himself to Ifeoma's bakery, hoping to talk with her. She always seemed so calm, no matter what happened. *Maybe she could share some of that calm with him.*

But when he rounded the corner and saw her shop, he stopped cold. The expensive glass windows in the front had all been broken out and her delicious breads trampled into the stones of the street. Everyone who passed hurried their pace as they went by the shop, like they feared being caught in it, too.

Gya paused. *What should he do?*

The shop was dark. Maybe Ifeoma was not there. He looked all around as his hands shook. If they would do this….

When he saw that no one payed particular attention to him, he ran to the shop and peered in. The destruction inside was complete. Even the door had been partially torn away from its hinges. No sign of the baker.

He spun around to look both ways along the street.

Passersby stepped widely around him and hurried on their way while they kept their gazes averted from him. Further down the street, one Keeper watched him with a wolfish grin, but otherwise did nothing.

Gya knew Ifeoma lived above her shop, but he feared to cross the destruction inside to reach the stairs at the back. Still, he needed to see that Ifeoma was all right. He took another look around, and when the Keeper's attention wandered, he slipped inside.

He hurried across the shop, trying to avoid stepping on the debris. When he reached the stairs, he stood a long time at the bottom, talking himself into climbing them. He was afraid to even call out.

But finally, he took the first step, and the next, and shortly stood before the door to Ifeoma's living quarters.

The door was completely broken away, and part of the wall too. The destruction he saw within her dwelling surpassed that downstairs by an order of magnitude.

He leaned in and softly called for her. Once, twice.

He received no answer.

He stood frozen at the threshold. *Should he go in to look for her? He probably shouldn't even be there.*

He heard voices. *Someone downstairs?* He crept to the landing at the top of the stairs and tried to see who was talking. *What if it was Keepers? He should not be found here.*

Gya listened but was unable to make out what they said.

The voices' owners must be close outside the shop. Hopefully, they would leave soon. He needed to be away from this destruction. He needed to return to Toa. Needed to see if his own dwelling and business might have suffered the same fate as Ifeoma's in the short time he had been away.

He shifted his feet. *When would those people leave so he could leave too?*

Then he remembered… Chizoa was supposed to have stayed with Ifeoma. *What if she had still been here?*

Gya returned to the baker's dwelling. He eased his way through the debris while he looked for any sign of what had happened to Ifeoma, and possibly Chizoa, too.

The living quarters were small, just two rooms. He found no indication of where Ifeoma and Chizoa might be. Their possessions were so broken and tossed around, he could not even guess if they might have left before the destruction. Gya spotted Chizoa's favorite hair stick where it lay almost hidden under the broken remnants of a table and chairs. A sinking feeling tore through him as he snatched it from the floor and fingered it to check for damage. *What if he never saw her again?*

He continued poking through the destruction but found nothing else intact. He did however find a door tucked away at the back that led to a narrow staircase that ran down the side of the building.

A quick look around showed no one nearby so he hurried down the stairs. To hide the best he could manage, he took the smallest alleyways and least-used streets as he returned to his own dwelling.

Back at the storehouse, Gya at first saw nothing amiss.

Then he realized he heard no sounds of activity, and the big double doors stood wide open. *But they only opened both when they needed to load carts, none of which they had any longer.*

He saw no one around, but still hesitated to approach. Finally, he slipped around to the side door, also open, he discovered. Inside he saw some of the destruction he had seen at Ifeoma's, but mostly he saw that the few goods that had remained in the storehouse had been cleared out.

Gya said Toa's name into the silence, his voice wavering.

After no answer, he called a little louder. Only the echoes of the empty storehouse answered him.

He dashed up the stairs calling for Toa, louder and louder with each repetition. Still nothing.

He stopped at the sight of his dwelling, feeling like he had been punched in the face again. The whole place had been torn apart, his and Toa's belongings thrown about with no care for them at all.

Gya wandered through his dwelling and randomly picked up things and dropped them again. *How could this have happened? How had the Empire discovered their secret?*

Had Ifeoma and Chizoa been able to escape the destruction? Or had they been taken?

He began to gather things here and there that he might be able to use, without giving much thought to his actions. He found a bag and stuffed it with any food that had not been ruined. He grabbed some clothes. On the floor by a broken chair, he found Toa's favorite bracelet, an intricate design that their mother had crafted from wire wound with rectangular yellow-brown beads. Gya wore a similar one made with rectangular purple-blue beads. He stuffed Toa's bracelet in a second bag with the clothes.

Where was Toa? Had he gotten away?

Right! The packs he and Toa had put together the previous night.

Gya grabbed a last bit of food and ran back downstairs to the hidden door to the tunnels.

A fear he had not acknowledged vanished when he saw the door intact and closed. It remained undiscovered in its shadowed corner. Or so he hoped.

On the other side of the doorway, Gya paused. *Should he find some way to seal it against the Keepers in case they returned and searched more thoroughly? But what if Toa needed it? How to decide the best action?*

Torn between the two choices, he stared into the darkness.

If Toa had taken his pack….

Gya felt his way in the dim light from the open door to the side tunnel where they had hidden their packs. Only his own pack sat there.

Relief robbed him of strength momentarily. At least Toa had been there and was away again. They had not settled on a specific place to meet if something like this happened, but they had discussed a few different possibilities. Gya hoped Toa would wait for him at one of them. *He'd check every one of them until he found his younger brother!*

He grabbed his pack, ready to head out, but turned back to retrieve the crystals and powders that he and Toa had hidden nearby. Some crystals and powders were gone. *Toa must have grabbed them.* What was left, Gya put in a satchel that he carried cross-body and that already contained his other crystals and powders.

Gya hurried back to the hidden door to the storehouse, pulled it closed and locked it with the locking kri-stone crystal in the secret keyhole on this side of the door. Then he dipped his first and middle fingers into one of the pouches of powdered kri-stone.

The powder clung to his fingers and he drew the same sigil he had used to open the door from the other side, but this time on the tunnel side of the door. He had practiced this one so much, he could almost have done it in his sleep. A good thing since it was too dark with the door closed to see his work.

The magic gathered as he followed the whirls of the complicated sigil, somewhat more elaborate than the one he had drawn for Alorsha. *Had that really been just a few days ago?*

When he completed the sigil, it glowed slightly. Gya pulled out the crystal that matched the powder and tapped it three times in the middle of the sigil to activate the magic.

He stepped back as the glow spread to the edges of the door and its frame to complete the lock. If Toa came that way, he would still be able to open the door, but the Keepers should not be able to even determine that a door existed there, let alone open it without magic.

At the appropriate gesture with the crystal, the powdered kri-stone lost its glow and streamed off the wall back into the pouch he held.

Without even a glance behind him, Gya hurried away from the only home he had known, feeling his way through the dark tunnel.

CHAPTER 13

Gya froze on the tunnel-side of the door to the cave they used for magic. *Were those voices?*

He crouched, setting his candle off to the side, and placed an ear against the cold stone to try to hear better. From the voices, he knew that more than one person was in the cave beyond, but he could not understand what they were saying. The voices were too muffled for him to tell whose they were, either.

What to do? If he opened the door, he might walk into a group of Keepers who waited for such a happening. He clasped his hands to stop their shaking. No one had ever again seen any Magicka taken by the Empire, as far as he had heard. No one knew what happened to them. But he could imagine far too many horrible things.

He stared at his hands. *Why was this happening? And what could he really do about it, when he came right down to it?*

His pack slid off his shoulder, knocked him off balance and caused him to sit suddenly on the dirt floor. As he gave it a glare, as if it had done that intentionally, he spotted the codices that he had grabbed when he had hurried through the tunnels to this point, codices that he and Toa had hidden so recently, with a couple missing that Toa must have taken.

He grabbed the one on top and flipped through it. Maybe he would find something in one of them to help. He found it frustrating how any sigil too advanced for his skills, or that he had not worked with for a few weeks, slipped away from his memory. That just seemed to be the way of the magic, but it meant a lot of looking back through codices of sigils for any he had not worked with recently.

In the third codex that he flipped through he found something useful. A sigil to let the Magicka who cast it look through a solid object. *Now, did he have the right kri-stone crystals and powders?*

He dug through his bag and found the two colors he needed, both crystal and powder in pale yellow and colorless clear. He hoped he had enough. Rare compared to the other colors, the pale yellow would boost the magic, something needed for this sigil to work.

He studied the sigil while he tried to calm his fears. The magic worked better if the Magicka managed at least a relative calm.

When he felt ready enough, and felt he should not take any more time, he meticulously copied the sigil onto the rock door. He smiled at the tingle of the magic as it flared. It settled as he finished the final part. Just as it was supposed to do.

Gya tapped his blue-tinted seeing kri-stone crystal on the key points of the sigil that the codex indicated. He placed the largest flat side of the crystal against the door in the middle of the sigil and leaned close to look into it with one eye.

At first, what looked like a gray swirling mist within the crystal filled his vision. But the mist cleared, and he could see into the cave.

He smiled. *At least Ekosua, Ayaru and Dakrei had also*

escaped Hawei.

Gya directed the streams of powdered kri-stone back into their pouches, and dropped in his kri-stone crystals too, before he tucked everything away again in his pack. Then he snuffed his candle.

Gya opened the hidden rock door to three surprised expressions accompanied by two knives held ready to attack. Dakrei and Ayaru held the knives.

"It's me. It's Gya."

The other Magickas nearly smothered him with welcoming embraces. A moment later they sobered.

"Where's Toa?" Ekosua said.

"I've not seen him since earlier this day," Gya said. "But a pack he had made up and some kri-stone crystals and powders are gone, so I think he's hiding somewhere."

"Didn't set up a place to meet?" Dakrei glowered at Gya.

Gya tried to give the older man a reassuring smile, but felt it came out more a grimace. "We talked about a few, certainly. But we hadn't decided on one particular one."

As the older Magicka turned away shaking his head, Gya added, "Of course, this place is one."

"So what now?" Ekosua sagged to the floor and clutched a small cloth pack to herself.

Gya looked at the others. Each also had a small pack, easily carried. They gazed back at him with questioning expressions.

Gya threw his arms up. "Why are all of you looking to me? I don't know."

Dakrei squeezed Gya's shoulder with a hand still strong in spite of his years. "Calmly, son. We look to you because you, at least, have more knowledge of what's out there beyond Hawei. From all the time you spent as a child on the various boats that visited and from all the people you've done business with."

Gya nodded at the truth of his words and plopped onto the floor. He peered toward the cave opening and tried to bring his thoughts into something coherent.

"Well now, we can't stay here," Ayaru said. "Not in the cave, nor in Hawei."

Gya nodded. "If we can, though, I think we should wait until dark to leave the cave. It might not be wise, but if Toa hasn't come before then, I'd like to check the other places we'd talked about. To see if he's waiting there or has left some sign."

Dakrei nodded. "We can be careful."

"But after, I just don't know," Gya said. "There's north to the barbarians. At least from what I've heard, they don't seem to care one way or another if someone's a Magicka. But we'd have to cross a lot of the Empire to get there."

"Not to mention the Mavkath Sea." Ayaru waved her hand in the general direction of the cave mouth and the sea beyond.

"Maybe we could take a small boat to cross the sea," Ekosua said.

"Possibly. But it's risky this time of year to be out in a small boat," Gya said. "Many of the merchants who've docked here have told me tales of sudden, dangerous spring storms that stalk the Mavkath."

"Long have people spoken of those storms," Dakrei said. "Must believe there's at least some truth in the tales."

"West isn't good," Gya continued. "The Empire claims the land all the way to the coast but there's really nothing much there. Drier even than here and I think only a few small settlements. East and south are about as bad as north – a lot of the Empire to cross to get beyond its borders."

"Can't we go to one of the other groups?" Ekosua said.

Dakrei shook his head. "Be very surprised if they weren't in the same difficulty."

"We don't know that, though," Ekosua argued.

"Well, we can't risk it," Ayaru said.

"Even if they're not in the same difficulty, can't just arrive in their town. Their Keepers would pounce on us there, and anyone with us," Dakrei said.

They fell silent. Gya tried to think of a way to choose the best direction, but nothing came to him to prefer one way over the other.

"I'd rather not go southeast," he said. "Going toward the Imperial Capital seems like the worst choice."

The others murmured agreement.

"What of that ship?" Ayaru said. "Did you get a chance to learn more of them?"

"Some," Gya said. "They do have some magic and they don't seem to come from someplace that's anything like the Empire, that hunts down Magickas. But I didn't learn where they *do* come from. They're here following a fugitive from their homeland, so the ship's owner told me."

Gya shrugged, his expression unhappy. "I don't know that we know enough about them to be able to even decide if we can try trusting them."

Ekosua giggled, which drew concerned looks from the others. She waved off their concern. "No, I'm all right. It's just how Gya managed to completely non-commit to anything in that last statement."

The others grinned, even Gya.

"Still," he said, "while a ship might be easier, if we walk as much as possible wherever we decide, might we not be harder to find in the end?"

"Oho!" Ayaru poked Dakrei in the ribs with a finger. "You'll have to move your lazy feet to keep up with these two youngsters, old man." She smirked at him.

He returned her smirk. "Keep up with them better than you, old woman."

Gya grinned. Ayaru had ten or so years fewer than Dakrei and neither of the two was lazy or decrepit by any means.

As they fell into a familiar, comforting banter, Gya eased over to the cave opening to look out. Ekosua joined him there.

"I'm so sorry about Chizoa." She gave his arm a motherly pat, although she was not more than ten years his elder, certainly nowhere near old enough to be mothering him.

Gya sighed and stared at his feet. "They took her, didn't they?"

"Yes, and others of Blighted families in the town. We're all that's left. With Toa."

Gya leaned out of the opening a little to peer at the *Deliberia. Was that much activity common on a ship for that time of day? What were they doing?*

Ekosua also leaned out for a look. "Would the Empire take their Magickas, too?"

"I hope not. But I wouldn't be surprised to see them try." He gave that some consideration. "But I don't really see them letting them."

With a nod, Ekosua returned to the cave. Gya followed soon after and the four Magickas settled in to wait for night.

~ ~ ~

Someone shook Gya's shoulder. He waved an arm without opening his eyes. "Go 'way, Toa."

But the voice that whispered at him to wake up was not Toa's. Gya struggled up from the grip of his disturbing dreams and opened his eyes... to a sunset glow on rock walls.

Right, the cave.

He looked at Dakrei. "I'm awake."

"Good. Need to see this."

The older man pulled him to his feet and toward the mouth of the cave. Gya realized as they got closer that the light he saw flickered. Not sunset, but fire.

He and Dakrei joined the two women to peer outside.

The fire that engulfed what had been his home caught Gya's attention first. Gya stared as the bright flames wiped out the building his grandparents had built, and his parents had expanded further to serve their growing business. He saw some people near the flames, but they just stood there and watched. When he realized his face was wet, he swiped the backs of his hands across his cheeks and scowled.

He looked further away, to the harbor.

"The *Deliberia!*"

Alorsha's ship seemed engulfed in flames. But something was odd.

Gya realized he could see people on the deck of the *Deliberia*... just walking about. Not acting at all like people on a burning ship. He saw other people on the dock, and they looked far more frantic. Many of them wore the uniform favored by the Keepers when they wanted to look their most imposing: trousers, boots, shirts and hip-length coats all in a deep, dark red, with their gray gloves the only break in the monotone color.

Gya glanced at his companions and they gave him astonished looks in return.

"Well now, I'd say the people on the ship have some magic." Ayaru's tone was dry.

"But look." Ekosua pointed to the figures on the dock. Some of the Keepers had pushed three people forward, closer to the ship. Even from this distance, Gya could see that those people held kri-stone crystals in one hand – the largest crystals Gya had ever seen, nearly the length of their hands. The stones glowed an angry orange-red.

The Keepers prodded the three Magickas—that had to be what they were—and, as one, the three raised their hands and began to draw sigils in the air with powdered kri-stone that streamed from pouches at their waists, seemingly guided by the kri-stone crystals they held. They each drew the same sigil, in perfect coordination.

Ekosua gasped. "The Empire's using Magickas!"

"Looks like they're forcing them to do what they want," Dakrei said.

"Where did they even come from?" Gya muttered. He had seen no strangers other than Keepers in the town mere hours before. No new ships sat in the harbor, and the Magickas did not have the look of people who had just ridden into town.

As the four watched from their hiding spot, the sigils drawn in the air glowed softly. The powdered kri-stone hung there without falling to the ground as it should have. When the Magickas on the dock completed the sigils, flames shot out from them, reaching for the *Deliberia*.

The flames joined the flames that already wreathed the ship and began licking at the ship's hull.

"Here." Ekosua handed Gya a seeing-stone.

When he looked through it, he discovered the magic on it let him see everything as if he stood much closer. As he watched, he saw Alorsha step onto the deck from the part of the ship that held her cabin. She handed something to several crewmembers who had run to her at her appearance. *Small vials holding some liquid?*

She and the others spaced themselves around the railing of the deck. Alorsha shouted something and they tossed up their hands to throw the liquid from the vials into the air. Alorsha stood with one hand on the ship's rail, the other raised.

The liquid from the vials hung in the air longer than it should have been able to. When he looked again at Alorsha, Gya saw that the liquid from her vial had formed a long stream that reached from her hand upward. It expanded and joined with the other drops hanging in the air to create a dome above the ship. Gya wished he had one of the other seeing-stones to see what the glow of the ship was doing.

After the dome held its position a moment longer, it stretched down all around the *Deliberia*. As the edges descended, they extinguished the flames that surrounded the large ship. Parts of the hull looked darker, blackened from the flames but not badly burned.

Everyone on the docks stepped back to put distance between themselves and the ship. With the flames no longer there, Gya saw that the ship's gangplank had been retracted. Alorsha stalked to the edge of the deck where it had been and regarded the Keepers on the dock.

She planted her hands on her hips and just looked at them. Her Ship's Master and Ship's Captain joined her, flanking her.

Then she and one of the Keepers—one Gya did not recognize—engaged in what looked like a shouted argument. It ended when the Keeper stomped away, leaving several of his fellows on the dock. Other Keepers prodded the hapless Magickas away from the dock and toward town. Alorsha watched them a short time before she turned back toward her cabin.

"Need to find a way to get on that ship," Dakrei said.

"But how?!" Ekosua said. "Surely they'll sail away as fast as they can after this."

Gya lowered his seeing-stone. "It doesn't look like they are. At least not yet." He glanced at Ayaru, who nodded.

"I agree with Dakrei. Let's see if they'll take us on."

They clambered and slid down the hill to the narrow strip of beach that ran beneath the rocks that concealed the cave. From there, they eased their way back toward the dock, eyes and ears alert.

After they had traveled nearly half the distance, they paused among some concealing rocks.

"It's too well-lit over there," Gya muttered.

"Maybe the Keepers expect something like what we're trying," Ayaru said.

"We could swim," Ekosua said. "It's not too cold for it. Or maybe borrow one of the small boats, just to get to the ship."

"But how do we signal the ship from the water, or even from a small boat, without alerting the Keepers." Gya frowned.

"Isn't there a way to send a message with kri-stone crystals?" Dakrei said.

"If both people have sister-crystals, crystals cut from the same original crystal, it's supposed to be fairly easy,"

Gya said. "Of course, that's to let them talk back and forth."

"But we just need a message to go one way," Ayaru said. "May I see your codices?" She held a hand out to Gya.

He dug them out of his pack and divided them between all of them. Only the rumble of the spume-dappled waves that came ashore and the susurration of the pages the Magickas turned in the moonlight marked the next many minutes.

"Here," Ekosua said. The others gathered around and read over her shoulders.

"Not too complicated," Dakrei murmured.

"But can we do it from this distance?" Gya said. "It's not clear about how far away it'll work."

"Well now, let's try here, with all of us guiding the magic, and see if it works," Ayaru said. "If it doesn't, we'll swim closer and try again. You saw how their Magickas drew the sigils in the air. We should be able to do so, too, if we need to."

Ekosua smoothed an area of sand. "Not the best surface to work with."

Gya shrugged and helped the others pull out the crystals and powder that they would need. This magic only needed one color for the sigil: white, the most common.

They worked together—as they had been practicing for many months—to form the sigil, and placed all but the final crystal, just as the codex showed.

"Gya, the *Deliberia's* owner knows you. You speak the message," Ayaru instructed.

Gya stared out at the ship as he decided what to say, then he placed the final crystal. He knelt next to the sigil, careful to avoid disturbing any of the lines, leaned over it, and spoke softly.

"Alorsha, it's Gya. I and three other Magickas request permission to come aboard, from the water to starboard. Please flash a lantern on that same side three times if you'll allow it." He had chosen the starboard side deliberately – the side away from the docks and best hidden from the milling Keepers.

His message completed, he sat back to watch the ship. After a time, he shifted to relieve a numb foot but never took his gaze from the ship.

"It doesn't look like it worked," Ekosua muttered after they waited further long minutes. "Or maybe she doesn't want us on her ship."

Gya shook his head against that thought. "I feel she'd be willing to help us."

"Maybe we *all* need to say the message," Ayaru offered.

"Maybe it needs to be shorter," Gya said.

"Was your whole attention on her, this Alorsha?" Dakrei asked Gya. "Maybe need to picture her in your mind."

Gya looked from one to another of the others. "Should we try all of that?"

The others nodded. After a brief discussion to settle on what they would say, they knelt by the sigil and leaned toward it as Gya had. Gya pictured Alorsha aboard her ship and nodded when he felt ready.

After a count of three from Ayaru, the Magickas spoke in unison. "Alorsha, Gya and three others request permission to come aboard, from the water to starboard. Please flash a starboard lantern three times if you agree."

Gya felt a small surge of the magic that he had not sensed the first time. When he glanced a question at the others, they each nodded. So they cleaned up the kri-stone and waited again.

After a much shorter wait, Gya saw a lantern flash three times from the starboard side. The signal repeated after a short pause.

"Swim it is." Dakrei led the way into the water.

CHAPTER 14

Gya clambered up the rope and stepped dripping onto the *Deliberia*'s deck. He was the last one on deck. One of the crewmembers threw a blanket around his shoulders and he nodded his thanks as he clutched it close. While the days had been warm, the spring nights still held a chill to them. After quick introductions all around, with the Ship's Master telling the Magickas to please call her by her first name Saevalde, Alorsha gripped Gya's shoulder.

"Come inside, all of you," she said with a nod toward the door to Saevalde's cabin and hers beyond. "I'm interested to hear what all this is about."

Alorsha sent a couple of crewmembers running for some food and dry clothes, then walked the Magickas to the cabins.

Inside Saevalde's cabin, Gya saw that the furnishings had been rearranged. The bed had been moved further to one side, with a decorated arras hung as a partition mostly hiding it. That left much of the rest of the room open, occupied by a table and several chairs and also left a clearer path between the door to the deck and the door that opened into Alorsha's cabin.

Almost on their heels, a crewmember followed them into the room and placed a platter of bread, cheeses, and dried fruits and a jug of wine on the table. Another followed behind with plates and mugs. A third followed that one, with a stack of clothing.

Saevalde nodded toward the curtained-off section. "Feel free to change into the dry clothes." She and Alorsha moved to the other side of the table and chairs where they seated themselves and spoke together in low voices.

The four Magickas exchanged looks and sorted through the dry clothes to find items that looked like they would fit. They took turns changing in the curtained half of the room, the women first, followed by the men.

"Where can we place these?" Ekosua held out her bundle of sodden clothes and tried to keep them from dripping much more on the floor.

"Just hand them to the crewmember outside the door," Alorsha said with a smile. "My people will rinse out the salt water for you, so they'll be ready for you when you want them back."

With a surprised glance shared with the other Magickas, Ekosua did as instructed, and the others followed suit. Gya was last to take his clothes to the crewmember and noticed that two of them stood outside, flanking the cabin's double door. When one ran off with the sodden clothes, another crewmember stepped up to the vacated spot.

Gya closed the door and joined the others at the table. The food was tasty, but exotic – unlike anything he had encountered before. Alorsha and Saevalde ate with them.

"Are we prisoners?" Gya gestured at the door to the deck.

Alorsha shook her head. "Not at all. They're there in case we need anything and also to let us know if anything changes out there." She waved a hand in the general direction of the dock.

"Thank you for all of this, and for the risk you take by

hiding us," Ayaru said.

Alorsha and Saevalde exchanged looks. The Ship's Master went to the outer door and told one of the crewmembers to ask Captain Ludek to join them.

"Captain Ludek—Mikolus—ensures our safety," Alorsha explained. "With Saevalde, he helps make any important decisions that affect the ship and her crew."

"Perhaps we should just gather our clothes and go," Ekosua said. "There's enough trouble without getting you further involved."

With a shake of his head, Dakrei pulled her back to her seat. "I think this isn't just concerning us."

Alorsha smiled and nodded. "Your Keepers want us to surrender ourselves and our ship to the Empire. The best I can tell, they came with their demands about the same time as the destruction in your town. Destruction caused by them, I might add."

"Several people from Blighted families are now missing, too," Gya said. "Including my brother. Although it looked like he might have left on his own and is probably hiding out somewhere."

The door opened and the Ship's Captain joined them. He took a position behind Alorsha and to her left and leaned against the cabinet there. Saevalde resumed her seat to Alorsha's right.

"Well, but you've not looked yet in all the places you and he discussed," Ayaru reminded Gya.

With a nod, Gya started to rise. "I should get to that. I have to know—"

"Bide a moment, lad," Saevalde said. "It's possible there's a better way to find your brother than for you to be running off back into that mess out there."

"Seems other things are going on here, as well." Dakrei directed a look of significance at Alorsha. "Why are they coming after you? Even before you showed any of your magics?"

Alorsha told them what she had told Gya, about

seeking the two men: Jarthan, her life partner and Devrand, the man who held him captive.

"Might be Devrand set this Empire on Hawei," Mikolus said.

"Why would you say that?" Ekosua said.

"He's done something similar before," Alorsha said. "To try to stop me—"

"To try to kill you," Mikolus broke in.

Alorsha shrugged with one shoulder, her expression one of discomfort. "I'd like to think not—"

"No matter what you'd like to think, lass, he *has* tried to kill you. Us," Saevalde said.

"You told me he was dangerous," Gya said.

"Yes." Alorsha rose and paced. "His magic is stronger than mine in many ways and he's just growing even stronger."

"Every place we visit, you're also growing stronger," Saevalde said in a low voice.

Alorsha gave herself a deliberate shake. "True. We'll get the blackguard, no matter what he throws at us."

"Be wary of the Empire," Ayaru said. "They've been taking unwilling Magickas for years now."

"Finding a way to make them work for them, too, so it seems from what we saw happen on the docks," Dakrei pointed out.

"We need to flee the Empire," Ayaru said. "You should, too, Alorsha."

"I need to know about Toa." Gya gave Alorsha a sharp look at a sudden thought. "How do you follow this Devrand? Do your magics let you see where he is?"

"Not in the way I think you mean," Alorsha said. "I have something that's connected to both Devrand and Jarthan. I use that to find a direction to Devrand relative to my location. Then I have to chase him down."

Gya slumped. "I'd hoped you might've been able to use the same thing to see Toa," he muttered.

"Well now, I think I remember some sort of sigil for

seeing at a distance in one of the codices," Ayaru said to Gya. "Different from what we use on our seeing-stones. More powerful. But we've worked long with seeing sigils so we should be able to manage it."

"But aren't they *all* just variations of what we do with the seeing-stones?" Gya objected.

"Perhaps," Dakrei said. "Should still look at them again."

So Gya and the other Magickas hauled their slim codices from their packs and handed them out to each other. The next many minutes, they flipped through pages and pages of sigils.

"Here it is. This one, I think," Ayaru held up her codex, open to an elaborate sigil in three colors. "It talks about using this sigil to discern something that's not close at hand. Also clarity of sight."

The other Magickas set their codices down and gathered around her to study the page.

"It's more complex than any we've managed so far," Ekosua muttered.

"Reads like it's more for gaining insight rather than seeing something far away," Dakrei said.

"The description's vague," Ayaru said. "That might mean it's versatile."

Alorsha stepped close to peer over Gya's shoulder. He glanced back at her. "I thought you couldn't read our language."

Alorsha smiled. "True. I can't. But I'm still curious. I can also admire the drawing."

Gya returned her smile. "That's the sigil we need to draw to work the magic."

Alorsha nodded and stepped back. "What can the rest of us do to help?"

"Ideal to have a large, flat surface to lay out the sigil," Dakrei said. "But not the floor, I think," he added as he scrutinized that surface. "As well fitted together as the planks are, the edges between would disturb the sigil's integrity."

He shrugged at Alorsha. "If we were more accomplished, more experienced, we'd be able to work around that. But as we are, we'll take advantage of anything we can to make it go more smoothly."

"Will the table be large enough?" Saevalde said.

The four Magickas conferred, looking from the codex to the table and back.

"It should be fine," Ayaru concluded eventually.

She and Gya pulled out the crystals and powders the sigil would need—blue, purple, and white—while the other Magickas returned the other codices to the appropriate packs. Saevalde and Mikolus helped them move the rest of the food from the table to the tops of the low cabinets along the walls. After he moved the last platter and grabbed more cheese from it, Mikolus stepped back to stand near the door and watch, his expression unreadable. Alorsha and Saevalde joined him when the four Magickas took places around the table.

Gya struggled to ignore their small audience and worked on laying out the sigil. Unlike the curvy, mostly circular sigils they had worked with so far, this one was basically square-shaped, although Gya spotted a star shape in it too, edges angled inward, when he looked at it a little differently. The square was turned to have the corners top and bottom and side to side and crossed by other parts of the sigil. The only curves in the sigil were the small detailed writings—some of which extended from the mid-point— scattered along other lines of the shape. All the other pieces were straight lines, something that would make this sigil more difficult than most to get right.

Matching the drawing, Gya laid out some lines of the sigil in the blue powdered kri-stone, while Ekosua and Ayaru added others in purple. Dakrei filled in the finest details with the white powdered kri-stone.

The Magickas took several minutes to compare their work to the diagram in the codex and correct a few errors.

Then they placed the crystals—white and clear—at the points indicated in the codex and held aside the largest clear, colorless crystal.

"All ready, except for the last crystal to seal and actuate it," Dakrei said.

"I'm not feeling even a hint of magic." Gya shared a worried look with the others. "Usually I feel the magic building, even before we place the last crystal."

"Perhaps not evident until that last crystal is placed." Dakrei nodded to the crystal Gya held. "For this sigil."

"Remember, they don't all work the same," Ekosua added.

"Perhaps," Gya acknowledged, his expression dubious.

"You place the crystal, Gya," Ayaru instructed. "Lead us in the magic, since you have the closest connection to Toa."

He glanced at the other Magickas. "Ready?"

With nods, they took places next to the table. He slipped into the gap they left for him and eased the crystal to its place in the center of the sigil where it touched powders of all the colors.

"I'd like to look for the others, too but I'm going to try Toa first," Gya said. "Let's all picture him as we saw at the last meet he came to before all this."

Gya glanced at his fellow Magickas to find their attention focused on the large crystal. He did likewise, remembering Toa's features and the smile he wore when he worked with the magic.

The magic ran through the sigil and an image formed in the crystal – something moved there.

Gya leaned close and tried to make out what he saw, but the image was too small. It might be Toa…. He focused harder, trying to make the image clearer, or larger.

More movement, indistinct and unrecognizable as anyone in particular.

Gya released the magic with a sigh.

"Was it Toa?" Ekosua said.

"Too small to tell," Dakrei said. "Could have been anyone really."

"Anyone have a larger crystal?" Ayaru said.

When no one did, Gya sank into a chair. "How can we find a crystal that will work here? I've not seen one suitable for the seeing magic that was any larger than this one." He gestured at the clear crystal in the sigil's center.

"You need something bigger for the image to form in." Alorsha stepped up to the table and studied the sigil and crystal. "Does it *have* to be a crystal?"

The Magickas exchanged startled glances. "Well now, could be that's exactly what the magic needs," Ayaru said.

"It's possible to adjust magics to stretch their original intentions," Alorsha said.

"Combine yours with theirs?" Mikolus said.

Alorsha nodded.

"Will that work?" Gya said.

"There's a good chance, I think. It's at least worth trying. I'll just get a few things." She headed to the door that led to her cabin.

While she was gone, the Magickas checked the sigil again and made a few more tiny corrections.

Alorsha returned as they finished thickening some of the lines of the sigil. She carried a shallow bowl, like a wash basin, although this one was made from some gray metal. A satchel hung from one of her shoulders.

"Would you be wanting water, then?" Saevalde asked Alorsha.

Alorsha nodded. "I think some of the sea water. Best to connect as much as possible to this place."

Saevalde nodded and went out on the deck.

Alorsha met Gya's gaze. "I can think of a number of possibilities that might work. Combining my magic with yours. Don't despair if we have to work through several variations that don't work to find one that will."

Gya nodded, uncertain that any of this would work. He watched as she set the bowl on one of the chairs and unloaded several small bottles from the satchel. Some contained liquids of various colors and others held what seemed to be crushed leaves. She placed the bottles on another of the chairs.

Saevalde returned with a bucket of water. Alorsha dipped a hand in it and brushed her wet hand across the table around the sigil, taking care to avoid the kri-stone powder lines. The water lingered there only a moment before it spread across the entire tabletop—even under the powdered lines—and sank into the wood. The four Magickas gave Alorsha incredulous looks.

She grinned in delight, the first such expression Gya had seen from her. "I should've warned you, I guess."

Mikolus grunted and she tossed him a quick grin over her shoulder.

"Because of a number of things we don't have time for me to explain right now, our ship acts like it's another place than your home here. Our magics are different. To be able to work with you and your magics, we need to connect. This is one way."

Gya realized then that the table was made of the same wood as the rest of the ship. He leaned over and touched the floor next to one of the table legs. He found it cool and slightly damp, like the water Alorsha had spread on the tabletop had run through the wood table and into the floor.

When he looked at Alorsha, she nodded. "The wood is called taiawood. It's rare and magical."

"But the *Deliberia* sits in the sea water. Why need this?" Gya gestured at the still wet-looking tabletop.

Mikolus chuckled and Alorsha shrugged. "I can't tell you always the why of my magics. But I've had a lot of practice figuring out what works. This is a way to indicate that we are going to do a specific magic that involves yours."

"Indicate to whom?" Ekosua whispered to Gya, who shrugged.

Alorsha opened one of her bottles and poured a drop of the pale blue liquid it held into her palm. Her gaze unfocused, as Gya had seen in the woods outside Hawei.

A touch on his arm startled him and he jumped.

"Attend closely," Ayaru said in a quiet voice. "You see what you might learn of this other magic."

So Gya watched to see what Alorsha would do. She repeated her actions with each of her bottles and dried her hand after every one that held liquid. He felt the waiting magic in the sigil behind him but could not feel what Alorsha was doing.

When she reached the last bottle, Gya became aware of Mikolus's gaze on him. When he looked up, the Ship's Captain just nodded at him.

Alorsha set aside a bottle that held pale blue liquid and another with a pale blue-green powder. She smiled at Gya.

"These two should work best with your magic, perhaps even enhance it a bit. Do you ever scry in water?"

Gya gave her a blank look, and she nodded. At what, he had no idea.

"I'll put some of the sea water in the bowl, with a small bit of my concoction and the powdered leaves here. The bowl will go into the sigil's center to connect to your magics. Atop your crystal, I think. I hope then you'll be able to clearly see your brother."

"Me?" Gya's voice squeaked a little. *How embarrassing.* That had not happened in a number of years. "I'd thought to have one of the others try. They've more practice than I have."

Alorsha only gazed at him. "That might well be, but you're closest to him and you know the places to look. I'd think that you have the best chance of getting this to work and let you know what you need to."

Gya rubbed his hands on his borrowed trousers and swallowed. "If you say so."

With a small smile for him, Alorsha lifted the bowl and gazed into it. "If you have something of his, that'll help the magic."

Gya gave her another blank look, then remembered the bracelet. He dug in his small pack until he found it all the way at the bottom and pulled it out. "This is Toa's. He seems to wear it pretty much every other day."

Alorsha nodded and handed Gya the bowl, which he only then noticed had a highly polished interior. He clearly saw himself, although upside-down, in the curved inside. Under her guidance, he placed the bowl in the exact center of the sigil atop the large clear crystal there, taking care to keep from smudging any of the lines of the sigil.

Alorsha poured some of the sea water into the bowl, only about two fingers' width in depth. She nodded toward the bracelet Gya still held in his hand.

"Slip that into the center of the bowl."

After he did as she instructed, she placed her hands on his shoulders and nudged him a little to the left and up against the table's edge. "This is your best spot."

She dipped two fingers in the water in the bowl and clasped that hand around Gya's wrist. "Connections help with my magic," she explained at his startled look. "Now rest this hand on the bowl's edge."

When Gya did as she directed, she nodded and looked to the other Magickas. "Please gather around as you did before. I'll next add the seeing concoction to the water." She indicated the bottles she had set aside earlier.

At their nods, she grabbed the bottle with the powder and sprinkled a light coating of its contents atop the water in the bowl. Then she poured a single drop from the other bottle into the center of the bowl.

"Now look into the water, Gya, and think of who you want to see. Think of Toa, just like you did with the crystal," Alorsha instructed in a voice not much above a whisper.

Gya followed her directions. He watched the powder sink to the bottom of the bowl and the blue liquid spread out through the water. He glimpsed Toa's face—clearer than in the crystal—in front of the bracelet where it sat in the bottom of the bowl, but then his brother was gone again.

Ekosua gasped and Gya almost lifted his gaze from the surface. But he felt more than saw Alorsha shake her head.

"Yes, the others saw him, too," Alorsha said in a low voice. "Keep at it. This is new to you. It might take a little time for you to see anything of use."

So Gya looked into the water and turned his thoughts to Toa, to his desire to see him again. His brother's face began to take shape again in the water, but the image faded into a blue-gray haze that filled the bowl. When it dispersed, Toa was gone.

Alorsha stepped back. "It's still not enough," she muttered. "Let's take a short rest."

Gya slumped into one of the nearby chairs. "What more can we do? Maybe the sigil's just too advanced for us."

"One more thing I can think of to try," Ekosua said. "What if we draw the sigil in the air? Like those Magickas did to throw the fire at the *Deliberia*. From seeing the fire they directed at the ship, I'd guess that drawing it in the air somehow made the sigil stronger."

"But how did they even do that?" Gya said.

"Well now, a sort of reversal of how we gather the powders and return them to their pouches, I'd think," Ayaru said.

"We can do this." Dakrei pulled out the pouches that held the powders. He handed one to each of the other Magickas and kept one for himself. "Just like we did on the table," he instructed. "But need not make it so large."

Gya clutched his crystal and peered into the bag of powder. *Just like they had drawn the first one?* That meant he had to go first. A light touch on his shoulder startled him.

"You can do this," Alorsha whispered and stepped back out of the way.

First, the Magickas gathered all the powdered kri-stone

from the table. Then Gya stepped again into his place near the bowl and concentrated to reverse as exactly as possible the motions he used to gather the powder back into the bag. He pointed one end of the crystal to the small bag and drew it away in a slight arc, traced a loop in the air with the crystal, and made a tapping motion at the point he wanted to start drawing.

To his surprise and delight, the powder followed the crystal in a thin stream. Gya focused on the shape of the sigil and drew it in the air as if his crystal was a pen. The powder continued to follow and formed the lines of the sigil – just hanging there.

The others joined him and constructed the rest of the sigil in the air above Alorsha's bowl. After Dakrei finished the last detail of the sigil, all the powders that had not been used in the drawing streamed back into their respective pouches.

"Do we place crystals again, like on the first one?" Gya gave the hanging sigil a dubious look.

"The Magickas on the dock didn't, that we saw," Ekosua pointed out.

"Let's try with this," Ayaru said.

The Magickas set aside the pouches and crystals and again gathered around the table. Alorsha took her place by Gya and placed her fingers on his wrist. "As before, then," she said.

When Gya placed his hand on the edge of the bowl he felt the magic much stronger than before. He gazed into the water, looking through the sigil in the air, and focused again on seeing his brother.

Toa's face formed in the water, faster than previously and much clearer this time. In the water's image, Toa turned his head and said something with a smile. Gya tried to get a look at where Toa was, but his brother's surroundings were indistinct in the water. Alorsha dipped a finger in the water and the image of Toa grew sharper still, but his surroundings remained blurred and hidden.

"We should look at all the places you and he said you might meet," Ayaru said. "Can we do that?"

"Should be able to," Alorsha said. "Same as with Toa, Gya, think of one of those places."

One by one, Gya pictured the places he and Toa had discussed as possible meeting spots. The images formed in the water, but all were dark, barely visible in the dim moonlight. All were empty of people.

A sense of defeat washed through him and Gya closed his eyes. When he opened them again, he gazed back at the water. One more seeing. He pictured Chizoa, her smile, the way her eyes crinkled when she tried so hard not to laugh at him. The water seemed to ripple although the surface stayed smooth.

"What is this?" Ayaru said.

"Chizoa," Gya whispered. He remembered that Toa's bracelet sat in the bowl, but he had Chizoa's hair stick. He pulled the bracelet from the bowl and set it aside, then dug Chizoa's hair stick out of his pack and placed it in the bowl.

He turned his gaze to the water again and focused on how much he wanted to see Chizoa again, how worried he was about her.

The ripples reappeared, intensified, and abruptly cleared. Everyone stared at the image in the water.

"A wood door?" Ekosua said.

Gya shrugged and next tried to see Chizoa's grandmother Vabena. He had nothing of hers, but maybe it would work since Chizoa was related. A different door appeared in the water, similar to the first but with a color and grain not quite the same as the first. On the off chance it might work, he looked for Ifeoma. That produced an image of yet a third different door, and the image was hazy and wavered in the water. He switched back to Chizoa and tried to concentrate harder. Still a door and the image did not change.

When Gya's knees buckled with exhaustion, Mikolus

caught him and helped him to a chair.

"Was that all of them? All the people and places you wanted to see?" Alorsha asked.

At Gya's nod, she sank into a chair, too. Saevalde handed her some bread and cheese and passed some to Gya as well.

"We'll clean up in a minute, then," Alorsha said.

"Well now, we can start on it." Ayaru pulled the hair stick from the water and dried it off before she set it next to Toa's bracelet. "Is there anything special that must be done to clean the bowl?"

Alorsha shook her head. "Just pour the contents onto the deck outside, rinse it out with more sea water, and pour that in the same spot."

"Should any of them be going on deck?" Saevalde said.

"I think we're far enough from shore that no one will be able to distinguish who's on deck," Alorsha said. "But let's run with the minimum lights, anyway."

"A moment, then," Saevalde said to Ayaru and stepped outside.

"You can set the bowl in a corner for now," Alorsha said. "It can wait the short time Saevalde needs."

She watched as the three Magickas put away the crystals and powders. She sighed when the powdered kri-stone flowed from the sigil back into the appropriate pouches.

Gya chuckled at her expression. "You don't have anything that does that?"

"No. It would certainly make it easier, though. Cleaning up and using fewer materials for the magic."

"It's a necessity for us," Ekosua said. "Or we'd have run out of the kri-stone long ago."

Alorsha raised her eyebrows in a questioning look. "Oh?"

Ayaru nodded. "What we have has come to us from other Magickas. Mostly from parents and grandparents. Although sometimes teachers who weren't relatives. No new kri-stone has been found for many long years."

Saevalde returned, with a crewmember in tow. "It's safe now to be going on deck."

The crewmember walked to Ayaru and gave her a slight bow as he smiled at her. "May I escort you? Walking aboard ship can sometimes throw one's balance off." He extended an arm to her. She lifted the bowl, with a quizzical look for his arm. He smiled and gently clasped one of her hands, drew it to his arm and wrapped her fingers around his arm.

"A custom of ours," he said with a smile. "If you need the steadying."

As they stepped out on to the deck, Gya noticed that Dakrei watched Ayaru leave with an odd expression. *So it was that way with them, or at least with Dakrei, anyway.* Gya smiled to himself. A second thing that Gya noticed was the motion of the ship. He realized he had been feeling the slight rocking and swaying for some time.

"We've left the dock?" he said after he swallowed the last of his bread.

Saevalde nodded. "Aye, we have."

"We thought it prudent to put some distance between us and those Keepers and Magickas," Alorsha said. "Don't worry. We're not going far right now. We can put you and your friends back ashore whenever and wherever you want."

Gya nodded while he wondered exactly where he *did* want to go.

CHAPTER 15

Odd creaking sounds disturbed Gya's sleep and his bed rocked beneath him. *Where was he? What was that scent of cinnamon?* He blinked, trying to focus on his surroundings.

Then the meaning of the motion he felt penetrated his sleep-fogged senses. It was the motion of a ship.

With that, all that had happened flooded back to him. As he came fully awake, the ship's motion seemed less noticeable than before he slept. *Perhaps he was getting used to it.*

The previous night, Mikolus had given up his cabin—situated below Saevalde's and Alorsha's—to the four Magickas. Ekosua and Ayaru had taken the bed and a couple of crewmembers had provided Gya and Dakrei with some comfortable bedding for the floor.

Gya rolled over and looked around in the light from the windows. Sometime in the night, someone had placed all their clothes atop the cabinet that ran along the wall below the cabin's side windows. Gya hopped up to change back into his own clothes. But then he paused. *Maybe he should stay with the clothes that blended in here on the ship.*

He decided to wait until he could speak with the others, who even then were stirring. He grabbed his clothes, added them to his pack, and peeked out one of the windows. From there all he saw was water. *Would the Empire send its ships after the* Deliberia?

Gya watched the waves until he heard a knock on their door. Dakrei opened it to admit Alorsha and Mikolus who each carried a large plate piled with food.

"Thought you might be ready for the morning meal." Alorsha placed her plate on a cabinet. Mikolus set his next to hers and returned back out the door.

Alorsha followed him. "We can talk more after you've eaten." She closed the door behind her.

The four eagerly sampled the food and found it as appealing as what they had enjoyed the previous evening.

"I've been thinking about what we saw." Ekosua spoke around a bite of fresh bread. "Did anyone else notice. Toa's face seemed lit by lantern light. Like he was inside somewhere."

Gya paused in taking a bite. "It did, didn't it? He also looked like he spoke to someone."

"Didn't look worried or scared," Dakrei said.

"Well now, he didn't," Ayaru agreed. "Might he have found some of the others before the Keepers did? Could he be hiding with them?"

"Seems possible," Gya admitted. "I just wish we could've seen his surroundings. He could be anywhere!"

"What of the doors when you tried to see the others?" Ekosua said. "What do they mean?"

"They're behind those doors?" Ayaru said.

"If so, why didn't the magic go through them? We saw Toa just fine and he seemed to be in a room," Ekosua said. "So I'd assume we were seeing him through the walls or door."

Gya shrugged.

"So what shall we do?" Ekosua said. "Try to find everyone? Leave the Empire?"

"Well now, could try the magic again," Ayaru said.

"I think we should," Gya said. "And maybe visit those places we looked at, just in case. To try to find Toa, at least. Maybe come across something to help locate Chizoa."

After a moment of silence, Dakrei said, "I'm sorry, Gya. Don't think I can stay with you. I'm for getting out of the Empire as quickly as I can."

Ayaru placed a hand atop his and nodded. "I'm with Dakrei. I think staying is too dangerous, too likely to end with us doing the Empire's bidding. With them making us use our magic against others."

Gya nodded. "I don't disagree. If it weren't for Toa and Chizoa…."

"Of course," Ayaru said. "What of you, Ekosua?"

Ekosua scrunched her face into an expression that reflected her indecision. "I'm so scared. I don't know which way to go, what to choose."

"Come with us," Dakrei urged. "Find a new place to make a new home for yourself. Find a place to be safe."

Ekosua looked to Gya. "What about you?"

After further thought about his options, Gya shook his head. "I can't yet. I feel I've got to discover where Toa is. Maybe I can even get to the others, too."

Dakrei nodded. "Better chance without us tagging along. Without *all* of us trying to stay hidden. Easier to hide one."

"But I wouldn't send you away—"

Ayaru interrupted him. "Of course not. We know that. It's just the best we can all do for all of us right now. Part ways."

"Once we decide where we'll head, you'll know, too," Dakrei said. "Then you come find us when you can."

Gya frowned, not at all happy with the idea. But no better idea came to him. At least this way he would not drag his friends into the increased danger he suspected he might encounter. He nodded, and their discussion turned to the merits of the various places outside the Empire while they finished their meal.

Ayaru, Ekosua and Dakrei finally decided that they would go east. If the *Deliberia* would take them, they could go ashore at the port of Azkra and only face a week, perhaps less, of further travel east through a sparsely populated area to leave the bounds of the Empire entirely.

Based on some of the information Gya had learned from the various traders that came to Hawei, they agreed that Suor, a trading center a few days east of the Empire's eastern border would be the best place for them to plan to meet again. They settled on the fifteenth of every other month to try to meet, or at least leave a message at whichever inn in Suor was the largest.

Further, they planned to make copies of the few codices they carried between them, so both Gya and the other three would all carry the information about sigils that they currently owned.

Having made these few plans, however tenuous, and finished their meal, they headed out on deck. They spotted Alorsha standing alone near the bow of the ship and stumbled only a little with the unaccustomed motion of the ship on their way to join her.

She smiled a greeting.

"Have a request of you," Dakrei said. "We three." He gestured to himself, Ayaru and Ekosua.

Alorsha gave him a questioning look accompanied by a slight lessening of her smile.

"Gya would continue to look for his brother and our missing friends, go after them if possible. But we three feel we cannot stay within the Empire any longer. Would you be willing to sail us east to the port of Azkra? Still within the Empire, but very close to a border. We can escape from there. Afraid we don't have much beyond our gratitude to offer in return, although we do have some coins between us."

"No need for any coins." Alorsha waved away the

suggestion with one hand and turned to Gya. "I don't know this port. What can you tell me?"

"It's a larger port than Hawei, so the *Deliberia* will be less conspicuous there. It's in the easternmost part of the Mavkath Sea, this sea we're on right now. The sea is almost completely bounded by lands of the Empire, but it's possible to sail the middle without coming in sight of Imperial lands until we near Azkra. From the tales I've heard, it takes about a week and a half to sail there from Hawei, depending on the winds, of course. I've got a map. I can show you—"

"Yes. I'll look later. Saevalde will certainly wish to see it, too." Alorsha stared out at the water, her expression thoughtful.

"What will *you* do?" she asked Gya.

"I'd like to try the magic again, to try to see Toa once more, see if I can see Chizoa and the others, before the *Deliberia* leaves this area, assuming that you agree to sail the others to Azkra. Then I'd ask that you put me ashore either close to where I find Toa, if I do, or at someplace I'll figure out later so I can check all those meeting places in person."

Alorsha nodded and glanced over her shoulder to where Saevalde stood in conversation with a crewmember. As if she had called her, the Ship's Master turned to her almost immediately and joined them. She and Alorsha eased away from the Magickas, but Gya sidled a few steps closer to them so he could still hear what Alorsha and Saevalde said.

Alorsha explained what the Magickas asked of them while Saevalde listened with a solemn expression.

"And what of our purpose?" Saevalde said. "We can't always be helping everyone, lass. There's just not always the time."

"I know," Alorsha said. "But in this case, we're already involved and *can* help. Besides, Devrand's not gathered any magic yet. I haven't felt it through the connection yet."

"Will sailing that direction help you better determine the miscreant's location?"

Gya glanced at the two women and saw Alorsha give a curt nod.

"You're not worried that we'll be too far if he starts gathering the magic?" Saevalde said.

Alorsha shrugged. "Some, yes. But I don't like the idea of just stranding these people. It's always taken him some time once he begins to gather magic to himself. I think we'll have enough time. But if that changes, we can still find a place for them that's at least closer to where they're headed. Help them that much."

"Aye, lass, I'd not be liking to strand these fine folks either, if we've the choice. We're seaworthy enough, that's true," Saevalde said. "Although I *would* have liked a bit more time before we headed out on a longer journey again."

"Those Keepers seemed disinclined to give it to us," Alorsha said.

Saevalde chuckled. "Aye, you speak true, lass." She led the way back closer to the group of Magickas, her attention still on Alorsha. "So, anything pressing that you need to finish so our *Deliberia* can be hitting her speed again?"

"I'd like to work on that spot in the hold this morning. Strengthen it some more. Then she'll be ready enough. I can catch up on the rest as we sail."

Saevalde nodded and smiled at the Magickas as she and Alorsha joined them. "We're happy to help you out. Why not keep those clothes to wear while you're aboard? Anyone who spies us from a distance should be thinking you're one of us."

"What do you mean 'strengthen' a spot in the hold?" Gya asked after Saevalde returned to the crewmember she had been speaking with previously.

Alorsha gave him a sidelong look and his face grew warm when he realized his comment told her he had eavesdropped.

"We've not finished our repairs," she said. "We can sail, as you can see. But the *Deliberia*'s not yet ready to go at her top speed."

Gya pictured the condition the ship had been in when she limped into Hawei's port, the damaged mast, holes, and smashed timbers. He looked around the deck, and at the mast, and saw no sign of all that damage.

"Care to come with me while I work in the hold?" Alorsha said with a grin. "That'll go a long way toward answering the questions I see in your expression, possibly better than if I try to explain it with words."

Gya looked to his companions, but they opted to stay on deck. He retrieved his map from his pack and passed it to Saevalde before he followed Alorsha into the ship.

They made their way through the hold, more crowded than when Gya had been there the day after the *Deliberia* arrived in Hawei.

"You restocked quickly."

Alorsha nodded. "Chasing someone, we like to be ready to move at a moment's notice when at all possible. Here we are."

She led Gya around some stacked crates and was forced to dodge two cats who ran in front of her and almost tripped her, one chasing the other. Both were black and white, but one had only the smallest patch of white fur in the midst of the black. They were larger than the cats Gya had seen on other ships and looked sleek and healthy.

"No problems with rats, I'd guess."

"Not with those two and their siblings aboard." Alorsha shared a brief smile with him then led him to the curved wall of the hold. She ran a hand across a spot at about waist level. Gya saw nothing different there from the rest of the wood.

Alorsha must have seen his confusion. "You have something that lets you see magic? You can do that here, if you want. To see what I do."

Gya nodded. He took out his blue-tinted seeing-stone and some powder, drew the sigil on the stone and held it to one eye. Through the seeing-stone, he saw that one portion of the wall looked rough and damaged compared to the rest.

He looked a question at Alorsha.

"We had a boarder make it all the way down here. He seemed determined to chop a hole in the *Deliberia*, to flood us. Almost managed it, too. Now watch, through your stone."

Gya stepped back and watched as she instructed.

Alorsha placed both hands on the damaged section and closed her eyes. At first, Gya saw nothing different. Then wisps that looked like smoke wafted out from the wood. The same color as the wood, they wrapped themselves loosely around Alorsha's forearms and glowed softly. In the faint glow, Gya saw the edges of the damaged parts in the wood stretch and repair themselves, becoming sound and strong, as if nothing had happened. He felt more than saw it when she finished, when it was whole. Healthy, too. He would have described it that way. It had that sense to it. For a moment, the scent of cinnamon became overpowering, then it faded into the background again.

When she pulled her arms away, the smoke wisps retreated back into the wood. While he looked at her, feeling somewhat in a daze, he realized something.

"The ship's alive somehow? The magic...."

Alorsha just smiled slightly and led the way back to the deck.

~ ~ ~

Gya and the other Magickas set up for the seeing again on the table in Saevalde's cabin. This time Alorsha did not directly participate, but she guided Gya through the parts she had done the night before. The Magickas also chose to draw the sigil only in the air above the bowl rather than both there and underneath it. It did not seem to affect the strength of the magic.

"From what I can tell, you seem to connect with the magic in the kri-stone to bring it out to do what you want, is that right?" Alorsha said.

The Magickas exchanged looks and all nodded.

"A good way to describe it. As good as any," Dakrei said. "Never heard it explained that way, though."

"I haven't heard it explained in *any* way," Ekosua muttered.

"No one really to teach us," Gya explained to Alorsha.

"The old woman who showed me a few things, back before the Empire got so bad, just literally showed me," Dakrei said. "Never explained anything."

"It was the same for me," Ayaru said.

Gya had been thinking about Alorsha's description. "I think I'd have to say the magic in the kri-stone doesn't need us much to draw it out. Especially with the powdered kri-stone, it seems to come to meet us, sort of halfway."

Alorsha's eyebrows rose. "Interesting."

She stepped back to let them finish setting up.

As before, Gya guided the seeing. This time he started with Chizoa. He still saw only a wooden door, although it seemed to be the same one they had seen earlier.

After he tried again, and failed again to go beyond the door, Gya sought Vabena, then Ifeoma, with the same results. Finally, he sought Toa. The images of all the places he and Toa might have met appeared and disappeared in the bowl, with no Toa at any of them. Then Gya focused on Toa specifically.

His brother's face took shape in the bowl, and Gya was able to make the image pull back a little to show a wood wall behind his brother. Toa sat in a chair and looked at ease.

But then his expression changed. He reached out, out of sight of the image, and when he pulled his arm back, he held a distinctive red kri-stone crystal.

Gya groaned and almost lost the image. "No. How?"

Ayaru gasped and Dakrei placed a hand on her arm.

"What is it?" Alorsha spoke softly, but the urgency in her voice still came through.

"One moment," Dakrei murmured. "Look." He directed their attention back to the image.

Toa looked at the stone with recognition clear in his expression. Then his gaze turned somewhere they could not see, and he seemed to be listening. His expression changed and ran through several aspects from astonishment to sorrow and ended with fury.

"He knows," Gya murmured and the image vanished.

Gya sank into a chair and hid his face in his hands.

The others' expressions were worried while they cleaned up from the magic. Alorsha helped but gave them questioning looks as they worked.

"Did you know that Gya's father was taken by the Empire?" Ayaru said finally to Alorsha. "This was, oh, ten, twelve years ago."

"Fifteen, more like," Dakrei said.

"It was all my fault!" Gya raised an anguished face to look at them. "I did it to him and now Toa knows."

"Hush now." Ayaru patted his arm. "It was just one of those things. You didn't intend it. You were just a child."

"It's still because of me." Gya hunched over in his seat while he avoided meeting anyone's gaze.

"May I know what happened?" Alorsha said.

The Magickas exchanged looks and Dakrei cleared his throat.

"I'll tell it." Gya spoke to the floor. "I was about seven years old, I think. Our da was outside our home talking with a Keeper. I was stuck inside watching Toa while our ma worked in the storehouse. Toa had gotten into their room and was digging around in a box. He pulled out that crystal."

Gya ran his hands through his hair with a sigh.

"I'd never seen anything so pretty. I wanted to show

da. I didn't know it was kri-stone. I didn't know what kri-stone was. I ran outside with it, yelling for da to see what we had found, Toa and I. The Keeper saw, too, and knew it for kri-stone, I know now. When da answered the Keeper that yes, it was his, they took him away right then. All my fault. We later heard he had died while they held him somewhere."

Gya dropped his head to his hands and his shoulders shook.

Ekosua wrapped an arm around his shoulders and gave him a squeeze.

"But you and your brother and your mother *weren't* taken," Dakrei said into the uncomfortable silence. "You get your magic from both your parents. Your da kept the rest of you safe and out of their hands. The red crystal belonged to your mother."

Gya looked up sharply at that. "What? It did?"

Dakrei nodded.

Gya looked back at his feet. "I wish I'd known before they were both gone—"

"Wait!" Ekosua broke in. "I just realized something. Someone *gave* Toa that crystal, handed it to him. We saw it. He was also talking with someone."

Ayaru shook her head and a sad expression crossed her face. "The Keepers took the crystal when they took Gya's father."

Gya groaned. "So they *do* have Toa."

CHAPTER 16

IN THE IMPERIAL CAPITAL

As she had before, Imperial Minister Arizu led the way to the Imperial Council's small meeting chamber. She walked briskly, her pace just short of a jog, eager to get there without delay, eager to distance herself from the anger that followed so closely behind her in the person of Dev.

At the door to the chamber, the attendant tried to step in front of Dev, but Dev gripped his arm and easily moved him aside. With a slight nod, the man backed away. Dev stepped in front of Arizu then, yanked the door open, and stalked inside.

The three Councilors gave him startled, alarmed looks, but calmed when he exchanged the formal greeting with them one by one. Belying his gesture, though, he still fumed – Arizu saw that in his glittering eyes and furrowed brow.

Dev seated himself at the small table and sharply gestured for the others to also. His man followed close behind him, as usual, and took a spot by his left shoulder. He glanced at the others in the room, then seemed occupied with staring at his feet. Arizu still had no idea what his name might be. Most of the time she did not even wonder.

Dev let his flinty gaze rove across the three Councilors until they shifted uneasily.

"Those pet Magickas of yours that you sent to stop the threat, your touted, controlled Magickas, were completely ineffective. Useless! The woman escaped. With little difficulty, it seemed. Who knows where she'll end up next," he said.

The Councilors exchanged glances.

"What can we do?" the elder Imperial uncle spoke when it became clear the others would not. Arizu nodded in approval. *Wise of him to ask Dev how to handle the problem.*

Dev frowned at him a long time before he responded. "Gather together the rest of the Magickas in your lands, their families, anyone who might be able to do the slightest amount of magic and keep them away from the rest of your people. Hold them in a place more isolated than you have used to this point. Even better, use multiple locations so they're not gathered all together. Limit the people who interact with them, more than you have before. But don't bend these Magickas to serve the Empire as you have been doing. Leave them to me. I've a better use for them."

"By all means." The elder Imperial uncle smiled at Dev. "An excellent plan."

The younger Imperial uncle nodded several times. "The best plan for this situation assuredly."

"Without a doubt, you're best suited to handle the Magickas," the Imperial aunt added.

Dev smiled in satisfaction.

"You are aware, of course, that the crystals known as kri-stone are vital to Magickas for the casting of their sigil magic," the younger Imperial uncle spoke up. "It's generally believed that the stones originated from some lost, forgotten caves. Those few the Magickas hold currently, they've passed down in their families, or from teacher to student, for years. A new source of kri-stone would assist the Empire's Magickas in overpowering those rogue Magickas still out there."

"Perhaps the histories contain clues that someone from out-Empire like yourself, someone of your acumen can decipher," the elder Imperial uncle said.

"Certainly, you'll be able to discover what our poor scholars have overlooked," the Imperial aunt assured Dev.

Arizu looked to Dev. *Might he want to try to find those caves? That would surely let them deal with the threat handily. What a thrill it would be to accompany him on such an adventure.*

Dev stood and waved his man to exit the room ahead of him. "I thank you, Councilors, for the information, and the offer to let me study the histories. Please ensure that the best of the Keepers are put at my disposal."

The Imperial aunt and uncles acted only too pleased to agree.

After that, Dev took his leave of them and of Arizu. For only a short time, he assured her. But she feared he meant to leave for good. Unable to articulate that fear, however, she only watched him walk out the door. His unspeaking man took his place at his shoulder.

CHAPTER 17

The *Deliberia* turned east not long after the Magickas finished their seeing. From what little they had seen of Toa's surroundings, no one had been able to tell where he might be, but they argued reasonably that he seemed unharmed and unrestrained where he was, although obviously furious at what he had learned.

Gya fretted. *If only he could talk with Toa, try to explain. Maybe someone else had gotten the crystal somehow and then given it to him.*

Gya told himself that but did not truly believe anyone other than the Keepers had that crystal.

He had decided to travel with the ship to the port of Azkra. He no longer saw any need to personally check the places he and Toa might have met. Clearly Toa was elsewhere.

After Gya let Alorsha know that the *Deliberia* need not set him ashore anywhere on the way to Azkra, he eschewed the other Magickas' company in favor of leaning on the ship's rail on the highest stern deck and letting his thoughts wander. *There had to be some way to learn where*

Chizoa and the others were.

As midday approached, Mikolus sought him out.

"We need to settle on a better cabin arrangement for the time you're with us. I'd certainly appreciate having my cabin back." Mikolus grinned. "Some of the other crewmembers with compartments on the main deck level have offered to give you and your friends their compartments for the duration of the voyage. Would that be acceptable?"

Gya ducked his head. "More than acceptable, but no, please. We wouldn't want to put anyone out of their compartments, their homes aboard ship. Certainly, you have some corner of the hold we could partition off to use?"

The man clapped him on the shoulder and the strength of the gesture startled Gya.

"Your friends said much the same. There's no chance we'd do something like that to our guests. But if you won't take the larger compartments on the main deck, we can offer you some smaller ones below." He held up a hand to forestall Gya's next words. "No concerns that you're turning anyone out of their homes. These compartments are not in use right now, and they're comfortable enough, if small. You'll have to share, though."

Gya glanced at the man and met his smile with a small one of his own. "That would be fine."

So Mikolus sent a crewmember to help the Magickas move to their own compartments below decks. They were able to have two compartments next to each other that each held two hammocks, a bench, and a narrow storage cabinet. Gya wondered how comfortable such a sleeping arrangement would be. He supposed he would find out that night.

He plopped onto the short bench that sat along one wall and stared at the ceiling. He barely noticed when his companions left the room.

Toa's face, his fury, haunted his thoughts. *Now his*

brother knew what he had done. He would hate him for it. His guilt threatened to smother him, along with remorse and a sorrow at what his father's loss had done to them.

He absently pulled his token from beneath his shirt and stared at it but did not really see it. In sudden anger at the situation, at what it represented, he yanked it off and stuffed it into the bottom of his pack. Removing it did not change anything, but an unexpected lightness washed over him at the small act of defiance.

That drained away again, though, under the burden of his worries.

Sometime later, someone knocked at his door. He glanced at it but lacked the interest to go open it, or even call out to the person who knocked.

The door opened and Alorsha came in. She sat on the edge of the bench.

"We're making good speed. Although we're not sailing at *Deliberia's* top speed right now. The best I can tell, it will take that week and a half, perhaps a bit more if we don't reach top speed much, to reach Azkra."

Gya nodded.

"I'm sorry," Alorsha said, after silence had stretched between them for a time.

Gya turned slightly so he could see her without twisting his neck. "Thank you, but it's nothing of your doing."

Alorsha nodded, her expression sorrowful. "Both of my parents are gone, too. Dead." She got to her feet and stepped back out in the passageway. "Your friends plan to practice the magic, now that you can do so without fear of discovery. The weather's good so they're on the deck, if you want to join them." She closed the door.

After only a few minutes, Gya realized he did not want to stay slouched there making himself miserable. So he headed to the deck, pleased to find that he seemed to be walking better. *Must be used to the ship's motion now.*

As he climbed the steep stairs, he brushed his hand along the wall and tried to feel the magic in the wood.

Nothing at first, then he felt the faintest touch of something. His fingers tingled where they touched the wood. *Did something brush along his arm?* Another moment and the sensations vanished. With a slight smile, he continued his climb to join the others.

~ ~ ~

That day, Gya and the other Magickas enjoyed the unaccustomed freedom to practice their magic, although they devoted many hours to making the copies of the codices, too. They spent their time mostly on the deck—at one side to stay out of the way as much as possible—and soon discovered that they could wear themselves out with too much magic-work in too short a time.

Gya worked with Ekosua, something he had not done much before. They worked well together, but as the hours passed Gya's thoughts wandered more and more to the times he and Chizoa had partnered for the magic.

Was she all right? He shouldn't have waited to tell her how he felt about her. If he'd said something earlier, they could have been gone before everything fell apart. He only hoped he could find her again.

Ekosua gently squeezed his arm. "Perhaps time to stop for the day." She gave him an understanding smile. "I think we've made some progress, but I've had enough for now."

Gya nodded agreement. Some of the sigils they tried had been more complex than any they had previously worked with – not counting the seeing one they had used to see Toa. They had been able to draw magic from all of them, even if they had not achieved the sigils' final purposes yet.

He glanced at the other two Magickas. Ayaru and Dakrei both seemed pleased, if tired, as they gathered their crystals and powders.

Although well after midday, the Magickas visited the

ship's galley for some food. After they had satisfied their hunger, they separated to offer to what help they could around the ship and perhaps learn a little of sailing a ship that size.

Near the end of that first day out of Hawei, favorable winds allowed the *Deliberia* to achieve her top speed, so one of the crewmembers informed Gya with a grin. She also told him the evening meal would be ready soon. That turned out to be a rather boisterous affair with many of the crew eating at the same time in a space with several tables just for that purpose.

Gya clambered into his hammock that night sore and tired, but with a strange sense of peace, too. The lingering wonder of having been able to work magic openly without fear, combined with deep but satisfying aches from helping around the ship, accompanied him into a dreamless sleep. But near dawn, the sounds of people hurrying through the corridor outside the room he shared with Dakrei interrupted his peaceful rest.

He slid out of his hammock, careful to avoid Dakrei's below him and peered out their door.

"What's wrong?" he asked a passing crewmember.

"Don't want to be late," the woman said as she headed up the steep stairs.

Gya glanced back at Dakrei, who had not stirred from his hammock. "Go on," the older man urged. "I'll just get a little more sleep and you can tell me about it later."

Gya hurried into the clothes that matched the rest of the crew's and scurried after the last crewmembers.

It was not much past dawn, with just enough light to see what looked like far too many people gathered on the deck.

Were they fighting?

Gya scurried up the ladder to the raised deck at the ship's bow. From there, he perused the scene before him.

The crewmembers below him *were* fighting, Alorsha among them, he was surprised to see. Gya also spotted

Saevalde in the group. But this was not some brawl, he realized. They had paired off and were practicing weapons-work, just as the Magickas practiced their magic. Mikolus led the practice.

Ekosua and Ayaru joined Gya there and together they watched this early-morning activity. After a good couple of hours, the activity ended, and everyone headed off to whatever came next. Alorsha joined the Magickas at their vantage spot, wiping sweat from her face and neck with a cloth.

"You're welcome to join in sometime, if you'd like," she told them.

They gave her vague, polite responses that made her grin.

"It's certainly not a problem if you don't want to. Breakfast should be ready any time, if you are. Your work yesterday was very helpful. You have my thanks for it. There's more, too, if you're so inclined."

She headed down the ladder with a wave.

The day took shape much like their previous day had, with magic practice, codex copying, and helping around the ship.

The next few days, they fell into the crew's pattern of rising at dawn, even Dakrei, although they only watched the varying contingent of crewmembers who gathered on the deck to fight. While Gya saw many of the crew there only once or twice in those days, Alorsha participated every morning. As did Saevalde and a couple of others.

Gya found it interesting to watch the different attacks and defenses with a variety of handheld weapons, but he delighted in the archery. He noticed that, while Alorsha seemed adequate with the blades—the best he could tell— she was skilled with the bow and eclipsed the others he had seen so far.

~ ~ ~

The morning of their fifth day out from Hawei, after the morning's weapons practice and breakfast, Gya sought out Alorsha. He spotted her in a sunny spot in the bow of the ship and joined her there, where he found the sun a pleasant offset to the chill morning air.

"Why have we stopped?" he said. "Is there a problem?" He looked around, expecting and dreading to see ships of the Empire coming for them.

With a smile, Alorsha shook her head.

"No, there's no problem. I just need some time without eastward motion for my bit of magic. Perhaps you'd like to see this."

She gestured for him to follow her and led the way to that incongruous pole in the rigging that Gya had noticed his first visit to the ship.

Alorsha lifted the chain she wore around her neck, pulled it off over her head, and hung it from the end of the pole. She gave the lightest touch to the magic in the stone in its double frame. Gya smiled to himself: he could feel the magic with little effort. The pendant swayed back and forth several times, after which it began to inscribe a circle.

It spun at first, then the chain jerked straight out, nearly parallel to the deck. It swayed and formed an arc directed roughly south and ranging back and forth from east to west at the ends of the arc.

Alorsha nodded slightly and grabbed a small, square box that sat at the base of the mast nearby. Gya had not even noticed the box until she reached for it.

She set the box on the deck beneath her still-swaying pendant and removed the lid. A square metal plate concealed the inside bottom of the box and filled it from side to side. The metal had a circular smooth part in the middle, with the rest marked by engraved lines and other marks that Gya assumed was writing of some sort. A metal spoon with a short handle sat atop this square base and swayed back and forth balanced on its bowl, its motion similar to Alorsha's pendant.

Alorsha shifted the spoon to the center of the box and nudged the box around until the spoon's handle lined up with one set of lines that ran from the circle to the edge of the square. With that, Gya realized that this was some form of compass. He had seen something similar on other ships, although those had used metal needles that floated on water.

Alorsha then pulled a folded piece of paper, and a pen and small jar of ink, from a pocket and knelt on the deck to draw some lines on the paper. Gya peered over her shoulder and saw only two overlapping triangles, both with one curved side and two straight ones.

When she finished her drawing, Alorsha looked up at him.

"What's that way?" She pointed the same direction the compass spoon's handle did, the same direction that the pendant roughly pointed also.

Gya pictured the map of the Empire and tried to guess how far the ship had sailed in the few days they had been on board. *That way would be south....*

"I think maybe the Imperial Capital," he said finally. "I'm not sure exactly, but it's more or less that direction."

Saevalde joined them. "Better idea of Devrand's whereabouts?"

Alorsha nodded. "Between this and what I figured when we came to Hawei. He doesn't seem to be moving around much. Wonder what he's up to."

With a nod, Saevalde left them to speak with a small group of crewmembers.

"You can use that to point to where Devrand is?" Gya said.

"To some extent," Alorsha said. "As I've mentioned before, I can point to where he is relative to where I am. But I can't tell distance. Still, it's a useful bit of wayfinding magic."

"May I see?" Gya said.

At Alorsha's nod he stepped around the compass and

paper on the deck and closer to the chain and its pendants to study them.

"What's this stone?" Gya pointed at the double-framed pendant without touching it. "I've not seen one like it before."

Alorsha grabbed the chain and popped the center frame with the stone out of the outer wooden frame that held it and made it a pendant. She set it atop the plain ring on her thumb, right on the gray circle on the ring, and tugged gently on it to show Gya that it stayed there.

"The stone's called erythros," She held the ring out to Gya. "Somewhat common in my homeland. They use it in all the mage rings. It can assist in a variety of magics."

Gya gingerly touched a fingertip to the stone. He sensed the magic in the stone, but it felt very different from kri-stone magic.

"You use it to tell the direction to your fugitive. Could it work for Toa?"

"It works to locate Devrand because it has a connection to his magic. Also to Jarthan's magic." Alorsha popped the stone in its metal frame off her ring and placed it back again in the wooden pendant-frame. "It wouldn't work for Toa – no connection. But you've got that bracelet of his. That has a connection to him. Maybe there's some kind of locating sigil in one of your codices? Different from that seeing one you used?"

Gya shook his head. "I've seen one to help locate lost things, but nothing for locating a person."

"Maybe that sigil could be changed, adapted to work to help locate Toa. Or maybe another one."

Gya gave her a dubious look. "We're still working at getting a lot of the sigils to work just as they are. I don't think we're ready to adapt any."

Alorsha smiled and nodded. "In time, then." She looked past him. "It looks like your friends are ready for today's magic work, so I'll leave you to it."

She patted his shoulder and descended the steep stairs

to the main deck. Gya watched her exchange pleasantries with the other Magickas before she headed below decks, after she waved to Saevalde. He longed to figure out some way to do something like what she had done to get at least a rough idea of Toa's whereabouts, and Chizoa's. *Did that magic require the erythros stone?* He'd have to remember to ask where that stone came from. He hoped he could get some for himself. *Or could kri-stone be made to work somehow?*

The other Magickas called to him before he could pursue that thought further. He greeted them when they joined him and together, they moved to their accustomed spot to practice their magic – following the usual pattern they had fallen into these past days aboard ship.

CHAPTER 18

A fierce sense of unease jerked Gya out of a sound sleep and crawled over him and chilled him. *Something wasn't right.*

As he struggled to shove through the remaining disorientation of deep sleep, his overriding first impression was one of noise, loud, almost rhythmic. A sense of wrong motion followed.

He shifted around in his hammock and peered over the side. Darkness. Not even the dim glow through the crack at the bottom of the door from the lantern that hung in the passageway outside.

A groan from his companion drew his attention as his hammock uncustomarily dipped and swung. His awareness finally caught up to his half-asleep impressions. Wind and water caused the noise. *They had to be in the midst of a storm.*

He leaned over the side of his hammock. "Dakrei? Are you all right?"

"Well enough," the older man mumbled. "Must be one of those spring storms you've told us the traders told you about."

"That's what I was thinking, too." Gya worked his way

out of his hammock. "I'm going to check on Ayaru and Ekosua."

"Be careful."

With a nod, not even thinking that the other man could not see him, Gya managed to get his feet on the floor without falling into Dakrei's hammock. He wobbled his way to the door after he first ran into the bench along the wall and corrected his direction, stumbling with the erratic motion of the ship.

The corridor was dark and the floor damp underfoot. Gya hoped the ship was not taking on water.

He used one wall of the corridor to guide him and help support him and edged along it to the compartment next to the one he shared with Dakrei. He knocked on the door, as loudly as he could, and barely managed to stay on his feet as the floor tilted, rose, and fell beneath him.

In the noise from the water and wind, Gya almost missed Ekosua's voice as she called out that they were there. He cracked open the door and peered inside. Dark there, too.

"Are you both all right?" Gya said into the darkness.

"Well now, as much as we can be," Ayaru's voice came back.

"How's the ship holding up?" Ekosua said.

"I don't know, yet," Gya said. "I wanted to check on you, first. The floor out here is wet, and I don't see any lantern-light anywhere. That's all I know right now. I'll see what I can find out."

"It might be better to return to your compartment and wait this out," Ayaru said.

"Maybe I can help," Gya said.

"We might be able to do something with a sigil, too," Ekosua suggested. "Ayaru?"

"Light, anyway," the older woman muttered. "We'll see what we can do from here. Wait a moment, Gya."

Gya braced himself in the doorway and listened to the rustlings and muttered comments from the two women.

Before long, a dim glow appeared and grew brighter to give faint light to the compartment. A second spot of light blossomed and Gya saw that each woman held a glowing crystal. They grinned at his expression.

"We'll teach you this one later. It's similar to that one you already know." Ekosua stumbled close and handed Gya her crystal. "Take it for now. Its light should last about an hour."

"Be careful out there, Gya," Ayaru said.

"I will."

Gya eased back into the corridor and struggled to keep his footing as he headed for the stairs to the main deck. He staggered the few steps to the stairs and started up, squinting against the cold spray of water that came around the edges of the hatch above him.

"Don't open it," a voice called from behind.

"I won't," Gya hollered back and twisted to see who had called to him. One of the younger crewmembers stood at the bottom of the stairs, a boy perhaps five or six years younger than Gya. He scrunched his face as the ship rolled and threw them both against one wall. More water sprayed them.

"Should this much water be getting in?" Gya asked.

The boy shook his head. "Something must have broken free above. The canvas over the hatch should have been secured to keep the water out. But we can't go up to fix it. That would make it worse. Assuming we didn't get washed overboard."

Gya nodded his understanding. "I might be able to help."

"If you can make more of those, that would help a lot." The boy nodded toward the glowing crystal that Gya clutched.

"I don't yet know how. But ask my friends if they can do more." Gya pointed to the door to Ayaru and Ekosua's compartment. "Is the ship going to be all right? If this hatch is leaking—"

The crewmember waved off his concern. "Nothing to worry about. We've weathered many storms. The *Deliberia*'s hardy. I'll just go see about those lights."

Gya nodded and turned back to the leaking hatch.

Another two steps put his head right below it. Gaps on two sides of the hatch, where it did not meet the frame, seemed to be the main problem. No light came from outside and the periodic tilting of the ship, accompanied by waves that crashed over the deck, complicated his effort to see what might be done.

What sigil would help here? Hadn't Dakrei once shown him a sigil to grow things? True, it had been intended for crops as he remembered. But if he could maybe adapt it, as Alorsha had suggested was possible. He still felt unready to work such magic, but another drenching of water convinced him he should at least do something. It could not be good to have that much water coming in. *Although, with the violent motion of the ship, would he even be able to draw a sigil correctly? He'd have to go back to get his powders and crystals and see if Dakrei had that sigil in his codex....*

The ship rocked again, harder than before, if such a thing was possible. Gya gripped the stair rails, dropping his glowing crystal at his feet, and hoped to keep from being flung down the steps. After the ship righted itself again, Gya felt that hint of something brush his arm. Where he clutched the rails, his fingers tingled.

He retrieved his light crystal and looked back at the hatch. *Could he possibly do something like what Alorsha had shown him when she repaired the wall in the hold?*

What he felt must *be the ship's magic. But would it respond to him?* He had only worked with sigils and crystals. Cold water drenched him yet again. *Should at least try.*

He tucked one arm between the stair rail and the wall to try to hold himself stable and gripped his light crystal in that hand. He spread his feet to either side, bracing them against the sides of the step he stood on. That should hold him securely enough to be able to concentrate. *Hopefully.*

He pulled a picture of the growth sigil from his memory, the best he remembered. He fervently hoped that what Alorsha said about adapting magic was true.

While he held the shape of the sigil in mind, he reached up with his free hand and placed his palm flat against the hatch above him. His fingers tingled even before he tried to reach out to the ship's magic and a smoky wisp ran along his arm from the hatch.

It tickled. The scent of cinnamon wafted past him.

Forcing his attention away from that, and the rocking of the ship, he closed his eyes to focus on thoughts of stretching the hatch so it better closed the gap, growing the wood as if it was still a tree. A breath of warmth wrapped around him and darted away again. *It wasn't going to work!*

Gya drew in a deep breath and let it out slowly to help him find a sense of calm. He sharpened his focus, the image in his thoughts, and his intent. Again warmth brushed him, wrapped around him, and this time rushed through him as he touched the ship's magic.

Bit by bit, so very slowly, the hatch grew and stretched at its edges and spread out to fill in the gaps on the two sides, until it touched the frame. The wisp caressed Gya's arm before it flowed back into the wood.

He opened his eyes.

When the ship next lurched in the heavy seas, no water smacked him in the face.

With a pleased smile, he clambered back down the stairs, barely keeping his balance. The storm raged above and seemed to have grown worse. But elation filled him. *He'd connected to this different magic! What else might he be able to do?*

He headed back to check on the others and found Ekosua alone in the room with one small glowing crystal for light. She told him Ayaru had gone to sit with Dakrei.

"He's not well. From the motion of the ship."

Gya nodded and sat gingerly on the bench in the

women's room, suddenly aware that his insides felt twitchy. Ekosua peered at him in the dim light and leaned over to hand him two leaves.

"One of the crew brought several of these by. Chew them. It'll help."

Gya followed her directions and after several minutes, his nausea did ease. But it did not go away entirely. After a time, Ekosua crawled back into her hammock to get what additional rest she could. She offered Ayaru's hammock to Gya, but he chose to sit on the bench for the remainder of that stormy night.

The storm blew itself out sometime the next morning. Gya woke stiff from having slept tilted against the wall. A rush of activity in the hall outside the compartment drew him from dreams of wisps of smoke and glowing sigils that hovered in the sky. After he checked on Ekosua, who somehow still slept, he eased out into the corridor and next door.

There he found both Ayaru and Dakrei awake, chatting. After greetings, he grabbed a fresh tunic and turned his back while he changed into it.

"Anything I can get you?" he asked, poised at the door to go back out.

Both Magickas waved him off, so he joined the crush of crewmembers who headed up to the deck, to see if he could help with any needed repairs.

He found far less damage than he had anticipated, although still enough to keep the crewmembers busy.

Gya stepped off to one side and tried to spot Alorsha in the bustle. He wanted to talk with her about what he had done with the hatch.

Just as he spotted her across the deck, deep in conversation with some crewmembers, another crewmember clasped his arm.

"Mind helping out?"

Gya readily agreed and became engrossed in replacing snapped ropes. From there, another crewmember pulled him into helping with damaged sails and the day passed without any opportunity to speak with Alorsha. When the time came for the evening meal, Gya was weary enough that he looked forward to sleep more than food and so forgot about seeking out the ship's owner.

The following days, while the crew still worked on lingering repairs, the ship mostly returned to its usual routine, including the morning weapons-work. Gya also saw Alorsha do her wayfinding magic roughly every-other day, with the ship's eastward travel paused briefly for her work. *There* had *to be some way to use something like that to get a better idea of the whereabouts of his brother and friends.*

~ ~ ~

The last morning before they were to arrive at the port of Azkra, after a little more than the week and a half of travel that they had anticipated, the weapons-work looked much different. The crew set up the targets much like for the archery, but only ten crewmembers assembled on deck that morning, Alorsha among them, as usual. Mikolus brought out a wooden box that contained several of those strange non-hand-crossbows. He handed one to each crewmember.

Then he moved from person to person and worked with them on something Gya could not clearly see from his vantage point with the other Magickas up one deck and near Saevalde's cabin door.

"What are those things?" Ekosua sat on the deck near him.

"Maybe some strange kind of hand crossbow?" Gya said. "I think."

"What is it they do with all those things," Dakrei said from nearby. "Are those bits of cloth? And metal balls?"

"That's what it looks like," Ayaru said. "I hope we're far enough away. That Mikolus acted so stern when he warned me to stay back this morning."

Gya nodded. The Ship's Captain had been stern with him, too.

The four watched as everyone finished what they were doing, lined up a fair distance from the targets, and all looked to Mikolus, who looked everything over before he backed up so he stood behind the line.

"From left to right, fire on the heels of the one before you," he said.

The leftmost crewmember held up the not-crossbow device. To Gya it looked like he just squeezed the handle on it a little.

The Magickas clapped their hands over their ears at the most horrific bang that came from the weapon. Gya never saw what it shot, but he saw the hole it made in the target across the deck, about halfway between the edge of the target and its center.

The next person in line squeezed her weapon before the sound of the first had died, and the next after that, all the way along the line. Well before the time the tenth person had set off his weapon, Gya's ears rang. His companions looked a little wild-eyed as they hurried to the hatch that led below decks and disappeared down the stairs.

Gya shook his head. The ringing faded some and he eased up to Mikolus, who still stood behind the others and watched them do their preparations without helping this time.

"What magic are these things?" Gya asked. "While they look somewhat like hand crossbows, I've never heard of one that would do that." The holes in the targets drew his attention again. Most were placed like the first one, but a few were closer to the centers.

Mikolus grinned. "They're called flintlocks. They shoot small metal balls. Somewhat more effective than a hand crossbow. Care to try one?"

Gya looked at him with wide eyes. "M-me? I've never used a weapon, not even a sling."

"Seems like these are dangerous times. You might want to learn."

Gya gave the ten people lined up a wary look. They looked ready to set off their weapons again. "Uh, maybe another time."

Mikolus grinned and clapped him on the shoulder. "If you sail back again with us, you're welcome at the morning weapons-work. We can find you a weapon you'll be comfortable with."

Gya thanked him and hurried away before they set off those weapons again, uncertain how he felt about all this. *He really just wanted things to go back to the way they were before.*

~ ~ ~

That night, well after sundown, the ship dropped anchor some distance from Azkra, but within sight of the port city.

The Magickas, Alorsha, Saevalde and Mikolus stood in the dark along the rail and examined the port from a distance. All of the Magickas had their own seeing-stones in use. Alorsha stood with her eyes closed. Gya had seen wisps of magic reach out from the ship through the water. Saevalde had a long tube she had named a spyglass and Gya was not certain how it worked without magic. He preferred his seeing-stone.

"Well now, there's a lot of activity for after dark," Ayaru said.

"It *is* an important port," Gya said. "Larger and busier than Hawei."

"Some of them are bringing out something," Ekosua said.

"Catapult! Alorsha!" Saevalde said sharply.

Alorsha clasped the ship's rail and called out *Deliberia*'s magic. The large rock that flew through the air toward them slid aside just a few paces from the ship and splashed into the water nearby. Then a vapor drifted up from the water between the *Deliberia* and the port.

Saevalde ran to the wheel shouting orders to get underway as she moved. Within minutes, the vapor thickened into a true fog and increased enough to cut off sight of the port.

When Mikolus shook his arm, Gya realized the man had spoken to him.

"What?"

"Which way is best to find a place to let you and your friends go ashore?" Mikolus repeated.

"Uh, north, I think. I remember from the map that there's a promontory that way. We can round it and be out of sight of the town without having to go too far away."

With a nod, Mikolus warned Gya to be quiet before he ran to Saevalde.

Gya edged over to his companions, who stood huddled together. Even those few steps took him far enough that he lost sight of Alorsha in the fog.

"Do you still want to go this way?" he whispered.

Dakrei gave him a firm nod. "Get out of the Empire quick as we can. You could still come with." He kept his voice as soft as Gya's.

Gya shook his head. "I want to, but I feel I can't yet. I need to find Toa. See if I can find Chizoa and her grandmother and Ifeoma, too."

With a nod, Dakrei clasped hands with him, but offered no words of advice or caution. They had already exchanged those words earlier. The two women each hugged Gya in turn. When Alorsha stepped out of the fog right next to Gya, the three Magickas grabbed their packs from the deck and looked at her, their expressions expectant.

"A few minutes yet, until we'll be able to put you ashore safely," she told them, her voice also close to a whisper. "Also, here's this back." She held Gya's map out to him.

He took it and handed it to Ayaru. When she protested,

he pointed out that she and the others would likely need it. "Especially since it shows roads for the eastern part of the empire."

Then he turned back to Alorsha. "We're moving that fast?" He felt the motion of the ship beneath his feet, but in the enveloping haze he felt no true sense of their speed.

Alorsha nodded. "Saevalde is exceptional at what she does, especially with a little help from the *Deliberia's* magic."

They waited in silence. Before long, the ship abruptly pulled free of the fog.

Everyone took a quick look around. Gya saw no sign of anyone coming for them, and no one else said they did either.

Alorsha nodded toward the dim outline of the shore that stood some distance off their starboard.

Gya perused it in the pale moonlight. "That looks like the promontory I was thinking of ahead. We should sail around it and find someplace to put ashore."

With a nod, Alorsha headed to Saevalde, spoke with her for a moment, and then returned.

"We might as well rest a bit." She plopped onto the deck where she stood. "It could be as long as an hour, Saevalde says, depending on the currents here."

So they settled on the deck amid their packs and chatted about what they might find beyond the Empire and what the trading center Suor would be like.

The ship rounded the promontory and they saw the land beyond, devoid of any lights. After roughly another half hour, the ship slowed then came to a stop and dropped anchor.

Alorsha rose to her feet as Mikolus joined them.

"We're as close as is safe and we're lowering the tender now," he told the Magickas.

He looked at Alorsha then. "Can you give us fog again, to help foil any watchers?"

She nodded and moved to the rail to work the magic.

Gya peered toward the land and pointed. "Maybe there? How's that for a good spot to get ashore?"

Mikolus looked where he indicated and nodded. "Looks good. From here, anyway. Looks like there's even a path or road of sorts not too far inland. We'll see if the area still looks as good when we get closer."

After they exchanged their last good-byes with Gya, the other Magickas followed Mikolus to the railing and climbed down the rope ladder there to the tender, almost invisible in the increasing fog.

Alorsha and Saevalde joined Gya.

"Last chance for a long while to go with them, lad," Saevalde said.

Gya nodded. "I know. But I need to find out about Toa, Chizoa, Ifeoma and Vabena. I can't just run without seeing if I can do anything for them. Maybe make things right with Toa. If I can...."

Saevalde clapped him on one shoulder, which knocked him a step forward.

"Responsible lad," She gave him an approving nod and smile. "We'll begin our return journey when Mikolus has brought back the tender."

"You can continue to stay in the compartment you shared with Dakrei, if you'd like," Alorsha said. "Or we can see about getting you a different one."

"What? Oh, no, that one's fine."

"I'm going to check Devrand's whereabouts again. See if I can get a better idea of where he is."

Gya nodded. "I think I'll just stay here for now."

With a nod, Alorsha left him to his thoughts.

CHAPTER 19

Turning back to the west, the *Deliberia* sailed through thinning wisps of the fog. Gya lingered at the stern rail and watched the dark smudge that was the land until it disappeared behind them.

Was he doing the right thing? What if he made it worse? Maybe he should have gone with them.

He worried at these thoughts, rolling them around and around until motion out on the water caught his attention. He peered into the gloom and pulled out his seeing-stone to confirm his suspicions. The magic on the stone was nearly spent for the night, but it was enough for him to see the two ships, dark against the water, which sailed after them.

He ran to find Mikolus.

When Mikolus heard what Gya had to say, he sent a crewmember running for Alorsha and Master Eztevo and all of them returned to the aft deck.

They passed around Saevalde's spyglass. Gya even took a peek through it, although gingerly, at first. He found it showed the distant objects clearer than his seeing-stone had.

"Warships?" Alorsha passed the spyglass to Mikolus after her turn with it.

"Might be." Mikolus peered through the spyglass. "I somehow doubt they have friendly intentions anyway."

"Looks like they're out of that port," Saevalde said.

"They could only have come from Azkra," Gya agreed. "It's the only nearby port that could accommodate ships that size. Can we outrun them?"

The others exchanged glances.

"I'd prefer that to having to fight," Alorsha said. "We have some capability in that area but we're no warship."

Saevalde agreed. "Can you create fog yet again, lass? Or boost our speed?"

"I'll see what I've got that can help. Also, I think turn a different direction from the one we actually want. If I can bring up some fog again, we can then turn back again and be that much harder to find. Better also prepare in case we *do* need to fight."

With nods, Saevalde and Mikolus strode off, calling for various crewmembers.

"Can you shift the wind or waves slightly to favor us and hinder them?" Gya kept his attention on the following ships.

Alorsha tapped Gya's hand to draw his attention to her. "Unfortunately, no. Those are rather large and involved magics. Not something I can usually do. Certainly not with so little time to prepare. Do *you* have anything that can help? Maybe a sigil to hinder them somehow? Or hide us? Anything?"

Nothing immediately came to mind, but Gya did not want to disappoint Alorsha, so he hedged. "Maybe. I'll need to look in the codices."

"Bring them to my cabin. We can maybe combine magics to better effect."

With a nod of agreement, Gya ran to his compartment to grab his codices and kri-stone crystals and powders. As he headed back to Alorsha's cabin, he dodged crewmembers hustling about with weapons and armor. Mikolus stood at the center of the bustle and directed the activity. The canvas had been pulled from both the bow and stern ballistae and a couple of crewmembers at each ballista prepared the machines for use.

When Gya reached the middle aft deck, he found the door that led into Saevalde's cabin ajar. He peered in and saw the door to Alorsha's cabin also ajar.

"Alorsha?"

"Come on back," she called to him.

Alorsha sat at her table with several piles of plant bits there, along with numerous small bottles that held liquids of various colors. She waved him to a seat near her, with a small cleared space on the table in front of it.

"We'll need to figure out something quickly." She sorted through bottles as she spoke. "After my recent magics, I'll not be able to do much more than more fog and perhaps something to help speed the *Deliberia* along. So anything you can come up with will be good."

Gya hesitated, then flinched when Alorsha gave him a questioning look.

"I do want to help," he muttered. "But it seems most of the time I do something, it's no good. Doesn't work right, or at all. I don't want to make things worse."

Alorsha scrutinized his expression. "It's your choice. But think about this. Not doing anything is certainly not going to be of any help. So it's worth it to at least try."

She turned her attention back to her bottles, sorted out several to one side, and combined plant bits in a small bowl.

After he watched her a short time, Gya decided he should at least see what he could find in his codices. He flipped through them, focusing on the names that most had at the tops of the pages to identify the main purpose of the sigils. He concentrated on the copies from the other Magickas' codices since, for a time anyway, he still had a pretty good recollection of what his own codices held.

Perhaps a quarter of an hour later, Gya looked up from his codices when he ran out of fingers to use as bookmarks – one hand, as he needed the other to turn pages.

Sensing his motion, Alorsha looked up from her own work. "Find something?"

"Maybe. But many of them seem better suited for support if we were to have to fight. Things like Courage and Strength, although that latter in particular could possibly benefit the ship anytime. Protection." Gya grabbed a couple of his other codices to replace his fingers as bookmarks. "This one for Swiftness might be good, and there's this one that's called Turnaround."

Alorsha gave him a thoughtful look. "Promising. If you can do Swiftness, that would free me from having to put my energy toward that. I can add a little something to the fog instead. I've got in mind something to dissuade them from following us."

Gya turned back to the Swiftness sigil and studied it. "I haven't done this one before, but I've already practiced a couple of simpler ones that are not too different. I think I can do it, and I can probably work one other."

He turned the pages to the sigil called Turnaround and re-read the description. "Turnaround might work to help encourage them to go another direction. Or maybe just change their minds about following, bolstering what you have in mind. I've not done this one either, though, and it's more complex." He looked back to Alorsha to see her reaction.

"If you can do two of them, that would help. So you don't need to hold either of them? Focus on it for an extended time like you did for the scrying?"

"Doesn't seem so. From what it says."

"Good." She gathered the bottles she had set aside, tucked them into a small bag, and grabbed the bowl of plant parts she had mixed together. "Let's get back above and do this." She carried the bowl in one hand and the bag in the other.

Gya grabbed the crystals and powders he would need, and the single codex, and scurried to catch her.

They sidestepped various crewmembers who continued to prepare for the possibility of fighting: handing out weapons, checking weapons, donning stiff vests that looked like some kind of leather.

"It doesn't look like much protection." Gya peered at the armor as he passed.

Alorsha grinned at his expression. "No, it doesn't. But it's been treated with some of my concoctions. It offers more protection than you might think."

On the highest aft deck, they found Saevalde at the wheel and crewmembers working at the ballistae there. Gya noticed the *Deliberia* had already turned from its original direction. Best he could tell, they headed north.

"They're gaining on us," Saevalde told them.

"We'll see what we can do about that," Alorsha responded and led the way to the aft rail. She sent a nearby crewmember for a bucket of sea water then set everything on the deck next to the rail, between the two ballistae. She motioned for Gya to do the same. "Is this enough room?"

At Gya's nod of assent, she sidled to one side and mixed the contents of two of the bottles with the plant bits in the bowl. She nodded toward the open space between them.

"Go ahead," she urged. "Turnaround first, I think. Try to focus on the idea of confusion to our adversaries when you do the sigil. Maybe that will help."

Gya agreed and drew the sigil on the deck as quickly as he could manage. The description indicated that it could work at some distance. *A good sign.* He had worried that it was one of the sigils that needed proximity, or even contact.

Halfway through the complicated sigil, Gya forced himself to slow down. Already he saw enough errors in his drawing that he knew speed was not helping him. He painstakingly repaired the errors and resumed laying out the powdered kri-stone at a slower, more methodical pace.

When he finished, and felt the tingle of the magic as it built in the sigil, he glanced at Alorsha.

She worked to mix the contents of the bowl into the bucket of seawater, pouring in a bit at a time before she swirled the water around in the bucket. She looked up and met his gaze.

"Go ahead and finish the magic," she instructed. "I'm almost ready here and the two magics can mingle as the fog spreads."

Gya again turned his attention to the sigil and placed the final crystal to call forth the magic. As Alorsha had suggested, he concentrated on confusion, and pictured the magic flowing away from the *Deliberia* and toward their pursuers. The magic felt thin, thinner than he had expected from the description. A bit of it swirled back toward him in spite of his efforts and bewilderment wrapped him in its grip. *What was it he was doing? Was he supposed to be doing something?*

With some effort, he managed to shake off the magic's influence and push it away again, the direction he intended it to go. He hoped it would work.

With a subdued splash, Alorsha poured the contents of her bucket over the rail next to him and into the sea behind the *Deliberia*. Still clasping the bucket's handle, she repeated what she had done before to draw the fog around them. It swiftly grew between the *Deliberia* and the ships that chased them.

After the haze closed around them and obscured everything nearby, Alorsha sat abruptly on the deck.

"That's it for me for a while. Can you do the Swiftness sigil now?"

With a nod, Gya hurried to clean up the powders for the Turnaround sigil and draw the new one. This one did require nearness. *Fortunate that he wanted to use its effect on the ship.* In his hurry he managed to smear some of the lines and had to gather all the powder and start again.

Alorsha watched without comment but gave him encouraging smiles when he glanced at her.

After more time than he thought it should have taken him, he completed the sigil and felt the magic build. Before he placed the last crystal, he again looked to Alorsha.

"I wasn't able to make the first one very strong," he told her. "I'm not sure this one will be either. It might not be much use."

"Even a little extra speed will be helpful," Alorsha told him. "Please. Whatever you can manage."

So Gya finished the sigil and guided the magic into the *Deliberia. Did the ship twitch beneath him?* Alorsha placed a hand flat on the deck and the sigil's magic flowed more smoothly into the ship.

When he finished, Gya sank back against the rail, his head pounding and his stomach queasy. "That's all I can do for now." With some difficulty, he managed to return the powder to the pouch, although the ill feeling interfered with even the slight concentration needed for that action.

Alorsha turned toward Saevalde and told her to proceed as they had discussed.

Gya felt the ship shudder beneath him and its speed increased. Must be rowers moving the *Deliberia*, since no wind to speak of fluttered the sails. After many long minutes, his headache subsided enough that he no longer felt ill and he drew himself to his feet with a tight grip on the rail. He peered into the heavy mist behind the ship.

A short time later, Alorsha joined him.

"Think they're still trying to catch us?" he asked.

Alorsha and Saevalde both hushed him.

"We don't have anything to keep sound from carrying," Alorsha whispered into his ear. "Listen."

Gya did as she suggested and even closed his eyes to help.

He heard the faint swish of their oars beneath them

and little splashes of the ship moving through the water. Nothing else. But just as he was about to whisper that information, he caught the faintest hint of a sound. So he kept quiet and listened harder.

Voices?

Hard to tell how close they might be, but they did not come from the *Deliberia*. He could not make out what they said, and the voices only came sporadically, but they sounded louder each time he heard them, like they were getting closer.

He shared a concerned look with Alorsha, after which she left him to speak softly with Saevalde. Then she beckoned Gya closer.

"Let's get you some armor," Alorsha whispered.

"But I'm no fighter," Gya protested in a whisper while he followed her to the main deck.

"You need not fight. It might not even come to that."

"Best to have some protection." Mikolus's low voice came from close behind Gya.

When Gya whirled in surprise, the man just grinned and handed him one of the stiff vests, and held out another one to Alorsha.

As he donned the vest, Gya heard a strange whoosh, followed by what sounded like pottery shattering. Firelight pierced the night and Saevalde shouted from her position on the aft deck.

"Stay here," Mikolus told them and dashed to join Saevalde.

Alorsha sank to her knees and placed both hands on the deck beneath her. Gya felt the tingle of *Deliberia's* magic as he dropped down next to her.

"Can I help?"

With a weary sigh, Alorsha shook her head no, but the next instant jumped to her feet and headed for her cabin.

"Come with me. There's fire above, some sticky goo that I can't put out."

She led him to the cabinet in her cabin and practically

tossed him various bottles and other containers that she grabbed from within.

"What of that liquid you used to quench the flames when the Magickas attacked the ship back in Hawei?" Gya said.

Alorsha shook her head with a frown tugging at her lips. "Unfortunately, that was the last I had of that one. No more of that plant to make more."

On the way back out, nearly running at that point, she swerved aside and grabbed the pot that contained her chervynai.

Together, they ran to the upper deck, where Mikolus stopped them.

"Tread carefully," he warned. "The stuff clings to everything."

Gya peeked around Alorsha to see what they faced.

Glops of fire burned in scattered spots around the deck, slowly blackened the wood beneath them. A dagger lay there apparently burning too. Saevalde stood by the ship's wheel, still guiding it, but a bloody cloth wrapped her forearm.

"I managed to scrape it off Saevalde's arm," Mikolus continued, "but it clung to the dagger. You've got *Deliberia* resisting the flames?"

"For now," Alorsha said. "But they don't feel like normal fire. It won't hold."

She grabbed some of the containers from Gya and handed them to Mikolus. "Find out what will quench it."

She included Gya in that mandate and the three separated to ease up to some of the smaller, isolated bits of the fire.

Gya methodically worked his way through all the containers he still had, but none doused the flames. At least they were not spreading, but when he glanced at Alorsha, he saw the strain wearing on her. Whatever she was doing with the *Deliberia*, it looked like she might not last much longer. A couple of times, he saw her brush her hand along the chervynai and she seemed more alert after.

While he worked, as fast as he could, he heard more whooshes and saw rounded shapes pass on either side of the ship. No others landed aboard.

Yet.

"Anything?" Alorsha asked after several minutes.

"Nothing," Mikolus said and Gya echoed him.

Gya picked his way back to the ladder that went down to the next deck and watched Alorsha try the last few things she carried. She even mixed some of them together to try. Finally, she turned to her chervynai with a speculative expression. She plucked one petal and dropped it atop one of the smallest burning globs. For just a moment, the petal completely covered the fire and looked like it had quenched it. Then flames burst through, brighter than before.

"Maybe just scrape it off and throw it overboard," Saevalde suggested.

"Can we get it back into pots?" Gya said.

"Perhaps smother it," Mikolus mused.

Alorsha grabbed her chervynai's pot and placed it atop one of the smallest burning bits. She stepped back and they watched.

After only a few seconds, the pot glowed red, as if it were firing in a kiln. With a loud pop, it shattered and dropped all the dirt, and the chervynai, where it had been.

Alorsha darted to her plant and grabbed it, cradling it to her chest. She paused to scrutinize the small pile of dirt, leaned over, and held her hand above it.

Before anyone could object, she brushed the dirt aside with her shoe to reveal a darkened, damp-looking splotch on the wood beneath. But no fire.

"Hold on!" Saevalde warned as more whooshes approached. She spun the wheel and turned them sharply starboard.

Gya lost his footing and sprawled too close to one of the burning globs. He scrambled back and sighed in relief when Mikolus dropped two handfuls of dirt atop the fire to smother it.

Alorsha ran back to her cabin and returned without her chervynai and with more dirt. They made short work of snuffing the fires that remained. Fortunately, none of them had grown much yet. Alorsha took charge of Saevalde and unwrapped her injury to coat it with something she poured from a small jar she pulled from a pocket.

At Mikolus's urging, seconded by both Alorsha and Saevalde, Gya took himself below, to the relative safety of his compartment. *He couldn't blame them for not wanting him there any longer, for wanting him to leave them to deal with anything on deck. Why couldn't he have done the sigils better?*

After another hour or so of sudden sharp turns this way and that, the ship settled into smoother sailing. Alorsha stopped by.

"I wanted to be sure to thank you for the help, and also let you know that we seem to have lost our pursuers. However, we're now much further north than we had planned."

Gya nodded acknowledgment of the information, then blurted out, "I'm so sorry that my sigils were so useless. So weak. I failed to turn away our pursuers and so allowed the ship to be damaged and Saevalde to be injured—"

Alorsha cut him off with a sharp gesture of one hand and a shake of her head.

"The damage and injury are *not* your doing. The responsibility lies directly on those who came after us. Your magic helped, never doubt that. This I say true. Our situation would have been worse, likely by a great degree, without your aid."

Gya studied her expression to see if she only tried to placate him, but her expression showed she was sincere. He nodded slightly. She wished him good night and left him to his solitary compartment, where he pondered long what he might have done better. Or whether he should even have tried to do anything at all.

CHAPTER 20

The next days, Gya saw little of Alorsha. She spent much of her time in her cabin where she examined the little bit of the fiery goo that they had recovered. She also settled her chervynai into a new pot. The plant looked little worse for its adventure.

Gya joined in the morning weapons-work but felt completely inadequate. Still he made a little bit of progress working with a lightweight club, mostly learning about blocking attacks. Most of the rest of his time, he worked with his magic. Once each day he tried to see Toa, Chizoa, Ifeoma and Vabena, but he only saw a door for each of them.

After a couple of days, he did manage to spend a little time with Alorsha and learned something of how to feel the magic within things, how to draw it out, some of which he had already been doing with the kri-stone although he had not realized it. He also watched through a seeing-stone when she checked on Devrand's location. He could now see, and feel, her magic when she did that. But that did not help him get any closer to doing something similar himself to find his brother and friends.

The third day away from leaving the other Magickas ashore, after he had debated with himself for several hours, Gya decided to see if he could expand on the seeing magic, as Alorsha had mentioned was possible. *He had not bungled the sigil again, so perhaps he* could *do this.* He set up the bowl as before, then looked through the kri-stone powders and crystals he carried to see what might work.

He considered the blue-green a possibility. Blue-green for truth. *Well, maybe.* He next considered the brown for strength. Might help, but did not fit as well as he would have liked. *Gray for stability or black for power?* Stability was always good when working with the sigils, but he did not think it would add anything here. More power might help him reach further. But he was uncertain that would help either. *Pink for love?* He did love Toa, exasperating as he could be sometimes. He was pretty sure he had been falling in love with Chizoa, and she with him. *So maybe the pink.*

But uncertain of the results of mixing the colors when the original sigil did not call for it, Gya finally just pulled out more of the colorless clear kri-stone powder, which in that form looked much like the white. He compared them to make sure he had the right one. *Maybe it would be as simple as adding the additional clarity.* He hoped so.

Gya added a pinch of the powdered kri-stone to the water to join Alorsha's leaves and concoction and Chizoa's hair stick. When he finished the last lines of the sigil, hanging in the air as before, the water in the bowl roiled immediately, before he even began to concentrate on Chizoa.

It continued its agitation, and this time affected the surface of the water rather than just rolling beneath the surface. Gya caught glimpses of things, small images that flashed in the agitated water and vanished again. He saw the door several times – at least he thought it was the same door that he had seen before when he tried to see Chizoa.

He saw several glimpses of her face, but not long enough to get an idea of whether she was unharmed. He saw someone's hands, the edge of a sigil done in blue powdered kri-stone. Gradually the fragmented images gave way to fragments of the door, until that was all he saw.

With a sigh, he replaced Chizoa's hair stick with Toa's bracelet and turned his thoughts to Toa instead. This time the water reacted even more violently and some of it splashed out of the bowl. Again Gya saw glimpses of things: a door, Toa's face, a red kri-stone crystal. The water grew more and more agitated.

With a bell-like gong, the liquid contents of the bowl exploded up and out. The water caught Gya full in the face and drenched him, burning with a heat that had not been there a moment before. He screamed from the sudden pain and wrestled off his shirt to try to wipe the scalding liquid from his face and arms.

The next moment, or so it seemed to him, a multitude of hands and voices surrounded him.

He heard Alorsha call out. "Hali, Parl, get clear water, drinking water, and clean cloths." Then she muttered. "Wish we had a real healer right now."

Gya suspected he was not supposed to have heard that.

"I have that salve." That was Mikolus's voice. "Someone get Kluir."

Gya lifted his head and tried to open his eyes. They burned and were too swollen for him to get them open.

"Bring it here," Alorsha said. "Gya, hold still. We've got to rinse this off you."

He nodded his understanding and gasped as someone poured cool water on him. But the burning sensation on his skin eased.

"Keep your eyes closed," Alorsha said. "One more time."

Cool water drenched him again. Someone took his sodden shirt and pressed dry cloth into his hands.

"Gently pat the water away," Alorsha said. "Don't

rub."

He did that and hissed at the pain the slightest touch produced, while someone else interfered by helping him into a dry shirt. He had not realized that he had been shivering until the warmth from the shirt calmed the shivers.

A new voice penetrated the hustle around him, a man's. "We need more cool water and more clean cloths."

That voice sounded familiar. Now who was that? After some thought, Gya was able to picture the face that went with the voice. A young man, probably still several years Gya's senior, with nearly white hair that had just a hint of brown to it and brown skin, lighter than his own. He had seen this man hovering near Alorsha, along with two other crewmembers – the ones she had named: Hali and Parl.

Gya stifled a groan as something touched one of his forearms. But then the cool wet cloth that someone wrapped loosely around his arm brought him some respite from the pain.

"Can I open my eyes yet?" he asked.

"Wait," the man said. Gya felt cool water dripping on his closed eyes before it ran down his cheeks.

"Good," the man said. "Try it now."

Gya had some trouble and felt like his eyes only half opened, but he looked around. Only Alorsha, Mikolus and this other man were close. He finally realized that this was the Kluir that Mikolus had called for. Gya had met him briefly but had not remembered the face and voice went together.

Kluir leaned close and Gya instinctively leaned away.

Kluir grinned. "Good, you can see. I don't see any of that shiny powder in your eyes, either. If you can take it, I would like to rinse them once more."

At Gya's nod, Kluir dribbled more of the cool, clear water into the corners of Gya's eyes and let the water run out the edges.

"How's that feeling?"

"Better," Gya said with some difficulty. His lips must be swollen, too. He glanced at Alorsha. "I thought you didn't have a healer." Alorsha grinned.

Kluir chuckled. "I'm not a healer. But I have some experience with scalds." He turned to Alorsha. "Does that salve have to go directly on the skin?"

"It works best that way, but it would work through bandages, soak through them, if we need to do it that way."

"Salve?" Gya said.

"It helps ease pain somewhat, nothing more," Alorsha said.

"I think it'd be best to put it in the cloth," Kluir said.

"Now that the water from the bowl's off me, it doesn't feel nearly as bad," Gya said.

"It's still not good," Kluir told him, but with a grin. "Going to be a while before you'll get looks from the women that are anything other than wincing sympathy."

Alorsha swatted Kluir lightly on the shoulder before she handed him a small pot with some kind of pale green cream within. He dipped two fingers into the cream and smoothed it into a strip of clean cloth.

"Tell me if this gets too bad," Kluir instructed as he lifted the cool cloth off Gya's arm and started to wrap that arm with the new, salve-soaked cloth. Gya got a look at the swollen, darkened and reddened, blistered skin of his arm and flinched.

Kluir immediately stopped and gave him a questioning look, but Gya shook his head. "Doesn't feel worse," he said. "I just shouldn't have looked."

With a nod and grin, Kluir continued to wrap the cloth, then reached for another one and the salve.

"Why not tell me what happened." Alorsha's request drew Gya's attention from Kluir's actions.

Gya frowned then winced as that hurt. "I decided to try to expand on the magic for trying to see my brother and friends."

"How?" Alorsha seated herself on the deck nearby. Gya had a moment to be grateful that she had told him not to work on magic in his small compartment. He could only imagine what might have happened in there.

"I took a pinch of powdered kri-stone and added it to the water. That kri-stone is good for clarity. I had hoped it might strengthen the seeing, help me learn where Toa is and see Chizoa. Then I could try for the others, too."

Alorsha nodded. "So what happened?"

Gya described what the water had done and the fragments he had seen, and the final result.

Alorsha looked away, a thoughtful expression on her face. Kluir had Gya lift his arms to let him wrap the cloths around them easier. Gya felt ludicrous sitting there with both arms in the air.

"Should I *not* have done that?" Gya asked tentatively.

Alorsha shrugged. "Not necessarily. Magic can be tricky and unpredictable when you're trying something new. I imagine you already know that."

Gya nodded.

"Perhaps next time, you might want me there, though. I think I've worked with magic much longer than you have. I might've been able to calm the water before it got so out of hand."

Gya nodded, and jumped when Kluir leaned close to look at his face.

"I need to wrap your face, too, for at least this first day," Kluir said and frowned at Alorsha. "So he needs to rest. No magic for a bit."

Alorsha gave an impression of chagrin, spoiled by the smile that teased at the corners of her mouth. "As you say."

Kluir snorted and shook a finger at her. "Now help me with these last cloths."

~ ~ ~

For the next two days, Gya rested mostly in his compartment, uncomfortable and fidgety, even with the bandages on his face removed after the first day. The morning of the fifth day from when they had left the other Magickas, Gya could stand it no longer. He wandered on deck to watch the usual weapons-work, although he took no part in it.

When they had finished, the crewmembers dispersed and Alorsha and Kluir joined Gya.

"We can try having the rest of the bandages off," Kluir said to Gya while he wiped the sweat from the weapons-work from his face. "I imagine you're ready to be free of them."

"Please," Gya said.

"Afterwards, if you feel up to it, please come back on deck." Alorsha headed toward her cabin.

Kluir took Gya back below deck to Gya's compartment, and carefully removed the bandages that they had been replacing every few hours.

Then he sat back and perused Gya's injuries.

"You'll still be very uncomfortable for a while longer, and the sun will hurt those burned areas. Wear a hat that can offer you some shade, have a shirt with loose sleeves, and the salve is here, if you need relief from pain." Kluir pointed to the small jar that sat next to Gya's bed.

"Otherwise, how do you feel?"

"Much as you said." Gya looked at the angry-looking skin on his arms. "But the air feels good. I don't have a hat with me, though."

Kluir nodded. "I'm off to get cleaned up. I'll send someone along with a hat for you. Have someone get me anytime, though, if you start to feel worse."

Gya nodded and found a shirt with long, loose sleeves. He waited until a crewmember brought him a hat, something made from straw, it looked like, and kind of pyramidal in shape. With it on his head, he returned to the deck, bringing some of his powders and crystals with him, along with Toa's bracelet and Chizoa's hair stick. The extended rest had let him solidify an idea for finding Toa. *And it just might work, even.* But he wanted to get Alorsha's help and advice.

He found her on deck where she worked her wayfinding magic with her pendant. When she finished, the pendant pointed basically south, as before, but still wavered back and forth, although perhaps not as far to the east as before. She gave Gya a quick nod of greeting.

Gya returned Alorsha's greeting. "I'd like to try something like that, like what you do with your pendant. Can you guide me? I do have Toa's bracelet. I've also been thinking – he and I both used the kri-stone crystals and powders all the time, the ones I carry with me. Maybe one of those would be something like your magic connection to Devrand and Jarthan."

Alorsha gave him a speculative look. "Maybe it would. It's worth trying. You do realize that it's not anything like your normal way of working magic."

Gya nodded, with a slight smile. "That's why I need your guidance."

She matched his smile then was lost in thought for several minutes. With a curt nod, like she had reached some decision, she told Gya to wait there for her as she headed to her cabin. When she returned, she carried some cord that she wound back and forth through her fingers. She handed it to Gya.

"It's not like what I've got so we'll have to make some guesses here. I suggest you pick one or two of the crystals that Toa and you both used the most, if you can. They have magic in them like my pendant does. This seems to need that. Wrap his bracelet around them and use this cord to secure everything together and give you something to let them hang by."

She watched as Gya followed her instructions. He chose the seeing stone that he and Toa used so often. *Its purpose might help too. Perhaps.*

When he had everything secured together, he shot Alorsha a questioning look.

She scrunched her face into an expression he had not seen on her before. "I'm just guessing. I'm not really a teacher of magic, but let's see what we can do. Remember how you were able to feel *Deliberia's* magic?"

Gya nodded.

"Concentrate on how that felt. Close your eyes and hold out the bracelet and crystal. Let them hang from the cord and try to relax. Don't anticipate the motion."

Gya did as she instructed and stood there feeling a little ridiculous while he hoped that this would work. When she spoke again, her voice was barely above a whisper.

"Do you feel any magic?"

"I think so. Sort of like what builds in the sigils when we draw them. It's in the crystal." His voice was a quiet as hers.

"Picture yourself touching that magic, drawing it out into the bracelet, and reaching out to the one the bracelet belongs to."

Gya tried to do as she said. He felt… something. Maybe. *But was it doing anything?*

"Slowly open your eyes and look," Alorsha whispered. "Keep your focus on what you want to do."

Gya slit his eyes open the tiniest bit. The makeshift pendant of crystal and bracelet spun in a small circle. He was certain he was not moving it. The circle widened then changed to an arc. It pointed the same general direction that Alorsha's pendant had but swung much wider.

It traced that arc a moment longer before it abruptly dropped to hang straight down, the magic no longer working on it.

He glanced at Alorsha, hoping she would have an explanation. But she only shrugged. "Sometimes new magics have some odd effects."

Gya nodded, but still wondered at it. He unwound the cord from the kri-stone and Toa's bracelet and grabbed

Chizoa's hair stick to see if he could make the magic work again for her. He used a different crystal – one that he and Chizoa had used most often when they had worked together on the sigils.

This second time he used the pendant resembled the first. But this time, it swung in an even wider arc, acting like it could not pinpoint Chizoa any more accurately. *Maybe she'd not been in contact with the crystal long enough. Or more likely it was due to his lack of experience with this sort of magic.* Again before too long, the magic slipped away from him and the pendant dropped to hang straight down.

He met Alorsha's gaze. "I imagine more practice will smooth it out," she said.

"Both times it pointed the same general direction." Gya unwound the cord. "I think I need to go ashore. Go south."

Alorsha nodded.

"One moment," she said and joined Saevalde at the wheel.

Gya put the crystal, cord, bracelet and hair stick together in a pouch at his waist and followed her. After some discussion between Alorsha and Saevalde, the latter turned the ship to the south. She called out for the crew to reduce the speed when Gya warned that they would be sailing toward Empire-held lands again.

Gya watched Saevalde send a crewmember up the tallest mast with the spyglass to keep an eye out for land and warn them at first sighting. Gya hoped it would mean they would find a place to go ashore undetected.

In preparation for that, Mikolus called a meeting later that morning, held in Saevalde's cabin; she had the best table for such things. Gya took a seat next to Alorsha and looked around at the others. Mikolus and Saevalde were there, as were the three crewmembers that Gya had noticed often lingered near Alorsha. Kluir Reez, Gya knew now, of course. Quick introductions reminded Gya of the others' names: Hali Arithi, the woman with yellow-brown hair, browned skin and blue-gray eyes; and Parl Smas, the man next to her, with black-brown skin, black hair and dark brown eyes.

Saevalde opened the discussion with a gruff comment to Alorsha. "You are set, lass, on this plan, even with this Empire hunting, perhaps killing, mages?"

Alorsha gave her a tired nod. "Yes. From what I saw in Hawei, and what I've been seeing here from my pendant, it's clear that Devrand is inland somewhere."

"Are there no rivers large enough to sail the *Deliberia* up?" Parl said.

Saevalde snorted. "She is *not* a river barge."

Gya shook his head. "There are a couple that are perhaps deep enough, but the waters are rough and the channels narrow, from what I've heard from merchants who tried."

"If it *is* Devrand who set these Keepers on us, he'll have described you to them, too, don't you think?" Hali pointed out.

"Might be disguises would work." Mikolus pointed to Gya. "Take that hat, for example."

"We have nothing like it in the Empire," Gya said with a smile. "Out-Empire travelers should be able to journey relatively safely. But they'd need the proper tokens."

"Aye. The cursed tokens," Saevalde muttered.

Mikolus gave her a sly grin. "We've got one or two crewmembers who can handle that particular problem for us."

Saevalde shook her head, but grinned. "I won't be doubting it."

"How would these disguises work?" Hali asked Mikolus, then looked at Gya. "Does your magic have a way to change someone's appearance?"

Gya's eyebrows rose at the question and stretched the too-tight burnt skin of his face. "If so, it's nothing I know how to do. And no, there's not a sigil in any of my codices that does something similar that could be adapted." Then he muttered, "Not sure I'm ready to try adapting anything again, anyway."

Alorsha chuckled. "I'm sure we can manage something. We have enough people from enough different lands to give us some exotic customs and attire to draw on."

"So who's going ashore," Gya said.

Saevalde snorted, and Alorsha grinned.

Gya looked around at everyone's expressions. "What am I missing?"

Saevalde pointed an accusing finger at Alorsha. "She'll be going, although she shouldn't."

Alorsha grinned again. "Which means they *all* will insist on going too." She waved a hand at the three who seemed to be guards for her.

"That they will. And I will, as well, on this one," Mikolus said.

"I'd rather you stayed with the *Deliberia*—"

Saevalde cut Alorsha off. "Lass, we'll stay out away from the shore. We'll be fine. You might need him with you. Especially if you *do* catch Devrand."

Alorsha looked from one to the other. "Very well."

"What of me? Toa and Chizoa are that direction." Gya paused at a sudden thought. "What if your Devrand's where they are?"

Alorsha frowned. "Everything does seem to lead us that direction. Are they strong Magickas? Devrand gravitates toward strong magics."

Now Gya frowned. "None of us knows how strong we might be in our magic. Hard to hide and test your limits at the same time. I can say that the magic has seemed to come easily to Toa. More so than to me. I-I'm not sure about Chizoa."

Alorsha exchanged glances with Saevalde and Mikolus before she turned back to Gya. "It does seem possible we might find them all together. So, will you be our guide in the Empire? Not a Magicka, of course, and not from Hawei, either."

"Definitely not," Mikolus said.

Gya considered it. "I'll do my best to not bungle anything. Although I've not been all over the Empire, I can still tell you about our customs and how things work. Maybe I'll hear something that can lead me to my brother and friends."

With his agreement, they spent the rest of the day gathering various clothing items from crewmembers and figuring out which they would use and how they would make this venture work. At Mikolus's recommendation, Saevalde turned the ship back a little east of south so they would not approach the Empire's shores from an expected direction, or so they hoped.

That solidified a concern Gya had that he had not been able to articulate earlier.

"If you can use your ring-pendant to find the direction to Devrand, does he have something to tell him where you are?" he asked Alorsha as they filled a couple of packs.

Alorsha paused and gave him an inscrutable look.

"That's a good question. He knows we follow. We've almost caught him any number of times." She pulled out her pendant and studied it, then rubbed her thumb across the stone. Gya could feel her working some magic.

After a short time, she looked up. "His magic doesn't work the same way mine does. I don't think he can use it to find a direction to me as I can for him. We've had no indication that he has done so in all the time we've pursued him."

She frowned. "I suppose he might be able to tell some other things, if he looks for them. Maybe whether I'm closer or farther away. Once I'm closer to him, I get a feel for that. He might possibly sense if I'm gathering magic – I can get a sense of that about him without much effort."

"That's not good," Gya said.

Alorsha smiled. "No, not particularly. But I've not been trying to sneak up on him, and the sensation of nearness is only relative to the last sensation. So if he's not paying much attention, he won't realize the difference."

"There are a fair number of 'ifs' involved," Gya pointed out.

Alorsha laughed. "Too true. But still, I must continue."

Gya considered her determined expression and nodded. Still, he wondered if the small group that planned to go would be enough. *He hoped they knew what they were doing.*

CHAPTER 21

As they sailed roughly southward, they made preparations for those who would travel through the Empire. They dyed Gya's hair an unusual red-orange that he assured them no one in the Empire was likely to have naturally, or wear by choice. His face was still reddened and a little swollen, which everyone agreed should help keep him from being recognized. The others who planned to go ashore also dyed their hair other colors. Part of their story, if anyone asked, was that it was a custom of their land.

Alorsha's concoctions had proven handy for all the colors, which ranged from greens in Mikolus's hair to a deep, deep purple in Alorsha's to a blotchy pattern of whites in Parl's. Hali had black streaks in her hair and Kluir had blue.

Hali borrowed some kind of cosmetic paste from one of the other crewmembers and traced designs on the faces, arms and hands of everyone except Gya. When the paste dried and flaked off after a couple of hours, it left the designs on their skins, darker on those with lighter skin and lighter somehow on those with darker skin. Hali told them the designs would last for close to four weeks, although they would be more faded after the first week.

With a laugh, Gya assured them that everyone would likely look more at the designs than at what they really looked like.

To go with the fanciful skin designs, the clothes they decided on were a fashion Gya had not seen before, long tunics that reached their ankles but had slits up both sides that reached their waists. These were worn over loose trousers that tucked into boots or were gathered close at ankles above low shoes. The tunics and trousers were all shades of pale blue and green, with bright, fanciful embroidery at the necklines, cuffs and hems. The tunics had various lengths of sleeves.

Mikolus found some more of the pyramidal hats for the men to wear, so Gya would not stand out so much from the rest of them. Alorsha and Hali packed a few colored scarves.

"Also a custom of our people – at least as of now," Hali told Gya with a wink.

A day and a half after Saevalde had turned *Deliberia*'s course southward, the lookout sighted land. Saevalde halted the ship and sent up a second lookout to help check the coast for a good place to go ashore. After the two reported back to her, she turned the ship further east and sailed slowly that direction while she followed shouted instructions from the lookouts above.

Near dark, she dropped anchor and joined those who would be going ashore. Narain came with her and brought with him two large stuffed packs and a smaller one. He handed the large ones to Mikolus, saying they held food for the journey. The smaller one he kept for himself.

"We've spotted a good little cove for your landing," Saevalde said. "Narain will be going along only to stay with the tender until you're well on your way, while we stay off-shore some distance. From the looks of it, there's a decent-sized village just a bit along a road that runs near the shore and turns inland."

"We'll stay with the tender while Parl gets us those tokens we'll need," Alorsha said.

"I should go help," Gya said. "You'll not know which ones—"

"Best you stay with the others," Parl said. "Unless you've got some sneaking skills?"

When Gya admitted he did not, Parl just grinned. "I'll be sure to bring back a variety and you can tell us which to use."

"We'll go ashore when it's full dark," Mikolus said, then turned to Alorsha. "Would you again give us some fog?"

She nodded and beckoned Gya to join her at the rail.

"You've seen and felt how I reach into the plants to draw out their magic. Water's similar, although I go through *Deliberia* to reach it. Watch with your seeing-stone while I work the magic and see if you can reach into the water's magic, too. See if you can feel it."

She waited while Gya drew the sigil on his seeing-stone before she set to work.

He watched the magic flow out from her, all glimmering greens. Iridescent wavy magic from the water rose to meet hers, coursing along *Deliberia*'s hull. The fog began to form. He looked over the railing at the sea below and tried to feel the magic he saw there, tried to call some to himself.

As the fog grew thicker, the magic he called swirled around below him, out of reach. He extended one hand toward it and tried to send out the magic he felt in himself to touch the water's.

He reached… further…. Then something snapped.

The water's magic leapt toward him, dropped on him, and drenched him in cool sea water, much more than the spray that had already been hitting him.

Alorsha gave him a startled look and tried unsuccessfully to stifle a laugh. He glared back before he laughed, too.

"That's one way to call it, I suppose," he said.

Mikolus handed him a cloth to dry off and returned to where some crewmembers lowered one of the tenders such as they had used to ferry the Magickas ashore several days ago.

When the tender had settled in the water, Narain, Kluir, Hali and Parl climbed down the rope ladder and caught the packs and goods that Mikolus dropped over the side to them. Gya moved to help with that. After Alorsha finished speaking with Saevalde, who looked unhappy but resigned, she joined Gya and Mikolus at the rail.

After all their packs were in the small tender and stowed, Alorsha, Gya and Mikolus climbed down the ladder as well, making the boat crowded. Narain eased around and over the others and took a place at the tiller. Everyone else, except Alorsha and Gya, grabbed oars and rowed.

Near midnight, they clambered ashore. After they unloaded the tender, they drew it above the waterline and hid it in some tall bushes that grew close to the water. Mikolus drew everyone except Parl a little further inland, further into the foliage that grew thick along a small stream nearby to stay hidden. Parl jogged inland the other direction to meet the road and follow it into the village Saevalde had mentioned.

The group hidden in the foliage made a cold camp in the mild late-spring night. Gya fell asleep to the low sounds of Alorsha and Mikolus talking.

Sunlight in his eyes woke Gya. He was not the first awake, but not the last either. He bundled the blanket he had slept on and joined Hali and Kluir at their packs.

Hali handed him some bread, cheese and dried meat and fruit. "No cooking this morning," she said. "Too close to the village to risk that someone might spot or smell the smoke from a cookfire."

Gya nodded and ate the food she handed him. He

looked at their still-sleeping companions and saw that Parl had returned.

"He got back just before dawn," Kluir told him. "Mikolus—"

"Mikolus is *trying* to catch some more sleep," Mikolus broke in. "But too many people are chattering nearby." He sat up and gave them a stern look, looking not nearly rested enough.

"Sorry," Gya muttered and jumped when Hali laughed right next to his ear.

"He's just pestering you," she said.

Alorsha rolled over and gave the small group a look that matched Mikolus's. Then she smiled. "At least everyone's in a good mood so far."

"We'll stay outside the village for the day," Mikolus said. "We can pass through the place under cover of darkness. Afterward, we'll switch back to normal daytime activity for further travel. Does everyone remember our story and the new names we'll use?" He directed his question toward everyone but looked at Gya.

"I'm Ganyai," Gya said. "From a small town 'you've never heard of it' that lies east and south, of the Empire. I have some knowledge of the Empire so this lot—all of you, that is—hired me to accompany them on their journey. All of you are from the land of Tanrith, which lies even further south and east." He pointed to Alorsha, then. "She's Asiva. Tanrith is a land of many different groups, each with their own customs, with only a few known to non-Tanrithans. Convenient for us."

Mikolus nodded. "Good."

Parl joined them and dumped a handful of tokens into Mikolus's hand. Mikolus, in turn, poured the tokens into Gya's hands. "Here are these. Please sort out which ones will serve us best."

Gya gave him an astonished look before he sat on the ground to sort through the tokens. It took him several minutes to pick out the best ones. He spread them out and explained them to the others.

"This one would be best to leave with you." He handed one to Narain. "It's for people who transport goods and other people and gives them the sanction of being in the countryside after dark. It's also not tied to a particular place, so you'll have no difficulties if someone from this village happens upon you."

Narain nodded and slipped the token's cord around his neck.

Gya pulled out eight of the other tokens and shoved the rest to one side. "Those won't work for us at all. They're for the folk of that specific village. But these are pretty much perfect." He spread out the eight that he had selected.

"These are all for travelers and allow for them to be out in the countryside after dark. Travelers pick up new ones from each town or village they pass through in exchange for the ones from the previous town. In the towns, travelers are expected to stay in certain inns. The only problem with these is that they're paired."

At the questioning looks from everyone, he continued. "They identify spouses who are traveling together."

"I suppose we can manage that." Alorsha frowned in thought. "Although, I don't like the notion of seeming to be with someone else."

Hali and Mikolus exchanged looks. "It'll only give others the impression, if they're nosy enough to pry into our business," Hali told her. "Doesn't matter what they think anyway, if it keeps them from hindering us in our purpose."

After she considered that, Alorsha nodded curtly. "I suppose."

"But if you hired me, then I'm unpaired, as is one other," Gya pointed out.

Kluir draped an arm around Parl's shoulder with a big grin. "Parl and I can make a good pairing, don't you think?"

Parl shook his head, but grinned, too. "We can pull this off. Just don't let Flenar ever hear of this. He'll ream me up one side and down the other that I didn't think ahead to bring him along instead of having to pretend to be with you."

Gya handed them one pair of tokens and looked at the others.

Hali grabbed a pair of tokens and dangled one in front of Gya. "You're with me, I think, Ganyai," she said. "We'll just change the story a little. Your town is close to the border of our land and we'd been meeting long before this against my family's wishes – you being an outlander, you see. We even wed in secret."

"Hali…." Mikolus's voice held a tone of warning.

Hali grinned back at him, unrepentant. "We need a little drama in our story. Anyway, when I learned of this journey, I made sure you knew, too, Ganyai, so you could come with us – knowing something of the Empire as you do."

Gya gave Mikolus a nervous look. The other man shrugged.

"It would work well enough," he said. "If you're willing."

Gya met Hali's gaze and smiled tentatively. "Certainly. I can do this. I think." He took the token she still held out.

"Oh, wait 'til I tell your Remdor!" Parl teased Hali. "What'll he say to you pretending to be wed when I know he's been working up his courage to ask you."

"That's supposed to be a surprise!" Kluir punched Parl's shoulder, and harder than just in fun, from Parl's wince.

"I already know," Hali told Kluir. "And the way it's going, I'll probably ask him first anyway." She turned to Parl then. "And don't you dare tell him. I'll tell him myself. *Without* making it sound like more than it is. I'd hate to have to mention to Flenar that it was you who pulled that prank on him weeks ago."

"Don't!" Parl's voice and expression both held panic. "I'll not say anything. You've my word!"

Hali glowered at him a moment, then gave a firm nod. "It's agreed then."

"That leaves us," Alorsha said to Mikolus.

"It's the best pairing," Kluir said. "With the way he gets all protective of you."

Mikolus just shook his head and took the token that paired to the one Gya handed to Alorsha.

"What of the rest of the tokens?" Hali asked.

"We could drop them somewhere back in the village when we go through tonight," Gya suggested. "Might lead them to think it merely some prank."

Mikolus nodded.

"Another consideration, though," Gya continued. "Most places seem to have something that spouses wear to show they are paired, like Alorsha's rings. In the Atturei Empire, we wear matching cuff bracelets of etched metal. We'll probably need to have something like that to help support our story…" he trailed off at the looks the others gave him.

"He's right," Kluir said, breaking the silence.

Alorsha looked at her rings. "I'm not replacing these, even with fake ones."

"We don't have sets of matching rings anyway," Hali said. "We also have no way to make them or metal bracelets. We'd better come up with some other custom."

"That we should. Among my people, the custom is to wear matching necklaces," Mikolus said. "Neckbands actually. Snug and with elaborate designs on them and often a small, carved stone hanging from them."

"We don't have the time or means to carve stones," Parl objected.

Hali pointed to a copse that stood between them and the village. "I can carve wood, though not nearly as fancy as that frame Grabe made you for your ring." She waved a hand toward Alorsha's pendants. "Might not take too long, either, I think. Especially if we cut disks from an appropriately sized branch for the basic shape."

"Do you still have that cosmetic paste?" Mikolus asked her. "We can draw designs on the neckbands with that."

Hali nodded slowly. "But we might want to keep that in reserve, in case we need to renew our own designs." She gestured to the fanciful shapes that stained her arms.

Mikolus nodded. "I've got scraps of sailcloth we can use. We can braid strips into neckbands that can be tied on."

"Get your branch, then," Alorsha instructed Hali. "Let's find a better spot for the day and we can get started on these neckbands. Tonight, we'll get beyond this village to somewhere we can settle in for a bit and finish them."

~ ~ ~

They packed up their minimal camp and headed into the trees, following Mikolus. Hali grabbed several sticks of various thicknesses from the ground as they walked. When Gya caught her eye at one point after she dropped one she had picked up to scrutinize, she grinned at him.

"Don't want any that are too green. It'll be best if it looks like we've all been paired up for a while."

Gya nodded his understanding and turned his attention back to keeping up with the others and avoiding tripping over the numerous roots that laced the ground. At least the trees did not grow too close together. Many stood not much taller than Mikolus, the tallest of the group. Gya decided the nearby village must harvest wood there.

After a couple of hours of this, Gya longed for a rest, but the others seemed uninclined to stop. So he stumbled on after them until Alorsha called a rest about a quarter-hour later, after she glanced back at him.

Everyone plopped down in shaded spots and dug out the waterskins.

"Do we need to go much further to find our spot to

settle in?" Gya asked. *He didn't sound like he was whining, did he? But his feet hurt!*

The others looked around.

"This place seems good," Parl said.

Mikolus nodded his agreement. "That it is. I deliberately brought us some distance away from the village. Might as well settle here for now."

"Good. I'd as soon get to work on the neckbands." Hali pulled the sticks from where she'd stuffed them into her pack and handed them out. With a grin, Mikolus handed his sticks right back to her.

"After I take a look around." He headed off into the trees.

Hali, Parl and Kluir exchanged looks.

"Right, me too." Parl clambered to his feet. He headed into the trees the opposite direction from Mikolus.

Hali directed the others to peel the bark from the sticks, then she rummaged in Mikolus's pack and returned with a small hatchet.

When Mikolus and Parl returned, the others had several wooden disks chopped from the sticks and were working on evening the edges. They used daggers for the work, under Hali's guidance.

"Found a creek nearby, so we're set there," Mikolus said as he and Parl each drank from their waterskins and rested for a bit. Then, Hali called them over to help.

Gya found the work interesting. He had never tried carving wood, although he'd be the first to admit that making the disk more circular was not much as wood-carving went. But he found a certain pride in seeing the circle take shape with his small, careful slices.

When he had finished with his disk, he placed it with the others Hali had laid out. They had eight smoothed disks of various sizes, although paired by size.

"So these will hang from the neckband?" Gya fingered one of the larger disks.

"We could attach them somehow to the front of the

neckbands maybe," Kluir said. "Or maybe weave them into the braid somehow?"

"Do they need to look like each other?" Hali wondered.

"Don't see why," Mikolus said. "As long as the pairs are clearly matched. Otherwise they can be distinct."

"We need holes in the disks, I think," Alorsha said. She looked at Mikolus. "Can we have a small fire?"

Mikolus looked off into the trees around them, gazing in the general direction of the village. "A small one."

"Good." Alorsha gathered some twigs and sticks.

"Good to have some heated food, too," Kluir said as he helped.

Soon they had their small fire. While Parl and Hali put together a hot meal, the others heated the ends of a couple of needles that Alorsha had, plus two pieces of wire that Mikolus had, and started burning a small hole in each of the disks, including the extras.

"Do you always carry bits of wire?" Gya asked Mikolus.

"A person never knows what might be useful when away from home," Mikolus said with a shrug and a slight smile.

After they ate, they took turns working on the holes, hoping to make it go faster. When Hali was not taking a turn, she traced designs in the dirt and asked the others what they liked for their disks.

"I like fish," was Parl's only contribution to that discussion.

"I'm not wearing some fish at my throat!" Kluir said.

"Ah, their first fight." Hali chortled.

The two men finally settled on a design that could look like a fish, if looked at with that in mind, but also could just be fanciful lines and swirls. When the first disk had a hole in it, Hali took it off to the side to carve the design. After he finished the hole for the next disk, Mikolus pulled some pieces of cloth from his pack and sat on the ground nearby.

"Braided or just a strip secured at the back?" he asked the group.

"Braided and dyed pink," Kluir said. "You can do that, right, Alorsha?"

She grinned. "I can."

Parl groaned. "Not pink. You know how I hate pink."

"Yes, I do! If I'm wearing your fish, you can wear pink," Kluir said. "It'll look good on you."

Parl groaned again.

"You carry dyes with you?" Gya asked Alorsha.

"Not exactly. I have various seeds, roots and leaves that I brought along. A few of them can also be used to dye things. I've also got some potions that can work as dyes or paints." She turned to Mikolus. "I think all of them braided. We can dye the strips different colors for greater variety."

With a nod, Mikolus tore the cloths into long, narrow strips and trimmed away loose threads.

When Gya and Alorsha finished the holes in the disks they had been working on, he helped her prepare small amounts of dye: the pink, a blue, a green, and a yellow. They dyed the strips Mikolus had made and draped them over branches in the sun to dry.

As the day wore on, Hali managed to finish one of the fish disks and got a good start on the second. Gya sat near to watch and they settled on a design for their disks. Alorsha and Mikolus picked one of the simpler designs that Hali had traced in the dirt for theirs.

Alorsha dyed some of the strips a second and third time to get darker variations in the colors. Mikolus and Parl left a couple of times to check around that they were still undiscovered.

They revived the fire and settled in to enjoy a hot evening meal and some rest before they headed out again.

CHAPTER 22

The group set out a little after sundown after they put out the fire, gathered everything, and scattered dirt and old leaves and other forest debris around to leave the place looking as undisturbed as possible. They reached the village close to two hours later. The streets were quiet and most of the buildings showed no lights at their windows.

Parl led the way, with Mikolus bringing up the rear.

They ran into no Keepers, a good thing, although they did see one walking about. Parl kept them to heavy shadows and away from what looked to be the main streets of the place.

When they found the village's one tavern, from which subdued rowdy sounds came, Gya scattered the tokens at the base of the back wall. A good-enough spot.

They left the village behind them less than an hour after they entered and pushed their pace on the road southwest the next couple of hours to put as much distance behind them as they could before they camped. Mikolus arranged with Parl, Hali and Kluir for someone to be awake at all times during the night with a plan to switch who stayed awake every couple of hours. When Gya volunteered to help, the other man thanked him, but said he preferred someone more skilled with weapons, just in case. Considering what that meant, Gya did not feel too bad to be excluded from that task.

Alorsha did not take a turn either.

The next day they stayed in their camp, some distance off the road and concealed in another copse of trees. They used the day to finish their neckbands, the carving and the braiding. Alorsha rubbed each disk with a cream from one of her jars, then rinsed it off, leaving the disks looking like they had not just recently been carved. After that, they used a few threads pulled from some scrap cloth to secure the disks to the braids.

Kluir's and Parl's braided neckbands were in shades of pink. Alorsha's and Mikolus's were blue and green and Gya's and Hali's were green and yellow. To help avoid any mistakes, they also reviewed their story and the names they would use: Asiva Talu for Alorsha and Mirov Talu for Mikolus; Ganyai Arikron for Gya and Hieva Arikron for Hali; and Kolyav Reesma for Kluir and Pashev Reesma for Parl.

When they felt confident that they would remember their names and story, they settled in for the night, with the plan to set out again about midmorning. During the evening meal, and for some time after, they shared jokes and fantastic tales and even a few tavern songs, mixed in with some gentle teasing of each other. Gya found that he enjoyed the easy camaraderie and he slept better that night for the relaxation he had gained from his companions' antics.

They traveled slowly the next day, both because Gya's feet pained him still from the unaccustomed time spent walking and so that they would arrive at the next town before sunset, but close to it.

The Keepers at the town gate looked them over curiously but accepted their tokens without any trouble.

Gya found it curious, the two looked younger than him. Younger certainly than any of the Keepers he had seen before. And they did not exchange the group's tokens for this town's tokens, unlike Hawei which did that sort of thing for any newcomers when they arrived. Gya frowned to himself. He'd thought that all towns in the Empire followed the same pattern. *Odd.*

In a small scroll that otherwise looked much like the tally scrolls that Gya used to use, they wrote some notes about where the group said they came from. After they had everything marked down, the Keepers directed them to stay at the Crossway Inn near the center of the town.

The entrance of four Keepers, led by someone obviously of higher rank, and older, interrupted their evening meal at one of the large tables in the inn's common room. The four spaced themselves around the room but looked only watchful rather than hostile. The ranking Keeper was a man Gya estimated to be about his own height but with skin a darker brown than his own and hair a shade darker than that. He hauled a chair to their table and seated himself.

"Welcome to Uboro," he said pleasantly enough, but he scrutinized them, the expression in his pale-blue eyes unreadable. They thanked him around bites of their meal.

Gya found the Keeper's uniform strange. Like the uniforms of the Keepers in Hawei, the man's trousers and coat fit snugly, with the high-collared coat reaching to his hips, and his boots were the same shiny black. But this man's uniform was the brown-red color of old blood. He wore the gloves that all Keepers seemed to have, backless gray ones, but many thin, black lines twisted into fanciful designs adorned his. Entwined chain and thunderbolt symbols decorated his collar. They were nothing Gya had seen any Keepers wear before.

"My people tell me you have a unique tale to tell," the Keeper said. "I've come to hear it for myself."

"Of course, ah… what shall we call you?" Mikolus said.

The Keeper gave him a tight smile. "I'm Commander Badrani D'saroa, of the Imperial Seekers."

Gya fought to hide his reaction, his sudden impulse to duck, to hide. *A Seeker? Of all the people for them to meet…. Could the man somehow tell he was a Magicka? Is that why he had come to them? He couldn't be taken by a Seeker!* Gya clenched his hands together under the table. Everyone else exchanged looks.

"The Imperial Seekers?" Alorsha repeated.

"Ah, of course, you're from out-Empire" Commander D'saroa said. "We're the elite group of Keepers within the Empire specially equipped to deal with the Magicka threat."

"Such a horrible thing." Alorsha shuddered before giving him a winning smile. "How daring of you to face them."

Gya squelched a smile at how her words could be taken more than one way. As she must have intended, the Seeker took them as perfect agreement with his views on Magickas.

Mikolus laid a hand on her arm. "It's safe here, Asiva, with such fine people to stand between us and the Magickas. You've nothing to fear."

The commander looked interested. "A bad experience?"

Alorsha waved a hand in the air. "Oh, no, certainly not. I'd not go near one. I most certainly have no wish to, either."

"Of course," Commander D'saroa said, then prompted, "The tale of your travels…."

Mikolus told him the tale they had so carefully put together. After he finished, the commander perused each of them again in turn and verified their names.

"And why is it you've decided to make the long trip to the Imperial Capital while you're here in our Empire?" he asked next.

Gya and the others all exchanged quick looks. *How could*

they have forgotten to decide on the answer to such an obvious question?

Alorsha giggled, drawing surprised looks. "You'll think it so frivolous," she told the commander.

His eyebrows climbed his forehead and a smile tugged at the corners of his lips, but otherwise he held his serious demeanor. "I assure you I'll think nothing of the sort."

Alorsha gave him a shy look. "Well, I've heard tales ever since I could barely walk of how wonderful your Imperial Capital is supposed to be. Surpassing all other cities. I decided long ago that I just *had* to see it for myself. Someday. And I finally got the chance, since Hieva's brother inherited their father's place in the business he shared with Kolyav's uncle and they sent us out to see what wonderful new goods we could find for their shops, goods from your astonishing Empire."

"They hope to set up a fruitful trade, if goods from the Empire appeal as much back home as they think they might," Kluir said.

"What of your horses or carts?" the commander asked, with a predatory expression. "Or a carriage, perhaps?"

"Cursed bandits!" Alorsha's expression mixed anger and haughtiness. "In Tanrith such a thing would never have happened. Stole the carriage in the night and left us walking for days now. No suitable mounts to be seen in the small settlements we've passed to this point. My feet are so pained I'm not certain I'll be able to walk to our room after this."

"Bandits? Are you sure?" the commander said.

"Who else could it have been?"

"Did you set no watch at night? Why not stay in inns?"

Alorsha gave him an incredulous look. "Of course we set no watch. And why stay in inns when the weather has turned suitable for sleeping outside, away from the noise and odors of a town full of people? It's what our people do. In *civilized* lands, one should be perfectly safe. Are you telling me that your Empire is unsafe?" She turned a wild-eyed look on Mikolus, who patted her hand. Gya marveled at her ability at pretense, and her quick thinking to come up with a reason for their traveling that the commander seemed to accept.

The commander looked a little wild-eyed himself. "No, no, of course not. I'll report this barbarity and we *will* catch the culprits. In the meantime, you should be able to find some suitable mounts at Ruznei's stable. Oh, and here are these." He dropped six tokens on the table for them, all gray with black markings, and no colored tints like other tokens. "These are the travelers' tokens for out-Empire visitors. Because they're from the Seekers, you need only show them in any towns from here to the Imperial Capital. You'll not need to exchange them for new ones. And please accept the hospitality of the inn for the night, with my compliments in the interest of fostering goodwill trading. I wouldn't think of having you sleep on the ground when there are perfectly good rooms going unused here. And now I'll leave you to your meal."

They murmured thanks as he stood. After another piercing perusal of each of them, he left, taking the other Seekers with him.

With a quick look around, Mikolus leaned forward on the table and spoke in a voice barely above a whisper. "We'll need to talk, but elsewhere." Then he resumed the solicitous spouse persona he had taken on.

Later that night, after everyone else in the inn slept and after Alorsha placed her hands on the wood walls to see if she sensed anything, anyone listening, they gathered in a tight huddle in the larger of the three rooms they had been given.

Gya pulled out one of the tokens the commander had left with them. "I've never seen or heard of tokens like these." He kept his voice low.

"Do they say anything that will cause us trouble?" Alorsha asked.

Gya shook his head. "Except the all-black design part

and saying they come from the Seekers, and that we, the bearers are from out-Empire, they're just like the tokens we had. Even down to being paired."

"Might they have any magic about them?" Hali said.

"The Seekers wouldn't use magic!" Gya said.

"Supposedly your Empire wouldn't either, yet we saw them using Magickas in Hawei," Hali pointed out. Gya had to concede the point.

Alorsha held out her hands for all of the tokens and closed her eyes while she held them. "Ceramic, like all the others. No plant bits, so I can't be certain, but I feel no hints of magic about them."

"Does he believe our tale?" Gya asked.

"Even if he doesn't believe all of it," Mikolus said, "Might be we've given him enough that could be true, if implausible, that he'll likely only want to watch us for a while. So we just need to be extremely careful and be completely who we pretend we are."

"Do we get some horses and ride out tomorrow?" Parl said.

"Might be we'll do that. But let's see what tomorrow brings first. We *would* do well to get horses for us."

"Since we're here to see about goods for possible future trade, perhaps we should look around the town for a day," Alorsha added.

"It could help our story seem more plausible to the commander," Hali said. "The people we pretend to be would likely not be hurrying from place to place, much as we want to."

"But let's keep any magic working for between towns," Alorsha warned Gya. "If the Empire has more Magickas doing their bidding, more than those we've seen, they could have them hidden anyplace. We'd not want to attract their attention."

Gya nodded. He did not feel inclined to try any magic anyway.

They separated then to get some sleep. Hali clasped

Gya's arm for the short distance back to the room. *The single room they were to share.* The thought made him twitchy.

Once inside the small room, with the door barred behind them, Gya found himself staring at the lone bed. It was wide enough for the two of them. Barely. *How could he have agreed to this deception? Now what was he to do?*

He cleared his throat and glanced at Hali who just stood looking at him. "I'm not going to attack you," she said.

"Y-you can take the bed." He edged over to the hard chair that sat near the small window. He wished it was Chizoa there and not this formidable warrior from an out-Empire ship. His face heated at the thought and he ducked his head. "I'll be fine here."

"I'd thought to offer you the bed," Hali said. "I'll sleep lighter in the chair, and should stay at least partially on watch anyway."

Gya tried to hide his sigh of relief that she did not expect to share the bed. "If you're sure."

A quick step and she brushed his cheek with her lips. "You're sweet, and I'm sure. Get some sleep."

~ ~ ~

The next morning at breakfast, the commander joined them again. This time he came alone, and he ordered a meal, too.

"I've spoken with Ruznei on your behalf," he said around bites of the excellent meal. "He can give you the Seekers' price for some horses."

Alorsha clapped her hands, with a delighted smile for the commander. "How wonderful of you. You're so generous to strangers to your Empire. Truly your Empire is as great as we've heard tell!"

"It's my pleasure, I assure you. We wish to ensure guests to our Empire have no reason to be unhappy with or regret their visit. If you wish, I can take all of you over to the stable after breakfast to choose your mounts."

"Such a kind offer. We'd hoped to also visit some of your shops, of course." Hali gave the commander a hopeful look. "Perhaps you can escort us around and show us all the best places in your lovely town."

D'saroa glanced at each of them in turn. "I'd have thought you'd want to be on your way to a larger town."

Gya did not like the way he watched them for their reactions.

"Are you saying we have to leave so soon?" Hali said, her voice heavy with disappointment. "I'd hoped to get to know you a little better. And smaller places often have hidden treasures for trade." She placed a hand on his arm.

"Hieva," Alorsha said in an odd voice, a hint of warning in her tone.

Hali gave her a brightly false smile. "What Asiva? You know my mother and two of my aunts all had more than one spouse."

Kluir and Parl both almost choked on their food. Commander D'saroa's wild-eyed look returned.

"I-I don't know…."

"Of course you don't." Hali patted the commander's arm. "That's why we should talk, get better acquainted."

So Commander D'saroa escorted them all about the town. He pointed out the best shops and the few places to get a good meal. They shared the midday meal, and he took them to Ruznei's so they could get some horses.

After they had each selected one, Ruznei gave D'saroa a nervous look and told them the cost would be two hundred thirty silver-spishas. His relief was obvious at Commander D'saroa's approving nod.

Alorsha turned to Gya for help with the coinage. She held her coin pouch while Gya selected the appropriate coins, two of the larger gold ones she had and thirty of the silver.

"These should do fine," he told her and reached out to hand them to Ruznei. But Commander D'saroa took them first and looked them over.

With a grunt and a nod, he passed them to Ruznei. "Close enough to our coins." He then instructed the stablemaster, "Come see me later to trade for spishas."

"Will you leave then tomorrow, Hieva?" Commander D'saroa asked as they walked the horses back to their inn.

Hali shrugged and exchanged a look with Alorsha. "Perhaps. Maybe not until the next day. What of you? Do you always stay in this town or do you get to travel the Empire for your duties?"

"I do travel. Mostly I stay near the Imperial Capital, though. This was a rare trip for me. I've had some unusual matters to look into."

"Oh? So you'll be staying here for a while?" Gya said.

Commander D'saroa nodded. "Possibly so. But if I'm able to return to the capital while you're still there, perhaps I'll see you there."

Hali smiled at him. "That would be wonderful."

Commander D'saroa stopped in the street and gave them a slight bow. "This has been enjoyable, but I should return to my duties."

The group gathered for the evening, this time without the commander's presence. Under cover of the noise from the other patrons, they were able to talk some.

"Seems there's an outlander who's eased his way into the Empire's business in the Imperial Capital," Parl said when they were about half-way through the meal.

Alorsha looked up sharply. "Did you get a description?"

Parl shook his head. "But I heard he's the reason so many Keepers have spread out to the outlying towns."

"Looking for us?" Hali said.

"Best to work on that assumption," Mikolus said.

"Should we avoid other towns, then?" Gya said. "The nights are warm enough that sleeping outside has not been much of a hardship. That should continue to be true."

Alorsha shrugged. "We've certainly done it before."

She looked at Gya. "Will it make us too obvious? If we continue to do that?"

Gya considered that. "While most travelers seem to prefer to stay at inns, it's not unheard of for people to sleep out during the warmer months. Helps save money."

"With horses, we're not going to look much like we need to watch our money," Hali said.

Gya shrugged. "Horses don't necessarily mean wealth. Just that you're planning to travel a distance. The ones we picked out aren't anything special, so they'll not give the lie to a story that we want to save money."

Alorsha looked to Mikolus, who shrugged.

"I think keep it as an option," he said. "But I saw no sign that this commander thought we're anything other than rather strange. And perhaps a bit concerning." He gave Hali a look of reproval.

Hali just grinned back at him. "Keeps him distracted from trying to pry into our story too much."

"We can hope," Alorsha said. "Still, we'll stay cautious."

CHAPTER 23

Gya and his companions left Uboro early the next morning after a last hot meal in the inn. Gya had not ridden much in recent years but found it easy to remember the little tricks to it and soon felt comfortable again atop a horse as they continued on toward the Imperial Capital.

The next towns on their way were spaced roughly a day's travel apart for people on foot, so they only stopped in every other town. None of the towns held extra Keepers and the group deliberately downplayed their more exotic aspects to avoid drawing too much attention from the Keepers they did encounter. Without being obvious, Gya kept an eye on any Keepers they passed, but none took any special notice of the group. Their tokens granted them easy passage through the towns they did not stay in.

As they traveled, Gya studied the townsfolk in each town. *Might he find another like him? Another Magicka? Probably wouldn't be able to tell from looking. All to the good, actually — Keepers couldn't tell either.*

The towns reminded Gya of home more than he had expected. True, they were built from different materials, painted in different colors. But all had a sense of wariness about them, with everyone—except for the Keepers—shooting glances from time to time over their shoulders and shying away from meeting others' gazes. A council hall with its pole of the Empire's mandates dominated the center of each town – just like Hawei. *Was the entire Empire like this? So full of suspicion, distrust and outright fear?*

A few times when they rested between towns, Gya tried the seeing magic with the bowl again, using a small bowl that Alorsha had brought along just for that purpose. Not as good as the larger basin on the *Deliberia*, he found, but much easier to take traveling. He kept hoping that he would somehow manage to actually see his brother and missing friends.

The images came quicker, easier, but otherwise looked little different from before. Even smaller, they were as clear as previously, but he still only saw the doors.

Although they ate in towns whenever they could, their food ran low a little more than a week after they had come ashore, so they decided to stay a couple of days in the next town they came to. Before they arrived there, at Alorsha's request and when no one else was about, Mikolus led them off the road and some distance into a thickly wooded area. They stopped in a small clearing so that Alorsha could work her wayfinding magic.

"To make sure he's not headed a different direction since I last checked." She slipped off her horse.

Gya joined her on the ground. "Perhaps I should check on my brother and friend, too."

Alorsha nodded agreement, so they took themselves off to the edge of the clearing while the others watered the horses at a brook that ran at the other side of the clearing.

Gya watched as Alorsha worked her magic, in case he might see something to help him more with his. He did not spot anything different, so after her pendant assumed its swaying arc—still pointing the same general direction it had before, although perhaps a little more to the west than previously—he prepared to do his version of the magic. With a little extra something he wanted to try. Before he wrapped Toa's bracelet around the kri-stone crystal, he traced the small seeing sigil on the crystal, as he would do if he planned to look through it. *Maybe it would help.* Then he repeated all that he had done before to make the pendant and try to locate Toa.

This time, the arc seemed smaller than before. *Must be getting better at this.* As before, the arc roughly matched the direction Alorsha's pendant had indicated. When the magic slipped away, the pendant abruptly swung back toward Gya. An odd tingle poked at his chest, gone in the next instant, and the pendant dropped to hang straight down. He looked to Alorsha, but she watched the others across the clearing and had not noticed.

Wondering at that last bit, Gya repeated everything with Chizoa's hair stick and the crystal he had just used for Toa. As usual, the pendant's arc swung wider than it did for Toa. It did indicate the same direction, however. When the magic slipped away from him, the pendant behaved as it had before, swinging back toward him before it dropped to hang straight down. This time a slight burning sensation accompanied the odd tingle, and he saw Alorsha notice the pendant's odd motion.

Gya rubbed the spot on his chest and felt the Seekers' token right at that spot. He pulled it out and saw faint markings on it, black like the rest, which had not been there before. They faded away so quickly he wondered if he had imagined them. But when Alorsha's hand covered his, he knew she had seen them too.

After a minute, she pulled back. "I still don't feel any magic from it," she murmured.

Gya tried to see if he did, but nothing was there. The markings had disappeared, too.

"We'll want to look into this further when we have time. But for now…." Alorsha pulled off her token and dropped it into a pouch at her waist, her expression troubled. "Maybe not wear these except if we have to."

With a nod, Gya copied her actions and dropped his in the satchel he used to carry his kri-stone powders and crystals. While she hurried to the others and had a quick conversation which resulted in them also removing the tokens, Gya untangled the cord that made up his pendant and tucked away the various pieces.

Again on their horses, they made their way out of the trees and back onto the road. With little conversation, they continued to the next town.

Before they reached the edge of town, with its customary Keeper guards, they again donned their tokens. But when they were out of sight again within the town, they returned them to their pouches before they headed to the inn they had been told to use.

The two days they stayed in town, a place called Farhani, they circumspectly purchased extra food to carry with them so they could avoid towns even more. The one time Gya tried to broach the subject of his pendants, Alorsha hushed him urgently.

"We'll talk after we've left town," she promised and turned her attention elsewhere.

While in town, they took the opportunity to clean their clothes, and to purchase a few less-exotic items to wear.

They also ventured out from their inn in groups of two or three to see if they could gather some information about the capital and what might be happening there, as well as anything that could give a clue about where the Empire took Magickas.

"The outlander in the Imperial Capital is real," Hali told Gya and Mikolus when she and Alorsha joined them at a table in the inn's common room the day before they planned to leave. "A lot of people had some pretty wild, unbelievable tales about him. But otherwise, he sounds like he might be Devrand." She deliberately kept her voice low, although the noise in the room probably meant they would not be overheard.

"One of the Keepers told me that they're finishing gathering up all Magicka family members. They're taking them to the Imperial Capital, he claimed, but no one knows anything beyond that," Alorsha said.

"Then we'll find my brother and friends there," Gya said.

Mikolus shifted in his chair next to Alorsha. "He's gathering these Magickas to himself, isn't he? Like he's done before."

Alorsha nodded, her expression one of misery. "I'm afraid that's so." She looked at Gya. "Where does the kristone come from?"

Gya gave her a surprised look at the change in subject. "It's passed down in the families, much as the sigil codices are. I've heard that Magickas used to also find more, sometime a long time ago, in certain caves, but I've never heard where those caves might be. Or how to find them. Some stories claim they were hidden or buried."

A commotion at the door drew their attention. Parl and Kluir hurried in, along with a few townsfolk who spread out in the room and spoke urgently to the people already there. Kluir and Parl rushed to their companions.

"You'd better come see this," Parl said in a low voice, his tone urgent, too. He spoke mainly to Alorsha, but his stance took in Mikolus as well.

As they rose to follow, many of the inn's customers also headed to the door.

"At least we'll not stand out too much in our curiosity," Mikolus murmured.

Parl led them through narrow streets toward the southwest portion of the town. As they got closer, Gya heard shouting.

Parl stopped them at a corner and eased around. "Best stay back here." He let them follow him just a step around the corner.

About a block ahead of them was a small market square. The shops had closed for the evening, but people thronged it, townsfolk and what looked like all the Keepers of the town. Some of the townsfolk hovered at the edges of the square as Gya and his companions did. Others huddled within the encircling Keepers, perhaps thirty townsfolk there, families. With weapons drawn, the Keepers forced the huddled townsfolk into three small, crowded carts that stood on the far side of the square, stuffing far too many people into them.

As Gya watched, one man approached the Keepers, waving his arms and apparently protesting their actions. Two of the Keepers slapped him with the flats of their swords and, over the protests of the woman who had been with him, beat him to the ground. Then they hauled him to his feet and dumped him into one of the carts, where he moved feebly. Gya winced at the sounds of pleading voices and crying children. He started toward them, but Mikolus blocked him.

"Too many for us to help here." Mikolus kept his voice low. "Starting anything will likely get too ugly and harm those we want to help."

He drew Gya's attention to the surrounding townsfolk who stood in the various streets that led to this square and blocked them completely. Only a few looked concerned, fear and sorrow in their expressions. Most of those gathered there seemed jubilant and cheered the Keepers on. The cheering grew louder when one of the Keepers lifted a fallen child and tossed him into a cart with no regard for his wails of fear or the people he landed on.

"It won't take much to turn this into something far worse," Mikolus said. "To turn those onlookers into attackers." Gya miserably nodded his understanding.

Mikolus sent Hali and Kluir back to the inn to get their horses and gear. The two ran off while Alorsha, Parl, Gya and Mikolus eased back to distance themselves further from the Keepers and the townsfolk who supported their actions.

"Families of Magickas?" Alorsha nodded to the people

crowded into the three inadequate carts.

"Can't tell by looking," Mikolus said.

"I heard lots of talk of 'the Blighted' earlier," Parl said.

Gya stepped back, shaking, unable to watch any longer. *That could have been him. It still could be if they were discovered.* He sank down against the wall.

What seemed like hours later—but Gya felt certain was not nearly that long—Kluir and Hali returned with their horses and packs. They stopped further away from the square and the crowd there.

Mikolus urged everyone over to wait with the horses. Hali knelt next to Gya and spoke softly to him, but he did not hear her words. His thoughts whirled, and his insides, too.

He wanted to help those people but feared discovery. *What could he do anyway, really?* He was the poorest Magicka, unable to work many of the sigils and fumbling most of the others. *What made him think he could even help Toa and Chizoa and the others?* Gya dropped his head to his hands and wished he could stop hearing the horrible sounds from the square.

Again a long time passed, so it felt to Gya, before the sounds around the corner faded, accompanied by the sounds of carts rolling across the cobblestone streets.

"They're headed southwest," Mikolus said.

"Isn't the Imperial Capital still south of us?" Kluir said.

Gya did not realize that had been directed at him until Alorsha knelt next to him and repeated the question. He roused himself enough to nod. "Roughly, anyway."

"Maybe the road curves around and goes more to the south after they're out of town," Hali said.

"We'll find out," Alorsha said. "Can we safely head out now?

Mikolus nodded. "Mount up."

They walked the horses through the square, empty of people, but littered with belongings. The Keepers had let their prisoners keep very little with them.

"Shouldn't we...?" Gya waved a hand at the scattered goods.

Mikolus shook his head.

"Lives have to take priority," Hali murmured.

Gya nodded and watched Alorsha lean from her mount to grab one small bag from the ground.

He gave her a questioning look.

She flipped open the top of the bag to show him two thin books that were certainly codices of sigils, and the pouches so like his that held his crystals and kri-stone powders. She tucked the bag away in her pack behind her.

Gya looked around. "Are there others dropped here?"

"That's the only one I spotted," she said.

They continued to walk the horses to the edge of town, to avoid drawing any unwanted attention. At the gate, the Keepers checked their tokens—which they wore again for that purpose—and wished them a good journey. They warned the group to stay well back from the carts that transported the Blighted and seemed satisfied with the assurances that Mikolus gave them.

After they were out of sight of the Keepers, and on the packed dirt of the roads between towns rather than on cobblestone, Mikolus urged the horses to a faster pace.

"We don't want to get too close," he said. "But we need to be close enough to see what's what, to see our opportunity."

"So we *are* going to help?" Gya said, hope and fear alike grasping him.

"To do so, we have to make sure that it's a time and place that will truly help and not make matters worse." Mikolus took the lead.

It took little time to reach a point from which they could see the dust from the carts. Mikolus had them slow, then, and rode a little closer himself. He rejoined them a short time later.

"They have ten Keepers," he told them. "Three of them drive the carts. Looks like they're still going to travel for a while, so we'll just follow along back here for now."

"What of the people in the carts?" Gya said.

"They're as well as can be expected," Mikolus said. "Good enough for now."

"We're still going southwest," Hali said. "I don't think they're taking them to the capital."

"Wonder where they're headed, then," Alorsha said.

They followed the carts, the dust really, until the sun set. Mikolus had them wait again while he rode ahead.

"They're still going," he said when he returned. "We'll have to listen more carefully for them as we lose light and can't see the dust."

"I've got a sigil that'll let me see in the dark with my seeing-stone," Gya said in a low voice.

Mikolus smiled. "Perfect. Please do the magic and ride in front with me."

Gya needed just a few minutes to work the magic, then he rode next to Mikolus and looked through his seeing-stone to follow the dust that hung in the air. A portion of his attention lingered on the road behind them, though, as he half-expected to hear Keepers coming for him at any moment.

After a time, the motion of the horse's walk soothed Gya and dulled his fear of being followed. He fell into a kind of daze but startled awake whenever the horse's gait changed even slightly or when his arm started to fall.

Roughly two hours after sunset, well into the full dark of night, Mikolus halted everyone.

"I no longer hear the carts," he said.

Parl slid off his horse. "I'll go see." He disappeared into the darkness.

Gya let his hand drop into his lap, hoping to ease the cramp from holding the stone up for so long. Mikolus gave him a sympathetic look and slid off his horse.

Alorsha followed his example. "We might as well take a little rest while we wait for Parl." She dug out some of their dried food and began to eat.

Gya dismounted and stretched out on his back in the grass at the side of the road. Bushes ran close to the road at this point, with thin trees beyond. He groaned softly as he stretched stiff muscles.

Perhaps a quarter of an hour later Parl returned.

"They're setting up camp," he reported. "With little regard for their captives," he added with disgust clear in his tone.

Mikolus rose from where he had been seated eating. "Let's move off into the trees while they're still making noise over there. Might be they'll not notice any we make."

He and Parl led them in a wide arc around the spot just off the road where the Keepers had set up their camp. Gya caught glimpses through the trees of a large fire with people gathered around, Keepers he assumed, and the carts together off to one side. The best he could tell, all the captives were still in the carts.

After they had circled the Keepers and carts and put some distance between them and themselves, Mikolus found a small clearing in which to make camp. Alorsha worked some magic with the plants to cover any traces of their path to that point.

"No fire," Alorsha told Gya as everyone cared for the hoses. He nodded his understanding. Too risky that the Keepers might spot it.

With some of the dried food they carried with them and waterskins, they found places to sit.

"So we'll wait for the Keepers to go to sleep so we can free those poor people, right?" Gya asked.

Alorsha and Mikolus exchanged looks. The other three glanced at them and then looked away, at the ground or their feet, every one of them.

"We can't always help everyone," Mikolus murmured. "As Saevalde has said."

Alorsha frowned.

"We can't just let the Keepers haul them wherever they're going. To whatever dire fate they have planned for them," Gya added when no one said anything.

"And what do we do with them after we've freed them?" Mikolus said. "They'll have to go somewhere. Not back to their town, I think. They'll need supplies, then. And we have just enough for ourselves."

"What of the food and whatever the Keepers carry?" Gya said. "I'd say they owe it to their captives. They can take that and flee somewhere safe. They'll probably know someplace – they live in this area, after all."

"The Keepers are carrying little enough with them," Parl said. "Maybe food enough for another couple of days, at most. And not much for their captives, from what I saw."

"Maybe they're going to wherever your friend and brother are," Kluir said to Gya.

"Freeing them now is a risk. To our purpose, certainly." Mikolus gave Alorsha a stern look. "It could be too much of a risk of bringing ourselves to unwanted attention. Burdening us with people we can't really help beyond a certain point. And that risks them, too. We can follow for a time. Maybe find where they're going and see if your people are there." He nodded to Gya. "Learn more rather than just haphazardly doing something."

"I don't like the thought of those people packed into those carts," Alorsha said.

"I don't either," Mikolus said. "But hasty action right now might lead to worse results. For everyone."

With another frown, Alorsha nodded. "We'll watch and follow, then. For now. It's not unreasonable to think they'll end up somewhere where we can learn more to help our purpose, too."

She gazed at Gya then until he reluctantly nodded.

When everyone had finished eating, they settled as well as they could manage for the rest of the night, with Mikolus, Hali, Kluir and Parl making arrangements for at least one of them to always be awake.

Alorsha sat near Gya and handed him the bag she had

retrieved. "Maybe something in there of use, if you don't mind taking a look at the sigils. But do rest, too." She wrapped herself in a cloak and stretched out.

Gya shifted his position until he sat in a patch of moonlight and flipped through the two codices from the bag. The first held the simplest of sigils, ones that he already knew from his own codices, but the second held much more elaborate sigils. He lost track of time as he worked his way through the codex, taking his time to study each sigil there. It was a thin volume, but what he found was extremely valuable.

He dug through his pack to find pen and ink and made copies and notes of the most useful sigils he found. He filled many of the blank pages at the back of his own sigil codices and had nearly completed his copying when Parl awakened Mikolus to switch with him for watching the camp. Mikolus peered at what Gya was doing and did not interrupt.

Gya finished copying the last sigil and some notes about it then tucked the codex back in its bag and returned his own codices and writing implements to his pack. With a nod to the other man, Gya stretched out to get some sleep.

CHAPTER 24

ELSEWHERE IN THE ATTUREI EMPIRE

Arizu smiled a greeting to the man at her door. "You came," she murmured.

Dev reached out and brushed her cheek with his fingers, although he did not smile. His gesture soothed her lingering worries, but she had hoped that seeing her again after so many long days apart would make him smile.

"You have news?" She drew him inside as she frowned out at the primitive arrangements around her building and Dev's ever-present companion who dropped to the ground nearby. Then she closed both out behind the door.

Dev nodded and this time she got her smile. Still, it was not the smile she had hoped for. This one looked more satisfied and almost feral, rather than pleased at her presence. There was also something about his eyes. A strange wisp of darkness flowed across both eyes, there and gone again. He caught her hand in a warm clasp, and odd smiles and wisps of darkness no longer concerned her.

"It looks promising." He caught her other hand. "Early signs are very auspicious, and the process is moving quickly enough."

"But isn't this linking too risky? What if the Magickas break free? Turn on us?"

Dev chuckled, a low sound that thrummed right through her. "Not to worry. They won't. They can't."

He lifted her hands, still clasped in his, and brushed his lips across the backs of her fingers.

She smiled in contentment. *Of course he had everything in hand. Those Magickas would learn, if they had not already, that he was in control. They would not cross him. That would be the height of foolishness. Even those dregs of the Empire would know that.*

With a gentle tug, she led Dev to the small table where she had already laid out some of the Empire's most delectable dishes in preparation for his arrival. He still clasped one of her hands as he pulled her close to squeeze into a single chair with him. He nodded toward the food.

She selected one morsel and fed it to him. At his nod and expression of pleasure, she fed him another bite and waited for him to finish that one. "So you *are* going to find where the crystals come from?"

"I am. The setup is nearly complete. I'm close to having enough to locate those caves. Your Keepers had all the information, the knowledge that the kri-stone all retained a connection of sorts. But they failed to find a way to truly use that knowledge, aside from keeping track of some people. I've been able to go so far beyond them with this linking. It's now just a matter of time to solidify enough links."

"And you'll be able to do so much more after. That's what you've told the Council, right? You'll do something amazing?"

Dev's disturbing smile returned, but Arizu did not notice it. "Oh yes. I do promise something amazing."

CHAPTER 25

Much too early the next morning, Gya woke to someone shaking his shoulder. He swatted at the hand and Hali chuckled.

"Time to get going," she said. "Parl's been watching the Keepers and their prisoners and just told us they're getting ready to move."

Grumbling to himself, Gya grabbed his stuff and scrambled onto his horse, which someone had tacked up already for him. Then he ate more of their dried provisions, some meat strips and hard bread, while he tried to finish waking up in the dawn light.

The day passed slowly as they again followed the dust of the carts, first along the road, then turning aside on a trail not much better than a path. It headed more west than south.

Those they followed did not set a fast pace, and did not stop for meals or rest. So neither did they.

Again when the Keepers stopped for the night, they set their own camp at some distance from them. While the others settled the horses and refilled waterskins from a small nearby stream, Parl went to have a look at the Keepers and their captives. He had nothing new to tell the others when he returned, so they ate and settled themselves for the night, with both Alorsha and Gya taking turns watching the camp with the others.

Morning was largely a repeat of the previous day. Gya joined the others to pack up to move on. He munched the food Kluir passed him as they worked but did not pay much attention to what he ate. Some kind of dried fruit. And they resumed following the dust raised by the carts and Keepers.

Near midafternoon, Mikolus led them off the side of the path and into the trees, where he called a halt and dismounted. Parl slid off his horse, too, and the two of them moved further into the trees after they waved at the others to stay put. They returned before Gya had time to grow too nervous.

"They've come to some sort of enclosure and looked to be unloading their captives there. We'll set up over there." Mikolus pointed roughly southeast. "They're off that direction." He pointed southwest. "We'll need to watch a bit to decide what to do."

His voice had an odd note to it and Gya wondered what caused it.

They made their way through the forest the direction Mikolus had indicated. They moved as quietly as possible while riding horses, startling a couple of rabbits and ground squirrels and a few birds from their path as they went. Parl found a sort of narrow trail that took them southeast, more or less. The going was better following it, but still slow.

After roughly a quarter hour of this, Mikolus picked out a spot for their camp, with a brook nearby, and they dismounted there. Parl stayed with the horses while Mikolus took the others through the trees to look at the enclosure.

They stopped at a rock outcrop and crawled to the top

of it to look out through the trees.

Below them, in a slight valley among these low hills, sat several long, plain, wooden buildings. A fence of rough wooden planks encircled the buildings. Gya counted four Keepers who paced along the fence, a sturdy-looking structure at least as tall as Mikolus, but with numerous narrow gaps between the boards that made it possible to see through to the interior. The area within the fence had been cleared of trees, although stumps remained, and the grasses had been worn down, in some places completely to the bare dirt. The Keepers who had been with the carts had their captives lined up near those conveyances.

Further within the enclosure, other Keepers ordered other small groups of people about. The groups seemed to be divided men and women, and they looked to be working on something, following the instructions of a leader with them. Everyone except the Keepers wore clothes little better than rags. When the wind shifted, Gya caught a foul odor from the enclosure.

As they watched, the Keepers with the carts separated their captives, men from women from children, and took each group to a different building, against their protests, sometimes having to drag people there as they struggled against the separation. They barred the door to the small building into which they shoved the children, while two of the enclosure's Keepers took positions outside the doors to the other two buildings that held the new captives. Gya could hear the children's cries from where he hid. He reached for his bag with its crystals and powder, but Mikolus's hand on his stopped him.

Mikolus shook his head. "No better risk than back at that square." He barely voiced the words. "We must wait and watch to judge if we might help."

Gya scowled but nodded.

The Keepers who had brought the carts chatted with a couple of enclosure Keepers for a time, then looked like they were preparing to stay the night, at least.

After watching a little longer, Mikolus shooed Gya and the others back down behind the rocks and they headed back to their own camp. Alorsha again used the plants to cover any traces that they left of their passage.

"What were they doing?" Hali asked in a soft voice when they had moved far enough away that it was safe to talk. "The ones who were already there."

"It sort of looked like practicing the magic," Gya said. "But not in any way I've seen before."

"They're certainly not keeping their captives in good condition," Kluir said.

"Keep them weak, keep them under control," Mikolus said.

Alorsha glanced at Gya. "How well does your magic work if you're exhausted or injured?"

"Not well at all. But it's still possible to work it."

"No one knew about this?" Hali's tone was incredulous.

Gya shrugged. "Not that I ever heard of. But, of course, the Empire knows. Certainly at least some of the Keepers, too. The Empire's been taking Magickas from their homes for a long time now."

"But didn't you wonder where they took those people? Didn't anyone ever try to find out?" Hali said.

"Of course we wondered. But we didn't dare try to learn anything. The Keepers made examples of those few who did. The lucky ones recovered. The others didn't, or they disappeared." Gya looked down at his feet. "We all learned quickly to fear trying to learn anything or do anything. Pretty much everyone who's not a Keeper is afraid of catching their attention. Their attention's never a good thing."

"From what I noticed in Hawei, and other towns, the Empire excels at employing fear to keep control of all of you," Mikolus said. "And to divide you, too. Fear of other groups turns you easily against them. Then they claim one group is the cause of all the problems and everyone else follows along with whatever they decide to do in the name of keeping everyone safe, and also to distance themselves from that one group."

Gya nodded sadly. "A good description. And too few to fight it, so what can we do?"

"Perhaps not much for the whole Empire," Alorsha said. "That will need the citizens to act. But perhaps we can manage some small help here."

"Back to our camp first," Mikolus said.

There Gya watched Alorsha check on Devrand's location. When the pendant snapped out parallel to the ground and wavered back and forth, as usual, it pointed roughly toward the enclosure.

"Doesn't mean he's there, though," she muttered. "He could be somewhere further beyond it."

"Any sense that we're getting closer?" Mikolus asked her when she finished working with the magic.

"No. And I would have expected something now, I think. Since he's not seemed to move much."

"Might he have found a way to block you?" Gya said. "Like that door blocks me from seeing Chizoa?"

Mikolus cursed softly and Alorsha nodded, with a frown, as she tucked her pendant away again. "Maybe he has," she said. "Although, there have been times before when I didn't feel any change in the nearness of his magic." She shook her head.

"Maybe I should try to see Toa and my friends again?" Gya said. "Maybe they're there and if so, maybe being closer will make a difference in seeing beyond the doors."

"Can other Magickas tell if someone is working your kind of magic nearby?" Mikolus said.

Gya thought about that a moment and shook his head. "Not that I've ever heard of. I've only been able to feel it if I'm very close to someone. Within just a couple of paces or so. Sometimes."

"Worth the tiny risk, then," Alorsha said.

Gya filled his bowl with water from the brook and

drew the sigil for the seeing magic in the air above the bowl.

The images came quickly, with him so practiced at the magic. But he *still* only saw a door when he tried to see Chizoa or Ifeoma or Vabena. However, he managed a glimpse of Toa in a room. This time, Gya saw the edge of a table near Toa, along with what looked like a sigils codex. He tried to see the codex more clearly, but the image fragmented and yet another door appeared and obscured it.

He let the images go. At least Toa had looked healthy and unharmed. "The wood of the doors looks *somewhat* like the wood of those buildings." He shrugged. "Maybe."

They turned their attention then to finishing setting up their camp.

"We've got to free the Magickas there," Gya said as they settled down later to another cold meal.

"I'm concerned that we might not be able to," Alorsha said, "with so many guards."

"We also can't trust that the Magickas won't use magic against us," Hali pointed out. "Like in Hawei."

Gya frowned but nodded.

"Can't you do something with the plants? Like you've done before?" Gya waved a hand in the general direction of the path they had taken to the enclosure, now devoid of traces of their passage.

"This enclosure is too big," Alorsha said. "I could hold maybe a third of it. Maybe. We'd have the rest on us with swords, maybe the sigil magic, and who knows what else."

"I'd like to try to see if any of the people we seek are here," Mikolus said. "Since the magic seems unable to tell us that, we'll need to do some normal sneaking and spying. We can also see what we can learn of the place to decide if it's possible to free them somehow."

Before going to sleep, Gya worked the pendant wayfinding magic for both Chizoa and Toa. Both pendants indicated the same general direction as Alorsha's had—

toward the enclosure—although with wider arcs than hers, as usual. Mikolus watched and noted the directions with a nod.

As the magic slipped away from Gya, just like before, a strange twinge struck him, a spark of magic from somewhere nearby. *Kri-stone magic?* But when he tried to focus on it, it vanished. Try as he might, he could not find it again, or even a hint of it, to be able to guess where it came from.

With a sigh, Gya tucked everything away again and settled in to try to sleep, vaguely aware of Mikolus slipping away from the camp into the dark forest.

~ ~ ~

The next day, they took turns observing the enclosure, with Parl watching the most while Mikolus prowled the forest around them and the enclosure. Kluir and Hali seemed to lounge while keeping watch on their own camp and Alorsha gathered and examined leaves, twigs and roots from every plant around them.

Gya looked through all his sigil codices to try to find anything that might help. He also reviewed the notes he had copied from the other codex and made some additional comments in places he had not copied well enough. He found a few possibilities among the codices, but really only one that he felt able to manage any time soon, not counting an easy sigil for unlocking that he felt he could work with no problems. He refreshed his memory of a sleep sigil he had learned some weeks ago but never really used and the trap sigil that he and Chizoa had worked on together.

He closed his eyes against an unexpected wave of uneasiness that surged through him at the thought of Chizoa. *He longed to see her again, hear her laugh, feel the touch of her hand. What did that cursed door mean that he saw when he tried to see her?* He hoped that she was all right.

He stared at the codex of sigils in his hands and took a deep breath to calm himself. *He would find her somewhere beyond that door. She would be fine.* Learning all he could, as fast as he could, would help. Another deep breath and he was ready again to get back to it.

When he tired of puzzling over more new sigils, Gya decided to practice and perfect those two sigils he already could do, at least somewhat. As for the new one that he had found, it was more complex than any he had accomplished alone so far. *But he could do it, couldn't he?* It would cause anyone who stepped on it to become confused. *That had the potential to be helpful.* From what he had copied from that codex Alorsha had picked up in Farhani, the sigil should be able to affect more than one person. *Even better.* So he worked on that one, too.

Sometime in the afternoon, he became aware that Alorsha watched him. He finished the last swirl on the sigil he was working on and gave her a questioning look.

"My wayfinding this morning again pointed toward the enclosure, but because I can't tell the distance to Devrand, I can't say that he's in that place," Alorsha said. "From where we are, can you tell me what might lie beyond the enclosure?"

Gya pondered her question. *Too bad he'd given the map to Ayaru. Should've thought to make a copy to keep for himself.* He glanced at the shadows from the sun to help him make a guess at the direction and frowned as he pictured what he could remember of the map.

"I'm not certain. I think we've come around enough that northwest is that direction. If it is, there are a few other towns of the Empire, and… Hawei also lies that way."

Now Alorsha frowned, too.

"I wonder…" she muttered as she wandered off in thought.

Gya finished his last sigil without success and realized he was too tired to work the magic well. So no point in continuing. He put away his kri-stone and the sigil codices and paced the camp a few minutes to loosen muscles held too long in one position. He grabbed the bag that contained the codices they had retrieved from the square and carried it over to Alorsha, holding it out to her. "I meant to give this back to you earlier."

Alorsha shook her head, with a smile. "Why don't you hold it for its true owner."

He nodded agreement and returned the bag to his pack with his own codices. Then he knelt by Alorsha, who had returned to her plants.

"Are you trying to find some magic that we can work to help?"

Alorsha nodded slightly. "Essentially."

"Can I help somehow?"

She studied him before she reached out to him. "Here." She handed him a few small round leaves, pale yellow-green with veins of a deep, dark green. "Do you know this plant?"

"I've no idea what it is."

"See if you can touch its magic, see what it can do."

Gya gave her a wide-eyed look. "How?"

"Remember how you touched the magic in the *Deliberia*. See if you can do that here."

Gya gave her a startled look. He had been alone when he had touched *Deliberia*'s magic.

She smiled at his expression. "When I'm on the ship, I can feel anything or anyone touching *Deliberia*'s magic. What did you feel?"

"Uh, a tingling in my fingers where they touched the wall. Maybe something brushed my arm. I felt much the same sensation when I fixed the hatch during the storm. You know about that, don't you?"

Alorsha smiled and nodded. "I should have thanked you long before this."

She turned her attention back to the leaves. "Remember what those sensations felt like. Remember what you saw when you looked at the *Deliberia* through your seeing-stone. Holding onto those memories, focus your attention on the leaves in your hand. Try to ignore anything else."

Gya followed her instructions and examined the leaves. They were pretty, softer than he had thought most leaves were. But nothing else. He remembered that Alorsha often closed her eyes when she worked to touch other magics, so he closed his.

In the darkness behind his eyelids, the leaves slowly came into view. But not as they looked in his hands. In this darkness, he saw a glow similar to what he had seen in the *Deliberia*. Fainter. A different color. This glow nearly matched the green of the leaves. Then, as if he had just opened his eyes, had just awakened from a deep sleep, the magic was there. He felt it. Not much like how it felt when he worked with the sigils. But similar enough that it felt comfortable, familiar. He realized that Alorsha had rested her hand on his arm.

He gave her a startled look again.

"Giving you a little help this time," she said. "I can draw to the surface and enhance magics from plants. Sometimes, I can also help other mages feel the plants' magic, if I touch them."

"So I can see the magic in the leaves now, and feel it. But I can't tell what it will do."

She smiled. "That comes with practice and time, just as with your sigil magic."

They brushed the leaves from his hand to hers. "These will calm someone. If they are upset or agitated. Not a lot, from first look, but still something that can be useful."

She gestured at the plants she had laid out on the ground and explained what the magic in each would do. Then she had Gya feel and see the magic in each one.

"Now, this one," she laid her hand on some branches with pale leaves and tiny purple berries. "This one will make a person very sick if eaten, even if I don't bring out its magic. But with its magic brought forth, the person will be incapacitated for a day or more, but recover completely after another couple of days, I think. With no lasting effects."

She met his gaze.

"If we could get that into the guards' food…" Gya said.

Alorsha nodded. "Of course, that would be the difficult part."

"What of this one?" Gya pointed to a neat pile of some brown-green leaves. "I think I felt that this would… affect what a person sees? Maybe bring on visions? If burnt, perhaps?"

Alorsha smiled and nodded. "Very good. Another that's also potentially useful, with the problem of making sure only the people we wanted affected got in the smoke."

Gya gave this some thought. "I remember you told me you can't adjust the wind, but would you be able to make a slight breeze?"

Alorsha shook her head with a grin. "Unfortunately not."

"But there *is* the fog," Mikolus said and Gya jumped. He had not realized the man had joined them.

Alorsha nodded. "Between the stream here, and all the plants, there should be enough moisture for me to work with. Not as good as at sea but might still be good enough."

Mikolus rose. "Let's all talk while we eat and see what we can come up with."

~ ~ ~

That night they had a small fire, since the slight breeze blew from the enclosure to them, and Kluir cooked some fish he had caught from the stream. As soon as he no longer needed the fire, they put it out.

They gathered close to eat and talk.

Gya and Alorsha told them of the magics they had found that might be of use, both Alorsha's plants and Gya's sigils. Then Parl and Mikolus spoke of what they had learned of the enclosure.

"As we saw yesterday, the men and women are held in different buildings," Parl said. "Men in the buildings to the right of the gate, women in those to the left. I saw no children other than those they brought in with the carts."

"The three buildings straight in from the gate, at the back of the enclosure, seem to be reserved to the Keepers," Mikolus said. "At least, I only saw Keepers enter and leave those. The additional Keepers from the town are still in the enclosure, and they brought out some food from one of those buildings. I'd like to get a closer look at the buildings after dark."

"Is that wise?" Hali said.

"Perhaps not," Mikolus said. "But they had far fewer Keepers out and about after dark last night than during the day. I counted six. Assuming the same is true tonight, Parl and I might be able to slip into the enclosure and get an idea of the interior of all those buildings. They do all have windows, with nothing blocking them."

When Alorsha gave him a look, he grinned. "Yes, both Parl and I took a look last night. But neither of us entered the enclosure."

"So we still need a closer look to see what might be possible," Parl said.

"Can the rest of us help at all?" Hali said.

Mikolus shook his head. "Parl is best at this sneaky stuff. I'm the next best. That's enough to risk right now."

Parl waved a hand at the small piles of plants that Alorsha had left spread out nearby. "Anything in these new plants to let a fellow become invisible?"

Alorsha smiled mysteriously and pulled two small vials out of a pocket. "Not invisible, but I *was* able to pull out magic from one of them that can help you go unnoticed, like you belong there. I've been able to make only the two doses, so far. Each will last about an hour after swallowed." She handed the vials to Mikolus, who was closer, and he passed one to Parl.

Her grin turned impish. "I'll apologize now for the taste. It's absolutely horrible. But I've not had the time to find what I can mix in to help with that."

Parl wrinkled his nose at her and muttered, "The horror."

But then he smiled. "An hour is good. Wait until the dead of night when most of them are not out and about and we should have plenty of time to see what we need."

Mikolus nodded agreement. "Watches as usual tonight. Gya and Alorsha first this time, so you can be well rested for any magics we might need tomorrow."

CHAPTER 26

In the morning, they gathered together, with a cold meal this time, to learn what Parl and Mikolus had discovered during the night.

"The buildings where they're holding the Magickas have only one large room on the inside, with mats for sleeping," Parl told them. "One door each, which is barred at night. Two guards at the gate who change roughly every four hours, and they're not precise about the timing."

"From the way all of them move, I'd say roughly half of these Keepers are good enough with their blades to worry us. That's too many to consider doing something openly," Mikolus said. "The buildings at the back of the enclosure opposite the gate are divided into rooms with a hallway running the front length of the building. A single door into each building and one door for each room. They were all closed so I couldn't see in any of the rooms, no windows there. Windows into the hallway only. One roaming guard who walked from building to building and checked the doors of the rooms inside, which all seemed locked."

Mikolus turned to Gya. "Don't get your hopes up, but the doors *do* resemble what we've seen when you try to see your people."

Gya nodded. He understood Mikolus's point, but he could not contain his smile at the thought that Chizoa might be that close.

"Can you make enough of those 'we belong here' potions for all of us?" Kluir asked Alorsha.

"I'll work on that today," she said, then looked to Mikolus. "Assuming we're doing something tonight?"

He nodded.

"How many sigils can you draw and use in, say, about an hour?" Hali asked Gya.

"Part of it depends on which ones we want to use, and how. If I'm floating one through the air, with the concentration I need for that, I doubt I can begin another without losing the first. Of course, I can wait until it's done its magic before I work on the next. The sigils I draw on the ground stay and work until people walk across them, however many the sigil is set up to affect. As far as I know, they won't vanish or lose their effectiveness if I begin another sigil."

"What of yourself?" Alorsha said. "Every piece of magic takes something out of me until I'm exhausted, if I let it go that far."

Gya nodded. "Same for me. I don't actually know how much I can do how fast before I'm unable to focus enough to work the sigils. I've done three in an hour before and still felt able to continue, although none of those was one of the 'in the air' types."

"Can you be ready for three, then?" Mikolus asked. "On the ground certainly, and whichever you feel you can best do in the air."

Gya nodded.

"What of that seeing-stone?" Kluir said. "The one to let you see in the dark? Can someone without magic see thorough it?"

Gya shrugged. "I don't know. We can test that tonight before we go, though."

Mikolus looked around at the small group. "We'll do as much preparing, and magic practicing and testing as we can get done during the morning hours. Maybe an hour or two after the midday meal, too. After that, rest as much of the afternoon and evening as possible."

"As much as doesn't drive us crazy, anyway," Hali muttered, drawing grins from the others.

Mikolus agreed. "We'll also pack up, including making sure the horses are ready to go. We'll see about getting those people out of there after the moons set."

"Some hours after sunset," Kluir said.

Everyone looked to Alorsha, who nodded her agreement with the plan. "Count me out of weapons-work this morning. I'll need the time for my magic."

He nodded and led the others, minus Gya too, away from their camp, and further from the enclosure, for some weapons-work. Gya moved to a clear space at the other side of their camp to work on his sigils. But from time to time, he watched Alorsha gather more plants and make them into potions, sometimes using a tiny fire.

While he took a break from the magic about mid-morning, Gya watched some of the weapons-work, awed by what he saw. With no need to teach any other crewmembers or allow for their lack of knowledge or experience, Mikolus, Hali, Parl, and Kluir sparred with a speed and skill that was nothing short of amazing.

Gya had not been around warriors much before, had certainly not seen them when they faced their fellows who were as accomplished as they. He had no doubt that they, at least, would be able to accomplish their goal that night.

Later that afternoon, even tired as he was after his work to learn the sigils, Gya had trouble resting. He worried whether he would be able to do *his* part that night. *What if he messed up a sigil? Or, worse probably, stepped on a twig?* He had no illusions that he could be as silent as Mikolus or

Parl.

He tried to reassure himself that they could do this, that *he* could do this. The others carried those flintlocks, although they had not practiced with them recently. Still, Gya had seen them on the ship. All of them hit the targets more often than not. *Those could make a big difference even being outnumbered as they were.*

Gya rolled over and told himself firmly that he needed to get some sleep. A short time later, he rolled over again, frustrated.

He jumped when someone touched his shoulder.

"Let's walk a bit," Mikolus said in a soft voice and offered him a hand up.

They stopped a short distance away from the camp, where the others seemed to be resting well, and Mikolus turned to him.

"It's normal to be nervous before something like this."

Gya nodded but gave him a look full of misery before he blurted out his thoughts, surprising himself but unable to stop. "What if I bungle it? I might draw the sigils wrong and not be able to call the magic. Or I'll trip on something and alert all their guards."

"We'll adapt." Mikolus gave the younger man's shoulder a comforting squeeze. "We start with a plan, but anticipate that things won't go as we thought, or hoped. Prepare yourself to be flexible, expect that things won't go as planned, try to be as ready as possible. We can't do much more than that."

"I suppose." Gya frowned at his shoes. "Have you done much of this sort of thing?"

Mikolus chuckled softly. "Not exactly. I'm more accustomed to being on the defending side. Still, I think we can make this work. Especially at night with many of them asleep."

Gya nodded. "I just wish I could keep all the what-ifs from twisting my thoughts into knots."

"That's a problem, true. Everyone finds their own way

to deal with that sort of headache. Might be you can try looking at each what-if by itself and come up with one or two things to do for it."

"So that's what you do?"

"That it is. A lot of the time. It helps me feel that perhaps I'll be ready for whatever way something will go wrong."

He grinned at Gya, who managed a chuckle.

"Just try to run through them only once. Don't keep going over them. Then try to get some real rest."

They headed back to their camp. "I'll try," Gya said.

~~~

They did not have a fire for the evening meal, so their meal was cold again. Not that Gya really noticed as they discussed what they hoped to accomplish that night.

"What magics have you decided on?" Mikolus looked to Alorsha and Gya.

Gya shrugged. "I've got a sigil that I know how to do that will trap someone who walks across it. Although I've not set it up by myself before. And I found another one for confusion. Works much the same way."

"Those could be useful," Kluir said. "Put them where Keepers will likely step on them."

"How many will they affect?" Alorsha said.

Gya gave that some thought. "As many as five for the trap sigil, from the description. But I've not tested the truth of that. I *do* have the kri-stone to create two of them. For the confusion sigil, it didn't say."

"Hold those ready, then. What else?" Mikolus looked to Alorsha.

She grinned. "Two things. There are the plants, of course. While the grasses are meager, I can still do something with them. Just in small patches, though. And then I've got something that will make a person sleep, long and deep. Maybe avoid having to fight, and avoid possibly being seen and identified. But it requires touch."

"I've also got a sigil to cause someone to sleep," Gya said. "There's a way to cast it from a distance. It doesn't last for long, maybe an hour, but could still help."

"Do you have what you need to do it?" Mikolus said.

Gya nodded. "But I've not done the distance version of it before. But now I understand how it is supposed to work, after seeing those Magickas draw their sigils in the air when they attacked the *Deliberia*."

"How sure are you that you can do this?" Mikolus asked.

Gya swallowed and looked around at all of them looking at him. "Pretty certain. I've gotten it to work, just not the extra part of being at a distance."

Mikolus glanced at Alorsha, who nodded.

"I'd say use it on sentries," she said. "We can use my salve on those who are already asleep to keep them that way."

"We'll hold the trap magic in reserve, I think," Mikolus said. "Wouldn't do for one of us to accidentally run across it in the dark. Same for the confusion. How long do you need to set up for the sleep sigil?"

"Several minutes. But I need to be able to see the person I want to send to sleep."

Mikolus nodded. "We'll all go to the enclosure. Spread out around it. Parl, stay with Gya. Gya, do you have to work this sigil again to catch another person?"

Gya considered that. "I'll draw it in the air and send it to the person to affect. It goes in a straight line, so if I can be where more than one person would be lined up for me, and they're not too far apart, I think I can send it to affect them before it breaks apart too much to be effective. It will affect three people, at most."

"We'll see if we can get you into a position for that, then," Mikolus said. "Downing any sentries is our first task. Then we see if those rooms in the far three buildings hold any of Gya's people."

"And we free the others," Gya added.

Mikolus gave him a long look, then looked to Alorsha.

"I don't see that it'll increase our risk," she said. "Not at this point. If we are able to free them, I don't see that we can leave them here. They'll have the food from that one building to get away."

"And away to where?" Mikolus frowned. "We can't take them with us."

"Why can't *they* decide where to go?" Gya said. "Once they're free from the Keepers. Why do we have to plan it for them?"

"It's unthorough," Mikolus muttered.

"But not unreasonable," Alorsha said. "We know it's unlikely this will go to plan, so why not see where it does go?"

"Well, with some little plan in place, anyway," Hali said with a grin.

Mikolus acquiesced with a slight nod.

"We'll need to wait a bit for the guards to settle in for the night. That will offer us our best chance," Kluir said.

"Pack up camp as much as we can and then rest again until time," Alorsha said.

After they packed everything, ready to go, they settled back to wait for the moons to set.

"Nap if you can," Parl told Gya in passing. "The rest of the night is likely to be a bit lively." He plopped onto the ground nearby and seemed to go right to sleep.

Gya saw the others, except for Hali, settle in to rest. She smiled at him and set herself to watch.

CHAPTER 27

Taps on Gya's shoulder woke him. He was surprised to find that he had been able to fall asleep. Mikolus moved on to rouse Alorsha and Kluir when he saw that Gya was alert.

Gya looked around. "Where's Parl?"

"Off taking a last look at the enclosure before we get there," Mikolus told him. "He should be back soon."

While they waited, they saddled and packed the horses to ready them for travel. In his satchel, Gya placed the sigil codex he needed along with the required kri-stone crystals and powders, organized so he could quickly grab what he required for the magic.

Then he pulled out his white-edged seeing-stone and traced the sigil to see in the dark on one side of the crystal using the proper powdered kri-stone.

He handed the crystal to Hali. "Can you see better through it?"

She tried, first looking with one eye, then the other, then both while looking somewhat cross-eyed. "No. Still can't see in the dark."

Gya sighed. The others tried it then, with no different results. Even Alorsha.

She patted his shoulder as she returned the crystal.

"Some magics just don't work for others," she said softly.

Everyone turned back to their tasks to get ready.

Parl returned just as Gya began wondering what was taking the other man so long.

Mikolus gave Parl a quizzical look as he joined them, then gathered everyone close to hear what Parl had to say. Hali handed out food, and passed around some drink too, to anyone who wanted them.

"Looks pretty good. Actually, better than before," Parl told them around sips of water. "The extra Keepers seem to be gone – at least all their horses are and the carts, so most likely they are, too. They've got just four guards awake, that I could see, and they don't act like they expect any trouble. None of the Magickas in sight. All in the buildings like we saw the last couple of nights."

After Alorsha had eaten a little—Gya noticed everyone ate only a little—she handed out three small bottles to each of them.

"The bottles with three ridges below the corks will ease pain," Alorsha instructed them. "If you need some, first try a sip and see if that's enough to ease the pain. The smooth bottles with square bases hold the 'I belong here' potion."

"Need a better name for that," Hali muttered.

Alorsha chuckled and agreed. "As before, it still tastes awful. The aftertaste fades faster than before, though."

"Good!" Parl said.

"I don't know how useful it'll be, though. With fewer guards about, it might not override their natural suspicion at seeing someone in an unexpected location."

"Might be they could still be of use, though," Mikolus said. "I'd prefer to have them along."

Alorsha nodded. "The third bottle, the round one with no ridges, holds a version of that plant that would make people sick if they ate it. Now this potion just needs to get on their skin. Make sure not to splash it on yourself. It should take only a few drops, but there's not much in each bottle." She next handed out small torn strips of cloth.

"If you like, dip one of these in that last bottle and just brush the wet portion against the skin of the person you want to make sick." She herself pulled on leather gloves, then pulled out two small jars. She handed one to Mikolus and kept the other herself.

"Finally, these contain that sleep salve I mentioned. Don't get any of this on your skin, either. Anyone it touches will sleep deeply for at least eight hours. I could only make this small amount, so the rest of you will have to get it from one of us if you need it."

"Good enough," Mikolus said. "Gya, try to stay close to one of the rest of us when we get there. Perhaps Alorsha would be best. She has some weapons experience if you two get into trouble and, of course, you've both got your magics, too."

Gya noticed then that Alorsha carried her flintlock—tucked in her belt—as well as a bow with a quiver of arrows. Her cross-body bag bulged oddly. *Carrying potions and such,* he assumed. Much like he carried his kri-stone crystals and powders.

Mikolus continued, "The rest of us will spread out. We want to down the Keepers before they see any of us. Incapacitate them, restrain them…."

Gya gave Alorsha a questioning look. She leaned close and whispered. "We don't want to kill anyone, but if it's them or us…."

"I understand," Gya whispered back.

"Then we find Gya's people, if they're there, and get everyone away from the place." Mikolus looked at each of them in turn. "Ready for this?"

After receiving nods and murmurs of agreement, he grabbed his horse and headed toward the enclosure, the others following his example. They brought the horses as close to the enclosure as they dared before they left them tethered.

Gya tried to move as quietly as Mikolus and Parl did as they made their way through the trees and underbrush. Gya stuck close enough to Alorsha that he felt her sleeve brush his arm as they walked. The night was dark with the moons gone, but he found the stars provided a surprising amount of light to his night-accustomed vision. *Too bad he had not been able to make the night seeing-stone work for everyone.*

He shivered and tried to calm his thoughts. But the shivery feeling stayed with him, although the night air held some warmth in it. He glanced around but saw nothing amiss.

They reached the enclosure and Mikolus motioned everyone to spread out to circle it. He pointed Parl and Gya to a thick clump of trees. From there, Gya could see the two sentries at the enclosure's one gate. Alorsha stayed nearby.

Gya inspected the enclosure and the two still-awake Keepers. He shook his head slightly. He had not done anything like this before. *Could he truly manage it?*

A clap on one shoulder startled him from his thoughts.

"You can do this," Parl whispered in his ear.

He eased to the side and watched as Gya dipped his left forefinger in the powdered kri-stone and began to draw the sigil in the air. While he *could* use either hand to draw sigils, unlike many Magickas, Gya had found that he preferred using his left hand.

The closest sentry sat leaning against one post of the gateway to the enclosure and gazed somewhat off to Gya's left. The other stood beyond him, from Gya's perspective, facing away.

The last swirl of the sigil drawn, Gya took the crystal and tapped the middle cluster of powder that hung in the air, then blew on the sigil.

It floated away from him, and held its shape, right to the first sentry, seemingly passing through him without losing its coherence. His eyes fluttered once and he fell asleep, tipping over with a soft thump.

In the quiet night, the thump was loud enough to catch the attention of the other sentry, who turned at the sound.

"Magicka!" he shouted.

Gya heard a curse from Parl and ducked back into some bushes. He hoped the sentry had not seen him.

"Stay hidden!" Parl dashed into the trees, headed toward another part of the enclosure.

Gya peered through the bushes and saw two more Keepers running toward the gate from other parts of the enclosure, alerted by the sentry's shout. They looked around for the threat as they ran.

At the same time, Gya's sigil sailed through the air and through the second sentry before he moved away. He dropped to the ground asleep and the powdered kri-stone streamed back to Gya's pouch. The other Keepers drew their swords.

Gya started to move, then froze as he saw clumps of grass in the camp stretch and grow. The grass wrapped around the running Keepers' feet, tripping them, and bound the two who slept. Mikolus and Kluir appeared then, running from the left, and Hali from the right. *Must have climbed over the fence.* The three headed for the two armed Keepers, who chopped at the grasses with their swords.

Gya looked for Alorsha and spotted her a distance off to his right. She knelt in some bushes, her hands on the ground. He edged toward her, but his attention stayed on the enclosure.

He saw Mikolus lean down to one of the struggling Keepers and the woman went suddenly limp. *Probably that sleep salve.* Mikolus repeated the motion with the other struggling Keeper then glanced toward the gate. Parl joined him and he and the others dashed toward the three buildings at the back, from which some commotion came.

Gya frowned. *Must be the other Keepers.*

He started when Alorsha stepped up to his side; he had been so focused on the enclosure.

"Better get in there and help," she said and led the way.

When they reached the gate, Alorsha dipped a gloved finger into the small jar in the top of her bag. She touched the first sentry on the neck below the ear, then repeated her actions for the second.

"That'll hold them now." She wiped off the salve residue left on her finger on one of the guards' shirts and grabbed their swords, tossing them to the side some distance away from the gate where they were lost in the gloom. She and Gya opened the gate and wedged it open, then entered the enclosure.

Together, they eased toward the buildings at the far end of the enclosure. From the noise that direction, Gya judged his assumption about more Keepers to be true. But in the darkness and at that distance, he could not see well enough to be sure.

When he and Alorsha reached the back three buildings, Gya saw Parl and Kluir in a struggle with three people who shouted for help.

A woman managed to get free of the struggle but stopped just a step away, no longer shouting. Instead, she dipped her fingers in a pouch at her waist and started to draw a sigil in the air. Gya pulled the cork from the bottle that held the sickness potion and flicked the open bottle at the woman, hitting her in the face with several drops of the potion.

The woman froze a moment with a wide-eyed stare then began to cough and gag. She fell to her knees, unable to do anything but retch helplessly.

Alorsha managed to catch a half-clothed Keeper with the same potion, which dropped him to his knees as well.

Gya looked around, but Kluir and Parl had dealt with the remaining Keeper, leaving her also on her knees, helplessly sick. So far, no others had come running, but Gya heard a scuffle from within the building nearest them.

Kluir and Parl exchanged looks and headed inside.

"Hali's in there," Kluir called back over a shoulder and pointed to the rightmost of the buildings at the back.

Alorsha and Gya ran to the building Kluir had indicated. Sounds of a struggle came from there, too. Gya held the bottle with the sickness potion ready as he followed Alorsha into the building.

Inside, they found themselves in the hall that ran the length of the building. Not two paces in front of them, Hali fought with a man who was half a head taller than she was. While he did not wear his Keeper uniform—only a long loose tunic, likely for sleeping—he moved with the arrogance that marked him as a Keeper. Hali was holding her own, but she was hampered by the need to press against the door at her back that kept trying to open.

Their entrance caught the Keeper's attention and he turned slightly toward them, giving Hali a chance to lunge. Her sword sliced his sword arm and he howled. Taking advantage of his distraction, Alorsha darted forward and brushed the Keeper's arm with her salve. He dropped to the floor, snoring, as Hali narrowly missed skewering his chest with her sword. His sudden collapse threw her off balance and the door behind her was flung open, another Keeper there, sword drawn.

Fighting fear that threatened to paralyze him, Gya managed to dart close enough to flick some of the sickness potion in the Keeper's face. As the others had, she coughed and gagged and dropped to her knees retching.

Hali shoved her with a foot so she fell back into the room she had come from. After a quick look inside, Hali closed the door.

"Nothing else in there," she said in a low voice.

The three paused to listen, but heard no other sounds in the building. Hali waved a hand toward the door at the other end of the hall.

Alorsha nodded. "Need to check them all," she whispered. She took a position inside the outer door with an arrow nocked. Hali led Gya to the room she had indicated and tried the door.

"Locked," she whispered right next to Gya's ear. "Can you...?"

Gya nodded. He dipped a finger into the pouch that held the correct powdered kri-stone and drew the unlocking sigil in the air next to the lock. Then Hali easily opened the door.

Inside they found a small room that contained a bed, chair, table with a wash basin and one person asleep. Hali grabbed the clothes that hung over the back of the chair and took them to the door to the dim light that came from the windows.

When Gya saw that the clothes were a Keeper uniform, he got Alorsha so she could use her sleep salve on the guard.

"Wonder why he didn't wake with all the noise," Gya murmured.

Hali grabbed a jug from the room's small table and sniffed it. "This, I'd say." She tilted the jug over her hand and a few drops fell onto her palm. She licked them and made a face. "Pretty potent, but not tasty."

They quickly checked the other rooms. The one other room with the lock engaged held another sleeping Keeper—with a similar empty jug—who slept much deeper after their visit. The other rooms were empty of people, holding only similar furnishings.

They left that building and joined the others as they exited the middle building.

"None of your people in there," Kluir told Gya, with a sympathetic look for him.

"Just Keepers, all nicely sleeping now." Parl grinned. "And a few a little banged up."

Hali, Parl and Kluir headed to the buildings that held the Magickas; Hali to one of the buildings that was supposed to house the women and Parl and Kluir each to one of the buildings for the men. Mikolus, Gya and

Alorsha headed to the last of the three buildings at the back of the enclosure.

No guards lurked in the hall that ran the length of the building. As before, they worked their way through the building, unlocking all the doors. They found that all of the rooms were storerooms, mostly containing food, but also with other supplies, including some shovels and axes, wood, nails and spare clothing for the Keepers.

When they returned to the center of the enclosure, Gya saw people shuffling away from buildings all around them, gathering in the open areas where they seemed to be reuniting with friends or family. He and Alorsha had taken only a couple of steps following Mikolus to the women's buildings when they heard a scuffle behind them.

All three turned. A group of former captives struggled with each other. A couple shouted for the Keepers and seemed to be trying to work some sigil magic.

"Somebody stop him!" A voice behind Gya startled him. When he turned to look, he found himself facing an elderly woman who pointed across the enclosure to a Magicka who had nearly finished a sigil in the air in front of him.

Never reach him in time! Still, Gya charged toward the man, but skidded to a stop when a whoosh swept past his ear and an arrow sliced through the man's upper arm, disrupting his magic. Then Kluir had reached the man and downed him with a splash of the sickness potion. Gya turned back to see that the scuffle had resolved. The former captives who had tried to work sigil magic lay on the ground and did not look like they were breathing.

He caught a glimpse of Alorsha's anguished expression before she turned away.

"Grab food from the storehouse," Mikolus called out. "And anything else that might be useful, and everyone get out of here!"

"Stop!" A commanding voice rang out in the enclosure, squelching the commotion.

A woman's voice cried out. "He's got my baby!" Gya spotted her off to the side near the building where the Keepers had put the children.

A man also stood near the building, one hand gripping the shoulder of a small child, his drawn sword visible in the starlight.

"Back inside your lodges," the man ordered. "Or the children all die."

The captives muttered and backed away, but none headed into the buildings. Slight movement to one side caught Gya's attention: Parl, slipping through the gloom behind the building near the man.

"There's no need for such action," Mikolus said, stepping forward and catching the man's attention.

"You'll answer to the Seekers!" the man threatened. He brought the sword close to the child's face. "Do as I say."

Both the woman and the child whimpered. Everyone stood frozen a moment longer, then a few people turned back to the lodges.

"Drop the sword. Let the child go." Parl's quiet voice carried clearly in the stillness from behind the man. He stood partially hidden there, with a long dagger drawing a bead of blood from the man's throat.

The man swallowed and did as Parl said.

A mad scramble ensued. The woman and her child dashed to each other, while several other people swarmed the man that Parl held, shoving the *Deliberia* crewmember away. Many people ran to the storehouse, others still looked for someone in the crowd, and yet others darted into the buildings where the guards slept unaware.

Gya drew Alorsha's attention to the latter and they ran after them, only to arrive too late after having to fight through the milling mass of people. The blood splattered around inside those buildings left no doubts about what the former captives had done there.

Fighting queasiness at the sight and smell, Gya staggered back outside. Alorsha joined him a moment later.

"They've killed all the Keepers," she said.

A passing Magicka muttered, "No better than they deserved."

Alorsha stopped the woman. "What purpose did it serve? It doesn't change what they've already done."

"Keeps them from doing it again," the woman said.

Alorsha nodded thoughtfully. "True. But it also means they never had a chance to learn anything better, either."

"Doubt they'd have been able to." The woman shrugged and turned away, headed toward the storehouse.

"I can understand that point of view," Gya said softly.

Alorsha's expression saddened. "I can too, I'm afraid." A catch in her voice caught his attention.

"Are you thinking of that Devrand? Would you treat him the same way?"

Alorsha gave that some thought. "I'm not sure," she said finally, then muttered soft enough he almost didn't hear her, "I'm not sure *he's* the enemy." She turned away and raised her voice. "Let's get out of here."

They rejoined the others near the gate, where Gya saw those Keepers also lay dead. Alorsha gazed off into the distance, her expression pained. When the first of the former captives came to the gate, Parl and Kluir led them out and around the enclosure, away from the path and road.

"That could've gone better," Hali muttered as more people followed.

"Might be. But it also could have gone much worse," Mikolus said as they watched the stream of people pass through the gate.

"You go on," Alorsha said, after the last stragglers had left the enclosure. "I've an idea to leave confusion here for anyone who might come here after we've gone."

Mikolus crossed his arms and gave her a stern look. "You're not staying behind alone."

Hali glared at her and nodded agreement with

Mikolus's words.

Alorsha sighed. "Of course not. But I'll need all of you outside the fence."

When they had moved where she said, she knelt in the gateway and placed her hands in the meager grass there. For a moment, Gya saw nothing happening, then the boards of the fence and gate began to warp. Within minutes they were dried and crumbling, as if enough time had passed to rot them away. As the fence and gate fell, Gya could see all the buildings doing the same thing. And where the stumps were, new growth sprouted. Behind them, plants filled in the path that led to the gate, obscuring it, and also grew to conceal the bodies. Grasses reached high in the former enclosure, although the spots of bare dirt remained. When the saplings sprouting from the tree trunks reached twice Gya's height and the buildings had all been reduced to nothing more than flinders, Alorsha sat back on her haunches with a deep sigh. It looked like it had been years since the enclosure stood intact, rather than less than an hour.

"That'll confuse them!" Hali said.

Mikolus helped Alorsha to her feet, where she swayed, even holding on to his arm, clearly taxed.

"I've enough left to hide the path they've left." Alorsha waved a hand at the clear trail left by the former captives. "As long as we go now."

Hali and Gya led the way, following the clear trail of flattened grass and shrubs. Mikolus and Alorsha followed. He supported her as she magicked the plants to cover any traces they left behind that might show the direction they had gone.

When they reached the spot where they had left the horses, they saw the others had already gathered them up. They continued on, catching up to the large group, and traveled the rest of the night, headed roughly south. The going was slow, but they still put a good amount of distance between them and the site of the enclosure by the time sunrise arrived.

As dawn colored the sky, they stopped near a good-sized creek in a thickly forested area. Most of the former captives dropped where they stopped. A few, in better shape than the others, headed to the water to clean up. Kluir moved among the former captives, somewhat fewer than a hundred Gya estimated, and tended wounds, using that salve of Alorsha's to ease pain

Hali and Parl got a fire going and heated some food. Mikolus left to prowl around the edges of the camp and check back the way they had come.

Gya joined Alorsha where she leaned against a tree and perused the Magickas. He scrutinized every woman he saw but none was Chizoa or Ifeoma or Vabena.

A man and woman nearby got to their feet and joined them. "You have our gratitude for your help," the woman said. She held the man's hand tightly and kept looking at him with a wondering expression like she mistrusted what she was seeing.

"Why did those Magickas call for guards?" Gya said.

The man frowned and squeezed the woman's hand. Gya noticed odd wounds on each of their left arms, a single cut about the length of his thumb on the outsides of those arms near their wrists. The cuts looked recent, and the skin around them oddly discolored. *What caused wounds like those?*

"Some Magickas worked with the Keepers," the man said. "For doing that, they got better food, were treated better than the rest of us and granted some authority over the rest of us."

"Did we get everyone out?" Alorsha asked.

The man and woman looked at the people sprawled on the ground.

"All who would've wanted to leave, anyway," the woman said.

"Some went off with the foreigners before you lot came," the man added.

Alorsha gave them a sharp look. "Two foreigners? Men? One possibly looking ill, with gold-brown hair, light skin and green eyes, and the other with similar skin, red-brown hair and blue-green eyes."

The man and woman both nodded. "That's them," the man said. "Odd thing when they arrived, they just showed up that morning. No horses with them, just a couple stumbling Magickas. They left again sometime early day before yesterday. Or at least didn't see them again after that. Planned to head somewhere to the northwest, I think. From some talk I heard. One also said something about a gateway."

Gya and Alorsha exchanged glances.

"Why northwest?" Alorsha said.

"The foreigner in charge mentioned caves," the woman said.

"Was a woman named Chizoa held with you?" Gya asked. "Or Ifeoma or Vabena? Or perhaps a man named Toa?"

The man and woman exchanged looks and the woman shrugged. "Not that I know of, but the foreigners did take a few Magickas with them, the more accomplished of us. We weren't allowed to talk much, so I didn't know everyone's names."

Gya described the three missing women and his brother. When he finished, the woman nodded. "The one, Chizoa, sounds like one of the women the foreigners took with them. I'm not certain about the others."

"Did they say anything else about these caves?" Alorsha asked.

Both shook their heads.

"I did overhear something," the woman said after a moment of consideration. "Something from earlier. When the one foreigner was talking to the sick one. He said that they'd have to go there to be able to travel on. I didn't hear where 'there' was, but he might've meant the caves he mentioned later."

Someone called to the woman then, and after repeated thanks, she and her man picked their way through the Magickas to another woman who looked much like the first.

"A gateway?" Gya said after the woman moved far enough away to be unable to hear.

"I suspect they're again using Magickas' magic," Alorsha said. "Have you seen a sigil that lets you go from one place to another in an instant. Like going through a door or gate?"

Gya shook his head. "That would be very advanced magic, I'd think. Very difficult."

"That might be why the Magickas with them were stumbling. Maybe they were exhausted from such a magic."

Gya nodded his agreement and turned his attention to the Magickas who milled about. "Did you notice the odd identical cuts on their arms?"

They both watched the Magickas for several minutes.

Alorsha nodded. "I've spotted them on the others, too. Although not on any of them who came in the carts. Any idea what they might be?"

Gya frowned. "Not at all."

Alorsha's frown matched his. "Think I'll see what I can find out, before I have to sleep some."

"I think I'd better try to see Chizoa," Gya said.

Alorsha nodded absent acknowledgment and headed toward one of the groups of Magickas. "Let me know what you learn," she said over a shoulder.

Gya scooped some water from the creek into his small bowl and set it in a cleared space in the dirt at the base of one of the trees. When he began to draw the sigil, he attracted the attention of the Magickas nearby, who eased closer to see what he was doing. These Magickas also had the discolored wounds on their left arms. Gya started to ask about them, but then decided to continue with what he was doing. He got an impression of skittishness from the

Magickas who had edged close and did not want to frighten them off with possibly uncomfortable questions.

When an image formed in the water in the bowl, he heard murmurs of appreciation from those around him. He tried to focus on Chizoa, but just saw a greenish blur in the water. He saw much the same for both Ifeoma and Vabeila. When he focused on Toa, his brother's face appeared briefly in the water, with what looked like bushes behind him, before it dissolved into a similar greenish blur.

"I've seen him before," one of the men who watched Gya said. After some thought, he added, "He was working with the foreigner, I think."

Gya bowed his head and let the image vanish.

The man who had spoken rested a hand on his shoulder. "You know him. I'm sorry."

After the other Magickas had moved off to get food or to rest or wash, he cleaned up the sigil.

Maybe he should have seen this. Toa had always pushed to do something, to use their magic. Gya wondered what Devrand had offered his brother. He raised his head and watched Alorsha a short time. *He could ask her. She seemed open to sharing information.*

But as he studied her, he remembered things about the others that he had passed off at the time. Sudden silences when he came too near their conversation, breaks in what they said that might have been them choosing a different word than they originally would have.

Gya perused the others, Alorsha's people. Mikolus spoke with an accent different from Alorsha's and Saevalde's. On board the *Deliberia*, Gya had heard other accents, different still.

How did this Devrand of Alorsha's enter the Empire? He had not passed through Hawei, but Alorsha said they followed him. *And what of her magic?* Gya had heard of no place where anyone worked magic like hers. With all the merchants who had done business through his family's storehouse, he had heard a lot of tales of a lot of lands. But all their magics used kri-stone one way or another, just as the magic he knew did.

Who were these people? Where did they come from? Would he be better off joining Toa? But his brother seemed allied with this Devrand, another of these people.

Gya dropped his head to his hands. Maybe he should just ask them. But he was not sure he wanted to hear the answers.

Why would his brother be with this Devrand anyway?

Gya made a rude noise to himself and decided to find a time to question his companions. Soon.

He stopped in his tracks at the thought of caves. *Could they have found the legendary source of kri-stone? What damage might this Devrand do with that?* Gya hurried to the campfire, his questions feeling much more urgent.

But with all the bustle of getting everyone fed and wounds tended, people and clothes cleaned the best they could, and needed rest after the long night, Gya found no opportunity to speak with the people from the *Deliberia* that day. Mikolus returned around midday to let everyone know that there was no sign of anyone trying to find them or even looking at the enclosure.

At the evening meal, several of the Magickas, those who seemed to be leaders among the freed captives, sat with Gya and his companions to decide what came next.

"You have our gratitude," one man said. "But what are we to do now?"

"I want to go back home," a younger man said. Several others nodded in agreement.

"Don't we all," an older woman said. "But I doubt it's wise. Even if we were to make it there, the Keepers would just send us back to the encampments, as they call them."

"They've more of them?" Gya said.

The woman nodded. "According to talk I overheard."

"But couldn't we sneak back home somehow?" the young man persisted. "Hide out there?"

"She's right," Gya said. "It wouldn't be wise." And he

told them what had happened in Hawei, what they had seen in Farhani. That was enough to convince the doubters.

After some discussion, and consulting with some others who originally came from the regions nearby, they decided that they would do as Gya's friends had and try to escape the Empire entirely.

"We can't return to Farhani, of course," one woman said. "Those of us who're known in that town. Nor go further on that road back there, I think. Some of the Magicka families from our town went south and east some time back. I think that's the way to go." She looked around at the gathered people and received nods of agreement.

And so they decided to set off to the southeast, away from any known towns of the Empire, to try to get far away as fast as they could. Although none of them was in good condition—some had been in the encampment many months—they decided their chances were better to just go.

"Will you come with us?" the man who had just wanted to go home asked.

Alorsha shook her head. "We have other things we must do. Can you tell us anything more about these encampments? How many there are? Or where?"

The Magickas shook their heads.

When Gya tentatively asked about the strange wounds, the Magickas abruptly withdrew with guarded expressions and claimed they were nothing and they needed to get their rest. Gya exchanged glances with Alorsha who only shrugged.

"I wasn't able to learn anything more either," she whispered as she leaned close. "I didn't want to insist since they seemed very uncomfortable with the topic."

"Likely some torment the Keepers subjected them to," Parl murmured.

Gya agreed with that possibility, but something still bothered him about the wounds. He just wished he could figure out what.

~ ~ ~

The next morning, as the former captives finished sorting themselves out to leave, Gya remembered the bag Alorsha had found. He grabbed it from his pack and held it up. "We found this in the square. In Farhani. Does anyone know who it belongs to?"

A woman came forward. "It's my grandfather's. He hid it with us when they took him last year."

Gya handed it to her and she smiled her thanks.

When the former captives were finally ready to head out, Alorsha knelt to open a path for them through the plants.

"Join me and see what you can feel of this magic," she invited Gya, who then imitated her stance.

Her magic reached out to the plants she touched, to their roots all connected to the ground, and other plants nearby moved to her desire. The trees and bushes to the east bent away from each other to form a wide path. Gya could feel that the path extended far to the east of their camp.

Mikolus sent the former captives on their way with a wave. With Alorsha's guidance, the plants closed the path behind them, their roots even disturbing the earth, erasing all signs that the Magickas had gone that way.

After the Magickas were out of sight and the plants had all returned to the state they had been in before making the path, both Alorsha and Gya worked their wayfinding magic with their pendants. The pendants indicated the same general direction: northwest.

"Toward Hawei," Gya noted.

With a nod of acknowledgment, Alorsha joined the others to pack their camp. Gya took the time to dismantle his pendant and tuck the parts away in his pouch before he helped as they cleared away signs that they had camped there. The group then headed out themselves, riding northwest at a brisk pace. Except for Parl.

Mikolus sent Parl back north to the *Deliberia*, to inform Saevalde that they were heading back toward Hawei, so she could take the *Deliberia* that direction too, to be closer, if needed. Parl seemed the best choice, the others all agreed, since from a distance he looked much like the Empire's citizens, especially after they dyed the light blotches in his hair dark again, and his sneakiness might help him pass where the others would more likely be caught.

As they set out again, Gya wondered how best to begin his questioning of his companions.

CHAPTER 28

Gya found an opportunity for his questions when they slowed to share out a midday meal and ease the strain of their precipitous travel. None of them had gotten much sleep the previous night and they had become even more fatigued on the ride. Especially Alorsha, who had continued to work the magic in the plants to hide their trail.

As they ate, Gya looked from one to another as he tried to decide what to ask first, and who.

"What is it?" Mikolus said, not unkindly, after a few minutes of this.

"I have some questions," Gya began.

"Not surprising," Kluir said.

"Well… I—"

"Just plunge right in," Hali encouraged Gya.

"All right then. Where do you truly come from? Not knowing or using kri-stone, in a ship like nothing the Empire has ever seen? All of you have so many different accents. How do you even know our language in the first place?"

With a smile, Alorsha held up a hand to stop the flow of Gya's words. She guided her horse around a clump of bushes and turned her gaze back to him.

"So much to know," she said. "Where to begin?" She exchanged a look with Mikolus, who only shrugged.

Alorsha nodded as if he had told her something. "Well then, where do we come from? A variety of places, as you've guessed from our accents. None that you'll have heard of, so the names will mean nothing to you."

"But where?" Gya said. "Are you from beyond the Yuyur lands to the north? Or from the west? Are there lands beyond the great sea that we don't know of?"

Kluir chuckled. "Oh, much further than that."

Alorsha nodded. "Where we're from there is no kristone. As for how we speak your language, that's from *Deliberia*'s magic, one of the things she can do for us."

Gya looked around and saw that they were serious. "How?"

"When we… well—"

"Just tell him," Mikolus told Alorsha. "Easier than trying to talk around it and still make sense."

Alorsha nodded and looked like she was gathering her thoughts.

"We come from very far away," she said. "So far that only magic can take someone between there and here, open a path of sorts."

Gya pulled his horse to a halt. "Are you hidden-worlders?" he said, his sudden apprehension clear in his tone. "Sylphs or Pucks or some other denizens from the hidden realms?"

The others exchanged looks.

"If I understand you correctly," Alorsha said, "then, no. We're just people, like you. But we *do* come from another world. I don't think it's one of your hidden realms, though. Much further than that."

Gya gave her a doubtful look. "You're not numinous, then? Preternatural?"

Alorsha shook her head, echoed by the others. "Not at all. Just people with a rather unique magic that lets us travel to worlds not our own."

"She has the magic." Hali cocked a thumb at Alorsha.

"*Deliberia* has the magic," Alorsha countered. "Most of it. I've simply learned how to guide it, use it."

"So this Devrand and Jarthan, they're from your world?" Gya said.

Alorsha nodded again, but Mikolus shook his head.

"Her world," he said. "Theirs, actually." He waved a hand at the others and included Alorsha in the gesture. "I come from a different world and joined them on the journey."

Gya shook his head while he tried to take all this in. Of course, Sylphs and Pucks, the hidden realms, were all stories told to children. But this seemed just as fantastic, just as unreal.

"That's why my magic is so different," Alorsha said. "I carry and practice the magic of my homeland. Remember, I told you I'm called a coppice-mage there."

"One of the best, too," Kluir said.

Alorsha gave him a small smile.

"So you brought this Devrand here, too? And what? He escaped you?" Gya said.

"No," Alorsha said. "In my homeland, different people have different… talents, I guess you could say, with magic. Devrand brought himself here, no ship, and dragged my life partner with him. He's been doing this, fleeing us, through many worlds."

At the weary sound in her voice, Gya gave her a sharp look. "How long?"

Alorsha winced. "Around a year now, the best I can tell. It's difficult to keep track of the days when traveling from world to world."

"You've just dragged the ship and everyone on it along with you all that time to chase this Devrand?" Gya said.

"We've chosen to travel with Alorsha and the

Deliberia," Hali said heatedly. "I was a servant before. So dull. Tedious. Days of nothing much more than cooking and washing. But while spending some time with a town guard, who showed me some ways to defend myself, I learned I had a talent for weaponry. Coming aboard the *Deliberia* let me expand on that. And we've seen so many different places."

Kluir nodded. "Part of why I came along. As a merchant's guard, I traveled, but always to and from the same places. I wanted to see more. New places, not the same ones all the time."

"And Parl just sort of fell into it," Hali said with a grin.

"He was a stowaway," Kluir said. "A wharf-rat who hid aboard, not knowing what he was getting into. Hiding from the guards, I believe. After having picked some pocket he shouldn't have. We put him to work."

"But what of your families?" Gya said. "How could you leave them?"

"I don't think Parl ever knew his," Hali said. "And mine left me, dropped me off with an inn to be a servant. Too many mouths to feed."

"I was always the odd one," Kluir said. "Never fit in and always making the others uncomfortable. Wanting to travel rather than watch the sheep and goats. Left a long time ago and never looked back."

Hali leaned close to Gya, her expression intent. "She's not *dragging* anyone anywhere."

"That she's not. Anyone who wishes to stop, to leave the ship, can, at any time" Mikolus said. "New people can join us, too. That's how I came to be aboard. I stepped into the place of someone who decided to stay back in my home-world."

"Do you return to visit worlds you've been to before?"

"We tried once." Alorsha frowned. "It didn't go well."

Hali made a choking sound.

"It was a perfect disaster," Kluir said. "Not something any of us would want to repeat, I'm sure."

The others nodded their agreement.

"But what does this Devrand want with Magickas? Has he discovered where the kri-stone caves are? Why would he care, if you say your magics don't use it?" Gya said.

Alorsha winced again, but Hali gave him a sharp look. "Why do you think he might have discovered where kri-stone caves are?" she said.

"One of the Magickas told me she overheard him talking about caves. What other caves would he want?" Gya said and paused, staring into the distance as something came together for him. "The Magicka said he was heading northwest! What if he thinks the kri-stone caves are near Hawei?"

Alorsha and Mikolus exchanged glances and she called a halt. She pulled out her pendant, catching it momentarily on her shirt in her haste, then extended her arm to do her wayfinding magic. The pendant clearly inscribed an arc to the northwest.

"We need to keep moving." Alorsha urged her horse to a quicker pace and tucked her pendant away again as they rode.

Gya urged his horse faster to catch her. "So what does he want with them, the kri-stone caves, and the Magickas, if our magic isn't the same as yours?"

Mikolus answered for her.

"Devrand can make others' magics his own somehow. Even magics that are very different from whatever his original magic was. Likely he's planning to take the magics of the Magickas who travel with him, probably of any kri-stone, too."

Gya gaped at them, horrified. "He has my brother and Chizoa! Will this hurt them? Or worse?"

"I won't lie. It might," Alorsha said. "He's killed others."

"B-but why?"

Alorsha shook her head. "I don't know why. I do know he keeps gathering magic to himself, becoming more powerful. Some of it he uses to get to another world, to escape us."

"So stop chasing him and he'll stop taking others' magics," Gya said heatedly.

"From what we've seen, he wouldn't stop even if we did," Kluir said.

"I can't stop following him, trying to catch him," Alorsha said in an anguished voice and looked away. "He took my Jarthan, my world."

~ ~ ~

They traveled mostly in silence the rest of the day and gave the small towns they came across a wide berth. When they felt they could go no further without some rest, they searched for a place to stop. From the top of a low hill, they spotted a small collection of buildings through the trees. Mikolus called a halt and motioned them back the way they had come. He dismounted and eased back over the hill.

"Was that another encampment?" Gya whispered as he turned to eye the trees around them, starting at each small sound.

"Looked like it," Alorsha murmured, her attention also on their surroundings.

Many minutes later, a crack of a twig startled them, and they spun to face the threat… to see Mikolus sauntering toward them. "Letting you know I approached."

"Well?" Hali demanded.

"No one there." Mikolus mounted again. "Looks recently abandoned though. Might be an encampment. It looks similar to that one we know, from a distance anyway."

Alorsha frowned. "On we go, then. I don't want to stop too near that."

So they plodded further into the trees and after about an hour of travel, looked again for a place to stop. They finally found a hidden clearing in the thinning trees to make a cold camp. Mikolus traded Gya some of his out-Empire coins for the Imperial spishas Gya carried and slipped back to sneak into a town that they had skirted a little before sundown to get some more food for them. He planned to grab what they needed and leave the coins behind as payment. He returned about an hour later with a full bag and some news.

"Word is out," he said. "The townsfolk have some rough drawings of us hung on that pole near their council building. Good thing I'd planned to avoid towns the rest of the way, anyway."

He plopped onto the ground next to Alorsha. "I got enough food to give us another couple of days before we'll have to find more. There are plenty of plants around for the horses."

They shared out the food and ate.

"Any idea how long it will take us to get back to Hawei?" Alorsha said.

"These horses are strong and in good form," Mikolus said. "They should be able to make close to half the distance the *Deliberia* covered in a day when we sailed east."

"We've come a fair bit south of the coast," Kluir said. "So it'll take a bit longer to get back north."

Gya nodded. "We've come a fair bit west of the encampment already, but I think we're about a week from Hawei, give or take. That assumes we don't have to go around too many towns and so lengthen our journey that much more."

Hali sighed. "A week."

"A positive thing, though," Alorsha said. "I can tell that Devrand hasn't been pulling any of this world's magic to himself."

"Yet," Mikolus said.

"True, yet."

"So how is that a positive thing?" Gya asked.

"Means he's not getting ready yet to open the way to another world," Kluir said.

"Should even mean he's not found any kri-stone caves yet, either," Hali said. "Assuming there are any to find."

"From what the other Magickas said, he's only a couple of days ahead of us," Gya said.

"I saw no sign of them keeping horses at that encampment," Mikolus said. "So at least at first, Devrand and anyone with him would have been on foot."

"So we can catch up to them before they reach Hawei?" Gya said.

"Perhaps," Alorsha said. "It would certainly be preferable if we could."

"Do you have something to help sustain the horses if we need to push them?" Mikolus asked her. "Or you, Gya?"

"Possibly." Alorsha dug through her collection of potions and salves. "See what defensive sigils you might have, too, Gya. We'll need whatever we can use against Devrand when we catch up to him."

Gya nodded and paged through his sigil codices. He did find one sigil that was supposed to stave off fatigue for a time. It was more complex than any of the sigils he had successfully done so far, but he mentioned it anyway.

"Better start practicing it," Alorsha said with a smile, then shook her head at Mikolus. "I have nothing currently. But I'll check the plants as we travel and see what I can come up with."

"Are we continuing on tonight?" Kluir said.

Mikolus and Alorsha exchanged looks. "I'd like to for a bit," Alorsha said, "if the horses are up to it. Just let me gather some of these new plants around here, first."

Mikolus nodded. After Alorsha gathered the plants she needed, everyone mounted again. While they rode, Gya watched Alorsha as she lost herself in the new plants' magic. When it became clear she was too involved to manage her horse properly, he grabbed its reins to guide it.

After a couple of hours, he saw her focus return again to the here and now.

"Anything?" he asked.

"Nothing to help the horses," she said. "But possibly something to help against some magic. After we stop, I'll look into it further."

They rode until nearly midnight before they decided to rest for the rest of the night. Gya practiced the sigil a short time as he tried to fight off fatigue, until he could no longer keep his eyes open. Even as he drifted off to sleep, he saw Alorsha at work next to the fire. Looked like she was putting together a potion that used one of the plants she had gathered at their previous stop.

CHAPTER 29

Before they broke camp in the morning, Alorsha built up the small fire. To test her new potion, she told everyone. She spread the syrupy potion on both sides of one hand and, to Gya's shock, stuck that hand in the fire. In a panic, the others ran to her, but relaxed when she pulled her hand back, untouched. She gave everyone a tired, but pleased grin.

"Now to make it drinkable, if I can, since putting it all over ourselves would be problematic."

So they broke camp but spent about an hour before they left the area gathering as many of that particular plant's leaves as they could find. Alorsha showed Gya a way to tear them into small bits as they rode, provided they rode at a walk. They set out again, while both Alorsha and Gya prepared the leaves for the potion.

After he tore up all the leaves he carried, Gya tucked them away in a small pouch. He let his thoughts wander and eventually slipped into a hazy torpor. He still retained a vague awareness of his surroundings and the motion of the horse, but mostly rode in a daze and struggling to stay alert.

When the attack came, it took him completely by surprise. Several thuds on the ground behind them, close to him, were his only warning before something cold and solid slammed into the side of his head. He felt himself falling but could not stop it. He hit the ground, hard.

He lay there a moment, stunned, then the noise and confusion all around him registered. People shouting. Horses squealing. Pain pulsing through his body: head and arm, and his hip where he had landed on his satchel of kri-stone.

A hoof pounded the ground near his face, and he threw himself away, scrambling, with a yell of his own.

His frantic scuttling took him to the edge of the chaos and crashing against a tree, where he again landed atop his satchel.

Heat came from it. He felt it even through the leather side of the satchel, and it burned him where it touched him.

He yanked the bag away and dumped it out on the ground. His kri-stone crystals and the bags of kri-stone powder tumbled this way and that. Something dripped into one eye and made it hard to see. He impatiently brushed it away, paying little attention.

The token from the Seekers dropped out last from his satchel. As before, more faint black markings covered it. This time they did not fade.

Gya then noticed the tingle of kri-stone magic. *Another Magicka?*

As he tried to spot the other in the mess of tangled people and horses, the tingle grew stronger.

Some came from the token. But the rest?

There!

Two Magickas sat atop their horses on the other side of the tumult. Within the confusion, Gya's companions struggled against people in Seekers' uniforms.

Fear gripped him. *How had the Seekers found them?*

He should help. He clambered to his feet, wobbling, hissing with the pain in his head and elsewhere, but could do no more than cling to the tree to stay upright.

The two Magickas, a man and a woman, worked in complete coordination as they drew two sigils in the air.

"Beware the Magickas," he shouted as he looked around, making himself dizzy in the process. *What to do?*

The distinctive crack of one of those flintlocks followed by a scream yanked his attention back to the fight.

The female Magicka slid from her horse, curled around a bloody arm, and in the next second the other Magicka fell as well, for some reason. Gya did not think the second Magicka had been hit.

Someone else fired their flintlock and a Seeker yelled as his horse took exception to the sudden, unfamiliar noise and bucked, throwing him from its back. He landed off to the side of the fighting and curled there, groaning.

That seemed to be all it took to squelch the fight in the other Seekers. As they tried to break away, to run, Gya's companions caught them and knocked them to the ground using various means.

While Hali scrambled around tying the Seekers' wrists and ankles with spare bandages, Alorsha did the same to the two Magickas. She also swiped something across both their necks. *The sleep salve,* Gya guessed.

Mikolus and Kluir caught the horses, both the companions' and their attackers'.

Gya suddenly remembered the token.

It lay near his feet. The thin lines had vanished again, leaving it looking exactly as it had at first, when the Seeker had handed the tokens to them.

With some effort, as he tried to move past the pain, he gathered his kri-stone crystals and the bags of powder and returned them to his satchel. Even looking as it had before, something about the token bothered him. He was not sure it was safe to touch, but at the same time he was not sure he could safely just leave it behind. He left it for the moment.

He jumped at a touch on his shoulder and groaned at the pain that shot through him with the sudden movement.

Alorsha dropped to sit next to him as she called for Kluir.

Gya soon found himself the center of a bit of fuss as Alorsha and Kluir cleaned the wound on the side of his head and plastered one of Alorsha's salves on it. The others joined them, and they assessed their various injuries.

No one was unscathed, but Gya's head wound seemed the worst. One of the Seekers had hit him with the flat of his sword—mostly—when they had first ambushed the group. The others had a variety of scrapes, small cuts and bruises and their clothes looked worse for the scuffle. Alorsha sported a painful-looking scrape on the side of her face, and a nasty bruise there, too.

"We did come out rather lightly," Mikolus said. "For being caught so woefully oblivious. We won't be caught like that again."

"I think they meant to capture us," Alorsha said. "They did not seem to be fighting to kill."

Mikolus agreed with her assessment.

"What of them?" Gya waved a hand at the bound Seekers and Magickas. With the fuss over, he was surprised to count only four Seekers.

"A little worse for their attack on us," Hali said with a grin. "Nothing too serious."

"But you used those flintlocks," Gya said.

"Only grazed the one's arm," Alorsha said. "The Magicka. The other flintlock's ball went wide."

"Already wrapped the woman's injury," Kluir said. "She'll hurt for a while but won't bleed to death. As for the rest, scrapes, cuts and bruises like us."

While they had talked, two of the Seekers had been yelling and swearing at them. Gya glanced at them and realized he knew the one.

"That's that commander," he blurted out.

Alorsha nodded. "It's interesting how they claimed to be against Magickas and yet here they are using them."

"Yes, but 'here they are' how?" Hali said.

"Maybe something to do with that." Gya pointed at his token which still lay nearby, partly covered by dirt. He picked it up by its cord and stuffed it into a pouch at his waist. "I felt kri-stone magic earlier. From the Magickas as they were drawing the sigil, but also from the token. Those lines appeared again, too." He shared a look with Alorsha.

"Oh, will you shut it!" Kluir jumped to his feet and glared at their noisy captives. Alorsha grabbed his hand and put her jar of sleep salve in it. With a nod to her, he stalked to the bound Seekers and used a piece of their bindings to swipe some of the salve onto their skin. After that, only peaceful quiet came from them.

Alorsha hid a grin.

"We shouldn't linger here," she said when Kluir joined them again and returned her jar. "But where can we safely leave them?" She waved a hand at the captives.

"Are there predators in these areas?" Hali asked Gya.

He looked around as he considered the question. "We've certainly seen creatures that predators might eat, the rabbits and squirrels and such."

"That we have. I've also seen tracks at some of the streams," Mikolus said. "Some kind of feline, I'd say. More than twice as large as the *Deliberia's* cats, from the size of the tracks."

"So we need a better place than here to leave them." Alorsha tucked away the jars she had gotten out to tend wounds and strode to the captives. The others joined her there, all moving carefully to avoid aggravating their injuries.

"Maybe take them back to that abandoned encampment," Kluir suggested.

"I hate to backtrack so far," Alorsha murmured.

Mikolus grabbed one of the Seekers under his arm and hauled him toward one of their horses. "Get them on their horses and follow their path back. Might be we'll find something there without the need to retrace our own path."

Alorsha nodded agreement. With some difficulty, they got the four Seekers and two Magickas atop the horses they had brought and secured there. They led those horses and their own and followed Mikolus as he tracked their attackers back from the site of the scuffle.

The Seekers' trail took them roughly north. After a couple of hours, Mikolus called a halt and went on ahead alone. Gya jumped when something touched his hand. The Magicka on the horse he led had stirred. She had tapped his hand with her foot. He alerted Alorsha who joined him to look her over.

"The salve is wearing off. Sooner than it should have. Maybe losing potency."

"Or maybe doesn't work as well on a Magicka," the Magicka murmured and peered at them blearily.

"Please don't," she added when Alorsha reached for her satchel.

The Magicka lifted her bound hands and Gya saw she had that same odd wound on her arm. Although hers looked more healed than the others he had seen. "Can't do anything while I'm like this," the woman said. "I won't be made to, as long as they are out." She nodded toward the Seekers.

"So they *do* control Magickas somehow," Gya said.

The woman nodded. "We're a danger to you. You should get away before they wake."

"We can get you away from them," Gya said. "You don't even have to stay with us, if you don't want. You can go your own way."

"You can't take us with you." She lifted her bound hands again and inclined her head to indicate the wound on her left arm. "With that, they can find us."

"What is it?" Alorsha leaned close to study the mostly healed wound.

"Kri-stone crystal. They cut us and put one in each of us. They connect us somehow. Those gloves they wear let them keep track of us, and others." She glanced at her hands, then turned a sad, serious look on Gya. "They've used something similar to track you—"

"The tokens!" Gya broke in. He pulled his out of the pouch where he had stashed it.

"Yes," the Magicka said. "I overheard them talking about them. They used crushed kri-stone to make the pigments used on those tokens. They can follow you as long as you have them."

With a nod, Alorsha placed a hand on Gya's to get him to put the token back in its pouch. "We'll do something about that. But what of you? We could remove the crystals so you can flee."

"No! We can't. We can't flee. They've got our children, his little girl and my boy."

Alorsha's expression darkened at that.

"Then we can just get them away, too," Gya said.

But the Magicka shook her head against that. "You have my thanks, but they're many days from here. With the way they acted hunting you, you'd better run yourselves. We've been working on figuring something out. Leave us with them, asleep again and longer than they will be, if you can do that – to keep them from getting suspicious."

Gya felt someone next to him and realized Mikolus had returned. He glanced at the other man.

"There's another of those deserted encampments along their trail," Mikolus said.

"We stayed there," the Magicka said. "We'd do well enough there until everyone wakes and you can be long gone."

Alorsha and Mikolus exchanged glances and Alorsha gave a sharp nod.

Mikolus led the way through some thicker brush to reach the encampment. This one was the smallest they had seen, with only three small buildings within the fenced-in area.

The group followed the Magicka's advice and took their captives to the smallest of the buildings. They placed them on some low cots inside and tied them there. Mikolus and Kluir tied the horses inside the largest building with some feed and water in reach. They went through the Seekers' small packs but found nothing of concern. To help protect the Magicka from any suspicion on the part of the Seekers, they left the Seekers with their special gloves.

"We'll dump the tokens in a creek or river first chance we get," Alorsha muttered after she again brushed both Magickas' skin with the sleeping salve.

Mikolus smiled. "Hoping to send them chasing after us another direction?" He piled their captives' gear in a corner of the room, far from them, and collected their few weapons.

"Better take their powders and crystals, too," Hali said.

"I hate to leave them without," Gya said. "What if they need them?"

"If we didn't take them, the Seekers would certainly wonder why," Kluir pointed out. "That might lead them to suspect we learned something from their Magickas."

Gya had to admit the truth of that. So he gathered their crystals and powders and tucked them in with his own. They had one thin sigils codex, which he also took. He just hoped they already knew the sigils they might need and would not have need to reference the codex.

One last look to make sure they left things as they wanted, and they hurried away from the place. They decided to head directly north for a time, moving faster this time, until they found a creek that flowed with enough water to carry the tokens along. Mikolus made some effort to make their trail hard to follow without hiding it completely.

At the second creek they came to, much larger than the first, they pulled out all the tokens they had with them and dropped them in, watching as the swift water carried them away further to the north.

Then they turned back to their northwest path. As they rode, Alorsha leaned off the side of her horse to trail her hand against the plants they passed and magic them to conceal any trail they left behind them. Gya looked around from time to time, watchful for another attack.

~ ~ ~

The days that followed took much the same pattern, barring the attack. Everyone gathered leaves before they rode out in the morning. Gya tore them into small pieces as they rode, while Alorsha continued to urge the plants to hide their trail behind them. Gya struggled to rest when the time came, a sense that they could be attacked again dogged him and kept him twitchy. When they did stop for rest, Alorsha made potions and Gya practiced the sigil before getting what sleep they could. Every couple of days, Mikolus slipped into a nearby village to grab food and leave coins.

After the second night, Gya was able to form the sigil well enough to set the magic on all the horses, and their pace increased. After the third night, Alorsha had created a potion that they could drink to stay safe from fire. She made enough for everyone to have two doses and pointed out that they had already seen the Empire have their Magickas throw fire, so the potions might be needed.

"I had to thin the potion substantially to make it drinkable, so it won't last very long within a fire," she warned them. "If you find yourself in the midst of any fires, move away as soon as you can. Before the potion wears off."

She then worked on other possibly useful potions. At

the same time, Gya began to learn another sigil, one that should let a person hear sounds at a distance. *Could be useful.*

When they were still at least a day and a half away from Hawei, the best Gya figured, Alorsha suddenly halted her horse in the shade of a clump of bushes. She gazed straight ahead, her eyes unfocused. Mikolus eased his horse next to hers but did not touch her.

"What is it?" Gya asked.

"Is it Devrand?" Mikolus asked Alorsha.

For several long minutes, Alorsha did not move, did not answer. Gya could only barely see her breathing. With a shudder, she returned to them.

"He's begun to pull on this world's magic," Alorsha said.

"So we're too late?" Gya said.

Alorsha shook her head. "He's only started, and it feels like he's having some trouble drawing the magic to himself." She moved her horse out of the bushes and dismounted.

"Gya, please use that sigil that staves off fatigue on all the horses again," she instructed. "We're going to have to get there as fast as we can manage now."

The others dismounted so Gya would catch only the horses with the sigil. It would not do much for them to be caught in it, except it might weaken its effects spread out over so many beings.

"So he's in Hawei?" Kluir said.

"No," Alorsha said. "It feels like he's… lower? Underground? Maybe under the town, the best I can tell. I think he's in kri-stone caves under the town."

Gya momentarily interrupted his magic-working. "They're *under* Hawei?"

At Alorsha's curt nod, he returned his attention to his magic. The others refrained from any further conversation to keep from distracting him.

When he finished, they mounted again.

"How long do you think that will let the horses keep going?" Mikolus said.

"Half-again as long as if I hadn't done it," Gya said. "Although the description was not precise. They'll need extra food when it wears off, though. I think they can only tolerate this magic one or two more times before they'll need extra rest, or we'll lose them."

Mikolus nodded. "I hope that we'll only need do it once more after this. We should be there then?" He gave both Alorsha and Gya a questioning look.

Alorsha nodded and Gya said, "I think so."

They picked up their pace but alternated the faster pace with some periods of walking the horses. They also traveled much longer than usual before Mikolus finally called a halt.

"We've got to get at least a little rest. Won't do any good to get there exhausted," he said to Alorsha's resentful look. "I can tell the sigil is wearing off. We'll take that rest, eat, and Gya can place his magic on the horses again and we'll get there before it wears off again."

"Is he still gathering the magic?" Kluir asked Alorsha.

Instead of answering right away, she closed her eyes.

Probably checking, however it was she did that. Gya watched to see if he could get any sort of clue but saw nothing.

Opening her eyes again, she cupped the double-framed pendant in her hands and peered into the stone for a short time.

"He is." She slid off her horse. "Still with some difficulties, it seems, although I can't tell exactly what they are."

"Then we have some time yet." Mikolus set about tending to the horses and making sure they had plenty to eat within tether range. They had moved back into a drier region of the Empire, fewer trees and more brush, but the grass was still plentiful enough.

While Gya ate, he checked through his sigil codices once more and marked the pages of the sigils that would most likely be useful. He also flipped through the codex he had taken from the Seekers' Magickas but did not spot anything there that looked immediately useful.

Without using any kri-stone, he practiced drawing the sigils he thought he would most likely need, to try to make sure he would not forget a spiral or swirl. He reassured himself that if he did, he could easily find the sigils in the codex anyway to refresh his memory.

He tried to rest but found it difficult. He worried about Chizoa and Toa, Ifeoma and Vabena. *Would they be there with Alorsha's two men? Would they still be safe and unharmed?*

He had seen the Magickas the Empire had used to attack Alorsha's ship. They had looked broken somehow. He hoped his brother and friends were not like that. He hoped his brother would let him explain what had happened when the Keepers had taken their father.

At some point he finally fell asleep, to be awakened by Kluir.

"Time to head out." Kluir handed him some food that he barely saw in the predawn light.

Gya ate and again pulled out the kri-stone powder and crystals he needed for the sigil for the horses. That magic accomplished, he pulled all the sigil codices from his pack, save only his most-basic one, and managed to stuff them into his satchel. The he sorted his powders and crystals to place the ones he most likely would need at the top of the satchel. He slung the bag cross-body over his shoulder, as he preferred to carry it, and mounted his horse.

CHAPTER 30

They continued to ride through brush and stunted trees but moved faster than before. Mikolus led the way, with Alorsha right behind him guiding him. Gya followed, and Kluir and Hali brought up the rear. The trees continued to thin, and everyone looked around periodically. *Might the Seekers have found some way to still follow? Would there be another ambush, perhaps?* Gya's disquiet at the possibility seemed to pass to his horse which became a little hard to control. But he managed.

The morning waned and Gya fought to contain his twitchiness even as he feared he might burst from his nerves. Mikolus called a halt near a brook after Alorsha spoke with him briefly. He motioned for the others to gather close. They had left behind even the scattered trees and found themselves in low grassy and brush-covered hills that Gya surmised were the ones south of Hawei. *Certainly looked like them, anyway.*

"Gya, can you feel if kri-stones are nearby?" Alorsha asked.

Gya started to shake his head, then paused. "Not by

myself. But I think there's a sigil that might perhaps let me do that." He looked around at all of them. "Shall I try it?"

"Please," Alorsha said. "I'm feeling too much magic swirling around now. It's confusing."

Gya pulled out the sigil codex he had taken from the Seekers' Magickas and the needed kri-stone powders and crystals. The sigil reminded him of the one Toa had drawn not too long ago to use with the brothers' seeing stone to see the magic on the *Deliberia*. This one, however, surpassed that one in complexity and took three different colors. It was also more focused on seeing kri-stone. From the description, Gya suspected its main purpose had been to find lost crystals and powders. But it might work for what he wanted here.

As he worked through the various swirls that made up the sigil, he found it easier to draw than he had expected, even on the rough ground, although the dull ache from his head wound still troubled him and grew sharper when he tried to concentrate. The pain warned him that he would likely be unable to work much magic – still too soon. To finalize the magic, he tapped his seeing-stone three times on key junctions within the sigil before he held it to his eye.

He gasped as the area around burst into brilliant twirling colors. At first, he could make no sense of what he saw, but then he realized that they seemed to be swirling only nearby. Somewhat off to their left, toward low hills, they formed more of a line.

"I think I'm seeing your swirling magic," he said to Alorsha. "But over there"—he pointed—"I can see it's more organized. It seems to be flowing out from that direction in a kind of stream and dissolving into this confusing swirl where we are."

After everyone had dismounted, Mikolus tied the horses within reach of grasses and the brook. "We'll go on foot from here."

They unloaded their horses and hid anything they

planned to leave there. They took all the weapons and materials for treating wounds, and everything Gya and Alorsha expected to need for their magics. Gya gathered the powders from his sigil. The description in the codex said the magic would last for some time without the need to keep the sigil intact. He only wished it had been more specific about how long.

Still looking through his seeing stone, Gya led them to the place where the chaotic magics were calmer and aligned.

He pointed again. "It seems to come from over there."

"Is it one of the caves?" Kluir peered that direction.

"I don't see a cave opening," Hali said.

"Let's get closer, then. But cautiously," Mikolus said.

Gya still led the way, but now Hali walked next to him, her sword out and ready, and a flintlock in her other hand. Gya tried to move as quietly as Mikolus did through the grasses but felt certain he failed miserably. Still, no one came to demand answers of them, to know what they were doing.

The sight faded from Gya's seeing-stone a short time later, having lasted almost half an hour. He did not think it worth it to cast another sigil. He might need the magic for something more important soon.

They continued the direction they had been going and before long found themselves in a dry, rocky arroyo within the low hills, which now loomed above their heads.

A hint of something caught Gya's attention. He paused to concentrate on the sensation, to see if he could identify it. The others paused also and gave him questioning looks.

"I think I feel the kri-stone magic," Gya told them after a few minutes. "Coming from further that way." He nodded in the direction they had been going.

"Keep a look out for any opening that might lead to caves," Mikolus told them as they resumed their trek through the clumps of grasses and bushes scattered along their path.

Before long, Kluir spotted an opening in the rock wall to their left. They cautiously explored it, but it did not lead very far underground.

Traveling on, they found more such openings and took the time to investigate each one, trying to be as quiet as possible. They also found side gullies that met the one they walked. At each, Gya verified the direction from which he felt the kri-stone magic. They made only one turn off the first arroyo to follow another. After nearly an hour of this walking several steps and pausing to check out openings or attached gullies, Gya felt he might scream from the tension.

At the next opening they found, to their right that time, Mikolus told everyone to take a short rest while he took a look ahead. He confirmed with Gya that he still felt kri-stone magic further that direction then headed that way.

Gya and the others who waited with him sipped some water and checked weapons and magic implements but spoke little. There did not seem to be anything that needed to be said.

At a sound from outside their shelter, Hali jumped up alert and with weapons ready. A low whistle announced Mikolus's return.

He crouched in the opening of their shelter and pulled out his waterskin. "Might be I've found the entrance. The plants there are much disturbed, like several people trod them on their way through there, and it looks like there's been some digging to enlarge the opening." He drank some of his water.

"Devrand hasn't much cared before that I follow," Alorsha said, "so I wouldn't think he would start now. He *is* gathering the magic. It's slow, but steadily growing now. I can feel it."

"Then let's go," Hali said.

They held themselves ready in case anyone attacked and followed Mikolus to his likely opening.

Within, they were forced to walk one behind the other

to proceed through the cramped passage. The walls were rough stone, the same gray-brown color as the dirt outside and the floor they walked on. They encountered no side passages, but Gya felt certain the passage sloped down, taking them deeper underground. Once the light from the opening disappeared, they periodically passed small glowing kri-stone crystals stuck somehow high on the walls. The crystals provided enough light for them to see where they walked.

After nearly half an hour, the tunnel began to widen, and some light filtered to them from somewhere ahead.

"Ready?" Alorsha whispered to Gya, who walked close behind her.

He nodded and pulled the kri-stone crystals and powder for the sleep sigil from his bag. As they approached what looked like an opening into a larger area, he began drawing the sigil in the air. It moved with him, he was pleased to see.

Short of the opening, Mikolus motioned everyone to flatten themselves along the wall. He crept alone to the opening to see what they faced.

Two quick steps back to them and he held up five fingers. Then he held up three and pointed to one side, then two and pointed the other way.

"Magickas?" Gya mouthed the word more than vocalized it when Mikolus looked at him. Mikolus nodded.

Mikolus pointed to Kluir, Hali and Gya, and pointed toward the three Magickas that he had indicated to one side. Then Mikolus indicated that he and Alorsha would go toward the two. After everyone nodded their understanding, they crept to the opening.

Gya froze in shock at his first sight of what lay beyond the opening. The cave was huge! Kri-stone crystals, of all colors lined the entire space. Many of the crystals glowed faintly. Rocks that matched the tunnel walls littered the floor, many of them large enough for a person to hide behind.

Hali nudged Gya to a spot behind one of the large rocks and pointed to the Magickas further in, three men. Gya did not know any of them.

He studied them, bothered by something. All three Magickas stood next to the kri-stone walls, both hands flat on the crystals, but with their arms fully extended, looking like they were trying to pull away. The crystals beneath their hands glowed brighter than the surrounding ones. A spot on each of their left arms also glowed, about as long as Gya's thumb and in the shape of a kri-stone crystal. *The kri-stone crystals the Empire had embedded in the Magickas' arms.*

As Gya watched, an arc of light jumped from one of the crystals further away to the crystals beneath the Magickas' hands and to the small crystals in their arms. The Magickas shuddered and Gya realized the expressions on all of their faces were a combination of pain and terror.

Against Hali's frantic admonitions, Gya stepped out and walked toward the three Magickas while he held his nearly complete sigil ready in front of him. He felt that the Magickas were aware of him, but they did not turn to look at him. More magic arced to the crystals beneath their hands as he approached and to the crystals under their skin. An answering tingle from his nearly completed sigil poked Gya. He heard Hali and Kluir follow close behind.

"They don't seem able to move." Gya stopped several steps away from the Magickas. He completed his sigil, but still held it in the air instead of sending it at the Magickas.

Hali looked around the cave and drew Gya's attention to where the others stood near the far wall. The Magickas next to them, too, seemed unable to pull away from the crystals. Gya recognized those Magickas.

"Ifeoma! Vabena!" They did not respond, did not seem to have even heard him. *Where were Toa and Chizoa? Were they there, too?*

Gya peered around the cave but saw no one else.

"Don't send any magic at them," Alorsha called to Gya. Her voice was not loud, but clear enough in the cave.

"What are they doing?" Kluir murmured to Gya and edged closer to the Magickas.

Gya joined him. He released the magic of the sleeping sigil and caught the streaming kri-stone powder back in its pouch. Then he pulled out a different powder and worked a sigil on his seeing-stone. He looked through it.

"I'm not sure they're actually doing anything," he said. "It looks more like they're connected to the crystals, magically, and the magic is going through them."

"To Devrand, I think," Alorsha said as she and Mikolus joined them. "He's not in here."

"Maybe another cave nearby?" Kluir said.

Mikolus shook his head. "I've found no passage from this one, if there *is* another cave nearby."

Gya edged closer to the three Magickas nearest him and peered at them through his seeing-stone. "Above us somewhere. The magic's flowing through them and going up." He looked at the ceiling of the cave above him but did not see anything except rock and some more crystals.

"Another cave above this one?" Hali said.

Gya shrugged.

"Can we free them?" Kluir waved a hand at the motionless Magickas.

In answer, Mikolus first tried to pry Ifeoma's hands away from the crystals, then wrapped both arms around her waist from behind and pulled. It seemed that was starting to work, but then she shrieked as if in horrible agony. The other Magickas did, too.

Mikolus released her and jumped back. The Magickas stopped shrieking.

Kluir shook his head sadly and moved close to study the two women.

"They don't seem to be blinking," he said after a moment.

Hali stepped up behind the closest man and gave him a sudden hard rap to the head with the pommel of her sword. The man dropped to the floor as his hands came free of the crystals without any fuss or shrieking. Hali hauled the man away from the crystals.

Kluir frowned. "Effective, but not what I'd had in mind." He pulled a bandage from the bag he carried, whipped it in front of Ifeoma's eyes and tied it behind her head. She shuddered, her hands fell away from the crystals, and she collapsed. Kluir caught her and took her away from the crystals that lined the walls as Hali had the man she had felled.

Gya saw that Hali's man was already moving, trying to get up. He seemed groggy and confused.

"Why did you say to not send any magic at them?" Gya asked Alorsha as she grabbed a bandage from Kluir and tied it around Vabena's head, covering her eyes, as Kluir had done for Ifeoma.

"They just absorb the magic into what they're doing," she said. "I tried that a short time ago and learned that."

Mikolus caught Vabena when she collapsed after Alorsha blindfolded her. He carried her to the others. He and Kluir treated the two remaining Magickas the same and brought them to lie with the others, all of whom were moving, but groggy.

"Ifeoma? Vabena? It's Gya. Gyasi. From Hawei. Don't you know me?" Gya knelt next to the Magickas, who did not act like they knew he spoke to them.

None of them spoke or answered any questions the group asked of them.

Hali waved a hand at the Magickas. "Think it's safe to leave them here?"

"Well, definitely no Devrand close by," Alorsha commented after she had wandered around the cave to double-check.

"Five of them, five of us," she added. "Let's get them out to one of the other lesser caves in the arroyo. Leave their eyes covered until we're out of sight of these crystals, though, just in case."

Hali quickly blindfolded the first man, who had tried to

head back to his place at the wall. He subsided after she covered his eyes.

"Did the magic flow stop?" Mikolus asked Gya.

Gya raised his seeing-stone, looked all around the cave, and shook his head. "Still flowing up through the ceiling. But it *has* slowed."

"That's something anyway," Alorsha muttered as she got one of the Magickas to his feet, steadied him, and headed back toward the entrance.

They spent close to an hour taking the Magickas from the kri-stone cave and lodging them safely in a small cave nearby but out of sight of the large cave opening. They left some food and water with them and managed to get Ifeoma to respond, to understand to stay hidden, so they felt the Magickas would be fine for a time there. Gya did not think she had recognized him, though. They returned to the cave entrance but paused there.

"Gya, do you have a seeing sigil to tell if what you're looking at is real?" Mikolus asked.

"Thinking Devrand and his Magickas might have magically hidden another passage?" Hali said.

Mikolus nodded.

Gya shook his head. "Not one I can work yet."

"Devrand might not be in a cave at all. See there?" Alorsha pointed to the northwest, toward the cliffs that Gya knew rose above the sea.

Gya peered the direction she indicated. *Was that a glow? Difficult to see in the brightness of midday.* The others' comments confirmed they saw it, too.

So they headed that direction. After they climbed out of the arroyo, Gya could see that the glow was somewhat west of the cave he and his friends had used for their magics. That seemed so long ago somehow.

"Looks like it might be on the cliffs that overlook the great sea," he told his companions.

"How far away?" Alorsha said.

"Maybe a couple of hours walking," Gya guessed.

Alorsha looked back the way they had come. "I hate to backtrack. But how long to get back to the horses?"

"Close to just as long," Hali said.

Alorsha turned back toward the cliffs and pulled out her pendant. She concentrated on it and it swung out to point toward the cliffs, making only a tiny arc.

She exchanged a look with Mikolus and tucked it away again. He nodded and they hastened toward the cliffs.

"Hope we can get there faster than you estimated," Alorsha told Gya.

~ ~ ~

Gya and the others crouched in some scrub bushes in sight of the cliff edge. Devrand stood within a pace of that edge. Gya knew him from his description.

A second man crouched at his feet, his head down, with Devrand gripping his shoulder. Gya could not see that man's face, but judging by the hair color, he must be Alorsha's Jarthan. A glance at Alorsha's face confirmed Gya's suspicions. On the other side of Devrand, Toa and Chizoa clung to his arm, their expressions the same as the Magickas' in the cave, but their eyes were closed.

Although the magic of the sigil for his seeing-stone had worn off, Gya was certain they were caught in the flow of the magic from the kri-stone cave. Since their eyes were closed, he guessed that covering their eyes would not free them.

"Distance magic isn't likely to work," Alorsha whispered. "I suspect they'll simply absorb it." She pulled out her bow and some arrows.

"Not the flintlock?" Gya said.

Alorsha shook her head. "I'm much more accurate with the bow. If I manage to drop Devrand, be ready all of you to pull the others away." She pulled out a vial and dipped several arrowheads into its contents.

"You're trying that again?" Mikolus said.

Alorsha nodded. "I've been working with the elixir. It should work much faster now."

"What does it do?" Gya said.

"It interferes with a person's ability to draw on their magic, and others', too, I hope." Alorsha looked around at all of them. "Ready?"

"Better drink the potion against fire." Kluir followed his own advice.

The others emulated him and nodded their readiness to Alorsha.

She drank her own potion and rose to a crouch while the others scattered from the bushes. She shot two arrows in quick succession.

Gya ran toward Toa and Chizoa, making certain he did not get between Alorsha and Devrand. Kluir and Hali ran with him, while Mikolus dashed toward Jarthan.

While he ran, Gya pawed through his bag and pulled out some crystals and powders. A glance showed him he had grabbed the colorless, purple, and pink crystals and their powders. Clarity, connections, and love. They would have to do.

He began drawing a sigil in the air, pleased to see it keep pace with him as he moved, as the other sigil had previously. This sigil was a blending of two he remembered from the codices. He hoped that it might work, even if only a little, and in spite of Alorsha's belief that the Magickas—and Devrand too, he supposed— would absorb the magic. *Maybe for once he could do something effective.* Maybe he could free his brother and friend from whatever hold Devrand had on them.

Gya heard another arrow fly past and a hiss of pain. From the arrow striking Devrand, he hoped. The plants near him began to grow and sway. They stretched toward Devrand, crawled up his legs and wrapped around them.

When he neared the captive Magickas, Gya's sigil writhed in the air, twisted, then flowed toward Chizoa's arm, to the kri-stone embedded there under her skin. Gya briefly met Devrand's gaze and shuddered at the glee and triumph he saw there. The man had two thin lines of blood across one cheek and another along one arm soaking into his sleeve. *From Alorsha's arrows?* He seemed unaffected by any magic that might have been in the elixir she had put on them.

Gya shoved the remaining crystals and powders back in his pack and stumbled the last steps to the Magickas.

Hali and Kluir reached the Magickas at nearly the same time. They grabbed hold of Toa and tried to pull him away. Gya grabbed Chizoa's arm to do the same and gasped as kri-stone magic tore through him, flowing into him from the cave and through him to Chizoa and Devrand. Gya felt, and saw, something dark reach out from Devrand, a writhing smoky wisp that chilled him and numbed him. With a despairing cry, he let go of Chizoa.

But he actually did not.

Frantic, he fought to pull his hand from her arm, twisted and writhed, but he remained stuck. But somehow his head cleared, a little anyway. From the corner of his eye he caught sight of Hali as she swung her sword at Devrand's arm, above where the Magickas held it.

Time seemed to slow for Gya. He saw Devrand's hand tighten on Jarthan's shoulder. Jarthan raised his own hand – reluctance clear in his expression and his languid motion. Mikolus tried to stop him, to grab his arm, but something stopped him a step away. A faint, wavy shimmer appeared around Devrand. The sword rang like a discordant bell as it hit something a bare finger-width from the man's arm.

Sudden fire tore through Gya, through Chizoa, into Devrand. For an instant, everyone seemed suspended in motion, then the unseen fire burst out to throw Gya, Kluir, Hali and Mikolus nearly back to the bushes in which they had hidden. It incinerated the grasses around Devrand in a rough circle and scorched the ground.

Groggy, Gya tried to stand, tried to see what he could do, but his legs folded under him and dropped him back to the ground. Fire in a myriad of colors burst out of the bag he carried, burst from the kri-stone crystals and powder.

He panted from pain and fear as the fire began to eat through the defense that potion gave him and he scrambled to peel the bag from his body. When he managed to get free of it, he threw it away as far as he could. The fiery bag landed on the already scorched ground and an instant later was consumed by the flames. All his crystals and powders and the codices of sigils he had stuffed in there with them, gone in an instant.

Shrieks of pain, of horror, yanked his attention back to the Magickas, just in time to see them flare up like torches. Gya yelled for them, for his brother and the woman he had been coming to love. Gya screamed for them, shrieked their names.

But they were already gone.

The fire soared into the sky and arched over Devrand, who laughed wildly as he stood there untouched. The flames stretched further and struck the just-visible center of Hawei, then arched up again and soared out further. *Toward Ikkavai, the next town over,* Gya thought. Fire in all the colors of kri-stone burst from several places in the ground and engulfed Hawei. In the distance, Gya saw other pillars of fire climb to the sky.

Alorsha yelled something and scrambled to her feet. She charged toward Devrand from where she had been thrown.

The man just smiled at her and hauled the other man to his feet. The smoky wisp Gya had seen earlier swirled around Devrand then streamed out into an impossible hole that split the air behind him. Still smiling, he stepped backward through that hole, some kind of opening to another place, it looked like. Although the other man with him attempted to twist away from him and strained toward Alorsha, Devrand yanked him through the hole with him.

As Alorsha lunged for it, the opening turned hazy around the edges. With a whoosh of air, it snapped shut before she reached it.

For a long, silent moment Alorsha stood and stared at the place where Devrand and Jarthan had disappeared. Her arms hung limp at her sides and a helpless look of despair mixed with anger twisted her face. Without a sound, she sank to her knees and pounded on the ground with both fists.

Gya stood at the edge of the rounded blackened area, the taste of ashes in his mouth, keenly aware of his inability to offer Alorsha, or himself, any comfort or hope. His tears for Toa and Chizoa fell unheeded, streaming down his cheeks. A scream built in his chest, clawing to get out. But he swallowed it as unhelpful and just stared at the devastation.

CHAPTER 31

How long he stood shrouded in dark anguish, Gya did not know. What brought him out of it was a small sound, a whimper, from somewhere nearby. He looked around and spotted something brightly colored, oranges and yellows, in the tall grasses to the east of the blackened patch of ground. Motion caught his attention as Mikolus stalked that direction.

He must have heard the sound, too.

Gya followed but stayed back at a gesture from the other man. In passing he noticed Hali and Kluir both crouched near Alorsha, talking softly to her.

Gya stopped a step behind Mikolus as the other knelt and parted the grass. The oranges and yellows turned out to be the fine clothing worn by a woman. From the richness of the fabrics, Gya surmised she must be someone important in the Atturei Empire.

She lay huddled in a ball, rocked back and forth, and whimpered and muttered. Gya spotted a small patch of burnt ground near her, the exact shape and size of one of the Empire's tokens.

When Mikolus placed a gentle hand on the woman's shoulder, she jerked with a shriek and unfolded. That motion let Gya see the burned ruin of her chest and both hands. In those fire-ravaged hands, she clutched what looked like the cord from the token.

Mikolus called Kluir over.

Gya struggled to make sense of what he saw. All of the Empire's tokens must have had kri-stone pigments. Because this woman was certainly noteworthy in the Empire and so was no Magicka. *The Empire must have been keeping track of everyone!*

The woman's muttering pulled him from his musings. She seemed unaware of Kluir and his attempts to put some of Alorsha's salve on her wounds.

"He left," the woman repeated several times, her voice raspy. "He left me. Something amazing, he said." She seemed to focus on Mikolus then, but Gya wondered if she truly saw anything. Her voice rose to shriek and she shuddered violently.

"He took it all. Finally no filthy magic! All the kri-stone linked and eradicated!" She lurched away from Kluir and fell to one side. He reached out to help her, but she batted him away.

"Oh, it burns. All burning. Magic burning up." She whimpered again, shuddered and let out a long, rattling sigh. Then she lay motionless.

Kluir gently turned her over but no breath moved her chest. She was clearly gone.

He and Mikolus exchanged glances and turned to Gya.

"Do you know her?" Kluir said in a low voice.

Gya shook his head. "I've not seen her before. By her clothes, I'd say she was someone rich, important. Not from Hawei."

His voice cracked when he said the name of his town, his destroyed home. He turned away to compose himself.

"What customs do your people have? For your dead?" Mikolus asked.

"I—" Gya could not continue. *Why should this stranger— who had probably conspired with that Devrand—why should she get a proper burial when Chizoa and Toa wouldn't? It wasn't fair!*

Kluir patted his shoulder. "How about we just take care of it? Bury her."

Gya nodded and turned back to watch Hali and Alorsha. He heard soft rustlings behind him and the low murmur of Kluir and Mikolus talking, but when he glanced back after many minutes, they had already gone down the slope. He watched them as they took the woman's body in the direction of one of the arroyos. *To one of those small caves there*, he guessed. *That would do.*

Needing to do something useful, but something that did not require him to think, he decided to retrieve what they had left behind in their last push to reach this place quickly. His tread heavy, Gya headed back to where they had left the horses.

~ ~ ~

When Gya returned with the horses a few hours later, he found his companions huddled in the untouched grasses between Hawei and the scorched area where Devrand had been. All of them were soot smudged, their expressions weary and discouraged.

Mikolus greeted him with a nod and rose to his feet. "Better find a place to camp." He took the reins of his horse from Gya. The others did likewise.

Gya looked around. He winced when his gaze passed the scorched area. "What of the other Magickas?"

Hali shook her head, her expression saddened. "They burned, too. Nothing left in their hideaway except scorch marks."

Gya blinked against the tears that stung his eyes as another stabbing agony of loss ripped through him. Toa and Chizoa, and now Ifeoma and Vabena. *Was he going to be the only one left?*

Kluir gave his shoulder a pat. "Come on."

Mikolus led the way to one of the creeks that flowed near Hawei and followed it a short distance away from the ruined town to a place to camp.

After everyone cleaned up, getting rid of grime and soot, they gathered around the small fire to eat. Conversation was subdued, but Gya did learn that the others had looked through Hawei and also returned to the large cave of kri-stone.

Everywhere they had found the same, complete fiery destruction. They had found no one alive in Hawei, and no bodies. They had apparently burned away in the kri-stone blazes. While most of the buildings in town were also broken and burnt, Alorsha hoped they might still find some additional supplies for the *Deliberia*, when the ship arrived. She planned to begin looking in the morning.

With that meager plan in place, they settled in for a sad, troubled night.

~ ~ ~

The *Deliberia* arrived at the ruins of Hawei early the next day. With a sense of barely restrained frenzy, Alorsha and her crew dove into preparations to leave, to sail away, driven by Alorsha's need to be after Jarthan, to stay on Devrand's trail. They spread out through the ruination that had been Hawei and scrounged supplies from the few buildings around the edges that still stood, somewhat.

The devastation shocked Gya and tore even more at the losses that ate at him. Nothing was left of the bulk of the town, of the people who had lived and worked and argued and laughed there. Just soot and broken stones everywhere, with a burnt miasma that hovered in the air and stung his eyes and nose. Gya could barely look at the blackened, sunken ground where his town had once stood.

Gya tried to help the *Deliberia* crew, where he could, but he soon decided to just get out of their way, so he returned to the place he had last seen Chizoa and Toa.

Now he could never explain to Toa what happened with their father. Would never be able to ask his brother to forgive him for his role in it. All their times when they laughed together, and badgered each other in fun, those would never happen again.

He pictured Chizoa as he had known her. He pictured her soft smile, her pretty amber eyes, remembered the sound of her delighted laugh. She was gone and he had never told her how he felt. If only he could even see her one more time, touch her fingers, bask in her bright regard. But now he would never share any more moments with her. He fingered the hair stick she had loved and let his tears fall.

He had not known Vabena well, and now he would never get the chance to. Chizoa had always held her grandmother in high regard, and Vabena had always had a gentle smile for Gya. While a lesser pain, her loss nonetheless ripped through him.

As did Ifeoma's. Ifeoma, who had loved baking and always bustled about her shop with her bright beaded bracelets a soft clacking and tinkling accompaniment to her motions. He did not think he would ever smell freshly baked bread again without thinking of her.

All of them… just gone.

Gya remembered then talk among the townsfolk of the hidden realms. Many claimed that those realms held places where the spirits of the dead lived in happiness. Gya hoped that Toa and Chizoa, Ifeoma and Vabena were happy there, hoped Toa had found their parents there. Maybe they even now knew the things he had not been able to tell them.

He hoped so but that did little to console him.

The day wore on with Gya mostly lost in memories. He did join the others for an evening meal at the harbor and soon a murky dusk blanketed the destruction of Hawei.

With the arrival of that dusk, the ship was ready. Gya

wondered at the wisdom of setting sail in the heavy mist and with night rapidly approaching. A glance at Alorsha's determined expression kept him from questioning her about it.

He watched in silence as the last of the *Deliberia*'s crew went aboard and prepared to cast off. The docks had not suffered as the town had but looked forlorn with just two slumped structures near them. The sadness and loss that welled up in him at the thought of the *Deliberia* leaving surprised him.

He took a hesitant step toward the ship, nearly tripping over the pack of food and some clothing that sat at his feet, then stopped himself.

What use would he be where they were going? He was a merchant, a trader. With no goods to trade. He knew prices and negotiating and goods, not weaponry, fighting and sailing a ship. Without the kri-stone, he was not even a Magicka. True, he had the horses – Mikolus had said they could not take them with them on the ship. Gya could sell the ones he did not need to help him start over. Somewhere.

He started to turn away, to go somewhere—although he had no idea where—when he heard someone coming toward him. He knew the cadence of her footsteps.

He turned back. She stopped a pace or so away from him and gave him a strangely hesitant look. He returned her gaze, curious and saddened at the same time.

Finally, Alorsha smiled slightly. "I'm sorry that I've been so distant this day."

"I understand. You don't need to—"

"Yes, I do. We're leaving, probably never to come this way again. I wouldn't leave this standing between us." She looked at her feet. "Your friendship's meant much to me. I'm sorry about what it's done to you."

He waved a hand in the air, dismissing what happened, though he felt hollow inside from the losses. "The things that have happened weren't your fault."

"They happened because of me being here, so I have some share in the disaster. I just wish I could fix everything."

"No, this just happened." He held up a hand to stop her when she would have interrupted him again. "Please, let me speak. I appreciate the apology, but I don't hold you responsible. For any of it. In the time you've been here, I've learned and seen many wondrous, and yes sometimes frightening things that I would never have known about otherwise. I value your friendship. If you ever do happen to return this way, you can always come see me. I imagine I'll join the others east of the Empire. Assuming they were far enough away to escape the disaster. Maybe we'll come back west to start over."

She gave him a sad smile. "Again I must apologize…. No, hear me out. I wasn't entirely truthful just now when I said we *probably* would never return. There is no 'probably' about it. As I told you a while ago, I've pursued Devrand for many long months now, and never once, in all that time, have we passed back through a place we've been before."

Gya stared at her as he absorbed her words.

"So this is truly goodbye." She touched the back of his hand lightly and turned to return to the *Deliberia*.

After a couple of steps, she turned back.

"One thing I can do, to go a little way toward helping, is offer you passage back to Azkra. It will save you a lot of time traveling there to meet with your friends and would mean we need not say good-bye quite so soon."

"But what of catching up to your Jarthan?"

Alorsha sighed. "Over those long months, I've noticed the magic that takes us to same world Devrand has gone to always takes us to within a few weeks—at most—of his arrival. Even when we've delayed longer in leaving. Although I don't wish to delay too long as it makes the magic more difficult. I wouldn't leave you stranded in this destruction. We can certainly see you well on your way. If you wish."

With a slight grin and a nod, Gya grabbed his pack. Together they stripped the horses of all their tack and shooed them in the direction of the closest stream. Then they walked to the waiting ship.

~ ~ ~

Gya found the voyage back to Azkra much like the first one. Unable to practice any of his magic this time, he still watched the weapons-work every morning and even allowed Mikolus to persuade him to join in as he had before to learn a few more basic things.

He discovered that he liked the archery but had no desire at all to get anywhere near the flintlocks. Mikolus only grinned at him when he emphatically expressed that opinion.

At first, they sailed just within sight of the southern shoreline, wary of any Imperial encounters. But after they passed port after port and town after town that were as devastated as Hawei, they eased closer to shore. While it necessarily slowed their journey, at each settlement they paused and perused what remained, looking for any survivors from the safety of the ship.

They found none.

"This could mean the end of the Atturei Empire," Gya murmured to Mikolus late the sixth day of this, after they scanned yet another dead port.

The tall man glanced at him and nodded. "That it could. If there's less destruction further inland, they could still rebuild. But it won't be a fast thing."

Gya nodded in turn and gazed back at the ruined port as it slowly fell behind them. He did not want to speak it—that would make it real—but he feared for Ekosua, Ayaru and Dakrei. He feared the destruction had caught them, too.

Much of the journey, Alorsha kept busy in her cabin,

only coming out regularly for meals and every couple of days to join in a weapons-work session. From time to time, Gya felt that odd sensation through the *Deliberia*. Alorsha working some magic. His inability to work his own ate at him, but he saw no point in asking to do more with hers. All too soon the *Deliberia* and her people would be gone forever from his life.

He found the notion disheartening.

As they continued east, they saw fewer coastal settlements. They even spotted a few people, who paid no attention to the ship. Gya dared hope his friends would be well and unharmed.

They made good time on this eastern voyage. A few days shy of two weeks out from Hawei, a day shorter than their previous voyage and an estimated day out from Azkra, they turned north to stay out of sight of the port and sailed to the landing they had used before. They arrived there in the early morning, just as a hint of dawn colored the sky.

As before, they lowered a tender to sail to the shore in the water too shallow for the *Deliberia*. This time Gya and Alorsha rode in the boat, with Mikolus, who rowed. Gya had already thanked everyone and made his farewells to the others aboard ship.

As the small tender moved away from the ship, Gya looked back and saw the crewmembers he had traveled with and come to know looking at him over the railing. They raised hands to wave and he returned the gesture as a sinking feeling washed over him. *But this was the right thing to do, wasn't it?*

The short journey to the shore seemed interminable to Gya. He firmly squelched doubts that threatened to overwhelm him. *He belonged here, not sailing away on a magical venture to who knew where.* As the tender moved closer to the landing spot they had chosen, Gya spotted something that he did not remember from before.

"What's that?" He narrowed his eyes to try to better

make out the dark smudges where they had previously guessed a path ran.

Mikolus motioned for them to crouch down. Alorsha gripped the edge of the tender and called on the wood's magic to bring vapor wafting up from the sea's surface to help hide them. Mikolus wielded the oars to send them gently, and almost soundlessly, to the shore, changing their approach to an angle that set them ashore a little further to the east from the spot they had used before.

After he exchanged a look with Alorsha, Mikolus slipped over the side of the boat and moved off into the thickening fog.

Gya tried to watch the dark shape that was the *Deliberia*'s Captain, but soon lost him in the grayness.

"Do you think it's the Empire?" he whispered to Alorsha as he leaned close.

She answered with a shrug, pulled a bow and quiver of arrows from beneath her seat, and nocked an arrow. Gya had not even seen her bring the bow with her.

Before Gya had time to wonder or worry much more, Mikolus returned, startling him as he seemed to just appear out of the murk.

"Travelers," he told them. "Just a few of them. Might be a family group. From the looks of them, they escaped their town's destruction with little more than what they could carry. From the tracks, they came from the west and follow the path east. Maybe they're heading to someplace near where your friends were going." That last he directed to Gya.

"They look safe to travel with, if you want," he added. "None of them are Keepers and none wore those tokens."

Gya nodded and grabbed his pack. "It would be good to go with a group. Even if only part of the way. My thanks again."

Alorsha nodded acknowledgment. "I wish you success and happiness in your life," she said in a soft voice. Gya found her expression hard to read. *Might she be sad at this parting? He was.*

Mikolus helped him out of the tender and gave his hand a firm clasp in the process. "You'll want to circle around to approach them from the west, I think. Be careful how much you share with them."

Gya nodded and hefted his pack.

Mikolus leaned close to him. "You're sure about this? Once we've gone, we won't be back."

Gya frowned but nodded again and Mikolus returned his nod. Gya started the direction that Mikolus had indicated but paused and turned back. "You'll catch him," he called to Alorsha. "I'm certain of it."

Alorsha nodded and waved back when he waved to her. Then Gya picked his way along the shore so as to approach the group on the path from the west.

~ ~ ~

Walking in the pre-dawn dimness with the soothing, familiar sounds of the Mavkath Sea flowing around him, Gya's thoughts returned again to those who were gone. An empty heaviness settled in his chest, an ache that tore at him.

He remembered playing with his brother as children, carefree, before the Keepers took their father, before they had any knowledge of the hardships of being labeled Blighted and Magicka.

In memory Chizoa gazed at him again, her expression beautiful with her regard of him. He again heard the sweet sound of her voice, again delighted in the shared stolen glances, the touch of her hand.

Vabena shared her gentle smile with him; Ifeoma presented a specially baked treat, her bracelets clacking and tinkling.

If only….

He shook his head at himself. *'If onlys' wouldn't do any good. But why had this Devrand done this?* Questions that

Alorsha and the others had not really answered. *They did not seem to have those answers. Could he ever get those answers?*

Why did he have to kill them?

The ache deepened, weighing him down and slowing his steps as he headed toward his future that loomed bereft of so many people important to him.

~ ~ ~

Gya slowly approached the other travelers, wanting to avoid giving them any reason to fear. If they were Magickas too, they had likely had enough of fear recently. If they were not, he did not want to get too close in case he needed to get away.

His thoughts drifted back to the people of the *Deliberia*. He had enjoyed his time with them, even as they seemed to run from one danger to another. They were good people and for a time he had been part of doing something worthwhile. They had helped those Magickas escape. *Was it always like that wherever they went? What would he do now? Go back to being some kind of merchant? Was that what he wanted?*

His mind circled around this dilemma while his feet carried him closer to the strangers' camp. When he spotted the figure of someone standing watch some distance ahead, he stopped and waved.

"Hello?" he called out, not too loudly. It looked like some of the group might still be asleep.

The figure raised a hand in return and came toward him. He stayed put and let the other approach, a young man he soon saw. His skin was a shade or two darker than Gya's own—hard to tell for sure in the dim dawn light—and his eyes looked to be a light brown. The stranger's dark hair was cropped close to his skull and he wore no beard. He held a thick stick in one hand and gave Gya a wary look as he stopped well out of reach.

Gya held his hands out to both sides to show they were empty.

"Hello," the stranger said after they each studied the other a few minutes. "You escaped the destruction, too?"

Gya nodded. "I did. I'm hoping to reach Suor. When I spotted your group, I hoped we might travel together. Even if it's only for a short distance."

The stranger frowned and shifted his feet. "I don't know where Suor is. We're just looking for a new place. Nothing left of home."

"I'm in the same state," Gya said.

The stranger relaxed enough to share his name, Suyei. He did not offer his second name and when Gya introduced himself, he did not either.

"Come ahead and meet the others." Suyei lowered his stick from its half-ready stance. "We can talk about traveling together."

Suyei led the way to his group's small makeshift camp. The others had begun stirring and soon everyone was awake and busy.

Gya helped them put together a meal, offering a lot from what he carried when he saw they had next to no food. Those not involved in assembling and warming the meal, gathered the group's few belongings in preparation for moving on. In the midst of all this activity, Gya met the others.

Suyei, it turned out, had almost eighteen years, so close to a man grown but still with the features of a boy. His sister Atieno was older but declined to say how much. Gya found himself much observed by her and she smiled when their gazes crossed. The siblings' cousin Yaa, the youngest of the three, looked away in shyness when Suyei introduced her and did not speak.

With them traveled an older couple, Ekua and her husband Okinyi. Gya guessed they might be twice his own age, perhaps a little older. Their expressions showed weariness and sorrow, but they greeted him easily enough. Gya learned they had been near neighbors to Suyei's family in the town they came from. All of them were the last of their families. No others had survived the destruction that had swept through their village.

The last member of the group was Kofi, a boy of about ten years. He was not related to any of the others. They had found him alone as they had journeyed from their homes. He, too, had no other family left.

As he helped the group, Gya's thoughts returned to the *Deliberia* once more. *What were they doing now?* Surely Alorsha and Mikolus had already returned to the ship. They had presumably already sailed away. Maybe they had even already sailed through their own hole in the air in pursuit of Devrand.

He looked toward the shore but the fog that lingered there obscured everything.

Maybe they had not yet left. *Might they have decided to wait in case he changed his mind? Might he be changing his mind?* The idea that they were gone hit him like he had been punched.

He imagined he could hear Toa telling him to just do something. The ache that weighed on him morphed into a heat that flushed through his body. He pounded a fist against his leg. *That Devrand shouldn't be able to just go his way. He should be held answerable for what he had done!* Gya needed to be part of that. *He needed to go with the Deliberia.*

With that, he made his decision. If he hurried, maybe he could still catch them.

Forgoing the rest of his meal, Gya tore a blank page from the back of the single sigil codex left to him – the one he had previously left with the horses when he and the others had gone after Devrand. He dug out his one remaining pen and a small jar of ink and wrote a quick message to his friends in Suor telling them of Hawei's destruction and that Toa, Ifeoma, Vabena, and Chizoa were gone. He concluded by wishing them well and letting them know he would be journeying on the *Deliberia* and so would not see them again.

He handed the sloppy note to Ekua and Okinyi. "I'll not be coming with you after all," he said. "Will you please see this note gets to the largest inn in Suor? And tell them to pass it then to Dakrei, Ayaru or Ekosua."

Looking surprised and confused, the couple did not ask any questions but did agree to carry the message. He thanked them for that and for sharing their meal, grabbed his pack, wished the small group luck, and ran toward the fog-hidden shore.

It had not seemed long when he walked it earlier, but now the path stretched out in front of him. *What if they'd already gone? There really was no reason for them to have waited.* He had to hope that they had. If not, he was stuck here. He would travel with the small group to Suor and just have to find something to do with himself, something different. He did not think he was a merchant any longer.

He fell into a rhythm with his steps pounding the dirt, the grasses and brush he ran through rustling against his legs.

From his angle, he could not see the waterside yet, and heavy mist still lingered so he might not see it until he stumbled on it. But he smelled it, that familiar scent of the sea. A few seagulls called in the mist. He imagined they urged him on.

He plunged into the haze that thickened the further he went. He stumbled over things unseen and hoped against hope that he could call Alorsha and Mikolus back. Hoped that he would find them before they left. As he struggled, his head and heart pounded and almost drowned out the soft sounds of the water at the shore.

Then he plunged into the small waves, sloshing water into his shoes. He slid to a halt and tried to see through the fog.

"Mikolus? Alorsha?"

His voice seemed small in the grayness, lost in the murk. *Was that the sound of a boat in the water?*

He called again, his voice cracking as it hadn't done in years, and stepped back out of the water.

Trying to ease his pounding heart and heaving breaths,

he strained to hear voices, a boat, anything. But he heard only the sound of the water lapping ever closer to his feet and seagulls still calling somewhere nearby. A heavy misgiving took root in his gut.

He sank to his knees, heedless of the water that soaked them and sat back on his heels. He'd dithered too long. He was too late. If only....

"Gya!"

That was Alorsha's voice.

Hope surged through him and he jumped to his feet. "I'm here! This way."

He definitely heard the sound of oars, a boat coming toward him. Then the tender, and Alorsha and Mikolus, loomed out of the haze to touch ground right in front of Gya.

They gazed at him, hints of smiles quirking their lips.

Suddenly tongue-tied, Gya croaked, "You waited!"

Both Alorsha and Mikolus nodded.

"We did," Alorsha said simply. Something in her expression, and Mikolus's, said they were not surprised. *Had they known somehow—maybe all along—that he would need to pursue that man?*

Gya glanced back toward the small group he had just left. An image of the destruction that had been Hawei came to him and he pondered the loss of all that kri-stone, from what they had seen probably all the kri-stone anywhere. Even if other Magickas survived, they would no longer be Magickas. *He* would no longer be a Magicka here.

He brushed a hand across the grasses at his side and felt the tiniest hint of the magic within them, the magic Alorsha had shown him resided there.

He grabbed his pack. "I'd go with you, if I might."

Alorsha slid to the side of her bench to make room for him. Mikolus clapped him on the shoulder as he stepped into the tender.

The small boat practically flew across the water to the

waiting *Deliberia* as the fog tattered around them in the new day's sunshine. Before he knew it, Gya was climbing the ladder back onto the ship.

As he basked in the welcome of his new shipmates, Alorsha pulled out her double-framed pendant, removed the center frame with the stone from the outer wooden frame, and returned it to its place on her thumb ring. She then moved to the bow and placed both hands on the ship's rail.

Gya felt her draw forth the *Deliberia*'s magic. He could feel some magic from her ring, too, as it blended with the ship's magic and guided it somehow. He turned toward the bow to watch the air split open in front of the ship.

A sudden gale smashed into them and kicked up high waves, as clouds built right above them. With a crash of lightning, the wind caught the sails and sent the *Deliberia* careening through the hole into another place.

~

Pronunciations

Alorsha – uh LOHR shuh
Arikron – AHR ih krahn
Arithi – uh REE thee
Arizu – AH ree zoo
Asiva – ah SEE vuh
Atieno – ah TYEHN oh
Atturei – ah TOOR eye
Ayaru – AY uh roo
Azkra – AHZ kruh

Badrani – BAH druh nee
Bayo – BAY oh
B'Jen – buh JEHN

Candwi – KAHN dwee
Charnov – CHAHR nahf
Chizoa – CHIH zoh uh
chervynai – CHAYR vih nay

Dakrei – DAHK r-eye
Deliberia – dehl ih BAYR ee uh
Dev – DEHV
Devrand – DEHV ruhnd
D'saroa – duh SAHR oh uh

Ekosua – uh KOH soo uh
Ekua – EH koo uh
erythros – AYR ih throhs
Eztevo – EHZ teh voh

Farhani – fahr HAH nee
Flenar – FLEH IN uhr

Ganyai – GAHN yay

Grabe – GRAYB
Gya – G-EYE uh
Gyasi – g-eye AH see

Hakizi – hah KEE zee
Hali – hah LEE
Hawei – HAH w-eye
Hieva – HYEH vuh

Ifeoma – ih fee OH muh
igyelan – ihg YEL uhn
Ikkavai – ih KAH vay

Jarthan – JAHR thuhn
Jwanu – JWAH noo

Kalbei – KAHLB eye
K'lar – kuh LARH
Kluir – KLOOR
Kofi – koh FEE
Kolyav – KOHL yuhv
kri-stone – KREE stohn
K'rond – kuh RAHND

Layakei – lay AH k-eye
Limbani – lihm BAH nee
Ludek – LOO dehk

Mavkath – muhv KAHTH
M'bweyo – muh BWAY oh
Mikolus – MIII koh luhs
Mirov – MEER uhv

Narain – NAHR ayn
N'lela – nuh LEH luh

Okinyi – oh KIHN yee

Omondu – OH muhn doo

Parl – PAHRL
Pashev – PAH shehv
Pumza – PUHM zuh

Razaya – ruh ZAY uh
Reesma – REES muh
Reez – REEZ
Remdor – REHM duhr
Ruznei – ROOZ n-eye

Saevalde – say VAHL deh
Shala – SHAH luh
Smas – SMAHS
spisha – SPEE shuh
spishas – SPEE shuhz
Suor – SOO ohr
Suyei – SOO y-eye

taiawood – TAY uh wood
Talu – TAH loo
Tanrith – TAHN rihth
Tanrithan – TAHN rihth uhn
Tavano – tuh VAH noh
T'narm – tuh NAHRM
Toa – TOH uh
Toabi – toh AH bee
Triloa – TREE loh uh
T'rojim – tuh ROH jihm

Uboro – oo BOHR oh
Usrai – OOS ray

Vabena – vuh BEH nuh
V'sar – vuh SAHR

Wambua – WAHM boo uh

Yaa – YAH uh
Yakwes – YAH kwehs
Yuyur – YOO yuhr

Zawdi – ZAH dee

~

TITLES BY S. LYNN HELTON

Wild Heritance fantasy series

Duplicity of Power
Power Awry
Power Redeemed

Trial Run (prequel novella)
Trial and Tribulation (prequel novella)

The Deliberia Chronicles fantasy trilogy

Crystalborne Sigils
Songborne Gates
A Galeborne Resolve

Author's Note

Thank you for reading my book. I hope you enjoyed it!

Please consider leaving an honest review on the book's
product page at your favorite online bookstore
and on Goodreads. Reviews from readers like you are
powerful and greatly help other readers
discover books they might enjoy.

-Lynn

About the Author

S. Lynn Helton lives in the foothills of the Rocky
Mountains, U.S.A., with her family and a couple of crazy
cats. Lynn enjoys camping and hiking, playing games,
crafting, reading (a lot) and, of course, writing.

Read more about her books on her website:
www.slynnhelton.com

www.ingramcontent.com/pod-product-compliance
Lightning Source LLC
Chambersburg PA
CBHW071100250626
47159CB00002B/531